The Confessions of Sherlock Holmes

THE THEOLOGICAL ODYSSEY OF THE GREAT DETECTIVE

Volume 3

Dr. Watson's Mission to Rome

THOMAS MENGERT

BLUE FORGE PRESS
Port Orchard, Washington

Dr. Watson's Mission to Rome
Copyright 2024
by Thomas Mengert

First eBook Edition April 2024
First Print Edition April 2024

ISBN 978-1-59092-999-5

For information about film, reprint or other subsidiary rights, contact: blueforgegroup@gmail.com

Blue Forge Press is the print division of the volunteer-run, federal 501(c)3 nonprofit company, Blue Forge Group, founded in 1989 and dedicated to bringing light to the shadows and voice to the silence. We strive to empower storytellers across all walks of life with our four divisions: Blue Forge Press, Blue Forge Films, Blue Forge Gaming, and Blue Forge Records. Find out more at www.BlueForgeGroup.org

Blue Forge Press
7419 Ebbert Drive Southeast
Port Orchard, Washington 98367
blueforgepress@gmail.com
360-550-2071 ph.txt

Acknowledgements

The Confessions of Sherlock Holmes has, for all of its primary theological intent, a subtext that emerged in the course of the writing. That subtext is the decline and fall of the British Empire and of the imperial family structures that once supported it. The three Holmes brothers each manifest the end result of the system of primogeniture and the conflict present between art and reason in their blood. Each brother in his own way manifests the conflict entailed in finding a place and an identity in opposition to their father and his estate.

The character of the Holmes father remains distant and perhaps finally indecipherable. As the reader will discover in the course of reading the book the parental figure looks beyond his own sons in order to find an image of a substitute son that would meet the requirements and the pattern that the father needed each of them to represent. Unfortunately, each son manifested instead a diluted solution of traits that drew more from their artistic mother and her French heritage than from their stern father and his code. The individuality and character of the brothers manifests a freedom from convention that the father perhaps wished that he could have claimed for himself, but to see it present in his sons seemed both indulgent and a betrayal of his own strict principles. He valued rebellion, but not within his own house and among his own progeny. For this reason both Mycroft and Sherlock are comparative exiles, while Sherringford is saddled with maintaining Sigerside, the Holmes estate. If the Christian religion can be seen as the process of overcoming exile from God as Father through the sacrifice of a Son, the parallels will be immediately apparent.

I doubt that I would have been able to compose this book if it were not present as a reflection of the dynamics of my own family. So for this reason I dedicate this book as with all my efforts in life to my parents and grandparents and especially to my two grandmothers who each nurtured my early love for literature with their deep love and affirmation.

The support of my parents made my life possible in every way imaginable.

To my Father's mother, Tilly, who read me Longfellow's poetry on sunny afternoons.

To My Mother's mother, Gerda, who gave me the Doubleday Edition of The Complete Sherlock Holmes.

To my Father's father, Otto, who shared his library with me and taught me the value of family heritage.

To my Mother's father, Fred, who instilled in me a love of the sea and for his humor and love of stories.

To all of these my everlasting thanks.

"What is the meaning of it, Watson?" said Holmes, solemnly, as he laid down the paper. "What object is served by this circle of misery and violence and fear? It must tend to some end, or else our universe is ruled by chance, which is unthinkable. But what end? There is the great standing perennial problem to which human reason is as far from an answer as ever."

—From *The Adventure of the Cardboard Box*

"There is nothing in which deduction is as necessary as in religion," said he, leaning with his back against the shutters. "It can be built up as an exact science by the reasoner. Our highest assurance of the goodness of providence seems to me to rest in the flowers. All other things, our powers, our desires, our food, are really necessary for our existence in the first instance. But this rose is an extra. Its smell and its color are an embellishment of life, not a condition of it. It is only goodness which gives such extras, and so I say again that we have much to hope from the flowers."

—From *The Adventure of the Naval Treaty*

"The greatest schemer of all time, the organizer of every deviltry, the controlling brain of the underworld, a brain which might have made or marred the destiny of nations – that's the man!"

"Barker beat his head with his clenched fist in his impotent anger. 'Do not tell me that we have to sit down under this? Do you say that no one can ever get level with this king devil?' 'No, I don't say that,' said Holmes, and his eyes seemed to be looking far into the future. 'I don't say that he can't be beat. But you must give me time—you must give me time.' We all sat in silence for some minutes while those fateful eyes still strained to pierce the veil."

—From *The Valley of Fear*

ℑreface

It has seemed to me that a few words of preface should precede all else. My initial intention was to bring the book forward in a limited edition to be sold directly by the author to the purchaser after an appropriate lecture by way of introduction to prepare the reader for the unique demands of its content and length (over 800,000 words and some 2,000 pages) to explain my intentions in writing the book at all. The function of the present brief preface is to turn aside those readers who may imagine that a novel featuring Sherlock Holmes must of necessity be merely a tale of amusement and diversion rather than one probing into the very depths of the character of the man himself and the deeper mysteries of life. These readers may be distressed and disappointed if they expect only a vapid adventure tale and may attribute failure to the author, expecting him to have undertaken what he never undertook to do at all, simply to amuse and not challenge the reader.

The ideal reader of the following volume will be one who is willing to enter upon an intellectual adventure of no mean magnitude and to suspend his disbelief to the degree that he will find the Sherlock Holmes contained herein to be deeper in character and more worthy of esteem than any accolades ever afforded to him by Dr. John H. Watson might justify and to find herein a solution to many mysteries left unresolved in the original canonical tales. Since the present work exceeds the length of the entire corpus of the original tales, its existence may be very good news indeed to that ideal reader who wishes to hear more of Sherlock Holmes and Dr. Watson.

I shall here revive an old 19th century custom by greeting you dear reader. I trust that you will find a great intellectual adventure in reading the text that lies before you. It is no easy matter for an author to entrust his creation, formerly visited only by the mind which conceived it, to those he hopes will prove to be an indulgent public. A few introductory words before you begin seem in order. You are about to read a mystery that returns to the origin of all mysteries in the Mystery Plays of England, which attempted to explain the mysteries of the Christian religion by combining theology with popular entertainment and spectacle. The following story is told in two different voices with two different narrators: Sherlock Holmes and Doctor Watson. There are no chapter divisions. Instead there is a prologue, epilogue, and sixteen books. The span of time covered is from 1891 – 1899 with some short selections from 1914 through 1917 when both narratives were assembled by Doctor Watson. Together the two manuscripts constitute what may be called a discursive or picaresque narrative where ideas may be fully explored and examined. This type of book was quite common in the Victorian era but is less so today, though the need for such books is perhaps greater than ever before. I have long been concerned that with the decline of leisure, which is after all the basis of all that is most civilized within us, that we have forfeited as well the craft of the baroque prose of the 17th and succeeding centuries until the dawn of the contemporary literary scene. Even as late as the Victorian Age in England, some last vestiges of this sophistication and balance remained in the writings of men like Matthew Arnold and novelists such as Thackeray, Dickens, and Henry James. The work that you hold in your hand will I hope recall a vanished era, a more graceful period in the history of our common literature. Having made this brief apology for its ornate style I must move ahead to consider the extraordinary length of the complete book. Had this book been published in the 19th century, it would have been published in multiple volumes as was common for many of the books written by Charles Dickens and his friend Wilkie Collins, the originator of the modern detective story. I have often lamented the passing of that more discursive era when there was time and leisure to enter another world when reading a novel and to count on dwelling there for some time. I hope to have re-created something of that experience for the modern reader by writing this book in the fashion of an era, which I trust is not forever lost to us, when ideas might be fully explored to their furthest limits.

Any introduction should serve the purpose of explaining to the prospective reader the intentions of the author. It allows the author the liberty of an advance apologia, to deflect from the beginning any criticism for failing to achieve what was in fact never intended. Since the novel of ideas has become a rarity and since a didactic format has become unfashionable, I have thought it best to admit quite frankly that this novel is meant to take its inspiration from models whose several excellences have inspired my own effort. That a novel may include elements of the essay and extensively explore ideas is common in the Russian novels of Tolstoy and Dostoyevsky. The French also allow for the scope necessary to explore ideas in the works of Victor Hugo. English Literature is also not without models to inspire an endeavor such as the one that lies before you in this work. The primary genre or rather mix of genres, since I have taken instruction from several sources, includes the picaresque novels of Tobias Smollett, the writings of Samuel Johnson particularly *Rasselas*, and such unique works as *Tristram Shandy* by Sterne and *Vanity Fair* by Thackeray. The novel of ideas has been best represented however by the German writers. I have a special affection for two great German contributions to the novel of ideas: Thomas Mann's *The Magic Mountain* and Robert Musil's *The Man Without Qualities*.

To allow form to be flexible enough to allow for such content as I have intended here means to take liberties with the tradition of the novel of detection. Ordinarily the experience of the detective novel is considered to entail light entertainment or to be concentrated around adventure and romance. The appeal of Sherlock Holmes however exceeds both of these, for in the last analysis it is Holmes and Watson themselves who emerge from these narratives of Sir Arthur Conan Doyle as characters of such a unique and complete set of individual traits that the reader comes finally to have an affection for them far beyond perhaps any other protagonists in literature. It is for this reason that the focus of the present book is upon those very characters and the opinions and inner struggles that may have lain latent in the original tales, but that may now be explored in depth.

The present book is an effort to account for many problems of improbability or inconsistency in the original narratives of Sherlock Holmes. There are many cases that Doctor Watson mentions in his narratives of the great detective which he might have included in the annals of Holmes but never did. I have long thought it time for someone to attempt a grand synthesis using some of the brief and fragmentary hints provided by the established Canon. Although Sherlock Holmes appears occasionally as the narrator of a story we do not possess a sustained narrative in the Master's own hand until now.

Many readers of the Holmes saga may have wondered as much about the haunting character of Holmes himself as they have been curious about his untold cases. To round out the character of the man I thought it time that someone probed those moral obsessions and that hunger for the deepest meanings of life that evidently possessed him. Drawing on hints in the original stories I have therefore pieced out a narrative that I hope will reveal Sherlock Holmes in a deeper light and to solve mysteries that no previous chronicler has attempted to probe.

In writing this book I hoped to explore how Sherlock Holmes might have grappled with that most elusive problem posed by philosophy and by the many religions of the world, viz. how to account for the human condition and to explain the problem of evil. I thought it only appropriate that the greatest detective the world has ever known be given a chance to resolve these matters to the best of his ability and I thought it likely that he would have done so. What better time for him to have made this effort than during his long hiatus from London between the years of 1891 and 1894?

I have no desire to add mystification to mystery. This book presumes a certain knowledge of the original tales just as a symphony by Vaughan Williams depends upon a certain acquaintance with English folk melodies and the chromatic scale. For devotees who have loved Sherlock Holmes for years yet detect a certain mendacity and improbability in some of the endings as hitherto received, this narrative may pose some valuable answers. My desire is with this narrative to create a new unity where chaos and contradiction have reigned. May I not be thought presumptuous to undertake this task and may it serve to bring to rest the shade of the great detective who has no doubt asked why no one has yet followed up the clues so liberally sprinkled through the familiar accounts of Dr. John H. Watson. I hope that these will show how deeply imbedded in the original narratives is my own text, which growing from this fertile soil, will attempt to be true to the spirit and flavor of the original narratives and in addition serve as a substantial addition to the Canonical tales which with hopefully little effort of imagination on the part of my readers might be ascribed to the original characters brought to life by Sir Arthur Conan Doyle. If I appear to take liberties with the genre of the detective story by dwelling at length on matters of philosophy, of history, and of theology, then pray allow me to defend myself here before the bar.

Originally the mystery genre, of which the detective story is only one late example, referred to the religious mystery plays of the middle ages. These plays had a decidedly didactic purpose. Wonders and surprises were meant to widen the horizons of the audience to entertain the possibility of the miraculous and the wonderful. Are not these the very emotions we feel when we see Sherlock Holmes solving seemingly impenetrable puzzles? But more than this, the detective story has as its theme the struggle between good and evil. Nowhere is this dualism clearer than in the struggle between Sherlock Holmes and Professor Moriarty. I have taken the opportunity offered by these two icons of the moral struggle between good and evil to write a book in the ancient tradition of Christian apologetics to probe the nature of good and evil and explore in detail the Christian account for the origin of this struggle. In doing so, I have taken the model of the book of confessions such as that most famous example, *The Confessions of St. Augustine*, as my model. These confessions are meant to be the reflections of Holmes as recorded in his journal during his long sojourn of several years between 1891 and 1894 and continued in 1896 and 1897. Along with this account of what Sherlock Holmes scholars have termed, "the great hiatus," I have woven a tale told in the traditional manner by Doctor Watson that takes place primarily in the years 1897 and 1898. Together these twin narratives may answer some of the most perplexing problems left within the Canon of the original tales of Sir Arthur Conan Doyle. I have long been a devotee of those masterful stories and have wished to fill in certain lacunae that exist to complete the picture of Holmes' career. Sherlock Holmes is often spoken of as the most famous character in English fiction. The man who appears to wish to be thought of only as a scientific student of crime is fascinating because his own habits are so unusual. Does every detective study medieval music, ancient British charters, palimpsests, and do chemical research on coal-tar derivatives? Do they play the violin, attend concerts, and keep their tobacco in a Persian slipper? Are they beset with addictions, melancholia, and deep speculations upon the reason for human existence? Do they at once solve the crime and forgive the criminal in case after case? Do they enjoy the performing arts and masquerade? Do they have a sense of humor and enjoy teasing members of the upper crust? Do they enjoy horse-racing, fencing, single-stick, and boxing? If we eliminate these fascinating personal characteristics and the unique relationship with Dr. Watson, what would remain? Would the Master's immortal appeal be what it has been? Then why not, I asked myself, explore these ultimate questions of religious truth and ultimate meaning in a text written by the hand of Sherlock Holmes himself in the form of a journal accounting for the years spent on what has become known as the great hiatus, those years between 1891 and 1894, while not denying the pleasure of an old-fashioned Watson narrative at the same time in a parallel text occurring in 1897 and 1898? The result is the twin-narrative that now lies before you. It is my hope that the reader will find within this book not only a revival of the lost discipline of Christian apologetics but also that by meditating on the challenging thoughts and feelings of both Holmes and Watson this book may explore the deepest dimensions of human experience wrestling with the eternal problems. To use characters of fiction, well-known perhaps beyond all others, to enunciate and give form to life itself would surely be within the ambit of Sherlock Holmes, the greatest detective of all time. I also desired to explore the parameters of Holmes' relationships, the better to vindicate him from easy charges of vanity and if anything to make him more beloved when his unique personality is shown in greater clarity than ever before by revealing the hidden facts of his life, now hopefully revealed through the interlocked cases that lie before the reader in this long-suppressed account.

The reader will note that many ideas will throng these pages and it would be surprising if every reader agreed with the opinions that I have portrayed as existing in Holmes or in Dr. Watson. I have tried not to place opinions within them that would contradict what we already know of their established characters but I do admit to a didactic purpose in many of their discourses. This account may then be considered a fantasia of my own construction upon the essential themes provided by Sir Arthur Conan Doyle. That gentleman was known for the courage of his convictions that often led him to espouse extreme opinions in his own day and I claim similar latitude in exploring my own characterization of Holmes and Watson. It is the prerogative of the author to write his own book and to set before the reader only what the author possesses. If it be too much to hope that the graft will take in the original body of work, I shall be content if the indulgent reader will treat this account as a mere suggestion of what might have been and not what was. There will remain Sherlockian fundamentalists who will always look askance at the temerity of any additions to the Canon. For this reason all additions must be seen as what they are, an attempt to gratify the hunger of those who would wish for true immortality to descend upon the great detective so that there will always be another tale to read. May you enjoy reading this tale then as much as I have enjoyed writing it and hearing again, as if I were merely a channel for them, the old voices and feel again that sense of adventure known first to me in my youth when I feared to read the last Sherlock Holmes mystery and to know irrevocably that there would be no more.

Here again then, the curtain rises upon what I trust will reward the discerning reader of the old tales who has hungered for more, not merely of the stage props of Holmes and Watson in new and improbable adventures, but to find instead an answer and a completion in this addition to what has become the larger Holmes peripheral canon. May this contribution attempt an answer to the deeper mysteries posed by the original tales themselves. It is for the ideal reader who having read with a discerning eye the original tales and also for those specialists known as Sherlockians, but also for new readers, who will take this work as a useful hypothesis for what may have actually happened, that I have the pleasure to announce in that immortal phrase: the game is afoot!

Dr. Watson's Mission to Rome

Thomas Mengert

Book Six

The African Adventure
to
Sudan and Egypt

Dr. Watson's Narrative Continues

Note from Doctor John H. Watson

In the previous two volumes of the extensive multi-volume book, written at the time of the Great European War that began in 1914 and has yet to reach its conclusion at the time of this writing, a book collectively entitled, "The Confessions of Sherlock Holmes," I have gone a great way into all that I have learned of life and death as well as presenting the thoughts of Sherlock Holmes in a journal that he kept at the time of a secret wager contracted between Sherlock Holmes and his arch-nemesis, Professor Moriarty. This journal will forever be the closest thing that my friend Sherlock Holmes has ever provided to the world in the form of an autobiography. I would like to point out to the attentive reader that far more men have ever lived than have ever given a coherent account of their lives, let alone having actually contributed to the collective wisdom of the world. Sherlock Holmes was one of these latter individuals without whom the world would be a more vacant and desolate place.

As this third volume opens I had been reading Holmes' journal until late in the evening in our old rooms at 221B Baker Street to which we had just recently returned. The sounds from the busy traffic had gradually faded away below me and at last I decided to seek refuge in sleep from his travels through the exotic regions of Persia and Arabia as recounted in the journal. I was determined in my book to interweave his journal with my own account of an adventure that began for both of us in 1897 and was not completed until the new century. I will not say that my thoughts and choice of subject matter were independent of those of Holmes, because his influence upon me and perhaps my own influence upon him brought us to a state of a meeting of the minds that few men ever share.

I recall that my sleep was troubled that night because of my fear for the health of my friend and the shadow cast upon him by a recurrent lung ailment, perhaps contracted in his youth, or even from that period of dissipation and over-exertion that characterized the time of our first years together. I had long made his survival and retrieval from early vice one of the goals of my life. I had watched my own brother weaken and die from dipsomania and I had no doubt transferred some of that early affection and sorrow at his loss to Sherlock Holmes. His own proud nature would not easily suffer any direct intervention, but he was not beyond noticing how deeply affected I became when he would wander aimlessly about our rooms on winter nights lamenting the lack of imagination among the criminal caste of London. On such occasions he would wait anxiously for the sound of a carriage drawing up frantically outside our address and the sound of hurried footsteps on the stairs leading to our suite of rooms where he held his consultations with new clients. It was on just those restless occasions that he might reach for the syringe and ignoring my protestations retreat to his private chamber to seek in stimulation or in dreams what life could not provide. At last my ministrations seemed to wean him from his dependence so that at last I was able to decrease my sentinel-like watch over him and even to marry and to live an independent life. He always remained in my life however and many of the cases that I have recounted for the Strand Magazine were drawn from the days when I would leave home and hearth in order to accompany him on a new adventure.

It was often years before I could present the facts of a case before an avid public, sometimes changing the dates or names or circumstances as necessity required.

In the present case the magic of time has worked its wonders and the late Victorian Age already seems to be as distant as a fanciful vision, when life was far more simple and coherent than the present dreadful tumult and its denouement promises to be. I am not one who seeks his answers in dreams or in the stars. I am overall a man of science and reason, yet Sherlock Holmes is always upbraiding me as a romantic. His own nature can seem abrasive when it is only the natural impatience bred from his genius that makes him appear to be intolerant. I have seen him look aside where others might condemn and to condemn when self-seeking sycophants would be willing to dissemble or ignore the vices of the powerful and well-placed in society. Holmes always understood passions that he did not share, but he was irate with instances of carefully planned or systemic oppression over those who were ill-placed to resist.

After these few introductory comments I think that we may return to my efforts to share with the world a unique blending of two texts as each of us attempts to explore what is at stake in any religious commitment, particularly when religion is itself in many respects a moving target, as much at times a creature of history as of God.

On the following morning Holmes was already up before me. I had only heard occasional coughs during the night, but I had slept well so I was prepared for whatever challenges the day might bring. We both enjoyed a hearty breakfast before descending and catching a hansom cab to take us to Harley Street for Holmes' examination by Dr. Moore Agar, the famous lung specialist. Holmes had made his acquaintance some years before. He had met him during the year he had spent in

France and Italy in the year of 1893.

At that time he was living in Montpellier on the south coast of France and doing research into the coal-tar derivatives while also visiting the various monasteries of the region. He had first become acquainted with Dr. Moore Agar at the University of Paris. Holmes was attending a medical gathering there and the two great investigators found themselves in an immense surgical-theater listening to a presentation on microbe dyes. Holmes had brought along several slides with a blue dye that he had prepared and that he felt were quite promising.

The cellular-casing of the tuberculosis bacillus is remarkably resistant to various stains and as a result it is often invisible, which makes diagnosis and study difficult if not impossible. It is difficult to fight a foe that cannot be seen. If it became possible to obtain an inexpensive and reliable test for the presence of the microbe, it would make possible a more certain differential diagnosis and early treatment of the insidious disease that has killed millions and is second only to malaria or the plague in the catalogue of infectious human mortality.

There is a persistent resistance unfortunately among chemists to the productions of outsiders and Holmes' slides had drawn only a modicum of interest before Dr. Agar looked at the slides. He showed immediate enthusiasm and as a result Holmes was able to gain a hearing from some of the most important men in the field before leaving Paris. Holmes and Dr. Agar had immediately agreed to dine together after the final session of the day and the brief conversation of the afternoon continued well into the evening. The result was that the two men made a connection that was resumed in London upon Holmes' return from his long exile to London in 1894. How natural it was then that Holmes should turn to the great lung specialist for diagnosis and treatment when Holmes himself developed signs that he had possibly become infected with the very bacillus upon which he had spent a year of chemical research. It is possible that he had contracted the disease in obtaining samples from known cases or in the course of his extensive travels. In any case he became quite ill in 1896 with the result that Dr. Agar had prescribed a year of complete rest as both a prudent measure and as a remedy for the incessant demands made upon Holmes in the following years for services to some the royal houses of Europe.

I am sorry to report here that Holmes had given this cure at most a six-month period before entering a new period of intense activity. I hoped that the morning would end by Dr. Agar adding his disapproval to my own and that he would convince Holmes to abandon his plans to go to America. It was with this hope in my heart that I escorted Holmes up the steps to Dr. Agar's surgery. We were admitted at once and led back to the cold and spare consulting room. Dr. Agar listened to Holmes' breathing and his face showed the very concern that I myself had felt over the past months.

"There is a most decided congestion in the upper right lobe and you are running a slight fever. Have you lost weight recently? I thought so. I must of course obtain a sample of sputum to make a positive diagnosis but I can tell you that I have little doubt of the results. I am afraid that your case is likely to be recurrent and is presently in the active stage. If my conclusion is confirmed, I must prescribe three weeks of complete bed rest. After that time we will look at the sputum again. As an active case you are of course contagious and it would be most irresponsible to go about in crowds and I recommend that your close contacts should be limited."

I could see how displeased Holmes was by this information.

"Doctor, I am currently engaged in a most serious investigation and it is most inconvenient for me to abandon my present activities."

"Yes, but I am afraid, that you will have to do so," answered

Doctor Agar, "Or I shall not be ready to answer for the consequences. I am sorry to see that you have not followed my earlier advice to you. I will place you in charge of this gentleman." He said, referring to me. "Dr. Watson shall report to me how you progress. In the meantime, I fear that you will need to act through him in any action you propose to take upon your present case. I know that you have the utmost confidence in him and that no man knows your methods with greater familiarity. I am sure that he may bring your case to a happy conclusion. Your responsibility now is to yourself and to your own healing and I entreat you to take my words to heart or I fear that next year may not find you among us."

His meaning was of course clear and even Holmes was forced into silent compliance. I could of course see his disappointment. At last he spoke up.

"Very well Doctor Agar, I shall do as you suggest. I am grateful that you are not exercising your prerogative of sending me to hospital or to a sanitarium. I shall put up in my rooms at Baker Street and place the investigation of which I have spoken in Watson's capable hands if he will be so good as to assume its tasks."

Dr. Agar answered, "I am afraid it is quite necessary. After your initial rest if your samples show that you are again negative you may return to Devonshire, but even there you must resume the course of rest and research that you promised me last spring you intended to pursue. You may take brief trips to London to see me, but you will need to limit your caseload. We shall then see how you progress over time. I can see that you are distressed, but you must understand, Holmes, that no man may do all things. You may at least take comfort that your microbe dye has proven most useful to me in my practice and that I will use it to confirm the conclusions that I have reached this very day in your own case. You need not look chagrined for it is upon early detection that all hope of survival depends, and you have made that possible by your own research. Many lives have been saved already by your efforts and many more will be saved in years to come. The greatest murderers among us are the microbes. I believe that disease plays a role in the providence of God. It keeps us focused on the horrors that lie about us and not upon those that originate within ourselves. It reminds us of the limitations of our nature and produces within us a salubrious humility. In this manner tuberculosis is the primary agent for it strikes all social classes and conditions. It is the universal killer among the microbial infections. We have yet to find any agent of treatment. We may only use the characteristics of the disease against itself. Tuberculosis kills by degrees. It plays with its victim over years until the lungs are a mass of scars and cavities. The microbe must have oxygen however and it divides slowly in its metabolic processes. It lies in wait for years after initial exposure and then steals forth to destroy the lives of young and old alike. I have come to hate it Holmes, and it distresses me to see that it has fastened itself upon you. I shall do all that I can to treat you. I can at best though for the present advise the traditional remedial measures of rest and plenty of good food. Avoid all physical exertion and avoid all excitement and stress. There's a good fellow. I will bid you goodbye now and will send over the results of my lab tests by telegram later today."

With that we were dismissed and Holmes and I returned despondently to Baker Street. I insisted that Holmes take to his bed at once and instructed Mrs. Hudson that she must guard Holmes in the days to come if I should be engaged in furthering the case. She showed that maternal concern that she had always shown to Holmes and agreed to prepare a list of foods that we had received from Dr. Agar to build up Holmes' strength in the weeks to come.

I returned upstairs to find Holmes lying on the settee. "This will suffice, Watson, for the present. I shall go to bed presently.

Pray allow me to explain what you have undertaken, for the next weeks will be critical in our efforts to make Baron Maupertuis answerable for his crimes." He then proceeded to outline his plans and to give me instructions for their implementation.

"We are fortunate in that the market price of the new shares will indicate to us when the Baron is on our line. The great fish will nibble at first and there will be increased activity in the stock. He will try and pick up as many shares as possible without causing a general rise in the price and attracting other speculators. Eventually however word is bound to leak out; other speculators will scent the blood in the water and begin to circle and to buy. The price will begin to rise day by day until it begins to ascend rapidly. At that time the Baron will throw all caution to the wind and enter orders to buy shares in increasing amounts. The tide of the stock's ownership will shift in his direction until he obtains a controlling share in the company. He will no doubt wish to proceed with all haste to begin negotiations for the Dutch canal while the American position is still weak. He will wish to strengthen the very conditions for that weakness by publishing an account of the existence of the Murillo Papers in the European press and perhaps even issue a small press edition of the American chicanery in developing the railroads of Costas Rica. He will suggest of course that the same parties may advocate and profit from the building of a canal at public expense and that they will no doubt again attempt to use slave labor to do so as they did in the case of the railroads."

"This prospect will be very embarrassing to any American administration. We must not forget our recent discussion on the war between the American States in the 1860's, that it was the Republicans who saved the union under the guise that it was undertaken to free the slaves rather than to preserve the economic hegemony of the Northern States and to decide which part of the union would play a dominating role in the development of the American West. If then this new and extensive project of building an American canal can be shown to violate those very ideals that were used by the early Republicans to plunge a nation into civil war, it will be very embarrassing to the Republican party and may swing future elections to the Southern Democrats and cause a rebirth of southern influence in the American union."

"The President will of course offer assurances that no slave labor will be used to build the proposed canal but there will be at least a crisis of confidence and the Southern States will use the opportunity provided by the conflict to revisit old grievances. Baron Maupertuis will hope to use this period of internecine conflict in order to advance a Dutch bid on the canal and to pre-empt any American attempt in obtaining the necessary permission to begin construction. The Baron will press for his own candidates upon the Board of Directors and will urge immediate action and the force of his reasoning in the light of the events that will have been emerging in America will sway the other shareholders to follow suit."

"It is then, at the very height of excitement that we will strike. When the European powers are taking note of events and lending their support to the Dutch Company in order to prevent the threat posed by American control over the canal and the American's ability to dominate trade with Japan, the Baron will feel in complete control and at the head of events. owHHHHWhat a shock it will be then when the Murillo Papers are revealed to be … a forgery! The Americans will insist upon inspecting the copies that are in the Baron's possession and when it is revealed that they contain internal inconsistencies, and other elements which I had inserted when the copies were made, that will suggest fraud, the Americans will rejoice. They will arise in a mass to support an American canal and the price of the shares in the Dutch venture will consequently collapse. Now that a real war of interests is in prospect and having lost confidence in the Baron in the light of his part in publishing the fraudulent Murillo Papers, the price of his shares will collapse in the general flight. The Baron will face financial ruin and we will have achieved our objective."

I did not like the resurgence of excitement in Holmes as he outlined the above sequence of events that he hoped would follow upon our intervention in the Baskerville affair. I took the opportunity therefore of shifting the conversation to the main point at issue so that he would reach a speedy conclusion and go off to bed. "I see of course the line of events Holmes, but when will I need to leave for America?"

"Your part, Watson, will be to carry to America the original copies of the Murillo Papers. It is then that we must decide whether to produce them in order to bring about a resurgence in the price of the Dutch shares, or instead to obtain other concessions from the Americans in return for their suppression. It would be well if you were in America making the necessary preliminary contacts. I am still engaged in discussions with Mycroft over the proper course to pursue in light of the present complex state of European affairs. It is not impossible that our plan to destroy Baron Maupertuis might be foiled should any of the other European powers wish to purchase shares at the height of the scandal over the forged papers. We must then make it quite clear to them *en camera* that the Baron is a swindler and that the shares of the company are honeycombed with deceit and fraud. The newspapers will help in this effort should it prove necessary."

"But Holmes, the company and the Baron himself will be vindicated if the original papers are ever published," said I.

"It will be small comfort to the Baron to achieve a moral victory having already suffered economic ruin, Watson. He is a man who values money over even his own reputation. I do not think that he will step again into the fray and purchase shares again, nor will his presence in the company be welcome to the other shareholders. He will no doubt slink away to one of his villas in Italy for a time. We will follow his movements closely and take further actions against him should the need arise or the opportunity present itself," Holmes stated grimly.

"Then the date of my departure depends upon events and I shall at least be able to be with you for the early days of your convalescence," I reflected.

"You shall, but I will not have you hovering about, Watson. It would fret me to distraction. I assure you that I will keep you busy between the stock market and delivering missives to Mycroft at Whitehall. I meanwhile will sit here and spin my webs...not strenuously, I promise."

With that our discussion ended. I knew the tasks that lay before me. I could only hope that our elaborate strategy would be successful. We had had no word of Charles Augustus Milverton beyond the fact that a man meeting his description had taken the boat-train for the continent. We had lost all track of Roger Baskerville, I am sorry to say, although Inspector Lestrade himself was making inquiries as to his whereabouts now that the transfer of the papers had no doubt been made.

I could do little more that night. I helped Holmes to his feet after we both enjoyed a final nightcap of Cognac. I supported him as far as his bedroom door and there wished him good-night and a peaceful sleep. I then retired to my own chamber. The days that would follow would be busy ones as this present account will reveal. They involved much waiting and observation at the stock exchange and I carried nightly reports back to Holmes. I also spent time in the august antechambers of Whitehall. I carried the manuscript of Holmes' odyssey with me and was able to fill the long hours of waiting with perusing its contents, some of which I will include here.

His time in Mecca seemed to indicate a high-point had been reached in his theological reasoning. I did not agree with every point that he made. For instance his grasp of the divisions that still persist in Islam was somewhat tenuous at the time of the writing of his journal. The supposed unity of Islam has if anything been more tenuous and fractured than that of Christianity. There had been a profound tension between the lands of the Ottoman and Safavid Empires and as is usual it has been difficult to separate the sources of conflict, the theological from the material interests involved. The teachers and scholars, the ulema, have tended to adapt their teachings to the administrative orders of the Moslem state under the various sultans and shahs.

Whenever a society attempts to embody theocratic principles in the form of a state, there is a tendency to adapt doctrine to secular imperatives. There is a further tension between individual mystical experience and the necessary unifying function of defined dogma. Deprived of the unifying influence of the Holy Spirit and the functional and administrative unity provided by the successors to St. Peter, Islam had only the example of Mohammed and the complex poetry of the Koran from which to construct a body of common belief.

Even the question of the legitimate successor to Mohammed was in doubt from the beginning. Without the racial unity of the Hebrews and the doctrinal unity of Medieval Christendom the early military victories of the Islamic warriors could not be sustained over the centuries to the present day. Pushed back from enlightened modern Europe the followers of Mohammed now inhabit primarily those extensive and undefined regions of plain and desert that are central Asia. Their very fragmentation is the guarantee that the spread of Islamic teachings and military incursions can be successively kept at bay when they are too vigorously prosecuted.

Resistance to Christianity is a colonial threat when the cultural emerges as a political question in those lands subject to European rule. As such they are an inconvenience but not a substantial threat to western supremacy. The primary level at which Islam's contribution can be evaluated then is therefore as a unifying political and cultural force in the great landmass of Asia. However Islam has contributed much to the West as well. If Mohammed had never lived the world would have been deprived of certain valuable trends in mathematics, in art, and in architecture and Asiatic tribal warfare would no doubt have been even more pervasive and persistent than it has proven to be.

After his visit to Mecca about which he had been most reticent upon his return to London in 1894 Holmes had undertaken a mission to the Sudan at the behest of Mycroft Holmes. Now I hoped that his journal would provide greater details regarding his mysterious journey to Africa. He had already traversed Tibet and Central Asia, looked in at Mecca, and had now begun his journey across the wilds of Abyssinia to the desert city of Khartoum where General Gordon had met his heroic end. We both admired that central figure of the late-Victorian age, "Chinese Gordon," a man whose defiance of orders had brought about his own death in Khartoum. In the encounter between Gordon and the Mahdi could be read a parable of future relations between Mohammedans and Christians. I fear that the spirit of ancient religious antagonisms is not easy to lay to rest and will manifest again from time to time even in our modern materialist future as it has been outlined by such figures as Mr. Thomas Huxley and Mr. H. G. Wells. These gentlemen may someday realize that religions have laid the basis for human history and that no facile secularism is likely to lay them soon to rest.

From the Journal of Sherlock Holmes

February 18, 1892
Jeddah

Our withdrawal from Mecca was a timely retreat, for in the days before our departure I began to notice that both Colonel Moran and I were under increasing scrutiny at our lodgings. Now and again I would notice familiar faces in the crowds and wonder if we were recognized. Further delay would not have added to my knowledge of Islam and it was pointless to run unnecessary risks after having come so far. All in all we have been blessed in our journey. Beyond a few alarming incidents in Afghanistan, we have had little trouble thus far. The presence of Islamic beliefs among the populace and the rules of hospitality to the stranger have protected us from theft and violence and our only concern was not to violate any customs that might have brought tribal laws down upon us. I fear that these protections will not avail us in the Sudan. This region, though touched by Islam, has yet to be converted to full Islamic civilization. The British are distrusted and to venture into these regions is to court death. Why then am I going? Can it be to advance my religious quest? Perhaps not, but the question of Africa is crucial at this time to the politics of England. The struggle for colonial dominance is an intense one and could over time even result in a general European conflict. Faced with such a terrific calamity my loyalties must remain with England. A further reason for my expedition into the Sudan is to honor a promise that I made to Mycroft before leaving. He requested that I. "Take a look," as he put it, at the Sudanese situation, if I as he again said, "should be in the neighborhood."

Only one who lives in the antiseptic world of the Diogenes Club would have put the matter in just those terms. He explained that the Sudan is the great hinge of Africa. The very centrality of the location of Sudan and its immense size indicates that the long term disposition of Africa will follow the fate of the Sudan. Ever since the expulsion of the British after the fall of Khartoum there had been a fear of German or French dominance in the region, or worse still, that some sort of Pan-Islamic federation would sweep Sudan, and Egypt along with it also, into Moslem domination. If British forces do not control ready access to India through the Red Sea, then the British Empire's jewel, India, will be at risk. The fate of Sudan then is the key to the security of the British Empire.

I posed the matter to Colonel Moran in discussing my plans. He scoffed, "Still serving the Empire, I see. You are mad, Mr. Holmes. Do you think that you can simply walk into Khartoum as you have done here at Mecca? The place is a fortified camp!"

I pointed out of course that even fortified camps need trade-goods and that Mycroft had seen fit to place goods even now awaiting us in Jeddah brought in from India. We needed only to present our papers to make a claim upon these goods. Mycroft had also secured for us a sum of money sufficient to set out upon the expedition. These funds were in the keeping of an officer of the British Navy whose vessel was to remain throughout the late winter months in Jeddah awaiting our eventual arrival.

The vessel had not been in port weeks ago when we had passed through Jeddah, but we were happy to discover its presence upon our return to the Red Sea port. The young officer on shore was most cooperative. We were put up aboard in a proper British stateroom until the time of our departure for Ethiopia. He had aboard some canned tin goods from home and some biscuits and other treats that awoke in me a passion to return to England. There is a great comfort in the minor pleasures of life and the familiarity of various staples. I am not sure that one's customary food and drink and the mere sound of one's native tongue are not the greatest pleasures of life.

We had a most excellent discussion on that first evening and I slept well under the gentle sway of the vessel at its berth in the harbor. Even Colonel Moran set aside his usual saturnine ways under the influence of a proper Scotch Whiskey. The night breezes of the sea carried all the warmth and moisture of the abundant life about us. We sat on the deck and told of our adventures thus far. I entrusted to the young officer a few dispatches by the now notorious explorer, Sigerson. I was surprised to hear that my early communiqués have drawn a great following. It appears that this man Sigerson is already a somewhat romantic figure. Even young British ladies are reading purloined copies of my dispatches and hoping for news of harems and other Arabian Night entertainments. How Watson would chide me if he knew that I have become a figure of romance among the fair young things of this year's debutante season! Ah well, I must not disappoint them. Perhaps I shall have to include in my next dispatches some reference to desert sheiks and scimitars and daring escapes. But then again perhaps reality will provide these elements to my tale without the aid of my imagination. We will soon venture into dangerous lands indeed and we must be resourceful if we are to manage to escape down the Nile to Cairo unscathed and alive.

February 20, 1892
Jeddah

I have spent considerable time of late thinking of the concept of romance. The beginning of all romantic thought is the belief in the significance of the individual, that each life has within it a story and a purpose. Against this view we have that of historical reality which shows us for the most part only the lives of the few men and women of property, power and influence and of course the story of the vast institutional forms such as monasteries, armies, and nations. Against this background most lives have been lived in illiterate obscurity, disease, and premature death. There is little room for romance in the face of this fact of human historicity. But it is because of this fact that there is every reason to see in, not the futility of life, but rather its eternal significance, for despite the failure of most people to leave any lasting impression upon the recorded course of human events, they are retained in the only record that really matters, in the mind of God. Religion alone exalts all human life to equality as men and women before God and gives the lie to the inequality so prevalent among us.

For this reason religion has persisted, even in the face of its imperfect comprehension through the ages, for it alone offered hope that unlived lives might find solace in eternity for the deprivations present in their lives upon earth. Horror at the injustices of human life is the father of the religious attitude. It forces us to turn to God in order to request divine vindication. The very word, Hosanna, is an invocation that God will render justice to his people. It contains within itself praise and thanksgiving, as though judgment had already been rendered and the new era of the Reign of God had begun.

How strange it seems, that whereas the many far outnumber the few, it is always the many who suffer and the few that prosper. Does man readily accept slavery or is it the systems that are put into place that determine this seemingly universal phenomenon? Why should the few hire the many and be allowed to oppress them? What is a king without an army of chamberlains and minions to do his bidding? Strip a king of his robes and pretensions and you have before you only a man, naked and alone as are all men. The power of the ruler then is derived from the idea of sovereignty, from the faith and awe of the many before that which in the final analysis is only an idea. The idea has about it the pageantry of ceremony and the bestowal of robes and jeweled crowns. But they are not in themselves sovereignty but merely the symbols of power and the supposed right to rule. Once the system is put in place however, men and women come to accept their places in that order of things and events and yield to the naked man who becomes a king by virtue of their servility.

So it is with riches and with laws as well, for what are laws but mere pronouncements, a collection of sayings in the imperative voice issued by proper authority. If I as a mere man were to issue the Codex Sherlock Holmesiensis, I would be held in ridicule; for who is Sherlock Holmes to impose a system of general laws for mankind? But if I am the Lord High Chamberlain, because the King has made me so, then the prisoner in the dock trembles and litigants in civil actions go away with a determination of their rights and duties determined under the rule of law of which I am the minister.

If these distinctions carry any meaning, then it is ideas that rule mankind. Change the ideas and you change the nature of man. Religious ideas however claim to be more than mere functional concepts, though function they may indeed have in the ordering of society, but as having their value by being an indication of the purpose for men and women as created beings. If God were merely the sum total of a collection of floating superlatives, then we might conclude that it is man that creates God out of linguistic forms as a stop-gap for all that remains unknown. God would be what we do not know rather than what we know. For this reason revelation stops short of clarity when it seeks to denote God. Religion is at its closest approximation to a divine definition therefore when it does not describe God as He is in Himself but only in His relation to us as believers; anything more than this is idolatry in disguise.

Religion must be confined to God's actual dealings with men and women and not speculate as to the characteristics of any supposed pre-existence, when God existed alone and all created being was only a vagrant thought in the Divine Mind. The writings of the Old Testament for the most part follow this norm. They portray God as defined by his actions and refuse to go further. The phrase used is for God is less a name than it is a description: I am that I am. God defines himself as independent being as such, as that which is not dependent upon something else in order to exist.

It is for God alone to define Himself and to share being only insofar as he wishes with those beings that are subject to creation. God alone is sovereign freedom and our relation with that unique freedom must be one of trust, that God will not choose evil, for evil has no part in God. As a basis for this confidence, we have of course only the scriptural record and our own innate sense of the metaphysical requirements of any absolute being. There does appear a gradual evolution though in the actions of God in scriptural history. The apprehension of God seems to follow the ability of the Jewish people to grow in their perception of God's hand at work in various signature events of Jewish history. God appears to share His goodness only to the degree that it can be apprehended as such by the Jewish people. What begins as a narrow and particular deity, one serving the tribal needs for the acquisition of land in Canaan, ends finally with the proclamation that all men and women who wash their garments in the Blood of the Lamb of God will be saved. Surely there is a great progression here in just who we consider God to be. God of course remains God in any case, but it is the ever-increasing abilities of humans to comprehend these perfections that dictate the nature of Divine discourse.

If this observation is correct, then we may still not fully possess the revelation which is reserved for unveiling on the Last Day. Mankind steps progressively and incrementally into the providential order, but the ground only appears in the instant just before the falling foot. God so orders revelation that we may only grasp and record it or extend it from the point of view of the stage of theological development that we have already reached. This is why the history of religion contains so much of atrocity, because God can only speak from within the mind of man at whatever level that composite mind has reached in its long evolution from tribal norms to universal ethical insights. We cannot see the mind of God as in a rear-view mirror, but only in front of us as we approach Him.

Our prayer must always therefore be one of penance and of subjugation and finally of petition that we not be put to the test or even led into temptation. It is well that men of power should recite and meditate often upon the words of the Lord's Prayer, for it is a great burden to be among the rich and the powerful. History is primarily a record of the path that the great ones have followed to perdition than it is a record of their joys and triumphs. Perhaps, the nameless masses of men and women who have lived and died in obscurity are fortunate in that their memory is preserved in its entirety only within the mind of God and not among the records of mankind!

If this observation is true, then striving for fame and glory are indeed the pursuits of folly. When one stands near the ancient places where the great events of revelation are said to have taken place, as I stood only a short time ago at Mecca, one is forced to think about the question of whether it is the revelations that are God or whether God must always stand beyond his own revelations. We may ask whether all that we say of God is not tainted by being passed through the mind of man. This is not to say that revelation is untrue, but rather to say that truth itself is only a dull echo of the celestial music of the Kingdom of God, and that God's very Kingdom is profaned because of its association in our minds with what we know of kingdoms upon the earth ruled by frail human rulers. It is then the God that exists beyond the written sources of revelation itself who must always be sought, if as the mystics believed, we are to encounter God. Even the greatest of them only managed to gain a fleeting impression of what God must be.

The search for a grounding basis for all of human experience is the task of philosophy. Descartes was right in his realization that the search for just such a ground is the beginning and pre-condition for every later statement about anything at all. The first step of the distinctively human rests upon self-awareness. Perception is then followed by linguistic formulation; what we do not perceive we cannot embody in words. However a language of perception prior to the invention of categories for expression and of words to express those categories does not exist.

Human experience therefore begins close to what animals feel: pain, pleasure, hunger, thirst, the frustration of unfulfilled wants, and the satisfaction of drives in order to restore a sense of peace and equilibrium. Conscious thought floats above a stormy sea of perceptions that are in themselves inarticulate. If this is so then it certainly seems to me to be the height of temerity to speak definitively about a Supreme Being that exists on the other side of necessity and contingency, somewhere beyond both perception and articulation. We are like a fish swimming in the depths of the sea trying to conceive what it is like to exist beyond the silvery canopy of the surface of the water.

Since the basis of western religion lies not in immediate perception, nor in the articulation of perception, but instead in a post-hoc and sophisticated attribution of historical events to a transcendent cause, it would appear to me that philosophy and theology will always be somewhat in conflict in their respective claims to the attainment of sublime and absolute truth. Sociology and politics as derivative sciences will in consequence be even further removed. This is why any mixture of religion and politics will be an uneasy alliance existing well beyond any adequate truth statement; yet upon both of these the conflicts of the world rest. People kill each other over affirmations from which they cannot rid themselves.

The basis of more primitive societies lies closer to the fundamental human experiences of wonder, dread, or affection. The encounter of the infant with its mother precedes all thought. Music and rhythm of any sort unite people in a way that no discursive rhetoric may ever accomplish. Humanity begins in the bonds of commonality; one must go alone to a desert in order to think. Religion in its higher forms will emerge only later, first from systems of native worship and only somewhat contemporaneously from wandering bards or from the prophetic insights of lonely individuals. In the later evolution of human consciousness in search of a ground the final step is the formation of structures of religious authority and from them at last we arrive at doctrines and dogmas that claim a right of ethical normative and political supremacy.

This stage of human development however immediately encounters two problems: the first is the desire of human thought to ground itself without reference to any transcendent cause or doctrinal base; and the second is that advanced human societies encounter complex patterns of scarcity and the inequitable distribution of resources. These in turn seek resolution at times by means of violence and retribution, in wars and revolutions, in imperial domination or in resistance to even the benefits offered by advanced nations and their productive capacities. Individuals and even entire societies may then regress through atavism into a more primitive state as the study of mental illness explores and as the folly of such preposterous pretend-sciences such as phrenology or other superstitions reveal.

February 21, 1892
Jeddah

esterday, I managed to set down a rough outline of my thought process as a sort of skeleton that I hope to flesh out over time. I hope to leave for Africa soon and fear that the leisure for such advanced speculations may soon, under the pressure of events, be denied me. Let me continue while I can record my thoughts in relative peace by exploring in greater detail the difficulty that I see posed by highly evolved religions that now act as the basis for entire cultures and societies as well as the source of individual mental stability and expectations for individuals that profess these faith structures. Christianity emerges from the confused situation that prevailed in Judea in the first century.

Multiple movements of liberation were in play at the time and expectations and messianic fervor were high. Various movements existed and it would be strange if the one gathered around John the Baptist was the most likely to succeed. The Jewish people had a well-developed belief that the prelude to any success in war or peace depended upon strict religious observance of the Torah and repentance from individual sin. The figure of Jesus, at least as recorded in the gospels, is validated by both prophesy at His birth and later by a voice from heaven at His baptism. The function of the gospels is to announce, to validate, and to confirm the startling mission of Jesus and its authority in both word and deed. However, the key element and the one that early converts found most attractive was the shift in the nature of the promise of the expected Messianic figure from that of a political figure who would usher in the exaltation and triumph of Judea over the other nations of the world to the concept of an otherworldly Kingdom of God, one where individuals would survive death and triumph over our present condition of limitation and pain.

It took centuries to express, to fuse, and to reconcile all of these functions and to show them as emanating from one particular event, the suffering and death of Jesus Christ of Nazareth on a cross and His Resurrection on the Third Day. The timing of this event was essential because the concept of the blood sacrifice in reparation for sin was essential to the Jewish religion out of which Christianity arose. The Passover from political bondage in Egypt and the passing over at death of the righteous soul are a natural parallelism and the sacrifice of a mere paschal lamb could not compare to the spiritual efficacy of the sacrifice of a human being, particularly if that person was the Incarnate Son of the God of Israel, equal in every respect to the God that had always been worshiped by the Jewish people. Never had heaven come so close to earth. Out of this central proclamation and to tighten the metaphors to that of a well-tuned piano the church that had its birth at the event of Pentecost has devoted nearly two thousand years of effort and has spread its message throughout the world. The basis of that affirmation of faith that is the *sine qua non* for incorporation into the Mystical Body of Christ is hearing proclaimed the message of salvation as elaborated in the dogma and doctrines of the Church.

The authority of doctrine exists more to protect us from manifest error than to adequately define what is true, finally and absolutely; the delicate balance of affirmation always requires a step into the darkness of incomprehension, because history plays such a large role in the final formulation of Christianity. In this sense all speech about God must have a negative flavor. Revelation can more easily tell us what is not The Way than show us the Way in every detail. We are led like blind men to God and our sole function is to remain attuned to God's voice whenever He may choose to speak and then to follow that path until further directions are given. All true romance is found in the love of man and of woman who find within each other some sense of The Other, of what lies not within him or herself. Similarly, we seek in God what is evidently lacking among us, virtue, goodness, light, fullness-of-being, and eternity. To say that these things are but projections of our own unfulfilled desires is to assume that desire may not finally be fulfilled and that the deepest aspirations of our being are born only to be denied and frustrated. Faith refuses such a supposition because such despair would bring to an end the project of history itself.

What is human progress if it only serves to increase the numbers of the fat and slothful monarchs whose immense posteriors have graced so many thrones? To believe beyond the confines of earth is to seek God. It is the purpose of mankind collectively to do so. Even the individual must find in God his only succor amidst this transient life, given for but a seeming hour, into his hands. It is this task that I have been about on this journey of mine. It was inevitable I suppose that I would apply the methods of observation and deduction to solve the greatest mystery that has perplexed mankind since the dawn of civilization. But in doing so I have been forced to ask that inevitable question: whether civilization itself is not the problem.

What was man in the times before written history? Men were then indistinguishable in their general makeup from what they are today. If one could reach back into time and take an infant from the Neolithic Age and transport that infant to the modern era and give it the schooling of any other child, it would develop in the same manner as a modern child. Is this true or does the collective mind itself evolve, not in the individual but in whole communities, so that such an infant would be lacking in the primordial memories that the evolution of his tribe would have required in order to create those inter-cranial structures capable of being enlightened by modern thought? Is the brain mere matter then waiting to be formed, or is it not itself a repository for the collective memories of the human race? Perhaps our dreams are not our own, but rather the projections into the individual person of the aspirations of the group. If that be so, then religion is the desire, not for individual destiny alone, but a means of bringing the solitary being into the communal structure of the tribe and finally of the entire human race.

This view of course may diminish the transcendent nature of the religious quest and make it a mere matter of social convenience and social structuring. There can be no doubt that some religions serve primarily these functions. Still, to take such a view of things is to silence any further speculation about origins and the significance of our place in the universe. It is necessary for us to believe that we are more than the transient product of evolution in a cunning primate.

But perhaps that itself is our problem? Do we so overestimate our worth that we are blinded to the truths of our contingency? Our rule of earth may be like that of the dinosaurs and be but temporary in duration. No, no, that I cannot believe; for man alone leaves a record of his thoughts and mirrors all of creation in his formulations. But is that mirroring not tainted by our aspirations and desires? Can even the coldest man of reason sit upon the limb that supports him and blithely saw away? Suppose that we might prove that man is merely a form among forms and thought is but an ordering of protoplasm within the cranium and that a sonnet is only a higher order of the grunting and chattering of the apes, what then? Would our thoughts carry less conviction that they were real, that the laws of mathematics hold true throughout the universe, and that something of the divine is stamped upon our very being?

So persuasive is our sense of truth as known within ourselves that we believe that things exist apart from us, that we may even have insight into what stands opposed to us by being greater than our imagining. This transcendent conviction gives us control of our lives. If we trust our knowing apparatus, why should we not doubt as well our sense of a moral order and the existence of God? Are not metaphysical truths as true as mathematical truths? Must we deny metaphysics simply because it is of a different order? We intuit the transcendent and feel its very presence in relation to us to be as essential as everything else. Why assume that all that is required of us is a sharpened spear and a dry hovel into which to creep at night? It is our hybrid state as body and as spirit that raises these problems and to deny either part of the nature of man is to distort our composite nature.

I have often wondered if the reason that Adam and Eve did not perceive that they were naked in Eden was because they were not yet burdened with bodies. Perhaps the fall of our first parents was the first occasion, when to humble us we were clothed with an animal nature. In rebelling we sunk one level in the divine hierarchy, still retaining of course our nature as the image of God, but now mired in all of the hungers and fears of the beasts, yet without their primal innocence.

God may have said in effect, "Thus far shall you fall but no further, you shall be wounded, but not killed or abandoned. You shall not enter into that strange state of being-nonbeing that is reserved for the Devil and his Angels, that strange inverted hierarchy of hell, which even to glimpse, would be to find oneself confined there for eternity. I shall not allow you to descend further, but shall complete within myself what is lacking in you. Your existence as image will so change the Divine order that My Beloved Son will become one of you, to so interpenetrate your nature that a great restoration will take place; even the body, the mark of your degradation, shall be elevated until it shares your original destiny, if you are found with my life within you on the last day when your death will be a transition into life."

In just such a way we may appreciate the doctrine of the Resurrection of the Body, which otherwise appears so absurd. Who would wish heaven cluttered up by bodies? But heaven for men and women is spoken of as a new heaven and a new earth, a second creation whose parameters we have yet to grasp. St. John says, "Beloved, we are God's children now, what we shall be has yet to be revealed." It is this that makes the arguments for heaven so persuasive. Christianity does not say what it shall be but only hints at the full extent of the intentions of God in our regard.

As such there is a lack of closure around Christianity, if it is properly conceived. Christianity cannot be evaluated in the terms of its social function or any other reductionist mode of thought. Christ beckons towards an undisclosed universe, one that has yet to be revealed. We cannot vault over the bars of our own nature on our own to attain it. Our images of heaven are as crude as the drawing of beasts by ancient cave-dwelling artisans. Even Raphael and Michelangelo could never paint it. Our business is simply to allow the possibility that our desires might be so elevated that they would be worthy of the gifts of God and to allow God to do the rest through the doctrine of Divine grace.

How crude have been our conceptions of eternity to date and how many have lost faith because of that crudity. In our desire for certainty we are always making golden calves! The mind of man must finally allow for a fundamental lack of sufficient data to comprehend the designs of God, which in Scripture are always indicative and not determinative. God leads us along a path, only condescending to give us what is required for that day alone. Man does not carry about a surfeit or a surplus that would allow him to turn his gaze from God and be for a short while at least in a state of complete independence. Jesus says, "Man does not live by bread alone but on every word that comes from the mouth of God." Our disposition then must be one of constant attunement to whatever we may hear of those words, to whatever faint sense we may have of the divine measure, the music of the spheres.

But I hear the heavy steps of Colonel Moran outside. He

may have news and will perhaps inform me that all is in readiness and that the expedition may begin as soon as tomorrow if I am ready to depart. I believe he has seen to all of the mundane tasks of our journey: food, porters, camels, and trade-goods. He has no doubt also acquired arms, which I trust we shall not need. We will travel through lands of brigands and of pirates, so that I may procure information to feed the aspirations for Empire of the greater brigands and pirates at home in England. My distance from England has given me a new perspective upon our homeland that I had not thought to acquire. I see now the relativity of our national aspirations and of how small and crude they are in the light of the insights gained over the course of my journey. How weary I have become of history. Is not history finally the account of our atavism after all? But these reflections are for another day...

February 23, 1892
The Red Sea

e are again at sea! The dry shores of Arabia have receded into the distant glare of sunlight and there is only the open and inviting blue of the waters to be seen. Our journey shall be a short one for we need only cross to Port Sudan where we shall unload all of our goods. We may acquire additional camels and local guides there but we shall not tarry there long. I am anxious to reach Khartoum and to finish my mission there for Mycroft. I can tell that Colonel Moran is impatient with these adventures that have always seemed to him from the beginning to be the merest folly. His impatience is more than the mere weariness of a traveler, for he alone knows, as I perhaps have yet to realize, how dangerous the next weeks may prove to be.

There are limits to the civilizing force of Islam. In Africa the gentler teachings of the prophet have given way to a fanaticism represented by the aspirations to power of the Mahdi and his successors. His desire was to make of Khartoum a fourth holy city of Islam after Mecca, Medina, and Jerusalem. The desire to unite all believers has created, among the many schisms within the faith, lines of drawn battle that have often been regional in nature. Africa, as the site of the fragmented animisms of the various tribes, was always seen as the natural goal of Islamic expansion and conversion, while Europe remained the bastion of Christianity in the west and Russia in the east. How strange it is that both great religions claim to worship the God of the Jewish people yet neither can quite manage to deal with the phenomenon of Judaism itself or the Jews as a people. How the chosen people must resent these newcomers! The Torah had always seemed to be all-inclusive and the final triumph of the Jewish people to be assured or only menaced by the pagan and secular power of the Roman Empire.

Then over the course of one hundred years Jerusalem lay in ruins and the zealots were driven to suicide rather than to accept defeat at the fortress city of Masada. Then began the great dispersion of the Jews, which in effect has made them missionaries to the world, yet the world does not listen, satisfied for the most part to be either Christian or Moslem. How long shall it be before these great western faiths are harmonized around a common narrative, for surely God must desire some sort of reunion of the faiths that claim to worship a common god. It is time for a cessation of the violence and oppression that have marred the history of the last two thousand years.

Each Abrahamic religion believes that God's will is true and unalterable, yet each has a different version of the response demanded of mankind by God. If we may imagine a prospective believer in the position of doubt that precedes belief, how shall he judge among the respective exclusive claims made upon him to believe? Certainly Christianity has the ability to reconcile the prophetic utterances with the advent of Christ, while Islam appears to rework salvation history and to make the Arabs a substitute for the Jews as a new chosen people.

Each newer religion has refused the dialogue with those who have remained Jewish, who would honor God's original intentions and first revelations to man. Instead both have treated the Jewish refusal as an act of pride rather than as a heroic loyalty to the only God they have ever known. Surely God did not train them in loyalty through so many persecutions only to abandon them for persisting in what His commands had trained them to do, to resist all incursions of any faith but in the God who had given them the Torah which they viewed then and now as the definitive revelation.

What is this antiquity compared to short and obscure ministry of Jesus? Could a story tied to an execution be expected to extirpate a history of over two thousand years! His seemingly new doctrines, centered as they are upon his own unique person as a historical presence, must have seemed just as blasphemous as they were judged to be at the time, and his death under Pontius Pilate might have appeared as only one more trivial demonstration of Roman power over a subject people on a hill that often witnessed these executions. Even on the day of Christ's crucifixion He did not have the honor to be crucified alone. His death was among robbers and rebels after a minor riot in the Roman courtyard. The entire event should have been set down as only one of the nameless cruelties of history.

But it was not. The elaborate reconciliation of the claims of Jesus to traditional Judaism demanded the elaborate theological vision of the evangelists and of St. Paul before Christianity as a separate religion could claim to exist on its own. Even then it took nearly three hundred years of combating various heretical movements within Christianity to create the orthodox version of today.

Even then the complex articulations of Christianity did not

cease. Thereafter the elaborations of Saint Augustine and of Saint Thomas Aquinas and others, now called Doctors of the Church, reflecting upon and reconciling philosophy with the actual presence in time of Jesus the Christ, are examples of the long embroidery surrounding the simple carpenter of Nazareth. But these events came centuries after the Christ event, so surely the Jews must be granted great understanding and compassion and be embraced always as the first of God's children and the first covenant, if expanded in its reach, must be honored in its promises to the Jewish people so that the Torah will remain in effect, at least in honor, until the Last Day.

It is said that God is the Lord of history. If this is true, then there must be a purpose served by the long tale of woe that history tells of the Jewish people. Perhaps it is only due to the machinations of the principle of all evil that cannot tolerate the peace of God, which has led to so much oppression of the Chosen People. Evil seems intent upon limiting the sympathies of man for man regardless of belief. This force or persona would demand a fierce and stringent orthodoxy rather than to leave each believer, and even the unbelievers, to God's final mercy.

For this reason hope is the virtue that precedes even faith itself, for hope must desire that God's will to save men be universally effected and surely the vagueness and confusions of our present state should not preclude a final and efficacious mercy to all. Even the Koran speaks first of mercy before its many grim warnings. If mercy is the very substance of Allah then that substance and will should not be easily thwarted by the paltry ignorance of men. If it is heretical to daringly hope for universal salvation, is it not equally presumptuous to believe that all of God's efforts are so often met with failure and the loss of souls? Is God not impatient above all else with the sectarian slaughter so often done in his name?

February 25, 1892
The Red Sea

I am enjoying this respite from travel by camel. To be at sea at last and to feel the winds bellying the sails is to feel a physical corollary to the action of grace in the soul. Just as we at times lie becalmed and the great vessel swings to the waves not knowing how to proceed, so is the soul at times left swinging in the tides of emotion and of circumstance. Why this should be so is a mystery. God might compel belief by various terrors of the supernatural order, but instead he leaves it to the human condition itself and the manifest evils that exist among us to create within us a hunger for a better world. Yet that better world never arrives, so in boredom and unable to resist the manifold desires of the world, the flesh, and the devil we attempt to advance the rule of God as interpreted and demanded of us under the aegis of the will of men. This is as true in the religious domain as in that of the secular domain and these two often overlap. This is the driving force of history along with a pure secular need for power.

Against this universal tendency God counsels patience and humility, the very virtues shown in the life of Jesus Christ. By complying with this counsel we may not advance the hour of salvation, yet we never learn this. How many men of God thrive on apocalyptic visions! How many Christian believers desire to be on the shore of the lake of fire and to see who is to be cast into it! John and James were not the only sons of thunder and the gentle reproof of Jesus is applicable to all who have arisen since who love to populate hell with their own visions of the damned. To this apocalyptic desire the greater saints counseled an attitude of mercy and we may hope that St. Augustine may not fret too much when he discovers that unbaptized infants are not to be placed among the damned. St. Bernard similarly should not be too distressed that the Moslems of his day might find a place in heaven. My desire for a final solution to the problem of evil demands some hope for universal salvation.

None of these theological preoccupations of mine seem to trouble that great pagan, Colonel Sebastian Moran. He is one of those men who seem quite happy to make up his own mind about the world. Having long since despaired of eternity, he would create as much justice as this world allows and for the rest have what he terms, "a bloody good time of it." He paces the deck like a tiger both by day and by night. I fear that my company wearies him greatly and I must tell the Professor upon my return how indulgent the good Colonel has been of my whims during this extraordinary journey that we have shared. I believe that I understand Moran although he I am sure resents my beliefs. Yet he has given up trying to convert me to his own stoic philosophy, merely referring me to Epictetus or better still to Epicurus or Lucretius should I wish to know his views. He also has a marked reverence for, "that sensible Chinaman Confucius," as he speaks of him. He is however not overly fond of the Buddha. I asked him in recent days why he is so resistant to any concept of a supreme being. I was surprised therefore when today he brought up the entire matter on his own initiative. It was a lovely evening and the sea breeze was blowing us gently towards the African coast. His back was to me at first as we looked out over the water, but his voice was clear.

"It is on evenings like this that I, and even you Mr. Holmes, can forego all questions. Isn't this enough?"

I agreed that it was lovely, but wasn't it precisely that beauty that summoned all of us to question the source of such beauty? I pointed this out to the Colonel and he turned to face me.

"Shall I answer you Mr. Holmes? To be frank, I doubt if you can bear my answer. The reason for my disbelief is to spare God from answering our questions, for if God existed I should be forced to take Him to task, oh not in the name of all the calm intellectuals such as yourself who may parse the wisdom of the world in the security of a monastic retreat, but in the name of those poor and illiterate folk who make up the majority of the world's population. What is it to them what Aquinas, Pascal, and Spinoza may say about God? They know only that if they do not bring gifts to the local magician or tribal priest that the crops will not grow and that consequently their children will die. Their deepest instincts are that God is greater than they are and so must be feared and placated. I suggest that this primal fear and mistrust is the origin of all religions. The genius of the Jews was to imply that God cares about the moral stature of human beings and hence evolved the concept of sin and of righteous living as the best way to placate God. In contrast the simplest human beings know little of sin; they only know that certain actions are taboo and carry an element of risk. Such people know shame of course, but they do not know sin. They possess no exalted belief in the stature of human beings as more than that of the animals and plants that share this world with them. Their lives are confined to the base struggle for existence and to adjust their actions to the demands of a pitiless outside world. The concept of sin is only another of the abstractions of the philosophers and the theologians. The simple people know the fear of something and they seek by all means to placate it, for it is ultimately this force that sends upon them drought and flood and pestilence."

He paused and then went on, "They in their simplicity cannot imagine a God, who is all powerful, yet allowing the course of events to proceed as they always have done. What has the all to do with them? Surely any God must be busy about his own business! Still they imagine that they are not without some ability to influence whatever negligent attitude any supreme force might take towards them if they might only find the proper formula to effectively placate him. Their entire lives are devoted to trial and error as they seek the universal solvent to the divine indifference to their plight. They know well the brutality of life and the constant presence of their poverty, real poverty Mr. Holmes, not some precious poverty of spirit that will guarantee blessedness. These people take comfort where they can find it. They may imagine a better world after death but for the most part they confine their efforts to the challenges of each day."

I pointed out that the advent of European culture had done much to free such people from a limited world without the benefits of true religion and the civilization that it brings.

He smiled at me and sneered, "Oh yes, if they are frantic with hunger or fear or even desire, then they are told by the missionaries of the Christian faith to get control over their concupiscence and God will remit the punishment due to them for following their desires. Concupiscence, bah, what the churchmen call concupiscence is simply human nature. You ask why I do not believe in God. It is because I desire to remain a human being and not some dry wispy abstraction of man drawn out of some dusty book or to revere the dried flesh of some desert hermit as a relic or to listen to hateful men such as Augustine or Calvin who are content to assign even infants to hell the better to protect their theories and to vindicate God. Does God's glory demand that infants roast on the spit of his wrath? Is God glorified by the slaughter of the desert tribes of Canaan so that a few ex-slaves from Egypt may have a homeland? Shall I believe that all of the rich species of life were once crushed together into a boat to escape a universal drowning? I wonder how many species failed to survive because some elephant in the arc stepped on either the male or the female of the pair. It is all nonsense, nonsense! And the tragedy is that men have given their lives for these illusions and have lost whatever tiny joys might have been theirs in anticipation of some reward to be bestowed by a deity, one whose miserly nature and vindictiveness virtually shout at them out of the Old Testament."

I pointed out that there was also much of mercy in the Old Testament as well; he needed only to read the psalms to discover it. The writings were complex and addressed to various situations encountered by the Jewish people and could not be judged by a simplistic outside and contemporary attitude of what would have been most meaningful to the specific needs of the target audience at the hour of their composition. He brushed this observation aside however caught up in the vigor of his own exposition.

He continued vehemently, "And what of The New Testament? St. Paul was merely a poor fool, one who was finally overcome with guilt for slaughtering Christians; he went on to take the local legend of a good teacher and made of the tiny surviving cult of his followers a core of early communities, each separated from the others. Paul, after listening to some legend believing that Jesus was raised from the dead, spread this folly throughout the lands of the Roman Empire and finally met his end in Rome leaving a chaos behind him of contesting beliefs. The early writings were followed by a second century of Gnostic chaos. It took the Emperor Constantine to finally knit together anything that one might call a universal church. Politics created religion, Mr. Holmes; religion by itself only foments dissension. If the Roman Empire had not been rotten to the core its final concessions to Christianity would never have taken place. The Christians only won out because they were willing to die for their faith, whereas for the good Roman citizens religion was simply a matter of good manners and good citizenship, as it is among most so-called Christians of today."

"Shall I go on? Very well, can you imagine going into any Methodist chapel or cathedral of the Church of England and asking anyone there today to die for their faith? The prelates are no better. If the collection plate was empty long enough, we would lose half the curates who had hoped for a good living from the church! No, Mr. Holmes, speak not to me of religion. I do not begrudge some poor widow if she can find comfort over her prayers. Perhaps even I, when I am finally lying on a pallet dying of fever some day on an island off of the coast of Malaya, shall mumble some sort of prayers in my delirium, but do not judge a man's faith when he needs a god but when he imagines that he does not; when he is in other words young, strong, virile, and still feels that life may offer him something. Religion is for the old and the sick or for women whose lives are one long trial."

He laughed. "What you call faith, I call the despair at life. You have often upbraided me for taking the law into my own hands, Mr. Holmes. You condemn the Professor and his organization for killing those who must be killed in order to spare the innocent, for it always comes to killing in the end; someone must die and someone must survive, either the strong or the weak. All of life is a great struggle. Do you think that even in America with its absurd talk of democracy and equality that the leaders ever intended to grant the means to achieve these noble ends to the majority of the population? Who controls the money and the power in that nation after a hundred years of democracy? A more unequal society has never existed than exists in present day America. If you wish to find gods then look to the mansions in Newport, Rhode Island; look to men like Morgan, Gould, Carnegie, and Rockefeller. These are the gods of this age."

He paused before adding, "But do not seek mercy from them, for they use men for the maintenance of their own glory. Having seen the face of God and how He plays with his creation, they have learned to imitate Him and to become gods of industry and commerce. They are above the law these men, so when the Professor and I and our organization on occasion killed a few of them, behold, the balance of nature was restored and they who but yesterday had been as gods, crushing workers unions, evicting sharecroppers from their lands, buying up politicians by the handful, were suddenly revealed to have been merely flesh and blood after all as they lay dead in their comfortable sitting rooms."

He again laughed grimly. "If you want to know why I have

come along with you on your absurd quest it is so that I may see you fail, Mr. Holmes. You shall soon meet the Professor upon your return, whenever you feel able to face him, and I shall stand at your side and watch his logic and breadth of knowledge wither you like the grass. You may go off to Mayfair and sip tea with some pious dowager and speak of God while some vicar fawns at your side, or some fat bishop, who barely knows his own diocese let alone the souls committed to his care as he entrusts his cloak to his butler and has his ring kissed; but do not think that you may present the thin milk of your faith before the professor and me and demand that we share your illusions and give up our useful work, which was to purge the world of men and even women who deserved to die so that the poor might have a better life and so that some measure of justice would prevail!"

He paused for breath. "Now, Mr. Holmes, now when it matters for them and not after the poor are dead and forgotten and beyond receiving any comfort or aid that they will ever know and enjoy."

I had long known that the Colonel possessed a passionate nature beneath his saturnine pose, but I had never heard him break his silence and grant me such a deep insight into his tortured soul, for so I found it to be. It is not possible to be angry with God without in some way believing in Him. Far from being stung at his blasphemies and misapprehensions of the true teachings of Christianity, I saw in his words a purifying vision, just as I have found in Kierkegaard's attack on Christendom a chance to recapture the true significance of faith.

Even Nietzsche has in his own way made a great contribution to Christian thought as did Pascal in his time and Spinoza in his, not because these men were always correct, but because even in error they managed to lay their finger upon the silent rot that often grows within religious organizations. The faith must be constantly purged and re-conceived, not changed but re-conceived. The two-edged sword of scripture must be sharpened against error. The deep hunger of the saints must be drawn forth again from the laxness of a supine laity and the complacence of the many in the hierarchy of the clergy.

I was therefore not shocked by the words of Colonel Sebastian Moran, nor did I doubt for a moment that I should prevail at last upon meeting the Professor. I did though feel a new respect for Colonel Moran and knew that in his own bitter way that he loved the human race. Many a man of religion is more like the demons who despise mankind than like Christ who loved men and women, even in their sin, and even from the cross prayed that his most cruel persecutors would be forgiven, for they knew not what they did. Perhaps, neither does Colonel Sebastian Moran know truly of what he speaks. Behind his evident anger at God is a desperate love. I feel certain of it and with God's grace I shall find a way to draw it forth in time.

February 28, 1892
Port Sudan

We are anchored in the harbor of our destination, Port Sudan on the coast of Abyssinia. The great grey mass of the land lies before us, rising to mountain peaks beyond the pale, brown-colored buildings of sand and mud that constitute the town. We will be kept in quarantine and our ship manifests will be examined by the local officials before we will be given permission to disembark. I am anxious now to get underway as soon as possible. I do not know if I shall have time to explore and to record these meditations of mine in the days ahead. Should we be captured or killed and this journal comes into the hands of strangers, I hope that they will see that it is delivered to my brother Mycroft Holmes in London. With that grim prospect in mind I desire to set down today, here on this ship my own response to the indictment and arguments of Colonel Moran that I set down in my last entry.

Colonel Moran's primary error is his assumption that the communication of God with man is of the same linear order as our communication of the ordinary events of history. As Christians we affirm that the man, Jesus Christ, was simultaneously the uncreated and co-eternal Second Person of the Trinity that is God. So much is doctrine, but when we come to consider what the inner experience of Jesus must have been and how a divine awareness manifests itself from within a human mind and body we are beyond our capacity to comprehend the subjective experience of Christ.

The inner experience of all humans is of course a private realm that cannot be penetrated except by that sympathy born to us, across the abyss of separation between souls, by the mediums of language, art, and music. Even then, we cannot know the precise associations that such instruments may awaken in another person; how much less then can we know what it was like to be the person, Jesus Christ. If the person of Jesus is the most direct statement, in his actions and teachings, of the intentions of God to man, then it is here that we may find the closest thing to that simplicity of revelation that Colonel Moran would dare to demand of God.

But even here we are beset with a lack of the degree of clarity that we would wish to possess. The full exposition of the nature and meaning of the life of Jesus was the product not of days but of centuries. Contributions were made by the entire Church and even with the aid and intervention of the secular ruler, the Emperor Constantine, whose relation to Christianity may have been largely pragmatic as a device to unify his empire. Thus we must view Jesus through the lens of the Church and its collective discernments. This may appear to be problematic, but in the light of the teaching of Jesus himself, in his own words as recorded in the Gospels, this is not so.

It is quite evident that the power of Jesus to promote his mission was always conditioned by the response of faith that he met in the people to whom he desired to minister. Again and again Jesus would locate the causality of a wonder, a healing, or even a forgiveness of sin to the faith of the one who sought that ministration from Jesus. One need only think of the question posed by Jesus to his disciples, "Who do men say that I am?" To this question and the further and more focal one, "And who do you say that I am?" The question is always referred to the freedom of man to accept or to reject.

Once again the freedom of man, first granted by the eating of the forbidden fruit in Eden, is affirmed. God will not contravene man's freedom to take a position towards God. It would appear that God, whose very identity is "I am that I am," must turn to man and request from us the nature of His own identity as God-For-Us, for the God-As-Event requires our participation. God can only be a God-For-Us if we admit the possibility and say that He shall be so. God offers but he does not demand our consent!

Our vision of God is the measure of His revelation, so that when Peter answers, "You are the Christ, the Son of the Living God," Peter provides the basis for all subsequent Church history. Jesus answers Peter that only God could reveal this to Peter and that his personal affirmation will now become his very identity, so that Simon will now be called by the name of Peter. This revelation by God of the true nature of Christ is rock and on that rock of affirmation Jesus will build his Church, one acting in opposition to hell, that very hell that is the logical result of man's being without God. By affirming the nature of Jesus in relation to us, our own identities are altered and so is our fate, for we are now in possession of the definitive gift of God to man in Jesus as the Christ. There only remains God's response to our act of faith. That response was and is the total gift of Christ upon the cross and the advent of the sacraments.

The first of these is Baptism, which symbolizes a new birth in faith. It effectuates a new reality within us so that our state is no longer that of the post-Edenic man and woman who chose to exist in opposition to God, but our state now is that of a newness symbolized by a new birth. Man is not merely restored to his state prior to original sin. His state is now one of being a child of God and capable not merely of enjoying paradise but of participation in the very life of God. It is not too much to say that the post-baptismal man or woman is so unified with God through incorporation into the very life of Christ that they become sharers of that mysterious existence of unity without identity that is the life of the Trinity itself. We are simultaneously united with all others in the extended and universal Church so that the fruit of evil, which is separation and the state of being a god unto oneself, is at an end. The bond of charity makes all men and women essentially one and operationally convicts the residual sin within us through forgiveness and opens the prospect of a renewed effort towards the works of charity.

All of the above merely shows that God's revelation is so conditioned by the results of our primary and secondary sins that God must in a sense seep gradually into our lives as water enters a parched land. Our condition in other words dictates the manner of our reception. God exists for us only insofar as we first exist for God!

This may at first glance sound Pelagian, but it is not for without the prior initiative of God in the Incarnation of Christ there would be no grace and our prior denial in Eden would be what it then was, absolute and complete while lacking only partaking of the Tree of Life's eternity to have made our rash decision in equating good and evil into an irrevocable one. Eternal life seals our decisions by cutting off the contingency to our nature that is granted by time. The great hope of the sinner is that he or she may in time change his or her mind and repent. Eternal life takes from us those blessed limitations of will and of intellect that makes possible the alternation of sin and repentance.

Eternity is quite simply God's own great amen to the type of being that we choose eternally to be. It is only at that point when no further final revelation of God face-to-face with us at death can have any further relevance to the decision that we have already made that can doom us to hell. It is thus not God who creates hell, but rather that we in our desperate desire to find a place and a state of being where God is not, who create it.

This is the great inversion process of Evil, which is only comprehensible from within its own logic of ill-logic. This is the great gulf that may not be passed, because it is self-imposed by a being willing to make of itself its own absolute as was done in Eden: to be like God knowing good and evil, which only God alone may truly do, for complete non-being can only be understood from the vantage point of complete Being, which only the Trinity possesses.

To see this vision clearly is to understand the destiny of man from outside of our historical experience in its deepest metaphysics. To ask then that God deal differently with us, as Colonel Moran requests that he should do, would be to change that very metaphysical reality, which is constitutive of human nature. History may not alter the substrate of all human action. Granted this primal fact, we must leave the final sorting-out of souls to God.

For this reason, the Church wisely teaches its doctrine of purgatory, that state that bridges man to God in the realm that exists beyond what we know of death. Purgatory may be considered to be the realm where God at last grants us the universal perspective that we never manage to see on earth. Here we see only "through a glass darkly." The divine perspective is so divorced from paltry personal gain and vanity that in purgatory we may atone for what remains of sin in our nature and through the salutary ministration of the prayers of the faithful and the special healing of God at last shake free from all of the shackles that have bound our individual natures and by this means enter finally into the presence of God and assume our unique place in the life of the Trinity.

So what is my answer to Colonel Moran, one who would make God conform to life as we demand that it shall be? It is simply this, that all of existence would pall upon us if this world were to close about us like a sea. We would drown in our very pleasures and in surfeit of comfort finally rend our very flesh through mere boredom and the knowledge that without God we are fatally incomplete beings. Even paradise would eventually become hell for us.

It is this from this insight that St. Augustine spoke truly (and its revelation to him may counter many of his unsavory teachings) when he said of God, "You have made us for yourself and our hearts are restless until they rest in you."

March 3, 1892
Port Sudan

We are ready to depart overland. A few days ago we were able to unload the vessel and a weary labor it was. Our expedition is complete and quite impressive. It numbers over 20 persons and at least 50 camels, each loaded with goods, arms, and the essentials of life. Colonel Moran seems pleased at the prospect of adventure and of action after our long days aboard the ship and there is no sign in him now of the bitterness and mockery of a few days ago. I feel again in command, although I will defer to his military experience should we meet any dangers. My desire is to present a strong and a prosperous front as traders, well-armed but with peaceful intentions.

We have obtained some knowledge of the best manner of

approach to Khartoum. We are prepared to treat the Kalifa and his deputies with all due respect, since after all they are in control of the region. I have of course papers with me to show that we may act as emissaries of the British government in any discussions that we may have with the men in power and to make it clear that any interference with our persons will be looked upon as an affront to the British Empire and will be met with stern reprisals. We shall only produce these papers if it should prove necessary to do so and in the meantime we shall be content to appear simply as merchants with valuable articles to trade, in order to open a path for further exchanges to come on other trips if we are well received on this first incursion into alien territory.

That is our plan, such as it exists at the present time, and I trust that it is a good one. We have chosen well those items that constitute our merchandise and have brought gifts from Mecca for the Kalifa that may earn us some measure of acceptance and protection. Still, I shall be glad when this mission is finished. I have grown weary of desert regions and I hunger for the green fields of France and a return to the amenities and comforts provided by European culture. I feel that I have always lived in these alien regions and if I am so blessed as to return safely to England I believe I shall settle for a time in Devonshire. How I long to sit upon a sunny terrace by the sea and to observe the couples walking by on the beaches of Polzeath or from the boardwalk at Brighton or Blackpool and to sip from an iced Pimm's Cup and to read Dickens, Thackeray, or Hardy and to have Watson again at my side.

Will that vision ever become reality? Where is the dear old fellow now I wonder? If he could see his old friend now, baked brown by alien suns, and smelling of camel-dung would he recognize the abstemious figure of Baker Street who once turned to the artificial stimulus of cocaine to escape his despair and ennui? Were those days only a prelude to the man I have now become, no longer a complacent agnostic, one nurturing a bitter comfort by reading "The Martyrdom of Man," but finding instead on this desert journey a latent but sublime meaning in contemplation of the Church of Rome? Surely, I have followed a crooked path to the attainment of faith. I have used all of my gifts as a detective to consider every possible solution to that greatest of problems, the problem of existence itself to which each man or woman must finally address themselves, if only at the hour of their deaths. I believe that so few do so until precisely that dreadful hour not simply as a concession to the inscrutability of the problem, but because they cannot imagine an end to their own existence. It is a remnant perhaps of being created in the image and likeness of God that death of all things is the most foreign to our nature and therefore the most unimaginable of fates.

March 6, 1892
The Mountains of Abyssinia

After having once traversed the Himalayan regions of the Hindu Kush and the wilds of Afghanistan we have become accustomed to mountains on this journey of ours. Those of Abyssinia are remarkable less for any obstacle that they might impose than for the harshness and cruelty of their dry and barren aspect. This land is not so much majestic as it is forbidding. We feel all about us that we are intruders. Those tribes that we have met thus far have not offered active resistance as yet, but their manner has made it advisable to keep an armed guard about the campfires at night and to guard our camels well against any incursion. We have, however made excellent progress in the last days and we should soon leave the mountains behind and be traversing the great Sudanese desert before reaching the oasis of Khartoum.

Khartoum is the anchor of the entire region and has been

occupied by Mahdist forces ever since the forced withdrawal of the British under Prime Minister, Gladstone. In many ways the death of Gordon was unnecessary since it was not followed up by action on the part of the government to recapture and completely subdue the Sudan. The supposed Christian incursion to end slavery in the region never occurred and Gordon's martyrdom was in many respects in vain. Even the Mahdi himself was not long able to enjoy the fruits of his victory since he succumbed to a death by natural causes shortly after Gordon's death.

Each man was remarkable in his own way. Both were men driven by an extremity of faith that is rare in these days of secular rule. I am not sure that the 19th century shall not be known as the first century in which man has claimed to exist and to be able to prosper and to repose his trust, not in faith in God, but solely in man's own inventions and concepts of legitimacy or even expediency. I fear that this attitude of mind and heart will exact a great price eventually for if man is not ruled by God, then all political arrangements are merely exercises in raw power. The phrase in feudal times was always that "the king ruled by the grace of God," not as now by the consent of his subjects. Their obedience in turn was not to the person of the sovereign but to the God who bestowed that rule to the king and guided his exercise of sovereignty in the paths of virtue. Will the laws of a nation have the same sacred character and claim on obedience when they manifest only a temporary balance in the ongoing conflicts of the people among themselves in the struggles within a republic? I think not.

America is the great example of this new idea that people may govern themselves, at least in the civil arena. It is the first nation to break free of divine rule and to reduce all citizens to mere economic entities whose individual choices as mediated by powerful political parties that define the parameters of choice according to positive law. What began as an assertion of the general will in the abstraction of "the people" has now been reduced to the rule of those larger entities that the masses have allowed to exist among them: corporations, trusts, and political parties.

Can it be long before political parties are themselves dictated to by these very economic entities, no longer subject to law, but rather determining the very laws meant to regulate and safeguard their existence for the common good? With great power and wealth these corporations and vast political parties will be able to so influence events that the voice of the individual will become insignificant. The citizen will become only a cell in the larger organisms that will dictate the course of his life. He will live in debt to that which pays his wages until a new serfdom will descend upon the body politic, and all in the name of the abstract demos divorced from the will of a God. This new vision of national identity will itself be then only the equilibrium achieved by market forces, the sum total of the exercise of individual freedoms now become the very substance of the state.

When a nation rules without God, there are no real limits to its power. True sovereignty is always derivative. Any claim to rule that is absolute will by its very nature be captured by the most ruthless and powerful members in a society and the ordinary people will consequentially suffer. In the last analysis, for the meek of the earth to prosper there is only God as a refuge. He is their treasure and their vindication. A society that has lost God will finally lose even the concept of humanity and what began as a struggle for liberation from the Church will end by bringing a new enslavement, one with no limits, for the desire for power in some men is unlimited. How strange it is that the Americans fought a civil war to end slavery and within twenty years of that war's end many soldiers now freed from military demands became slaves themselves to industry and to commerce. How much suffering has this not produced!

What was the economic panic of 1873 but a foretaste of the future course of secular economics? When a person's livelihood is no longer subject to his or her own control as a craftsman but dependent upon industrial market forces, then each worker will be severed from his roots in his local community. There will be no locus to which he may appeal should he be idle so that labor may be assigned to him for the common good. Each man will drift like a leaf upon a stream until it finds some part on the bank of the currency stream to which he may attach himself. The stream however will never be within the control of the individual; so ever and again he will be uprooted and drawn back into the currents of life in which many will go under.

When the feudal system met it final end at the time of the French revolution of 1789, this revolutionary process was extended throughout Europe until it is now almost universal. America of course began its first existence with the very principle that will finally destroy the very freedoms that the Americans so covet. They do not understand that the freedom to practice any religion makes religion merely a matter of taste and not of truth. If religion has no absolute claim upon men, then it cannot be the basis for order and loyalty in a society. Religion then becomes a mere adjunct to life rather than the very reason for life itself.

This will leave the secular state with all power and where power is focused there will be men who will covet that very power. The task of human life, if we assume that there is no God, is to wage the eternal war of each against each, as Thomas Hobbes truly stated in his book, "The Leviathan." All communities then become only temporary ports in the storm and all loyalties become defined by self-interest. Man without God becomes a demon to his fellows out of a fear that they will act in a similar manner towards him. The basis of all trust lies in charity and charity is only the fruit of the grace of God and not of the will of men. The great religions of the world are finally the sole guarantee of civilization. Without them we have only the prospect of marauding Huns and the rise and fall of empires that men seek to create. Religion then must inspire politics without becoming identical to politics. Transcendent aims are all too often dissolved and are re-branded as political expediency; when this happens a greater evil may result than that which would be ultimately traceable to a purely pragmatic nation-state that might at least be answerable to the indignation of a discontented democratic populace.

But there must be no more of this tonight. I am after all in Abyssinia where the rule of brute force prevails with every change of tribal influence. We shall have a long day of travel ahead tomorrow and I must sleep. How strange it has been though to write this entry in my journal in this desolate place. To write by a campfire here in Abyssinia is to know that empires always pass away, for was not Abyssinia itself once the glory of the ancient world? I think of that great poem by Shelley of the passage regarding power with its line, "Nothing beside remains. Round the decay of that colossal wreck, boundless and bare, the lone and level sands stretch far away."

Dr. Watson's Narrative Continues

For Sherlock Holmes there could be no greater torture than what he termed, stagnation of the mind. The days that followed his visit to Dr. Moore Agar were therefore trying ones for us both. His desire to know how our scheme was progressing demanded that I make continual reports. I on the other hand desired to avoid giving him any news that might increase his anxiety. Judging by the slow response of the market, the Baron had made no decisive commitment yet. This was bad enough in the first week but when the third week passed and the price of the stock, rather than increasing, instead dropped daily, Holmes' anxiety could not be repressed any longer. It was at breakfast one morning as we approached the one-month anniversary of the initial offering of the stock to the public that Holmes' patience finally reached a breaking point.

"This will not do, Watson," said he. "The price has been dropping daily and our funds to keep up the appearance of interest in the company are virtually exhausted. If the price drops too low, the Baron may discover that the offering was a mere device to snare him. We must I am afraid begin to spend money in the outfitting of an expedition to Central America in order to make an initial assessment of the best route for the canal. You will need to tell those directors of the board who are privy to our secrets to press for an immediate expedition of engineers. We must by all means keep the issue before the public and show that this creation of ours is a bona fide company. Even if the Baron has acquired the copies of the Murillo Papers he may be biding his time before fully committing himself. Still, I am surprised that he is not been using this time to buy quietly at least some shares in the company through various proxies on the continent."

"That will be difficult to ascertain, Holmes," I answered. "There has certainly been some interest there, but the company still has a decidedly British flavor. Most of the investors of record have been English and a few French."

Holmes reflected on this before he continued, "We are playing with a most cunning man, Watson. If we appear to have accepted our reverses too readily, he will certainly grow suspicious. I have received word from the Vatican that the Pope desires that I make an investigation into the recent death of Cardinal Tosca. If it appears that you and I are engaged in investigating that crime, then the Baron will make no connection of our involvement with our actual machinations in bringing him to heel by the means of our Trojan Horse, the Greater Dutch Canal Company. He will have had our movements watched."

"I have observed nothing," I answered.

"That is what you may expect if one is dealing with Baron Maupertuis," Holmes grimly answered. "And it is for this reason I am afraid that I will now have to send you off alone to Rome."

"But Holmes," I protested, "I must be on hand here in London to make my reports to you about the market and to carry messages from you to Mycroft at the Diogenes Club."

"We must work around that, Watson. I am afraid that your presence in Rome is quite essential and I have Mrs. Hudson here after all to look after my health and other minor needs."

"But will it not be discovered that you are still here in Baker Street?"

"I have asked Inspector Stanley Hopkins to impersonate me and accompany you to Rome. I have taught him many of my techniques in disguise through the years and this is an excellent chance for him to test his abilities. The man certainly knows my mannerisms and we are of a similar height and physiognomy. Now here are the tickets. You will leave tonight from Waterloo Station and take the boat-train from Dover to Calais. In two days you should be in Rome. Here is a letter to his Holiness explaining that you are my most able assistant. It further states that ill-health prevents my presence in Rome at this time, but that I have every confidence that you will be able to make progress in the investigation there without me."

"But what of the need for someone to carry the Murillo Papers to America as we discussed, what if I should be required upon that front as well?"

"Well you shall not be at the antipodes," he answered smiling. "You may take ship for America out of Genoa if need be. I can have the papers sent to Lisbon by a government courier and you may pick them up there without returning to London. I am afraid it is quite necessary; there's a good fellow."

As usual I could not but yield to Holmes' requests which were often in the order of commands and so it was that one evening in late January of 1898 I found myself at Dover with Inspector Stanley Hopkins enroute to the continent once again.

I recall that period of my life and the years immediately preceding it as a time of dislocation. I felt that my life was essentially behind me: my years as a soldier, my career as a medical man, my two marriages, even my exciting years as companion and colleague to Sherlock Holmes; all of this was past for me and my deepest desire was simply to attain that most elusive form of human happiness, peace. I had found a part of the world where nothing important or significant was happening. Cornwall existed only in legend and was sustained only by its fine seaport of Plymouth. The Cornish language was a mere antiquity spoken by few people and its history was unlikely to be obtrusive, unlike that of most of the world that is always seeking some form of revival, as if all the atrocities of the past are insufficient in their countless bids for glory and dominion. I wished only to gaze each day out beyond the sea cliffs at the great grey ocean and to tend my garden by day and my own hearth by night.

My evenings were spent by a pleasant fire with a collection of the classic novels by my side and a glass of Madeira close at hand. I had long since despaired of history ever achieving anything to substantially alter the condition of mankind. I realized that at any given moment atrocities were occurring that I could not change or diminish and that at any hour restless nature might through fire, earthquake, or pestilence kill thousands of people who were no different from me. Many deserved better and received worse. I did not expect any sudden awakening of civilization or any purging flood or fire to manifest the wrath of God with recalcitrant human beings. I knew only that we blunder about in darkness and in ignorance for the most part and that somehow the corpses are buried, new children are born, and the human race struggles onwards towards no discernible end.

My feelings towards Rome and to Italy in general were mixed. I am not Catholic and I must confess to having entertained at the time some dubiousness in meeting the head of the Roman Catholic Church. I had been taught in my youth to regard the figure of the Sovereign Pontiff with some distain. My father was a Presbyterian and I had always considered myself to be a member of the Church of England while my first wife was a Methodist. I had spent my life in that chaos of beliefs that succeeded the Protestant Reformation. The sole unity of Protestantism is in the opposition to Rome with its authoritarian superstitions.

I must also confess that I did not like to leave Holmes at this critical time of his convalescence. On the other hand he was not invariably the best companion when forced to accept the shackles of confinement and he more than once had said that my presence and solicitude when he was ill fretted him to distraction. In any case, there was no point in putting up resistance since everything had been already arranged and it was a pleasure for me to see Inspector Stanley Hopkins again, that most excellent pupil of Sherlock Holmes.

His impersonation now of Sherlock Holmes was excellent. His manner and style were duplicates of Holmes in every way and since Holmes' reclusive ways and avoidance of photographs had made only his costume and demeanor well-known to the public and not his face, we were able to carry the matter off quite well. We had in addition the advantage of a private coach upon the train and it would only be announced to the press after our departure that Sherlock Holmes and Dr. Watson had embarked for Rome to investigate the mysterious death of Cardinal Tosca, a leading prelate in the Vatican. Before we left Holmes at Baker Street that afternoon and entered the winter fog that obscured our features from any curious pedestrians and caught a cab at our door to take us to the station, Holmes shared with us his theory of the case regarding the fate of Cardinal Tosca.

"It may help you both in your investigation if you can place the present case in a wider historical context. The fate of Cardinal Tosca is similar to that of many Popes of the 14th and 15th centuries. To succeed to the supposed glory of the Papacy was quite often a death sentence. Those were the years when rival families coveted the worldly power of Rome that had passed to the successors of the humble fisherman St. Peter after the fall of the Western Empire. It was during those many years of scandal that the way was prepared for the Protestant Reformation."

"Christian history has always shown a strange ambivalence about the next world. On the one hand those were years of almost universal faith and conviction. On the other hand, life was short and bitter and human nature with its greed and concupiscence was little different from what it is today. Men have always hungered for power and the great families saw even the Papacy as a means to enhance their fortunes even in this world.

Cardinal Tosca was, if reports be true, merely a latter-day example of this frame of mind. His desire was to enhance the Papal revenues in order to recoup some of the loss of the Papal States. The Papacy has since their loss been even more dependent upon the various Bishops of the world to sustain the central authority of the Church with funds. Though its message has always been one of faith in a kingdom that is not of this world, there has still been the question of the freedom necessary to see that this teaching shall not be interfered with or diluted by the secular rulers that have always been jealous of Papal powers: the kings, the princes, the dukes, and the barons of the feudal order and now the rulers of the various nation-states.

This struggle for supremacy is what has created what we call European history. In that history we have the best evidence that man will never conquer sin within human nature. This is a dismal prospect I know but to be a realist is to accept what facts teach us about the nature of man. This is why I have come to believe that any effort to secure lasting justice on earth seems rather to create new injustices and why a desire arose within me during my year in France in 1893 to leave the world and to spend my last years in monastic seclusion. Only my wager with Professor Moriarty and the specific threat that he posed at home prevailed at last upon me to ever return to England."

"Even within the Church there has always been a division between those active men who will persist in seeking a glory for the visible Church and those who can find solace only in contemplation of the next world. I have long been concerned about this struggle so that I believe that I can understand the mind of Cardinal Tosca. Whatever his ultimate motives were however cannot diminish the foolishness of his assumption that a man like

Baron Maupertuis could ever be successfully managed or eventually outwitted.”

“So now the Pope desires that an investigation should be made, very well. You Watson will please explain to His Holiness that an investigation has already been made and those measures are well underway to apprehend the chief malefactor responsible for the Cardinal’s death. As for the instrumentality of that death, does it really matter? The actual assassin may now reside anywhere in Europe or may even be dead himself. There are crimes that may not be solved but only redressed in another manner and at another time. It is not for me to advise the Pope of course, yet I know from that affair of the Vatican Cameos, where I was once of some service, that the Pope does value my opinion, at least insofar as my practical capacity as a detective and sometime diplomat extends.”

“You may therefore tell him that it is my opinion that the Papal States can never be regained by force of arms or by the accumulation of wealth and power. It is just possible that an age of martyrdom may come upon the Papacy again, as in the first two centuries of the Church’s existence. All of the glory and yes even the treasures of art gathered through the ages may be taken finally from the Church and there would remain only Christ alone. This is a truth whispered behind walls of stone in the many prisons of this world.”

“Certainly there are evidences in Scripture for this view. Jesus said that no servant is greater than his master and Jesus of course died as a prisoner. Jesus also asked, and I do not believe that the question was rhetorical, if when the Son of Man returned he would find any faith alive upon the earth. Perhaps He will not. But if Christianity is defeated and the rule of force comes at last to rule the earth, even then the few believers left will shine like stars in a darkened sky and be the more precious for their rarity. Perhaps the age of power is coming to an end for both religions and for nations also and men will finally face the need to cooperate merely to survive at all. Who can say? I only know that the way of Cardinal Tosca has spoken of itself, for he is dead."

Those were the last words of sending forth from Holmes that I carried with me to Rome and I did not relish the idea of meeting that august and venerable man with such a prophetic message. I told Holmes as much just as we parted. I told him that if he wished me to go to Rome I would do so, but I felt that it would be a mission that would yield little.

Holmes grasped my hand in parting. "Still you must go. You may hear there something that will be of use to me. I trust that the Holy Spirit guides the Church and I wish news of what is in the mind of the Holy Father at this critical hour of history the better to guide my own actions in the years to come, for I must confess that I feel a great darkening of the prospects for the future of the European powers is pending." That was to be my last conversation with Sherlock Holmes for some time.

The journey across France was a comfortable one for Inspector Hopkins and for me. There had been an early thaw and the fields were clean and brown, awaiting the early growths of spring. Holmes had given me a volume of the writings of Cardinal Newman upon my departure as well as a selection of the sermons of John Donne for which he had a great affection. In addition I had brought Holmes' journal with me. I was more anxious than ever now to read of his time in Africa and later of his time in France after his return from the Sudan. I returned then as we traveled onwards toward Italy to the journal where I had left Holmes in Abyssinia crossing that dry and mountainous terrain to the Sudan.

From the Journal of Sherlock Holmes

March 10, 1892
The Desert

We are now upon the great floor of middle Africa, a vast plain stretching out in all directions with the great Sahara Desert to the north. It is a land of gazelles and wildebeests, of dry timber and occasional green oases. The sky seems somehow to be bigger than the land because it is domed. The nights are clear with a multitude of stars so that infinity seems more viscerally present here than I have ever felt it. Most days were free from excess anxiety although there were a few exceptions. We were tracked for a time by men, who may have been brigands, but we sent a few shots over their heads and they swiftly retired. Ambush is not easy when dust clouds betray one's presence hours before any encounter can take place.

We cannot be many days distant from our goal. We put in the long hours with all of the silence of men undergoing a great ordeal. The sun is merciless even at this early season of the year. This is not a land for an Englishman; this much I know. I cannot imagine why we have any aspirations here. Surely we would not venture this far afield if it were not for the wealth in gold and diamonds secreted below the soil. Can any slavery of the natives of the region be worse than to be condemned to remain here when the temperatures climb throughout the summer months? May my mission here be a short one!

In recent years I have found myself increasingly sucked into diplomacy and away from the simple personal dramas that my cases used to invariably present. I can see now how I always enjoyed the feeling of triumph when a small and insular drama like a sudden squall had exhausted its force. My cases for the most part possessed a sort of closure that world events never manifest. In larger affairs events simply succeed events. History has no natural terminal points. Wars succeed wars and dynasties follow dynasties; events may be deflected in their headlong course but never be permanently resolved. To seek for a meaning in history is to seek patterns where for the most part only chaos reigns.

The Chinese oracle book, "The I-Ching or The Book of Changes," comes as close to a rational account of history as may ever be given. It traces the forces operative in any situation using the analogy of the sixty-four hexagrams. Unlike the binary, either/ or approach of western thought, "The Book of Changes" retains the complex partiality and complexity of events that surround us. Unlike Platonic thought it does not seek permanent forms or categories of experience. The hexagrams are merely tools; they possess no innate separate existence divorced from the concrete circumstances where they may be applied.

The Chinese seem at peace with our world of change, whereas western thought seems determined always to transcend time. Perhaps this is why the Chinese embody in dynamic terms what we would call transcendent goodness as "good fortune." Acting at the proper time when it is safe to cross the great water is the key to success. There is no effort within "The Book of Changes" to account for the mere presence of evil in the world and to refer back to a primal state of virtue and innocence prior to a fall. Instead the mind sorts all experience according to higher order categories represented by the hexagrams. To imply that any all-inclusive term such as truth or beauty can exist apart from examples of actual conditions in which these characteristics are manifest is to believe in Platonic forms. I have always tried as a detective to resist unconscious Platonism, yet as a deductive thinker I must always refer back to general truths in order to solve particular problems. Of course the difficulty presented by generalities is that they cannot account for the exceptional. The task of accuracy is to come as close to the specific as possible without simply saying that A is A, which tells us nothing.

Zen Buddhism as the exact opposite of Platonism does exactly this: it refuses all generalization and asks that we concentrate so much on the particular that the mind elevates the unique into an absolute. Meditation attempts to so focus the mind that the mind loses in a sense its referential contents and becomes empty. This goal is a subset of the Buddhist belief that all is suffering. A corollary to this is that only a willed insensibility can cause suffering to cease through insentient participation in the non-dualistic and undifferentiated being of Brahma. Thus, the highest goal of the Buddhist is to escape the human condition, not to conform it to a set of normative commandments meant to structure our lives and to draw us closer to God. In contrast to this approach, Catholic thought makes no attempt to sound the mind of God or to determine its workings in itself, let alone to assume that we can share it as it is other than through a uniquely secondary and participative mode through the action of divine grace upon the soul. Thus eastern and western mysticism are profoundly different.

For western mysticism all transcendental truths can be applied to God only analogically because an essential gap always remains between an absolute being like God and a contingent being such as man. God evidently does not despise the human as human though since even heaven, that most transcendent of all conditions, is spoken of as a wedding feast. For this reason an infinite value may be assumed to radiate out of even the most humble acts of human virtue if they are done out of a spirit of love for God and in God for men and women.

A final and more daring Christian corollary might assert that God does not even despise those faltering steps that lead to him. Our sins are not so much obstacles to ultimate salvation as they are stepping stones. How else but by seeing how lacking is all that is not God do we come to move from partial goods to supreme goods? The ancients spoke of the great chain of being as a ladder to God. Surely there is a great wisdom in assuming in God an intense interest in our advancement rather than assuming that he stands contemptuously aside avidly noting our failures so that He can punish them. We rather are the source of our own punishment.

March 13, 1892
Khartoum

We have arrived at last upon the outskirts of Khartoum. I am gazing down even now upon the city from a slight rise in the desert terrain. It is magnificent in its way, primitive but with a strange vitality. I have long dreamed of being here and of standing upon the very stairway where General Gordon met his doom. I can only trust that I shall not be killed also in this perhaps too romantic attempt. Heroism is at best a doubtful commodity and gestures are seldom appreciated for long in the onward march of events. I have often wondered if we might as human beings simply dispense with history for it is always the great events that have brought so much sorrow to mankind. It is to my way of thinking rather the untold stories of each day's labor of the common people that suffices to sustain the great edifice of history with its elaborate events and plans of conquest and glory. Those plans are usually the fruits of power and violence and they always promise glory in the end but leave behind instead ruins and ashes for the common men to clean up before beginning again.

Yet in spite of these skeptical views I am here to attempt to change history. I shall seek an audience with the Kalifa and attempt to get him to accept terms that will place the Sudan under the support of the British Empire. Support not control is the operative term. Mycroft has asked me to express the intent of the British government to offer protectorate status to the Sudan to prevent French or German interference there. The agreement would leave the present rule intact and the Kalifa would retain his position as spiritual head of his people. I am to gently suggest that British rule would bring certain trade advantages that the French and the Germans cannot offer, that the slave trade is at best a doubtful base for an economy, and that within ten years some sort of foreign alignment is in any case inevitable for the Sudanese. The terms offered by the English will be inversely proportionate to the effort needed to impose them so cooperation would be advisable.

It is a message that I am not sure will be received and entertained with quiet and equanimity by the Kalifa. Since this possible affront and hidden threat will be brought to his attention by me, I fear that I may have to bear the consequences of his wrath. For this reason I have brought with me certain communications from highly placed clerics in Iran and in Arabia saying that I am under the protection of Allah and that several Sheiks have promised me their good will and that I am also an emissary of these Moslem brothers to bring greetings to the Kalifa and to wish him peace. In short, I am an emissary of many men highly placed in the Moslem world in addition to being a courier with a message from the Crown. I do not believe that the Kalifa desires to anger Britain and to create a blood feud with his fellow Moslems at the same time by killing me. He will therefore listen to my proposal and if nothing else I shall be allowed to leave Sudan safely.

The first task will be to obtain an initial audience with the

Kalifa. My plan is simple. We have brought trade goods with us that will interest him because of their splendor. His major-domo will hear of our expedition and that local merchants are outbidding each other for our goods. We will undoubtedly be approached so that the Kalifa may have the first pick of our choicest silks and brocades and it is then that I shall explain that our mission is to him, that it exceeds mere trade with merchants. I have explained all of this to Colonel Moran and it will be his task to see that our manner of approach is firm and dignified and betrays none of the fear that is appropriate in such a delicate situation. We can but proceed now; the die is cast.

In case this should be my final entry in this journal I would like to record my thoughts about history and the hope that must be present in order to take any significant action in this world. History does not often witness the triumph of virtue among the leaders of the world. Rather, it appears to be the task of the virtuous to bear witness to the sea of atrocities that is history. I think often of the words of Jesus on his way to Calvary: "Women of Jerusalem do not weep for me but for yourselves and for your children, for if they do such things in the green wood what will they do when the wood is dry?" I can think of no more prophetic utterance of Jesus, nor of one more full of meaning and of irony. That God can enter history is one thing, but to enter it precisely as a victim of iniquity and to pay the full price of that iniquity in death is an event so astonishing, so contrary to all expectations that we might have of an all powerful God, that the universe itself seems to be inverted. The immensity of God funnels down as it were into an abyss, and not a grand abyss, but the tiny cave in which they lay the body of Christ after his death. After that there is only the great question, was this the end?

All of human history lies poised over that abyss of that most fundamental question. If this was the end of Christ and there was no resurrection, then life for the man of sensitivity, conscience, and compassion is simply not worth living, not because of whatever atrocities that individual man may live to witness or to suffer, but simply because of all the atrocities that have already taken place in history, which must overwhelm us if it is not redeemed. The blood-stain of the deaths of the innocent will be always before such a man and will spread over even the tranquil blue of the sky, the green fields of spring, and the soft blanket of the winter snows. Upon this question of Christ's resurrection rests all of our hopes: if that cave is not the end and Christ is risen and alive, then all evil shrinks down into a hard, bitter kernel of hatred and is finally trodden underfoot by even the most helpless of victims, for they too shall someday share in the resurrection of Christ, since it is manifestly the will of God that they shall do so.

There are also grounds to hope for the salvation of even those whom we take to be the most evil among us. It must take great effort to adhere to sin and to enter hell. I trust that even at the portals of eternity the greatest of sinners may yet turn to God. Certainly the teeth of hell turn outwards to repel all virtues. Perhaps it is the exclusivity of hell that may spare those who retain some spark of virtue, some last remnant of charity in their hearts. One must truly love iniquity in order to enthrone it in the place of God. We look forward to a state of being where history shall melt away and become only a series of insignificant days and nights and the lands that have witnessed such great evils that seem to have effaced the memory alike of those who were victims and those who put them to death; then will remain only the mind of God that conceives all things and preserves all events for in God nothing is ever lost but only changed.

Later—

The mystery of forgiveness is as mysterious as the problem of evil itself. The accusation of our actions may not be removed by our own efforts alone for what is done may not be undone, such is time that it records but once and the record may not be effaced. How then, one may ask, is forgiveness ever possible? Can sin ever be effaced? Must not Evil finally triumph over the Good because of the sheer nature of time itself that bears always the imprint of every thought and action? This stone-like impermeability of events is what is meant by Original Sin because in the order of things created by that sin, where man indeed attempts to be like God knowing good and evil, we confront the seeming emptiness and vacuity and silence of God who has as it were stepped into the background and allowed us to create the world in our own image.

Man without grace has not within his capacity the act of forgiveness, even for himself. If the true nature of his acts is revealed to him he will know them as evil and that he is as naked before his own guilt as were Adam and Eve. Man is then bound by his own knowledge to condemn himself, for having separated from God he stands alone. He knows that he has exhausted his own inner resources and that from within himself he has not the wherewithal to create again that which has been murdered within him or to turn again from the lie that has allowed that murder to take place. The result is despair, and that despair is not only real, it is the inevitable awareness and clarity of his position before God unless God comes to his aid.

This is the state of being that John Calvin was describing in his view of the ultimate depravity of mankind and the need for divine grace to do all through an order of predestination resting entirely upon God's initiative. Calvin would have been correct in his view of salvation if salvation was an individual matter, a contract between the individual and God; but that would be to misunderstand the full significance of the incarnation of Jesus Christ. God's initiative through the incarnation embraces the human race as a whole. The great severance into individuality and the burden of our personal sins is remitted *en mass* through membership in the Church. Redemption is a collective affair.

This is not to say that there is no Particular Judgment, for the Church itself teaches that there is one without defining its nature beyond saying that its results are immediate for the individual regarding his inclusion or exclusion from the Kingdom of God after death and that this condition need not await in time the Last Day when body and soul alike shall inherit their ultimate state of heaven or hell. This doctrine was obviously arrived at in order to reassure the members of the church that their prayers for the intercession of the saints were not in vain, which they would have been if the souls of the blessed were understood to exist in the insensibility of the grave until the Final Judgment on the Last Day.

I believe that what is often called the doctrine of the Particular Judgment is simply the individual discernment of whether one is or is not part of that greater body of the Church in its furthest ramifications of all men and women of good will after death. To confront ourselves shorn of all efficacious means and modalities beyond that which grace and mercy can supply is to know our limitation as creatures in a way that is both metaphysically significant and concretely painful to the naked soul. The symbols used in the gospels of the closed door of the Wedding Feast and the unlit lamps of the foolish virgins are a symbol of what this experience of potential exclusion would be like. Only in the fullness of this experience would a definitive choice for one's abode in eternity be possible.

The Resurrection on the last day on the contrary is of the fully integrated and functional body of all of redeemed humanity as the Bride of Christ. We are told at the moment of Baptism that we will hereafter be part of something greater than ourselves by the ritual of Baptism, which opens for us access to all the other graces. Without this initiative of God in the New Creation, that great second chance for humanity as a whole, we would each have remained helpless before history and our condemnation would have been at our own hands because due to the legacy of original sin of knowing good and evil we must judge all things including ourselves. Alone we would in all justice condemn ourselves in sheer individual and collective nausea at our own record of history. We would again hide from God because we are truly naked and ugly in our own eyes. We are only truly beautiful in the forgiving gaze of God.

The perverse oppositional force of what we know as the Fallen Angels consists simply in this: that they turn to God and say in effect, "Look what we (for the voice of hell is always the "we" of Legion) have done, at our own cost. The triumph is ours for we have taken to ourselves what you created to be with you. Those who will come to us will never, anymore than we did, accept your forgiveness." To this discourse of silly pride that finally shows the utter madness and triviality of Evil, God's answer was given from the cross when Jesus said, "Forgive them for they know not what they do," and later cried, "It is consummated. Father, into your hands I commend my spirit."

At the uttering of those words hell as a condition broke free from all future recourse to mercy like a great ice-shelf in the Antarctic region breaking free of the land and spinning off into the abyss of the surrounding sea, for there would be no further temptations in Eden, the garden might now be pillaged at will for God holds nothing back at the end of time. The Tree of Life is finally revealed as the cross upon which the Son of God perished for love of all things.

Evil, which has made of history its own possession, will be finally defeated and revealed as what it is: a great nothingness. The gospels speak of only one sin as unforgiveable in this age or in the age to come and that sin is simply the refusal of the order of salvation by a definitive refusal, by despair in the power of God's love to forgive sin, and the refusal to accept it with the freedom born in man after the sin in Eden. This is also what the Church means when it speaks of the necessity of Sanctifying Grace within the soul for salvation to take place. The life of God within us is precisely the fruit of that second initiative, after the Fall of Humanity in Eden, as manifested in the Incarnation of the Second Person of the Blessed Trinity and made manifest in the Passion and Death of Jesus Christ.

To enter into the order of salvation is what is referred to in Book of the Apocalypse when it speaks of washing one's robes in the Blood of the Lamb. It means that the individual supplements his own actions of cooperation with grace by drawing upon the grace given to the Church in what is called the Communion of Saints. This blessed doctrine allows as it were for a transfer, within the Mystical Body of Christ, of that which is necessary to the individual to be saved. The Church through its saints intercedes constantly in one great prayer for each and every soul within that Mystical Body of Christ.

The doctrine of Indulgences, that once bred such scandal, was simply the material misuse of a spiritual truth , viz. that the Church is allowed to grant forgiveness out of the boundless riches of Christ and that without that forgiveness, which it must dispense with the very largess of Christ Himself, the soul remains as it would be had Christ never come at all, viz. that the soul by itself and in itself is bound in its sin and bound therefore to condemn itself before God and to hide itself from the presence of the God which is love. To truly know the difference between good and evil is to be forever a victim of that capacity. God alone can bear such knowledge for He alone is all Goodness and all Love.

The task of theology is a task of both the mind and what

may be called experience. It is always a mistake to read experiential conclusions into doctrines whose purpose is to preserve theological distinctions, for they often exceed our present experience and can only be apprehended analogically. This is not to say that they are mere imaginings though, but rather that they exceed unaided imagination and ideas. To see that all of the teachings of the Church are not mere phrases but finally correspond to our own inner dispositions and intuitions as to the nature of reality is to adopt a rational faith.

To accept the Catholic faith then is to find a transcendent way out of the human condition, not by obliteration into mere matter, nor by a series of rebirths into an unaltered world, but to truly escape the human condition by seeing that God has redeemed it and taken it to Himself in the person of Jesus Christ, so that on the Last Day, with all of creation that will share in the revelation of the Sons and Daughters of God made one with Christ in heaven, all things shall be completed and God's complete will be done and the story of created being will reach its proper end and final purpose.

This then is my final confession of faith. No man may legitimately choose the hour of his death and I pray that my own temerity and hubris in undertaking this strange Odyssey will not constitute an unjustified choice by me. May this not be my final entry in this my journal; but if events shall fall out that way, then farewell Sherringford and Mycroft and farewell my most excellent friend, Dr. John Watson, and any others who hold my life dear.

Sherlock Holmes

Dr. Watson's Narrative Continues

After reading these words I set the manuscript down. How appropriate it was that I should have read them just before arriving in Rome. Holmes had often told me that he was not a theologian and that his effort as a Catholic was confined to an effort to assimilate the teachings to all that he knew and to avoid the facile affirmation that is a mere lethargy of belief that is common to many believers. He often acknowledged that the way of faith is demanding and the temptation to set down the yoke that Jesus said was easy and light was one that often beset him and that he wished that he might be like the little children who through grace both apprehend the truth of Christianity and have no great difficulty being one with the Gospel. Holmes however was, by the simple fact of being a great rationalist, condemned to walk the path of the early Church itself amidst a sea of heresy and could only come to a safe harbor at last after a most dangerous voyage, perhaps not one so dangerous as that of Professor Moriarty (once referred to as an arch-fiend) but still a most arduous one.

It is said that one who leads one of these little ones to abandon the faith would do better to have a great stone tied about his neck and be thrown into the sea. It is also said that sins and scandals may come but woe to him through whose agency they come. Certainly to cooperate with the devil in the undoing of the work of Christ is to walk very near to the gates of hell. Our sins are troublesome less for what they are in us alone than in that they weaken the Body of Christ through its members. It was to remedy this fact (I could see after having read Holmes' journal) that Jesus entrusted the mission to the church, that through the salutary example provided by its saints, it would minister to both the sinner and to the furthest limits of the evil that individuals unleash upon the world through history. Through its collective ministry the church is asked to remedy the effects of sin through forgiveness and penance and prayer. To be a member of the Catholic Church is to have access to the forgiveness granted by the collective body through its ministers and through the sacraments so that the membership of the church, collectively and as individuals, may learn to exercise the compassion of Christ and make it efficacious in the world.

It was with thoughts such as these that I, Dr. John Hamish Watson, arrived in Rome. It may appear to be a strange circumstance, but I had never before been to Rome. I am afraid that I possess a somewhat stolid disposition and have that subtle contempt for the overblown Latin cultures that is bred of British pride and prejudice. I preferred to take my vacations by traveling north into Scotland rather than seeking the warmth of the Italian plains or even on the Riviera. There has always been for me an essential honesty in the grim beauty of Scotland and by the same token something of falsity in the overdone monuments of Rome and its worship of its own antiquity.

There are places so over-burdened by the past that they stifle youth. There is little room for new endeavors when all about one is the evidence that everything has been done before. Rome has witnessed every vice and known every virtue. The present may never hope to equal past glories. There has always seemed to me little room for the individual in such a place and even new discoveries and the practical results of industry find little nurture among a people who believe that they possess the entire truth of life and death and have reached the summits of cultural and artistic achievement.

Still, for all of my past reservations I found myself awed by what spread itself before me as Inspector Hopkins and I left the rail station and I entered the vast circular space opening out upon the many grand boulevards of Rome that stretched out in all directions. The scale of Rome dwarfs our concepts of everyday life. It seems to suggest that man may always be more than what he is. Yet, even with its entire massive splendor, there is a sensible quality in the Roman character and a humor that I found refreshing. The Roman citizens have learned to be at peace with the past and even to treat it in a homely fashion. I was surprised to see the presence of humble Trattoria and pensione cheek by jowl with the magnificent Fountain of Trevi. The Italians know of all people the joys of food and wine and since we were both quite hungry after our journey we entered one of the aforementioned establishments and sat down. We were served immediately with a great carafe of Chianti and a selection of delightful meats and olives while we scanned the menu and with the help of our guidebook's translation ordered a selection of pastas and a veal dish served with white grapes that I shall long remember.

Afterwards we proceeded by cab to the British Embassy where Mycroft had arranged for us to stay during our time in Rome. It was no longer necessary for Inspector Hopkins to appear as Holmes, for the press had been fooled at the time of our departure as we had intended them to be, and since then had moved on to other topics of the day, as I discovered in reviewing copies of the London Times forwarded to Rome. The news reports stated briefly that Sherlock Holmes and Doctor Watson had left England to spend the winter months in Italy seeking a much deserved respite from their active cases. I also had a telegram from Holmes assuring me that all had gone well and that he would now be free to follow events in England and the Netherlands while the Baron would be assured by Holmes' supposed absence that his own activities would be spared further scrutiny. Perhaps this supposition would allow him to begin the purchases of stock in the Greater Dutch Canal Company.

Holmes was candid enough to tell me in addition that he had little hope that the cold trail of the murder of Cardinal Tosca would yield much at this late date but he could not ignore a Papal request upon so delicate a matter. He asked that I greet the Sovereign Pontiff in his name and that I would please keep him informed by telegrams to Mycroft of any progress that I made in the investigation. These would then be forwarded to Holmes at Baker Street. I shared all of this news with Inspector Hopkins who said that he trusted that we might find some information that might prove helpful to Mr. Holmes after all.

So it was that on the following day we set out early for the Vatican where we met with a Cardinal Angioni who acted as a secretary to the Pope. He assured us that the Pontiff was grateful for our mission and that he desired to see us on the day following when he had set aside some time to discuss the case with us. The secretary provided us with the results of the investigations of the local police, which were he was sorry to inform us, inconclusive to date. There had been no leads and the conclusion had been reached that Cardinal Tosca had been assassinated by anarchists or by one with a grudge against the late struggle of the Roman Church in opposition to the growing Italian nationalism. The investigation was still open of course, but it was felt that there was little hope of bringing to justice those men who had been responsible for such a sacrilege. We were promised, however, every sort of assistance in our own investigation.

After this brief interview we were provided with identity cards that would grant us access to officials at the Vatican. We were then free to spend the remainder of the day as we wished and we spent it in visiting St. Peter's Basilica and the Cathedral of San Giovanni in Laterno, known as the Lateran. I will not add my own poor words in trying to describe what may be the greatest architectural achievements of mankind as well as being the center of the Catholic faith. Certainly if any mere outward sign might signify the grandeur and the universal nature of Christianity it is present in the great Basilica of St. Peter's and its open palazzo. I was forced to reflect though that conversion of heart is an intimate experience and that no mere symbol of inclusion, however grand it might be, can convey what the quiet whisper of God may speak within the conscience of each soul. For this reason, I cannot say whether so much majesty is not superfluous and whether the sheer weight and scope of the building is not an inadequate tool to impress a seeking soul with the true nature of faith.

I tried to picture Jesus standing in the great circular approach by Bernini and wondered if the same Jesus who was born in a stable at Bethlehem would not shake His head when faced with such splendor. It seemed to have little to do with the spirit of the Beatitudes, but then God may be tolerant of the human need to express the inexpressible by having at least one spiritual place equal to the greatest aspirations of mankind. Certainly if the great pyramids may exist to honor the bones of dead Pharaohs and if Napoleon, whose ambitions had cost the lives of so many, may rest beneath his tomb, and if the tiny figure of Her Majesty Queen Victoria may reside at Buckingham Palace, than certainly the earth may manifest some sign of the majesty of God in structures like St. Peter's Basilica.

We spent the afternoon touring many other monuments and I saw the grim Coliseum that had once witnessed such scenes of savagery wherein death itself became entertainment for a jaded people. The grandeur of the ruins that surround it seemed to me diminished by the pride that had erected them. I could see how such a city might have fallen to the Goths and to the Vandals who must have sensed how little such institutions had to do with the great forests of the Germanic lands from which they came. What to them was the Senate? What to them were the annals of the Roman

Gods or the achievements of the Caesars? They knew only their own brutish deities of the hunt and of the fire. They would emerge from the forests with their crude arms and in sheer ferocity overwhelm the troops of the empire.

Such there will always be, men who fight not for a civilization but for themselves. Their women will keep the life-cycle flowing and guard the simple vessels and adornments of the household arts. They will leave behind few great names and history will know them only as a force of change that disrupted empires. Who is to say then what is civilization if it is not simply the rule of conquest and of power. If even religion is held to be about power also, does it remain religion, or is it not also but a passing strand of historical remembrance? Religions always stand between cultures and the transcendent world it seems to me. But perhaps that is inevitable. A religion that was purely transcendent would never be embodied in human societies, but if religions are simply another product of culture, then they would have no final roots in God.

It was with this initial assessment that I returned to the embassy to devote the evening to the adventures of Sherlock Holmes at Khartoum. The Islamic faith believes that in the final days there will arise one who will restore Islam to its purity in preparation for the Day of Judgment, one who will then stand with Jesus, who Islam treats as merely an honored prophet. There will be many signs that the Mahdi, the one destined to unite all of Islam against the infidels, has arrived and there have been many claimants through the years. None though have caused the British government such difficulty in its desire to extend its control south of Egypt into the heart of central Africa as have the claims of Mohammed Ahmed who called himself the Mahdi. I was anxious to hear of that fatal encounter between the great detective and Abdullah Ibn-Mohammed, the successor of Mohammed Ahmed as the Kalifa of Khartoum.

From the Journal of Sherlock Holmes

March 15, 1892
The Palace of the Kalifa

Today I met Abdulla Ibn-Mohammed known as the Kalifa, the successor to the Mahdi. The meeting took place in the governor's palace where we, the Colonel and I, were received with surprising hospitality. Even our temperament and preferences as Englishmen were considered and we were offered tea and a sweet-bread flavored with honey. I was astonished to see that the Kalifa spoke English, which spared us the awkwardness of having a translator. We were quite alone with him except for a black servant in a turban who stood at attention with a large scimitar at his side. The Kalifa presented a handsome figure in white robes with a ceremonial dagger at his belt. His apartments were large but contained few furnishings so we reclined upon cushions situated in a circle upon a great central carpet.

After the usual invocation of thanks to Allah and the inquiry of courtesy as to our journey, if it had not been too arduous, we were assured of his hospitality and protection while in Khartoum. I knew at once that we were now safe, for the bonds of hospitality are of an absolute nature in Islam. I knew that I might speak freely, but with the usual respect due the Prophet and always manifesting a proper honor and respect for the sensibilities of my host. We were asked of course about the purpose of this visit to a place where Englishmen had not been encountered or desired for some time. So after the usual courtesies and amenities were exchanged we came at last to the purpose of our visit. I explained as well as I could the unsettled state of colonial politics in Africa and the ambitions of Germany and France. I even mentioned the Boers, those Dutch settlers who posed the only real rival for the English control of the region of South Africa. I emphasized that as the world's foremost maritime power an alliance with England might be of advantage to the Kalifa.

The Kalifa had listened with the closest possible attention to my summary of the international situation. He looked upward for a moment in thought and then spoke in a quiet and cultured voice. "So England has eyes for many lands, does it not?" said the Kalifa. "Perhaps that is why you have come, to warn the jackal that the lion approaches and that he should flee."

I answered him at once that England could be a friend of the Kalifa and of Islam, as witnessed by England's partnership and association with the rulers of Egypt over many years.

"But then we would be as Egypt is, dancing as you say to the music of the British," he answered with a knowing smile. "You are here to tell me that behind your so quiet words there are a great many gunships that can sail up the Nile and many British soldiers, is that not so?"

Once again I demurred and told him that British intentions were honorable and would protect the Sudan from the Dutch, the French, and the Germans.

"Yes, and if one of their emissaries was speaking to me now, he would assure me that he intended to protect me from the British. Fortunately Allah fights with us. We need, as you have said the word, protection, but ask for no assistance from you. We are not strangers to your ways. Have not the Irish been protected by you for centuries? Were not the Americans across the great sea once protected by England? It appears to be your view that all peoples but those of your own little island have no wits. So you come to me bearing gifts and then I, like a woman, must smile and dance for my silks and spices and perfumes. You have come to offer a marriage contract to Sudan, but we would not be your first wife. We would be there to serve you and to beg for whatever you would choose to give us, is that not so?"

I told him that it was in the nature of power to seek a balance and from that balance there would be peace. I told him that the Sudan was necessary to maintain that balance among the other great powers of the world and that wars would come until that balance was settled.

"So you tell me that I must choose among many masters and that I must do so because otherwise the masters will make a war upon each other. I in turn tell you that we have no fear of war, for Allah is with us and the death of a martyr for Islam is honorable. Even if your words are true and war must come, what is it to us if the Christian nations make war with each other? We may even desire it, may we not? The crescent of Islam would then be poised over Europe. We would come from the east and from the south and soon all of Europe would know to profess the true faith. Your subtle voice is that of the Shaitan and I shall not follow it. We know that Europe is dying. There are no alms for the poor even in your great cities. We know that you are ruled by a woman, which is against the order of the wisdom of Allah. We know that no one who has ever been weak has grown in strength by association with you, but that you drink the blood of the peoples you have conquered and turn their people into slaves. If our positions were reversed and I was to offer you my protection in London, would you take it?"

I spoke up then rather heatedly and told him that we British abhorred slavery and that it was he and his people who were engaged in the trade of human beings. Colonel Moran looked over at me with a significant glance and I wondered if I had just sealed our doom with my candor. Fortunately my comment did not produce outrage on the part of the Kalifa, who made no effort to hide the practice of enslavement of the local black tribes.

"So it is with us. The Prophet has not forbidden it. Do not even your own Christian writings speak of slavery and that slaves must be faithful to their masters to please Allah? It is the way of life that some shall rule others, but Allah it is who decides who is be a slave and who is to be a master. We sell only the black ones who have not accepted Allah. They are already marked by the fire that is to come for they have not believed. We do no evil in acting in this manner with them. We do not enslave those who have accepted the Prophet and who follow the way of the Holy Koran. But you enslave your own people. They work for money, is that not so? They do not make the money. It is thrust upon them, but only in such quantity sufficient to keep them alive. They do not prosper. They are not free to step aside and to say that the master should keep his money for are not the land and the sea the possessions of Allah and do not all men have a right to rest or labor upon the land and the sea? But if a poor man wishes to hunt even a rabbit upon a rich man's land he shall be called to answer before a magistrate. You do not say that such a way of life is the will of Allah, because even you know that this is not true. Allah does not will that any free man should know such dishonor. No man should ask another for the means of life for surely Allah has provided enough for all and Allah knows what is just."

He paused in his discourse to see the effect of his words upon me before continuing, "What does England know of the Koran or of the Hadith? Do your people bow in prayer at the times of day when all must acknowledge that the ruler of all is Allah? No, in your blasphemous pride you are busy all of the day with trade! You have gathered to yourself the treasures of your many mistresses of which the greatest is India. Now you come to me and you say, 'Be like India.' I tell you that we will never be like India to send you tribute. I was chosen by the Mahdi, peace be upon him, to speak the word to the north and to the east. Even now I gather about me the true believers. I shall, when Allah wills, march north into Egypt. We will seal the path that you use to subjugate the lands of Islam. You shall no longer be in Cairo or in Alexandria. But these are not my goal."

I inquired of him what his wider intentions were and it surprised me that he spoke of them quite openly.

"For those who fight in the way of Allah no secrecy is necessary. We recall the crusades. The domination of the lands dedicated to Allah is not a new idea with you. It has been revealed to me that all of Islam, yes even in India, is to be made free once more. After Egypt is subdued and returned to the truth faith I shall continue across all of the Arab lands. I shall enter the Holy City of Mecca and all of Islam shall acknowledge that my master was the true Mahdi and that I have followed the path that he spoke of before going to Allah. Do you see? I may even speak of this openly to you. It does not matter, for Allah blinds whomever he wills and Allah exalts whomever he wills and your people will not see that yours is the way of the Shaitan until your destruction comes at my hand. You will come against my followers, but you will be defeated and your defeat will be a witness to all of the lands of Islam that they must stir from their slumber and awaken at last. You will be cast out and your vaults will no longer be filled with the fruits of your many thieveries. Your men of learning who deny Allah will at last know his will and theirs will be a most grievous punishment. Allah sees what they do. Allah reads their books before they are written. Nothing is hidden. I knew that a man like you would someday come to me and speak to me with honeyed words that we might be part of the great British Empire. We do not desire that fate, nor shall we suffer it. This you may speak to those who sent you to us. Tell them that we do not wish any honor but that given to us in battle and may Allah be praised for the great victory that will then come."

At that he clapped his hands as a signal that our interview was at an end. I could see that further discourse would be pointless and I was sad for I could see greatness in this man and I could not but admire his faith and sincerity. If God judges men by the purity of their intentions, then this man would be no stranger to paradise and though I did not share his beliefs I was sorry that we might not find some common ground. How strange it is that the absolute duty that we owe to God is translated into such loyalty to the most minute of differences among us so that men will die for codicils yet miss the central doctrines of justice that are common to all faiths.

I have read the Koran, the Bible, the Talmud, the Upanishads, the Book of Changes, and works of the Buddha and Confucius as well and nowhere is it said that God desires human blood. Even Kali is balanced by Shiva and her destruction is merely meant to describe what is. Death only opens the path to fertility and to new life. Yet the nations and the peoples of the earth are divided out of loyalty to an absolute vision that belies the true nature of God. All would be well if there was agreement as to the nature and the demands of that ultimate being but there is not. God's existence haunts the minds of all of mankind but His nature and attributes are veiled by our perceptions until religions are as various as our languages.

Some philosophers contend that both language and religion are products of the same capacity of the human mind. Language develops because the mind has the capacity for symbolic realization. Perhaps then religion develops also because of the mind's need to have a name for those aspects of reality that exceed its grasp. That set of realities is then given the collective name of God. This would make sense if God were a mere collection of attributes, but the great western religions also attribute personhood to God. If God is not a mere set of superlatives but has the integrity signified by having an identity and self-awareness, then God is more than a mere mental device of the human mind to correlate various obscure but ultimate concepts. God then stands towards man in relationship and not as an object. For if God were an object he could be comprehended. To comprehend is to surround an object of thought so that it becomes manageable. God of course is by definition beyond the mind of man to comprehend for the finite may never encompass the infinite. This means that the relation of the mind of man to God is not one of comprehension, but is rather that of being comprehended by God. God knows man; man does not know God.

I have thought often about this problem of seeking a metaphysical ground for religion. Its final resolution might succeed someday in uniting the various faiths. If it is not our business to know God, but rather to rid ourselves of those aspects of our nature that prevent God from knowing us in that unity entailed in all perception, then the various religions would not grasp so ardently at the partial state that must always make relative our most stringent doctrines and temper our desire to impose those fragments upon others.

It is not that religious doctrines are all equal though. Some are clearly fallacious. God, for instance, does not desire the death of the innocent nor that the spirit of man should be subjugated out of fear. God might turn from this universe at will but if this was to happen, if grace was to be withdrawn from us, then non-being like a great tide would immediately submerge and overwhelm us; yet we dare to question God. Our existence is profoundly derivative. Of this we may be certain. However, God creates a zone of freedom within us so that we may approach Him with free-will and not out of a dull necessity. But, that tiny zone of freedom also leaves us free to create from within our own limitations, idols to worship. May it not be that what we call the rule of chance is a similar zone of freedom possessed by the universe itself? If God were merely to trace over the lines of a preconceived plan, then it would not have been important to create anything at all! The mind of God surely could see every ramification of any action that He might take. All of recorded time would then be as predictable as the path of the falling of a stone from a tower is to us. To make the trial would then be superfluous for God. But we know that creation exists and why? So that God may allow us the space to co-determine what shall be. This is what freedom means for man both individually and collectively to take a stance towards God.

God's position towards us does not alter. It is one of great concern and mercy; it would be beneath the dignity of God merely to make us and then to watch us squirm. It is rather the darkness of our own natures that creates confusion and separation. We desire to grasp what may only be given. We desire to be as gods ourselves and to tell the one and only self-subsistent being the terms that we will accept before consenting to be bound by an eternal contract. Only in this way may the problem of evil be explained. God has vacated a region wherein we may act. God has pulled away from necessity, just as the Red Sea withdrew at His command. We play upon the floor of an ancient sea littered with shells and bones.

Our lives are spent crawling through the mires of time. We are, as the great poet Gerard Manley Hopkins says, "Seared and bleared with toil," yet still in our freedom we have made our religions mere emblems of ourselves and we confine God to the limit of our conceptions. God meanwhile from outside speaks into our echoing abyss of a universe, occasional words of comfort. We cling to these fragments of revelation and call them the Word of God, whereas they are only statements about God that are adapted to the human mind. We take the part for the whole. From this way of relation come those divisions and altercations that sever the natural amity that should exist between all men. Shall a time ever come when men cease to kill in the name of what is best within them? Until then, the problem of loyalty to God, when translated into political action, which in turn breeds violence, may never be resolved.

March 20, 1892
Khartoum

erhaps in adopting the language of diplomacy that Mycroft in his correspondence urged me to employ when I came to address the Kalifa I misjudged my gifts for persuasion. I fear that I have failed in my mission to the Kalifa and that blood will be spilled in the future to resolve the issue of the fate of the Sudan. To accept defeat is never easy for me. Those who have read of my exploits through the efforts of my Boswell may have come to view me as an infallible oracle. Alas, such is not the case. The artist in any field of endeavor destroys those preliminary sketches that have led him down the darkened alleys of his mind to no good end. I have spoken often of the art of detection for such it is. The long chain of reasoning for a detective is of little use if the initial insight, the intuition of a nascent pattern to events, does not grasp at that trailing thread in the woven fibers of the fabric of crime. I have often found that it is a simple matter to trace cause and effect once that initial point of penetration is reached. I have known periods when I have been stuck in that sterile zone, that dullness of apprehension, that has often made it impossible for me to move forward to the solution of a crime. Though it might seem a source of solace to me that when I could not solve a mystery, neither could it be solved by any other agent, but I am one who expects success and takes it as my standard of performance. For me to fail is always bitter, because as I have grown in ability through the years of the practice of my craft, so have my standards risen apace until I am not willing to accept those areas of fundamental uncertainty that are the essential posture of human beings on this sorry earth.

I am like one who is forever treading water, just keeping

my head above the raging waters. How pleasant it must be to stand upon the shore in safety, to be free of those assaults of chaos that the existence of crime represents! However much I have cherished the challenge of a problem and relished the opportunity to confront it, I have had at my back the awareness that human suffering is involved though I have had to place this awareness aside at times in order to not bias my judgment and prevent the emergence of a solution in due time. This may have given the impression to my friend Watson's readers that I am cold-blooded and inhuman in my approach. Such was not the case.

If I might choose an image for myself, I am rather like those Scottish Deerhounds that once coursed with me upon the Yorkshire moors of my youth. These great beasts will spare nothing in pursuit of their quarry once it is sighted. They will break their hearts and run through bracken and heather for hours to bring down their prey. If they relish the chase it is not that the tragedy of life is not present in the heaving lungs and the stained and bloody fur. To look into the eyes of such a noble beast is to see a wisdom and nobility often denied to man. I hope that as I grow older that I may still bear about me some of the dignity and fervor of my youth and that I shall not someday grow to be a specter in whose aspect there is only the dying ashes of the fire that once burned so ardently within me.

It is the privilege of man to know of his end before death is visited upon him. Always the prospect of death lies before us to temper our pride with sorrow and humility. What man accepts the loss of the quick perceptions and vigor of his youth? What woman accepts with grace the sunken cheek, the dimmed eye, the mouth grown thin and pursed with time? She whose aspect once caused a room to grow still, whose blush would pale a rose, whose form might draw forth envy and desire alike, must finally become the ragged remnant of what she once was.

Do we burn out then like candles? Is it our function to be

reduced to vapor and to ash? Why must we age so that we grow to be a mockery of ourselves? Should not man and woman grow so that just prior to harvest the fruit is at its fullest? Such is not the case with human lives. Our bodies show every impact and scar of our days. We are like the naked moon, whose unforgiving light, a mere reflection of the sun, is not golden but instead a pale and garish silver. The moon carries its history upon its face in the pockmarked scars of meteors. Each collision has left its bitter mark, yet the moon shines forth for all of that and will so shine until the heavens fail and the stars fall to earth. So may I shine until my death and yet come to accept whatever fate awaits me.

Certainly there is dignity in acquiescence to decay. What would the world be if it was littered with those who still in the fullness of their power and beauty had to be dragged forth protesting to death and decay? Is it not kinder in the dispensation of God that we age first and then die? We are given time to develop a loyalty to another place where we shall abide forever. Life as the years pass by begins to show us that its passion-play is full of vanity and folly. We come finally to laugh at the scarecrow in the mirror. Beneath the blows of life though bowed we are not broken. While we do not relish our end, neither do we deny its claim upon us. The earth is no drawing-room where we might tarry at will, but rather is a great hallway, an entrance portal, a vestibule opening to that which lies beyond all experience. It is our function there to rid ourselves of whatever we have gathered so that we will find ourselves to be naked at the end. Often I have read and relished that marvelous poem by Francis Thompson, "The Hound of Heaven." No man has so encompassed all of human life in a single poem. Shakespeare would revel in the phrases that poem contains.

Words are all we have finally to capture and to hold what we once were. They are our cry against the night. They allow us to take a position towards destiny. In this sense all words are holy writ for God allows us to speak. Even in our most bitter protests against fate we are met with tolerance and if we are upbraided (as was Job) it is only after we have first dared to cry forth our pain and our sense of injustice. The Bible contains perhaps the greatest testimony that can ever be written of the desire of human life to validate itself and deny our own insignificance.

I dared in this journal to speak and to grasp and perhaps to find, if not God, then at least to touch His trailing garments and to attempt to make sense of the competing demands of the various faiths that present themselves to us and ask for our unreserved assent. I do not know if truth has hovered behind mere sincerity so as to crown my efforts here, but to be honest in my brief and bitter days in the attempt and to rage against the silence that will follow is no unworthy aim. It is the privilege of man to be offered a chance at a closing argument before the divine tribunal. I have availed myself of this gift in these pages.

I begin to trust that having passed safely through so many dangerous lands unscathed I may return at last and meet Professor Moriarty face to face again and present to him my thoughts and visions. I do not know if they will persuade him to give up his intended course, but I trust that his great scientific brain will not be immune to what I may say regarding the nature of life and death in these pages. I have at times during the last months often asked myself if this entire wager between my arch foe, Professor Moriarty, and me has been somewhat frivolous. Who has appointed us after all to arbitrate the lives of others?

Professor Moriarty said that he would, during my absence, concoct a plan that would destroy the British Empire. Even now he is no doubt weaving his web with his usual systematic dexterity. How will he strike I wonder? Meanwhile, here I am wandering about like that strange character in the Reverend Charles Maturin's gothic novel, "Melmoth the Wanderer." Watson has always told me that I have no sense for romance, but would anyone but a romantic cross oceans and deserts in search of the God whom he might worship at home in the nearest chapel? Could I not as well have summoned the local vicar and exchanged celestial pleasantries over a cup of tea in his drawing room? Perhaps it is because I have always felt that God should not be easy to approach if he is to remain God that has been behind this arduous Odyssey of mine. Could it be that a pious widow who simply places flowers on an altar knows more of God than I? Her faith is no trouble to her. It is simply the backdrop to the humble courtesies of her manner and her tiny unremembered charities. Is it then my pride that demands a canvass of continents on which to enact my quest? Is God amused by my antics? Is God a fisherman watching as the line squeals out as I once again make my run and leap into the air with my scales shining in the sun? But what then is Moriarty with his slow and ponderous evil? Is he like a great heavy anaconda of the spirit, wrapping its suffocating coils about England? What force for good might our joint conversion make? We share the burden of our fame and a great burden it is.

I often wonder at those who seek power in this world. Why seek what can only add to the weight on the scale opposing our good actions by which we are judged? Should we not rather cultivate obscurity and desire that our names should be swiftly forgotten and our ashes scattered to the winds? If we are not preserved at last within the heart of God where will we be? Of what good are our tombs even if they are as grand as the pyramids in the valley of Luxor if they only bear testimony to our tyranny and vanity? I often think that the earth should cease to turn, that all should be in suspension until mankind might as one great body return to God, to find again that center about which all of history turns.

History is nothing if it is merely the cycles of struggle, of the rise and fall of cultures. Who can read the heavy volumes of Gibbon and not find in spite of the perfection of his prose the weary metronome of human existence and the eternal folly of humanity? For this reason I have often turned to Robert Browning and fought by his gallant side for a strenuous religion, though in my heart I have been perhaps more inclined towards those grim and elegiac verses of Tennyson, whose somber music brings comfort to the weary. This has been the rhythm of my life: great bursts of energy followed by languor and despondence. It has not made me an easy companion and it is no surprise that Watson has deserted me on two occasions to find solace in a wife. I have denied myself marriage for I have known that the domestic hearth would seem like a prison to me, just as I have felt imprisoned at times by the formalities of any doctrinaire faith. I would if it was possible burst time and space asunder to seek that strange kernel at the center called truth. I seem to be able to accept anything but this endless mystification of God, this eternal game of hide and seek, this coy and maiden-like flirtation with the mind of man! God seems at times to invite blasphemy if only in order to bring Him forth snorting like a bull in a Spanish ring to vindicate His own dignity. Instead, he allows men like August Compte, Thomas Huxley, and the Frenchman Ernst Renan to reduce Him to a conception or a legacy of a past historical and economic order with no relevance to modern man.

I am tempted at times to seek to produce in this material world the good that I myself conceive! In this I am close to Moriarty. I can wait no longer, I demand justice now! Let the world pause and then go spinning off along a new and more perfect course and why? Because I demand it! But if even Christ allows time to unravel like an errant spool and will tolerate evils such as those that now throng down upon us and that I fear will in the new century bring even greater disasters still undreamt, then who am I to dictate to God or to seek an end to evil. I hope that He may bring forth in due season a greater good than my conceptions? Shall I ever simply say amen to fate and turning away from futurity leave everything in the hands of God or does He desire that I struggle and will He perhaps forgive my many impertinences knowing that I so desired the good that I would walk a path of peril in order to find it? Is God patient with those, who like me, spurn the easy yoke that Jesus promised and does He value the wild stallion as well as He does the patient lamb? Such is my prayer.

Dr. Watson's Narrative Continues

I turned from Holmes' journal to gaze from my window that looks out upon the vast panorama of St. Peter's square. How strange it was to read of Holmes' thoughts on theology and the personal importance of his faith while in Rome itself. Our times have witnessed a veritable rebirth of the Roman Catholic Church among the English beginning with the Oxford movement. I had been raised to consider Catholicism as an Irish aberration, an ancient Church of superstitions and excessive concern with externals. As a Methodist I had been taught to simply follow the gospel teachings, to keep my prayers short and simple, and to keep external worship confined to the singing of hymns and to listening to an uplifting sermon. Above all I learned to embrace a primal sense of justice and order and in the possibility for men and women of good will to improve social conditions here on earth. The endless complexities of the Catholic faith had formerly possessed little charm for me. The whole thing seemed bathed in excess and spectacle from the plaster busts of the saints, to the constant wafting about of incense, to the wearing of ornate robes, and the obscure and fantastic distinctions of doctrines speculating about unknowable topics. The aged Pontiffs who claimed the right to rule in St. Peter's place over the whole Christian church seemed antidemocratic and to smack of an outdated absolutism.

Now that I was actually in Rome these thoughts came upon me once again. I must confess that I had often wondered if the

Church had remained centered about St. James in Jerusalem if it would not have been better for Christianity and for the history of Europe. The bitter antagonism of the Roman Church towards members of the Jewish faith might have been avoided if the derivative faith of Christian observances had remained closer to its roots in Jerusalem. Was the first century world of the Jewish Diaspora really ready for Christianity? But for that matter is any place on the face of the earth really adequately prepared to embrace the full impact of the teachings of Jesus?

Perhaps Islam might never have emerged had a united Jewish-Christian front opposed it in its incipiency as a mere nationalist movement centered about an obscure oral poet and visionary. Rome was simply too far to the west to exert control over the region where all western religions have their origin, the region from Canaan to Egypt and across Arabia to Persia. The center simply could not contain so much diverse religious energy. Even the former primacy of Rome over Christianity was forfeited and the Eastern Church was surrendered to the control of Moscow and to Constantinople, which had been formerly called Byzantium. There followed the age in the Western Church of the great land-owning monasteries and the rule of the prince-bishops, each controlling vast quantities of land. Meanwhile the kings, princes, and barons of feudalism, who in their own turn claimed to rule by the will of God, held the feudal masses of believers in servitude.

Then came the Renaissance and the religious wars of the 16th and 17th centuries that fractured the unity of the Western Church Only in our own day may the individual seek to approach God directly and make his own decisions and not simply inherit his faith as a spiritual adjunct to temporal rule.

If I had been adamantly Protestant before coming to Rome it had been because I held freedom to be the first prerequisite of the dignity of man and I could have little respect for a Church whose inquisition and crusades were, in its centuries of triumph, the most visible outward manifestation of its all-to-human character and desire to rule over the consciences of men and the daily conduct of their affairs. Any social betterment for the masses was to be deferred to the final arrival of the Kingdom of God on earth with the Second Coming of Jesus Christ in Glory. Is it too much to say that for most human beings the fate of their lives was to be slaves so that the members of the nobility and the higher orders of the clergy might live well? Many a Bishop never even visited his diocese but was ordained to Holy Orders by a close relation merely to provide him later with an extravagant income. It may be said that this practice was an aberration, but it continued for far too long to be considered irrelevant to the claims made for the Roman Church. Would the Church have survived if the standard of the Cross had always governed or was a certain amount of corruption the only bridge across what are today called the dark ages? Perhaps those years would have been even more savage without the imperatives of clerical rule.

Still it is worth speculating whether the Rome of today would be so littered with pretensions if the simplicity of Christ had been the practice of nineteen hundred years? If it is maintained that these external growths were not due to God but rather to man's resistance to grace, even within the bosom of the Church, then what becomes of the teaching credentials of an institution so long defiled by such wayward` practices? Can a severance be maintained in the Roman Catholic Church between doctrine and history such that doctrine has remained pure throughout the ages while its history shows such great deficiencies, such a short-fall from of its august and perennial claims to possess holiness? Was not the Catholic Faith itself, like the city of Rome that lay before me, a mere hodge-podge of ruins and of outmoded forms of thought?

Even in his lifetime St. Thomas Aquinas spoke in his final days of his great Summa Theologica as mere straw. Perhaps, that most glorious churchman sensed what I was then so impiously asserting, that God might not be confined to forms and that our errors only increase with the degree of our elaborations and the systemic discourses of the God that lies beyond our comprehension. Certainly, Jesus told us that unless we approach the Kingdom of God as little children, we shall never enter it. If this text were carved upon a sign-post as one entered Rome, how many colleges might close, how many seminaries would empty, and be replaced by simple men and women such as the Martha and Mary of the gospels, who perhaps never even learned to read, yet their faith was sufficient to be an example forever afterwards to Christians.

Even today the masses of mankind are illiterate. Must they first learn Greek and Hebrew and parse out minute differences in codex texts to know of God? If God has written His name upon the hearts of all men and women, is not orthodox doctrine itself a mere matter of form for does not divine grace accomplish its essential ends apart from any missionary activity? Shall the heathen burn in hell because the missionary's ship was slow or because disease took the dispenser of Baptism before he might reach an outlying village? How many men of God have believed that God is so easily frustrated because of the accidents and fatalities of life? How many miscarried infants was St. Augustine content to consign to hell because of the sin of Adam, so that those who never lived to draw breath might awaken to torment because of what they were, human beings, and all of this so that the justice of God might be vindicated?

Surely if God valued His dignity so highly, then the coming of Christ would have been indefinitely delayed or if He had come, he would have come in power and not as one who gathered the children about him as the very image of heaven and spoke lovingly of His little flock. All of these considerations had made me wonder whether Jesus had become lost and remained in many ways lost today even within the boundaries of the church. But I was as impatient with the Protestants as I was with the Church of Rome. Those who claimed to reform the Catholic Church have done little more than to make an idol of Holy Writ. They were like Moslems at heart if only under a different name! Surely God must not be confined to the Bible or to the Koran because all texts only exist in relation to the hearer. Proclamation is confined to the capacity of that which receives it as the ocean is confined by the cup filled at the water's edge. By making the Words of God correlative to God Himself religion can curtail God's freedom to exceed his enunciations.

I do not know how I know this for I am only a modest practitioner of the medical arts and no philologist, but I have learned that the doctor must take the body as he finds it in order to heal it. If then God wishes to heal us and if Jesus Christ is the divine physician of souls, then He must take us as he finds us and adapt his means and message to our capacity to receive it. How many physicians have killed their patients by demanding an instant cure? Both the body and the soul heal by degrees. In past ages physicians were little more than vampires, bleeding off the forces of life in order to empty the body of vile humors. Do not the doctors of souls similarly kill the soul by attempting to strip the personality of human nature and to impose by sheer will a perfection of character that is only the fruit of years of conversion and with many failures? For this reason I am impatient with glorious one-time conversions or reformations and the presumption involved in claiming that one is definitively saved.

At least the Roman Catholic Church for the most part understands the frailties of men and women. The Sacrament of Confession is if nothing else an admission that the life of grace is often lost, not grace itself, but the efficacy of its presence within us. God's will as manifested in grace is confined and limited in its effects by our freedom. This is a sign of the great humility of God, that He allows this limited efficacy of grace to be so without giving up on anybody. I will go so far as to say that God does not even despair of the damned because His love is everlasting.

I had not read Holmes' speculations in vain, for surely his journey would not have been necessary if it were not to explore his doubts and fears even within his belief. I have my doubts also. Who but the blasphemous man doubts and questions his standing in the face of eternity? He is blasphemous because in the last analysis such a man mistrusts God. It is this very doubt however that can bring us to God in order that we may be comforted in our doubts. Though I will not go so far as to say that the man who is confident of salvation will never attain it, I will say this; we are advised to take the lowest seat at the table so that God will say, come up higher. How many men and women spend their lives polishing a halo when they will be lucky if they may but wear as a diadem only a single thorn from the crucified brow of their Savior as their only boast and perhaps thereby attain salvation as they lie in the silence of knowing that they are dead and beyond all human hope but are still aware enough to grasp at God's parting hand upon the very cliff-edge of eternity. That has long been my own belief and it has been a necessary one.

Perhaps only a doctor who has attended at so many death-beds can know the fear for their future state in the dying, which only adds to the last distress of a dying creature. The doctor does not often get to choose his patients in hospital work. Before engaging in private practice I spent time in various London hospitals and it was there in those hospitals that I was able to see the true spectrum of variety in humanity. Few of those whom I treated had spent their lives in customary piety, yet all of them still possessed rudiments of faith. Few had so dwelled upon death and judgment that they had purged themselves of every attachment to sin. Many were thieves and not a few were fallen women, many dying of unspeakable diseases before their time, or from the abuse of tyrants who held both their souls and bodies in thrall. To apply an external standard worked out by clergymen in silent dialogue with scriptural texts to them and to assume that the God that theologians have assembled out of the conflicting images of God present throughout the Bible is the God who we each must face in due time, to apply some measure of that standard to a living human soul with irrevocable consequences, such was not my province as a physician; nor I will be so bold as to say should it be the province of any man. It was my task to give my patients courage in their final hours, the courage to take one final step through the curtain of oblivion to find their God.

There is little of metaphysical subtlety that is appropriate in that solemn hour of the gasping breath and the cold and clammy brow. The whole vast system of the organism seems in those final minutes of life to fall into chaos. Everything is awry and the organism knows it. Instinctively the body grasps to retain its hold upon life, with each cell desperately seeking for that fragile web of cooperation that has so long sustained it. As the senses fail the entire structure of life falls in upon itself until finally the last blood pools, the pulse ceases, and we say that the man or woman before us is dead. In that moment we see our own future fate. It is ghastly and I have never learned not to hate it, to find in it a mockery of all theological pretensions. Yet, it is only to theology's teachings that we may turn for hope at that hour. We look then to the living body of the Church that proclaims the faith of Christ. We may turn at such an hour and hope that the wretched thing before us may have been delivered to a state in which renewal and continuance is possible. After that as a physician we can do no more.

The religious conflict and division within me had been beyond the comfort of an easy Methodism with its reforming spirit and talk of conversion and of inner light. I needed more. To look upon the majesty of Rome was to receive some foretaste of heaven created by artists, by architects, and in the elaboration of rituals through the centuries. How I wished that I might have brought the intercession of so vast a body of belief to bear upon the suffering of those I had once served and not ushered into the death chamber only a mere bald-headed and wheezing minister who would later collect his burial fee for reading a few verses to the dying from a worn Bible. For all of my Protestant scorn I was gradually coming to see in the Roman Catholic Church a triumph of the spirit of man that while accepting death still recalls that man is made in the image and likeness of God and has a certain indestructible stature for that very reason.

The iconoclast destroys more than mere idols for he destroys the symbol as well and before long he exists in a realm of cold and disconnected ideas without form or substance. Perhaps what I had been taught to regard as excess was part of what men and women of flesh and blood require in order to attain a fully embodied and vigorous belief. I will even go so far as to say that the sin of Adam was as it is said a blessed event, a *felix culpa*, for from that sin comes the struggle of life and the vast drama of salvation. What greater triumph though celebrated by no arch of triumph were the words of Jesus spoken from the cross when he gasped, "It is finished. Father into your hands I commend my spirit."

I like to think that the human-nature of Jesus spoke in that hour, no longer burdened with shame but glorious even in death, a death humbly accepted as the will of the Father for the salvation of all men and women, but also showing the dignity, the self-possession to stand before even the evil of physical death with confidence in the immortality of life itself, a gift that God will not withdraw from us. This gift allows us to scorn death, to trample upon its shackles when imposed upon our bodies, to kick away the life we have known and all its accouterments, this body made of dead chickens, turnips, and sour bread, and to say that our souls may pass and from the gravity of flesh emerge resplendent upon the plains of being where God alone dwells. Surely after knowing that clarity of being no one would willingly submerge themselves again in that cloudy swamp that is our being in the body. Fewer still, I trust, would feel more at home in those regions of chill despair where Satan huddles in desolate rule over his supine legions. These lost ones who have traded freedom for the vast feudalism of hell, where all know their place yet grate against each other in that cacophony of self-glorification and the desire to be their own end, must truly be feared for what an alien destiny they have chosen, to be lost forever in a choice that is irrevocable only because they choose to make it so.

These were my reflections as well, as I may recapture them here, during my first days in Rome. I have placed them down here so that my readers may know that I grappled at the time with the same thoughts that Holmes expressed in his journal. I had found in his manuscript the challenge of a lifetime. I had never reached such depths before in my study of his character, a study that had for so long fascinated me. I realized that although I did not share his genius I shared his same desire to seek an answer to religious questions and to explain why this great drama of human existence that we all share is as it is. Religion once provided the undergirding of all social action. This seems less so today. The great project of the French Encyclopedists and the age of reason had yet to deliver humanity from its attendant ills by providing a composite and adequate solution. Only religion can ever provide an answer adequate to our needs. As the complexity of life increases, just to that extent our theology must be applied and translated into modalities fit to address new questions as they are posed. I returned therefore once again to Holmes' journal with interest hoping to find the answers there.

From the Journal of Sherlock Holmes

March 28, 1892
The Great Nile River

We have left Khartoum. I had hoped to prevail with the Kalifa to grant me another interview, but my efforts were in vain. There are men who view themselves as the tools of destiny and he is clearly one of them. His sense for his mission and the divine aid that will be vouchsafed to him to help him attain his goal is adamant. He had promised us an escort to the borders of the land he now rules but he also intimated that another such mission as ours would not be welcome. Indeed, I now believe that his purpose in seeing us at all was to provoke that very confrontation with the British in Egypt that must finally come. His words to me were a challenge, which he hopes we will communicate to the British government. I have little doubt that the Kalifa will not be content to remain in his desert stronghold indefinitely. The rich lands of the Nile Valley and the Ports of Alexandria and Cairo lie before him as sources of rich booty from which he hopes to lead a new Islamic wave that will sweep all of Northern Africa before it and beyond.

It may seem strange to modern Europeans but the world of Islam has never relinquished its goals of conquest and domination. The vision of Pan-Islamic rule is an integral part of the faith. Jihad is a duty that rests upon all believers. If universal charity is the goal of Christianity and universal peace its emblem, then triumph instituted in the name of the prophet and the rule of force and of imposed belief has been from the very first the distinguishing characteristic of Islam. Mohammed was nothing if not a great general. Islam is an ocean lapping at the shores of Europe and of Russia. It breaks forth at times in great surges only to be forced back. I fear that the co-existence of two such absolute religions as Christianity and Islam represent can never be possible. Both presume to deliver the earth into its final days. World history is poised over the prospect of an apocalypse that both religions anticipate and desire.

There seems to be something in humankind that craves some final accounting and destruction of the earth. Even the French Revolution had about it a fury and an absolute trust in reason that could only be imposed by force and bloodshed. The idea that men and women might have a natural dignity and the right to choose their religion is alien to the instinct of many. Once a belief system opens itself to an absolute authority existing beyond space and time, the very source of all moral structure and duty, then anything that promises only earthly peace and prosperity and the best possible life in our short and bitter days becomes irrelevant. Instead men will seek to know the will of God absolutely and then not leaving their fate to providence will instead make every effort to advance the aims of God by their own force. They will even attempt to advance the divine intention by their political actions, mistaking their need for power with the august aims of God. This has been the source of much anguish in history. But even anguish is allowed to be permissible by religions that see happiness as a promise reserved for a future life and not something to know or be enjoyed here and now. By making any present desire for a better world pointless in the face of the annihilation promised by God such belief structures undermine human progress and give the lie to charity. Against such positions of moral absolutism rebellions are bound to arise. There have been many great benefactors of history like Voltaire who have denied all of the claims of religion in the name of human progress only to forget that secular tyrannies can be as brutal as religious tyrannies. Secular republics have put in the place of God a politically based but no less absolute vision without any intentions or plans beyond what is evident in the laws of nature. These men are called deists and they included many of the composers of the great Encyclopedia of France such as Diderot. Even nature has at times been seen by such men as inimical to human progress. If nature is red in tooth and claw, then only art and technology may create for mankind a tolerable world. This concept, that human life may define its own nature and discover its own parameters, has meant that there is no bridge beyond the visible world to any consciousness beyond our own. The moral sense then is not discovered or even intuited, but created out of whole cloth by a social agreement. This has in turn meant that we can only look within ourselves for the truth. The history of thought then becomes a pursuit of the excellent in the poets, the prophets, and even those who write or interpret our laws. Culture becomes the substitute for religion and science is finally the mistress of culture.

The world will then be what we make of it and we will deem ourselves to be answerable to no god but our own experience reflecting upon the results of our actions. Certainly many people today hold to this faith. It fails though to deal with the evil in man and the perverse greed and destruction that have again and again laid waste to human progress and dispersed the resources that have been so laboriously gathered by past generations to create a better life for all. Men will always fear each other and from that fear there always comes the desire to dominate. If any progress has ever been made in history, it has been made by men who feared God more than they feared each other. If the fear of God is ever taken away will we be liberated at last or will not a new dark-age descend upon the earth? Man is always insufficient to himself.

My melancholy thoughts were interrupted by Colonel Moran, who seems to be only too glad to be returning to lands not merely dominated by but inhabited by Europeans. I noticed the gloating smile upon his face.

"We were lucky you know in Khartoum. I do not think that you realize how lucky. It was the Kalifa's contempt for us that motivated the mercy that he showed to us in allowing us to leave with our heads intact. Otherwise our heads would be even now displayed at the gates of Khartoum and our bodies would have been fattening the jackals outside the walls. I wonder where you will go now, Mr. Sherlock Holmes. No doubt you plan to visit some out of the way place like Mongolia, anything to put off the day when you must confront the Professor with the vanity of this preposterous expedition."

I turned to him and replied. "I shall surprise you, Colonel. I intend to go now to France."

"You are hungry for some decent food, eh? I'll give the Frogs this; they know how to cook."

"As a matter of fact I am going because I wish to conduct some chemical researches into the coal-tar derivatives. If I may make no other contribution to the human race, I may at least bequeath to the world some new substances that may be of use in fighting disease, the universal scourge of mankind."

Colonel Moran laughed. "Can it be so? Will you now turn from the metaphysical to such a mundane goal? How have the mighty fallen!"

"My dear Colonel, you may recall that my quest was not to pose as an arbiter of the absolute but rather to follow existing traditions so as to ascertain a set of common truths that may persuade non-believers such as the Professor. I was not attempting to create my own religion of course, but simply to discern a unity between experience and revelation in all religions. I do not know whether I have succeeded in attaining that goal, but I do not believe that the quest has been in vain. To add to that metaphysical quest now some measure of concrete accomplishment is simply due to my desire to use my talents, such as they are, to serve mankind as my religion mandates. It is no small comfort to leave this world some small legacy of our passing and as it happens I am a qualified chemist as well as a detective, so I shall now make an endeavor in that direction."

"You may do so if you wish and since I will then be at liberty from my constant supervision of your folly; I in turn will seek out the casino at Monte Carlo and other enjoyments. I trust that you will be quite safe in France and will require neither a bodyguard nor a translator. There is one goddess whom I have always revered, the goddess of chance. If you promise me that you will remain quietly ensconced in your laboratory, I shall leave you to your own devices for a time. I need no longer act as your guide and protector, but we shall return to England together when you desire to return."

In that short conversation, our plans for the future were made and I turned in silence to contemplate once again the primal river and its great crocodilian guardians. The banks of the river are thronged with all manner of life, yet always before me was the ever-present pageant of death. The torpor of the great Nile crocodiles was interrupted now and again by a great surge of energy as some beast that had ventured too close to the river seeking water was blocked by its fellows as they made their escape from the lunging jaws. The unfortunate victim is then drawn into the depths in a cauldron of muddy foam. This was the operation in action of the goddess of chance that was so revered by Colonel Moran: chance, fortune, or destiny.

I thought once again of "The I-Ching," that instrument to guide the Chinese man of wisdom so that he may advance at the most propitious time. I wondered if the Colonel was right and whether my journey had been made at the best of times. Might I have reached different conclusions had I been another man or had I made this journey of my life in another era? Is what we call our personality or character more the product of chance rather than insight and effort? If the truth of the individual is contingent, then what may we say of the truths that we call eternal and unchangeable, but must first rely upon the human mind to grasp and the human hand to record?

It is no small thing to claim to speak absolute truths for all persons, times, and places as religion does. I must confess that I at times envy those who exist without questions, those children of every age who may simply take life as it comes and find in the baubles and glitter of the vast carnival of existence enough solace to enable them to face both life and death without the questions and dilemmas that challenge those of a more philosophic cast of mind. These former types swim easily on the surface of events, satisfied and distracted from the lunging jaws of fatality. I could well imagine the grim amusement that Colonel Moral would express if he knew the course that my thoughts pursued after each encounter with him. He would point out that it is only the vanity of man that expects recompense for suffering. He would advise that it is folly to look beyond circumstances for any purpose or for some final justification for the way that things are by concocting doctrines such as that of Original Sin. He would say that the final proof of God's non-existence is the suffering of the innocent. To this I would reply that if his view were correct then it would be unnatural to feel a sense of horror when we witness violence and natural tumults such as storms and earthquakes when they decimate human lives. We possess an inner sense that such things should not be. They awaken more than mere terror within us. We feel indignation. We feel that somewhere and somehow there must be an accounting. The beauty of the world only adds to its horror. Pleasure only intensifies pain when it comes. Love only makes us mourn its inevitable passing away.

The roots of eternity lie deep within us. Is this perhaps due to a memory of a prior state? Certainly it is more than mere desire for what we do not possess that tells us that all things fall short of our expectations and our hopes. The organism asks that it not be disturbed, yet it covets growth and change. This constant chaffing against restraint and disappointment makes every moment a compromise between the intolerable and the adequate. To the thinking man life is only a suspended state between boredom and misfortune. The slight admixture of joy never makes for clarity in the mud-laden stream of our days and nights. For this reason, I have often thought that true beatitude is found only in distraction. If we do not witness the approach of the assassin, we lengthen our last moments and preserve them from fear.

But what can we say to those who have awakened to the beast watching us with predatory eyes only to snatch us unprepared from life without a solution and the solace that it brings? What comforts can philosophy give? I have spent my life in the pursuit of crime. To solve the individual problem posed gave me as a detective a sense of control over the inscrutable. Ever and again though, I have been forced back to the daily round of purposeless atrocities, to crimes whose immediate solution was evident, but still not reversible. The malefactor may have even failed to run away. He might stand over his victim with a dripping knife as though his crime finally allowed him to express the entire desolation of his life. Such criminals make defiance their justification.

Such crimes speak a language of their own. They are the cry of brutal and blind human impulse. Can courts of law impose reason after the fact? Crimes contain within themselves their own logic. They are a statement as truly as is a doctoral dissertation. They are circumstance, naked, factual, and irrefutable of human evil; but are they different from a plague, a great fire, or a cyclone?

Are these phenomena any less evil because their agency is blind and rooted in the mere physics of matter and energy? The fact that one has a human agent is irrelevant to the victim. In fact, if it is a working out of natural evil, it is worse still; for we imagine that God might have intervened, but for some reason of His own chose to abstain, to allow the workings of the physical universe to continue undeflected by the miraculous. If God can work miracles at all, then why should they not be worked all the time? Who would not wish for a universal exception to be made in his unique case from the laws of fatality?

So thought spins around and about its own axis and the only answer seems to be that creation, once flawed by what we call Original Sin, must limp along as best it may. Perhaps somewhere there is an alternate world. We may be living in the first-draft of creation. We may be figures on an aging canvass long since put aside by its artist, one who has neglected to remember that the colors are still running together and then cracking as they dry. I am only too aware that the Incarnation of Jesus gives the lie to this somber point of view. A better version of events might be that God as the creator refuses to surrender us, even to the results of our own definitive acts.

Our universe may be an example of pentimento, a canvas painted over and over again and what we call evil is what shows, even through the new paint, the outline of a prior hope and intention. Taking God out of the equation answers nothing, because then we are plunged into a situation in complete passivity to a fate that will not even allow us to question it because it is unconscious and unaware of us. If we cannot ask questions about our state of life, it would be better that we should be insensate. Even the lowly worm must be presumed to have some intent as it crawls about and thus feel some measure of disappointment when a rock blocks its path. Even stones erode in patterns as their substance resists decay. How much more so should we demand an answer to the final questions of life and death? If life is like the Nile, rich and fertile, yet full of violence and terror, so be it; but it shall not escape my probing. I will sound its muddy depths. I will stand fast against the turbid flow. I cannot do otherwise and continue to exist as a human being.

April 4, 1892
The Nile River

My last entry was made in a mood of rebellion bred of disappointment and frustration. Often in the desire to do the good our pride is most manifest, for we demand results disproportionate to the stature of human life.

Today my thoughts take a gentler course. We have left the upper reaches of the river behind. We have left the Sudan region and the great river is wider now as we enter the ancient land of Egypt. There are signs of cultivation replacing the green tangles of jungle. Already I feel the comfort of man's intervention through agriculture, irrigation, and the domestication of animal life. The course of this great river might be said to follow the course of development of human history. When we come to Cairo and Alexandria we will have caught up again with the 19th century.

I am alas a man of my own age. Technology is dear to me. My mind dares not confront circumstance with no aid of prior inventions. Strip me of language, deny me the differential calculus, take away from me the list of elements and of prime numbers and I should be lost. These are my totems. I cling to them in the darkness while outside the lion stalks and the hyena mocks, and the great snakes coil. Perhaps the reason why faith is so difficult for 19th century man is that we are finally establishing a measure of control over human limitations. The arduous effort to simply sustain life is ameliorated and rather than using this precious leisure to worship God, who was once our only hope, our culture of science and our technical progress has only increased our desires. To imagine that our present life may be so comfortable that we may dispense with eternity entirely has now become a common view. Perhaps it is the desire for an effortless existence that possesses us, one immune from cause and effect, and one that is not subject to chance misfortunes that now teaches us to rely only upon ourselves and to ameliorate suffering, not out of charity, but with the desire to create a heaven upon the earth.

All of history denies this sanguine view of what the future will bring. Power, whenever it has accumulated has always been used to oppress the weak and to spread the web of conquest. Luxury does not make for happiness, but rather opens the vast dimensions of our inner void. Man cannot be an end unto himself. I believe that what may be the best explanation for suffering is that it calls us forth to battle our own desires. Suffering unites us to the pain of the other and awakens our compassion. How foolish it is then to upbraid God for the nature of things and to ask for a better world than the one that we know. The Cross is God's final answer to mankind.

That God is crucified by man and not that man is made to suffer by an omnipotent God: this is the greatest of all mysteries. The Cross is more though than a mere symbol. It is the actual course of an event, one in the shadow of which all of human history now stands. However much man might doubt Original Sin, we cannot doubt that salvation through the atonement for sin of Jesus Christ offers us a new chance, one that has been given us by God to attain His original intentions towards man and woman.

After the Resurrection of Christ a chance was given humanity that is once again being thrown away, not merely rejected, but rejected with contempt in every true sin. The refusal of all help from God, combined with the desire to claim as a right what is and always will be a gift, has been the posture of human nature before God in all times and places. It makes us crave power

and domination. It makes us turn to God in accusation rather than
to be grateful that life is not even more difficult for us. To embrace
strenuous virtue and not to count the cost, but rather to rejoice
that our efforts may cooperate with Divine grace and run parallel
to what God alone can accomplish is the task of right living and the
source of our only lasting peace.

Dr. Watson's Narrative Continues

It was on the morning of my third day in Rome when I received my first communication from Holmes in London. My days had been spent in wandering about the eternal city and experiencing that sense of wonder that must greet any first visitor to Rome. In the evenings I would read selections from Holmes' journal and compare his thoughts with my own. My visits to various churches and to the great cathedrals of St. Peter's Basilica and to San Giovanni Laterno had placed the questions of faith squarely before me. I confess that I had at last reached that time of life when my end, far from being a distant and hazy prospect, was now gradually appearing before me in all of its stark clarity and inevitability. It may seem a strange thing, but even doctors are not immune to the fond illusion that death will make an exception in their case. I still felt within me though the vigor of youth despite my years. Indeed if I noticed any signs of aging at all it was from my increasing nostalgia for the gentler age that I imagined had once prevailed in my youth. I felt then that it was not I but the world that was aging about me while I remained strangely unaltered. Each year seemed to increase the sense of a blind and chaotic urgency that was hurdling towards an end that I could not imagine. I recall that I felt at times like a rider in a runaway carriage about to plunge into an abyss.

For this reason as the days of my visit passed I began to set aside my first impressions of Rome as having been somewhat inaccurate and to maintain a somewhat milder assessment and outlook towards the city and its sheer power over heart and mind. Rome's very solidity and permanence came to speak to me of its eternal youth. Perhaps it was the mild Italian air that already breathed with the odors of spring. I could feel in the moist earth a sense of the budding life of the new year of 1898. It is those quickening hopes that we associate with spring that makes one feel that a new beginning can always be made in life and that makes of youth a perennial season of the heart. I will even admit that my state of mind at the time was such that my sense of the mission on which I was engaged was blunted and diminished by a more personal concern.

Inspector Stanley Hopkins had relieved me of the usual prosaic duties of any investigation. While I was engaged in sightseeing, he had bustled about Rome with the aid of an interpreter provided for us by the British Embassy. The good inspector interviewed representatives of the Italian Police and certain high officials at the Vatican Bank. He told me that he would share everything with me when the data began to assemble in his mind and to take some cohesive form. Until that time, I was at liberty to explore Rome at will.

My period of solitary freedom came to an end one morning. I had descended to the dining room to join the inspector for breakfast. I could see by his air of suppressed excitement that he was making progress with the case. He waited until we had been served before laying the facts before me.

"I have learned from your friend and colleague Mr. Holmes that half of the task of detection is simply to undertake the necessary leg-work and to talk to all the parties who may possess information. I assure you Doctor Watson that the master would be proud of my endeavors during these last days in Rome. I believe that I now have within my grasp all of the essential circumstances surrounding the death of Cardinal Tosca and have obtained, insofar as possible, some sense of the character and personality of the man."

The inspector then proceeded to outline the case as follows. "Cardinal Tosca was in a sense a modern version of Cardinal Richelieu of 17th century France. He was a man who valued power for its own sake. His initial position of course was quite within the circumference of his holy station. The loss of the Papal States had deprived the Roman Church of substantial revenues. One would hardly think when looking at the art treasures of the Vatican Museum that such a vast enterprise might suffer for want of funds, but it must be remembered that art works and buildings such as cathedrals for all of their magnificence do not yield dividends. The value of the more portable items is confined to what would be realized by a sale. Of what use though is a cathedral except for prayer. The space enclosed by St. Peter's Basilica would be absurd if put to any other use than to express the majesty of God and the universality of the Catholic Church. It is true that the art might be sold to satisfy present needs, but in that case the trust of centuries would have been liquidated to satisfy a momentary necessity."

"The mind of the Catholic Church is calibrated in centuries. Its embrace is all of time until Christ returns on the Day of Judgment. Is it any wonder then that the Church unites many of the glorious productions of mankind with its invisible mission to be the presence of Christ upon the earth until the final day? Cardinal Tosca therefore felt that it was his duty, as indeed it was his assignment, to help to restore the finances of the Catholic Church as an institution, but without parting from its patrimony held in trust for the entire human race. To that end he bent all of his efforts until he reached the point that he looked more at the return promised than at the character of the investment. His involvement with Baron Maupertuis in the scheme that led to his death was only the last act of a course of dealings that had existed for some years. It must be remembered that the Baron's status in the world of finance is international and that his probity and even genius is unquestioned. We may never know whether Cardinal Tosca knew all of the details of the Baron's plan to ravish England with plague but we may hope that he did not know. We know that the Baron felt that Cardinal Tosca's life posed a threat and that he was killed on the Baron's orders by a secret society with roots in the island of Sicily."

I requested more details and Inspector Hopkins continued his account of his investigation thus far. "I must tell you at once, Doctor, that so secret is this organization that although every peasant in the land knows of its existence if not its reach that we are unlikely to ever capture the actual agents involved in the assassination. That is a matter of little consequence though. We are here to discover items that may incriminate the Baron by showing a link between him and Cardinal Tosca. We need this evidence, not so that we may prosecute the Baron in a court of law, but as insurance against further retaliation by the Baron after he is defeated through our use of his own means against him, the Greater Dutch Canal Company, our Trojan horse. If all goes well, the Baron will soon find himself in greatly reduced financial circumstances, but there is still the possibility of physical revenge from so formidable a foe. Your friend, Mr. Holmes, told me in London before our departure that we must have in hand information that may act as a shield from that vengeance. That is why we are here. I must add that you were not burdened with this knowledge for a reason. Your friend has entertained another purpose for this journey, that you would become acquainted with the earthly site of the church that he has embraced. He mentioned that he has detected in you through the years a certain disapproval of his conversion to the Roman Catholic faith and he has asked me to express his private hope that by being at liberty to explore Rome on your own that you might discover some sense of the path that led to his embracing the ancient and original faith of Christianity that is still preserved among us."

He smiled at me before entrusting me with an interesting personal confession. "I am related to the Jesuit poet, Father Gerard Manley Hopkins S.J., who is a distant cousin. You see, Doctor, I too am Catholic. I hope that you will forgive our little conspiracy, but as you know Mr. Holmes holds you in the highest personal regard and your own embrace of the faith he shares would be a great comfort to him in his present illness. He considers the Catholic faith as the greatest gift he could ever lead you to embrace."

Strange as it may seem, I was neither surprised nor irritated by being kept at a distance from the true posture of the case at hand. Both Holmes and I had worked for years with Inspector Hopkins, so close in fact had been our connection that we might almost have been a trio. The public may assume that the Holmes and Watson dyad was always the case and that I would be put off by being excluded from any investigation. It must be remembered that my fascination with Holmes was akin to that of my readers and that it was often a pleasure to be kept in the dark until the final hours of an investigation so that I too could enjoy the surprise and as it were the aesthetic pleasure of seeing the fully-assembled the case told from beginning to end. It was Holmes' habit to titillate my curiosity the better to incite my wonder and applause when the solution was finally revealed.

Regarding the possibility of my embracing the Catholic faith, I am sure that Holmes would agree that the path of conversion is not an abrupt one, but rather the gradual accretion of many hours and circumstances and that a faith embraced under sudden emotion may pass as swiftly when that emotion recedes. For this reason the Roman Catholic Church has always been deeply grounded in philosophy and has through the ages contributed many of the best minds to the advance of human culture, literacy, music, and art. A conversion that embraces all of these, one that unites the epistemological with the aesthetic has always been the genius and abiding characteristic of Catholicism. Protestantism in contrast by embracing a covenant approach to conversion has concentrated upon the bare acceptance of the word of God coupled with an irrevocable personal assent, rather like being bound to a contract. So personal and individualistic is this matter that any intersession of saints or benefices of the wider body of fellow believers is considered incidental if not a distraction from the matter at hand. No real ongoing sacramental life is necessary to nourish the faith if salvation can be achieved in a moment and thereafter never compromised by later conduct; the hunger for an absolute determination of whether one is saved or not distorts human nature and compromises human freedom. Holmes was now adding the cultural panorama of the most ancient and rooted of Christian faiths to supplement and to strengthen any leanings that I might have in the direction of Catholicism.

To my questions regarding the nature of any further facts that Inspector Hopkins had been able to discover thus far, he answered, "I was able to discover that Cardinal Tosca kept a diary. It was entrusted to the care of a simple Carmelite Nun who acted as his secretary. She is a most formidable person and I am afraid that I needed to use all of the charm that I have seen Sherlock Holmes use when dealing with women to get her to reveal the fact of its existence. She had not read it of course. I am afraid that I was guilty of some duplicity in the matter. I implied through my able translator that I was acting (as indeed we are) in an investigation of the life and death of Cardinal Tosca at the direct request of His Holiness Pope Leo XIII. She of course must have concluded that the investigation was part of or acting under the direction of the congregation that investigates prior to the beatification or canonization of men and women of virtue. The devotion of the good sister to Cardinal Tosca and the respect that she had for him would hardly allow her to withhold documents that might speed her former employer's future course of being elevated to the honors of the altar as a saint. She gave me therefore, many valuable papers that are being translated as we speak. The ones that I have looked at so far have been most revealing. These papers may not result in the progress up the spiritual ladder for which his secretary hopes, but they may at least allow the Cardinal to make some post-demise reparations for his involvement during his life with that diabolical agent, Baron Athanasius Maupertuis. The existence of these papers will also ensure us a measure of safety if the Baron should come after those who have thwarted his plans."

Inspector Hopkins concluded his exposition by saying, "I am afraid, Doctor, that I must again leave you to your own devices for I must see how the transcription is going. I shall of course share their contents with you when all is spread out before us and we must then jointly decide how to present the matter before His Holiness and pick an appropriate time for that revelation."

After that Inspector Hopkins rose and left me alone over my coffee and pastry. The net seemed to be drawing tighter about the Baron. The hand of a dead man may prove to be a formidable foe when he keeps a journal as Cardinal Tosca had evidently done. Italy for all of its beauty is no stranger to evil. Perhaps some dark legacy of the Roman rule still afflicts the Italian mind. Intrigue seems to breathe from the very stones of the city. I know of no land more beset by the worst aspects of virility in men who value power over family duties. This characteristic when added to the beauty of the women with their olive skin and shy eyes make Italy a land of many children, including those deprived of a unified family life, since they are often the products of spurious relationships.

If time permits I may be able to visit the oratory in Torino of Father John Bosco who tends to the street urchins there as Holmes once did with his Baker Street Irregulars. I have heard astonishing reports of this man's ability to foresee events. I am usually skeptical of such things, but there is a universality in these reports that like those of the cures at Lourdes makes one wonder. If we may not demand the miraculous to assert its powers at will, neither should we adopt an attitude of contempt when they actually do occur among us.

I have heard that it is characteristic of those who witness such things that the agents of the miraculous are the least likely to wish to make anything of their own contribution as vessels of divine power. The truly holy men and women do not neglect the prosaic duties of everyday life waiting for God to show His hand. They act as if everything depended upon them while leaving the results in God's hands. Above all else they seem grateful for whatever comes and greet misfortune and good fortune alike, with an equal humility. If we are surprised by the rare occasions when God intervenes in a more direct manner in human fate it may be because God does not despise the natural order. Most of His miracles happen every day in the beauty of the world that surrounds us. It will be time enough when we have rendered sufficient thanks for these miracles to ask for more.

I had determined to press ahead with reading Holmes' account of his travels, for I desired to reach as soon as possible the story of his return by way of France to England and to close the gap that had so long existed in my knowledge of the life and history of my dear friend, Sherlock Holmes. The days that followed developed into a certain rhythm. The course that my life had followed seemed gradually to reveal a certain underlying harmony rather than the series of chaotic coincidences that had always been their aspect before when I took time to reflect. The timelessness of Rome seemed to penetrate to my very soul. I remember that I returned to my room that day and opened the windows to the balmy Italian air and to the accompaniment of the shouts of children from the street below I began to read.

Book Seven

Voyage to France

Extracts from Dr. Watson's Notebook

To indicate my state of mind during the time of my mission in Rome I include the following transcription from a notebook that I kept at the time.

Most people tend to stay with the religious communities in which they were raised. The wager between Sherlock Holmes and Professor Moriarty implied an objective stance that is usually not available or customary in the ordinary course of life. For all of its importance it is exceedingly unlikely that a pragmatic calculus determines the faith of the average man or woman. Even less likely would it be to engage in a risk calculus that would determine precisely how much sin might be committed before risking an eternity of pain in hell or a loss of the supreme good in heaven, yet wars have been fought over precisely these questions.

Part of the problem has been how the prospective believer is to approach an authoritative text that claims to be the definitive word of God. The early church held the texts of the Bible in such reverence that colorful and elaborate designs supplemented the august dignity of the words; only recently have the Biblical texts been subjected to the same level of criticism and analysis as any other written document. It is difficult to recreate the mélange of beliefs that floated about the Mediterranean Sea and to imagine the impact of various cultural and political influences on transcendent belief structures. The welding together of human history and the source of all creation demands that a position should be taken regarding the relative significance of human life when set against the sheer magnitude of physical reality. "What is man that you [speaking to God] should be mindful of him?"

Can any text capture the infinite? Can the human element be purged from a text so that some ideal purity of intention can be transmitted by mere words with all of their connotations and configurations in the minds of the audience that hears them proclaimed? Two idealisms have haunted the Western Church: first, that the text of the Bible is understandable on its face even by a naïve reader, and second, that Christian communities display no measure of bias or ignoble motives in interpreting the relevant texts so that the doctrines that celebrate and embody Divine Revelation are indeed adequate reflections of the mind of God and that God is in fact as He is portrayed in Holy Scripture. But is it ever possible to critique any text from within a culture that has already defined the measure of permissible argumentation and interpretation? These questions do not emerge from within a comfortable conviction that one's religion is true; it requires minds such as those possessed by men such as Sherlock Holmes and Professor James Moriarty to engage them and for men like me to record their discussions and hope in doing so to reach some valid conclusions regarding the deepest questions that beset every human life.

I do not know whether my own conversion is motivated by the pure love of God as it should be. It may be motivated rather by my own discontent with the human condition. I am one who is often beset with what I can only term vicarious shame. As my father's younger son I watched as my older brother descended into drink. All of his early promise was destroyed and I had the sad burden of attending to his burial in America when he died at an early age. Whereas Holmes came from a family of landed gentry, my own forebears were honest tradesmen who made up in virtue and industry what they lacked in hereditary fortune. My brother was not satisfied with his prospects in England and took ship at an early age for Baltimore in the state of Maryland where he hoped to become eventually a prosperous ship owner.

His very impatience for advancement ensured his ruin. His expectations were only matched by his confidence in his deserving to be rich. He expected to marry well and to live the life of an exporter of tobacco. Instead he married under the importuning influence of youthful desire a buxom bar-maid at a sordid public house that he frequented after his days spent laboring as an accountant at a large shipping firm. He spent his evenings engaged in boastful and drunken tirades before a willing audience of fellow inebriates who would gladly applaud his manner and his extravagant gestures until his money ran out. At last he was dismissed from his position and finding that he could not gain another he descended into that abyss of dissolute and constant inebriation from which eventually death by pneumonia delivered him.

It is a sad but common tale. That it biased my own views and expectancies towards those lives characterized by mourning and sorrow. Those who choose a life in medicine must deal with the human mechanism as it is breaking down. Life exists always in the shadow of dissolution and decay. I also chose a military career in an effort to restore the family honor. This explains much of my early life. Later, the example of Sherlock Holmes and the love of a woman of patience and courtesy showed me that a well-bred life need not be hypocritical, but was rather the path of sanity in a world showing little sense of order and justice.

My medical practice, though always small, was adequate to provide a comfortable living for us and I was fortunate in my assistants. I had the satisfaction of alleviating pain and of working among those householders who were seeking a better life through years of industry and lives of moderation. Though I often failed to follow the workings of the mind of Sherlock Holmes I was not lacking in my own small library of philosophers and I numbered among my friends many men of insight and progressive views. After I turned my hand to sharing his cases with the public I even gained some celebrity in my own right as a contributor to various periodicals. Still, I remained dissatisfied. My sense of shame often extended to my very surroundings so that all of the great city of London seemed immersed in a sea of squalor. Even the expansion of the empire seemed to me a cause for embarrassment. Who decreed that England should rule the world? Had we really brought civilization to our far-off colonies or only the brutality of our rule? Greed appeared to be our primary motivation and parsimony at home condemned many to lives of the most wretched poverty. I would have joined one of the low-Church sects but that I yearned to escape, to find and embrace a religious tradition that transcended England altogether.

Now in Rome I appeared to be finding a sublimity that reached back to the earliest days of the Catholic Church when England was only a frontier for the settlements of the Roman legions. England has known its own state of exterior colonization by a superior power. Christianity has grown apace since those early days. Perhaps it was never meant to be a religion of the intellect. If all that was necessary for salvation had been present in England for an uninterrupted millennium, then of what use were the insights and schisms of the so-called English Reformation. God, the Apostolic Succession of the priesthood, and the sacramental order were constants and these needed no reforming but only patient correction when the sins of individuals entered like an alien infection into the purity of the One Body of Christ. Schism was always contrary to the mind of the Church and to the admonitions of Christ who prayed, "That they may be one, Father, even as we are one." So it is that I find myself here in Rome with a two-fold task: to aid in the defeat of Baron Maupertuis and to complete a conversion long prepared for but too long delayed and to follow where my most earnest thoughts and most sanguine hopes are leading me.

How convenient it would be to imagine an ahistorical relationship to God, but to do so would be to deny one's humanity. We are encased in time. All of our concepts of causality and even the very idea of moral responsibility depend upon the existence of a sequence of events. If God exists outside of time and unconstrained by it then He alone can exercise a freedom that would allow Him to change events by acting upon their antecedents in the light of actual later results. The question would then arise of course as to what would become of the prior result if witnessed by any outside observer. Would the new result automatically expunge the memory of the prior sequence of cause and consequence or would it remain as a sort of ghostly image like the remnant of a dream after one awakens from sleep? Therefore, not even God seems to be capable of undoing what has already occurred by tracing events backwards to their most remote causes and changing them.

In any case it appears that there is only one real version of events, the one that we are living through during each present moment. Nothing that is done may, strictly speaking, be undone. Yet sins can be forgiven! What does this really mean? What after all is atonement? May the burden of guilt be simply dispersed in heaven as smoke may be so defused that the atmosphere becomes clear again? Yet even in this simile the particles of the smoke though defused must still exist somewhere. How then may our sins be set right so that some lingering remnant of them does not stain the white radiance of eternity? Even purgatory which allows us to expiate in some fashion the temporal penalty due to sin, though it may transform our lingering affection to the evil that those sins represented may not cancel the harm once it is done because time itself has received the irrevocable imprint of the event.

But perhaps heaven expunges time itself so that souls that have attained to salvation retain only their present immortal status before God, as though the path that had brought them to such an exalted state had never been. But in that case would not memory be the first casualty? Without memory of our former selves would we be grateful to God for the Incarnation and Sacrifice represented and achieved by the Cross of Christ? What of all that we have been can be translated into the *lingua franca* of heaven? Will a resurrected body be only an analogy of what we once were or will it bear the imprint of the former life as a lasting sign and legacy? But that imprint would surely be tainted by our residual dispositions that however adequate as adaptations to a temporal order would have no essential relation to a timeless realm such as heaven.

Perhaps Divine revelation indicates as much when it speaks of heaven as a place where the lion will lie down with the lamb. At first this thought brings me great comfort, for what more placid image might be conceived than that just stated; but upon further reflection I am gripped with terror that the imperfect being that I am will be so changed by salvation that it will no longer be the I which I have always known. What sense would it make to the historical me if the sanctified being that I will become after death shows only the dimmest resemblance to the poor struggling earthly creature whose faith, hope, and charity in this flawed and imperfect world made it possible for its soul to enjoy eternal happiness.

Is this strange contrast not the reason why the Christian creed has always assured poor benighted men and women that their bodies will rise again on the last day, lest they doubt that it is they themselves who are loved by God and not simply some abstract principle that animates our poor clay, our passing flesh, and all that we have ever known of heaven while we are still of earth.

We shall be exalted by divine grace to a status undreamed of and though we may refer to that process as atonement and salvation, we shall not understand its parameters while we remain alive, subject to time, and subject to our nature as men and women. What then is Sanctifying Grace but the internal pledge of a promise made by God and of our willing acceptance and the correlative desire to conform our future actions to God's dictates in spite of all that may have been true of us even a short time before repentance and if we fall again into sin a reminder to turn instantly back to God in whom is our sole reliance and hope.

Two problems exist *ab initio* when considering the claims of religion as regards dogma and its ability to compel belief. The first problem is that which arises if the doctrines of the religion and the duties that those doctrines impose appear to be too natural and to appeal as well to common sense as to revelation. The skeptic will then be led to conclude that the origin of the religion is imminent and resides in unassisted human nature rather than coming from and taking its form from the dictates of God. To believe this is to destroy the concept of revelation and substitute mere anthropology in its stead.

The second problem is that a religion that appears to be excessively arcane or arbitrary or that appears to thwart human aspirations and desires will similarly appear to yield rational grounds for skeptical rejection because the doctrines will be held to be absurd and to violate either the dignity and stature of man or to frustrate justifiable human moral or material progress. Where then will that perfect balance point lie between extremes where revelations from God will be acceptable and yet compelling the unbiased mind towards faith?

A further problem is that the ultimate locale where or when verification of the claims of any religion can be made is only after death, which appears to entail the complete dissolution of the very structure that formerly contained and made possible all human actions. To project our thoughts beyond death then is to cast a line outwards into a seemingly endless and empty abyss of time and space. That line, no matter what force is applied when it is launched, must lose momentum as it confronts our limited condition and after an arc, however long it may be, must finally be found arching downwards to rest at our very feet as we stand on the black cliff of death looking outwards toward the eternal.

How much easier it is to take the steps that lead to faith if one's individual decision is assisted by the common prayer of a community. The journey towards faith in God the Father proceeds in most cases by first bonding with the Holy Spirit whose gifts of life and love sustain the Church of God. The mind only fully engages in many cases after the soul is already substantially inclined towards rational assent by the living example of other Catholics. But mere social inclusion can never be adequate to provide the grounds to seek Baptism into the Body of Christ. The Second Person of the Trinity must be encountered through scripture and through the reflection upon scripture and sacred tradition in the writings of the Church Fathers and the teaching of the Church Councils. To this is added the teachings of the Popes as these are embodied in various writings through the ages. But true faith must sooner or later reach some degree of inner articulation for the individual believer. To achieve the illusion of faith without its substance is to open oneself to abandonment of the Catholic Church at the first sign of intellectual doubt or through encountering the often severe trials that life must bring in its train. The journey to the faith must then exceed any initial conversion experience and even exceed the formal moment of Baptism.

It is the belief of the Roman Catholic Church that faith may be attained through the use of reason and that to assume that the best evidence for faith is a collection of mere probabilities is inadequate as a basis for such an absolute commitment. It is not that merely probable reasons to believe do not exist, but that these do not exhaust the valid grounds for believing. True faith is a trans-rational process, but not an irrational process, nor a mere blind gamble on slim odds. Those who never attain personal certainty may still believe, but for those who demand certainty there are still valid and adequate grounds for belief. The point may appear to be one of great refinement and as such not an essential one, but it is one that the Church holds to be important because to believe the contrary is to feed the contempt of those who have made science the only ground for human intellectual certainty. Yet many simple souls seem to be called to faith by a process that is so subtle and gentle that it resembles most the relation of the sheep to their shepherd and faith that is found in this manner is not to be spurned or held in disrespect. Each soul is only called upon to nourish its faith according to its respective capacity. Therefore, a better guide to the presence or absence of sufficient faith for salvation in the final analysis can be judged by the presence and degree of our active charity in dealing with the world.

If religion could operate in a realm entirely divorced from the actual world that we inhabit, where the production of goods occurs, where trade is conducted, where legal disputes are resolved, it would be a better thing altogether because religion cannot provide adequate or complete answers to these questions. Christianity was originally predicated upon the idea that the Kingdom of God was at hand and the expectation of an almost immediate anticipation and conviction of the return of Jesus

Christ. The gospel in the meantime was to be spread to the ends of the earth, an idea that in those days reached barely into Asia let alone the full extent of the world that we know today. The entire Bible is oriented to the centrality of the Judaic regions and their significance to the entire world regardless of the existence of other languages, cultures, or particular national or tribal aspirations in different regions of the earth. The emphasis upon interiority and sin may be the one key aspect to the Jewish concept of God as Holy. No one expected the gods of Greece or Rome to be holy. Elaborate ritualism was the key to the priestly ideal of Israel. The pursuit of good public policy addressing the world as it is has very little to do with Christian ideals. Diplomacy and politics take human nature as it is presently constituted as their beginning and their end. Mistrust and a balance of powers are counteragents to venality, duplicity, and treachery. The world has little time to reckon up occasions of sin caught up as it is in disasters that dwarf questions of guilt or personal responsibility. These may interest psychologists or prelates, but they do little to advance the welfare of the world. The appeal to the Second Coming of Christ is therefore no immediate answer to present injustices or a remedy to armed conflict. For these reasons faith is primarily a personal affair and salvation is usually parsed on an individual basis

I would not consider taking the step that I anticipate taking here in Rome were I not persuaded that the arguments against religion made my Winwood Reade were not more an example of rhetoric than of logic. The world lost a valuable advocate or clergyman when it lost young Reade to atheism. I say young Reade because his book, "The Martyrdom of Man" is manifestly a young man's book. In spite of its vaunted stoicism and disillusion and its supposed readiness to accept the loss of all spurious consolations in the face of death it still has about it the frenzy of youthful ardor. The young are prone to various enthusiasms of which the most common is a desire to break utterly with the past and to disparage the naiveté of their elders. It takes familiarity with loss and tragedy to cure us from the complacency and pride that would dispense with what the young view as antiquated illusions. Sorrow chastens our arrogance so that both Pelagian confidence in the perfectibility of mankind and the gaseous generalities of Emerson's oversoul are seen as mere projections of desires that are far more naïve than are traditional religious beliefs. Many fall prey to this desire for a premature closure of the question of God, which is inadequate to our present abilities either to affirm or to deny.

Many contemporary theologians seem to be engaged in attempting to purify the images and concepts of Christianity from any mythic credibility so as to cast off the primitive beliefs that are termed "mythological" in the most disparaging of forms of language and from the platform of our present scientific progress; in doing so these theologians dispense with the true character of their task. Theology is not a science anymore than love is a science. Theology is a conversation between God and humankind. It possesses all of the spontaneity of conversation in prayer. Its imprecision is caused by the different levels of the nature of the creator and the creature each of which occupies a different level of apprehension. The edges of the concepts of theology are blurred by their very sublimity and not because they are necessarily vague or untrue. Our relation to the truths of religion must then be characterized by reverence and by trust rather than by a process of strict proofs. One does not ascend to God by the inductive method used by Winwood Reade but by first casting out into the abyss for the proffered grasp of God as depicted in the image of Adam and God on the ceiling of the Sistine Chapel in Rome as painted by Michelangelo.

inwood Reade has his deity, but it resides in the intellect of man, which he presumes can make progress on the infinite by endlessly but by slow degrees. He assumes that the individual is correlative to the mindless cells of the body. Christianity on the contrary presumes that the individual may take a position in regard to God and that even God Himself is bound to respect and to validate our choice in regard to each soul's eternal destiny. The author of "The Martyrdom of Man" in contrast cannot quite make up his mind as to whether man is a worm or a god. As a result he grants to the collective species a destiny denied to the individual man or woman.

Ralph Waldo Emerson makes the same error, but not consistently; he alternates between the proud attitude of the materialists and the romantic consolations of the oversoul. Both positions are reminiscent of Baruch Spinoza. Revelation is denied and reduced to poetry the better to allow the freethinking man to elaborate his own projected goal for the human race. What is this attitude but that of an impatient philosophy that demands a premature closure to all things the better to convince itself that the great picture of existence may be descried and consolidated, however fuzzy the details may be because they are still hidden in future events? Is this anything but religion expressed in other terms?

The very scalpel wielded by Reade may be turned upon himself! I have no desire to resort to *ad hominum* attacks, but I cannot but wonder whether the early demise of Winwood Reade may have been caused in some manner by a mysterious anticipation of the event of death, a sort of reversal of the ordinary workings of cause and effect, so that the obsession with death supplied that feverish ardor to the words through which his intention was expressed by the young author. His desire to grasp the whole must have been frustrated by his own foreshortened horizon, which if unknowable might yet in some mysterious fashion have cast a shadow upon him. His is a feverish prose reminiscent of a great marlin, one that is irrevocably caught by a fisherman's hook that leaps into the air with its great beak shaking as it attempts to free itself. What is that hook but the human condition itself that the young know only by rumor and anticipation? It takes actual experience to so humble the mind and heart of man that he may be brought alongside the boat defeated by struggle and hoisted aboard the barque of salvation. In our defeat is our victory, for who would swim endlessly in the seas of this troubled world. "Oh death where is thy victory; oh death where is thy sting!"

Even the presence of religious conviction is not to deny the implacable sorrows of life, for even Jesus wept at the tomb of Lazarus, and those who took the lifeless body of Jesus down from the cross must likewise have felt at the time to be without consolation. Why not simply leave open a point of access so that God may reach us, if any God exists? From whence comes this desire to foreclose all options but a sense of despair that casting its eyes in one exclusive direction, from the deserted isle on which we dwell, presumes that rescue will never come from beyond the bleak horizon of our expectations? Perhaps behind its very back a landing party has already put its boat upon the sands and is hastening to aid the castaway? Is certainty to be purchased at such a price by casting off all consolation from religion as contemptible when our entire nature demands it? Would it not be better to conclude with St. Augustine in speaking to God these most intimate words of relationship, "You have made us for yourself and our hearts are restless until they rest in thee?"

Whereas the religious impulse, in order to be meaningful at all to human beings, must of necessity lay itself open to critique as being merely human in origin, God must not be treated as though His existence is dependent upon any discipline which presumes to comment upon God's specific nature. These disciplines reflect only a human understanding of God and to that degree filter God through the dull medium of our modes of apprehension. Many scholars claim that God's humility in allowing communication with us must of necessity prove that God is a product of our understanding and hence is a projection of our own desires.

It can be seen immediately that this view would allow God only two practical options in dealing with mankind:

1. To avoid all communication with mankind and to remain in an absolute and inscrutable silence;
2. 2. To so exceed or contradict our divinely implanted sense of the divine that our own senses and conceptions would find God's communications to be essentially unreadable and meaningless.

Both of these solutions would preserve a sense of God as the fundamentally and absolutely self-subsistent other independent of all human affirmation and by doing so preserve God's dignity. Paradoxically then the skeptic, if he is finally to be satisfied, might be imagined as exclaiming, "God must exist because He does not care for me!" This is essentially the deist's position: to affirm a creator God but to refuse all further predicates as to His divine nature.

This manner of thought of course leaves the human problem of why we are here unresolved. It is no solution to simply say that man exists in unconstrained freedom to create his own nature and morality independent of God, because our own inner sense of truth and justice denies us that freedom. But let us assume that such absolute freedom could be predicated of man as Nietzsche suggests in his writings; who could tolerate such extreme freedom? Moral and cognitive navigation from point to point demand that at least one fixed point must exist and that fixed point is God.

To deny God then is to enter into such a state of mental vertigo as to explode all concepts and referents, because all of these are traceable finally to some inner sense of truth or principle of verification. If the highest truth which determines our origin and destiny is denied, then what subordinate truths can remain standing? So it is that the truly rational man accepts revealed truth, not because he despises reason, but because without revelation reason becomes a useless faculty seeking to compare and contrast incommensurable elements while floating about in the ether of final incomprehensibility.

Human choice at this point enters into the question as it evaluates competing claims to revealed truth. These in turn may collectively be referred to that inner sense of the divine that is retained in our very nature. In Christianity God is recognized as love because it is love that our nature craves above all things. The residual image of God in man is the love that remains unimpaired by Original Sin manifesting itself in acts of sacrifice, fidelity, and the desire to preserve and foster whatever is good, true, or beautiful within us. These thoughts are not my own of course but are rather the distillation of the treasury of western philosophical thought. How strange that so many modern thinkers hope to advance by denying the very bastions of truth as thus far discovered by far better minds than they have thus far proved themselves to possess for all of their brashness and fulminations!

I have been only too aware of the contrast between our respective pilgrimages, the one recorded in Holmes' journal and my own present mission to Rome. Holmes dared to enter an alien culture, whereas my journey has been to the very heart of Christendom. Yet my particular journey has not been without its fearsome aspects. On more than one occasion I have had reason to believe that I have been followed, but whether by agents of the Baron, or by other parties, I cannot say. Certainly the fear of death has been upon me here and I have taken to avoiding those romantic evening walks about the Eternal City that were my first joy after my arrival. There is something to be said for discovering the majesty of Rome beneath a chill evening moon and in comparative solitude. The noise of the day is followed by a sense that one is wandering through eras of history in a way that exceeds oven the majestic periods of Gibbon's august sentences. Never have I felt so burdened by reflection though upon the shortness of a single lifetime into which all of one's experience must be confined.

Rome endures while kingdoms perish and dynasties decay. Even the spectacular sepulchers of the Renaissance Popes serve only to mock the dust that they commemorate. How much more then must the average man such as I am be diminished when he recalls that he shall leave this world substantially unchanged by his sojourn here. I spoke to an Englishman yesterday who had but recently returned from a sightseeing trip to Palermo in Sicily. He told me of the shocking spectacle of the Capuchin catacombs there where the monks' bodies are propped up as though they still occupied their choir stalls, singing now with bony jaws agape a last chant to the glory of God. Modest and retiring to the cloister in life their bodies may now be observed by all who care to visit. If these holy men who once dedicated their entire lives to God seem to give but futile evidence of a resurrection by the witness of their long decayed corpses, then how may the worldly hope to thrive on the final Day of Judgment? Is their life of self-denial and penance rewarded even now by the Beatific Vision although their bodies remain behind and have not even the good grace to crumble into dust but rather still hang together as though some inner force of life still clings about the naked bones?

I have faced death more than once over the course of my life, yet each time I have felt as though danger could not touch me; I have even craved and savored perilous adventures by Holmes' side. I have often asked myself from whence has come this confidence of mine in my own immunity from the universal fate. Only in the face of the mass slaughter of war or the laying low of hundreds by epidemic illness is this illusion of singular immunity purged when one is face to face with momentary death. We look with curiosity at the funeral cortege as it passes, as though the one whose obsequies we celebrate possessed some strange affinity with oblivion, some love of death, which condemns the dead man or woman to seek this particular way of manifesting his or her existence. The dead whom we might have shared a cup with only yesterday are now, after we learn of their death, already separated from us by miles and by eons. They are now part of that endless procession of the years that will make them even more distant with each day, until their very memory is hung with encroaching ivy and with obscuring moss. As for we who remain among the living, we prefer to wake upon the morrow and to seek in the business of life our eternal way forward towards an indefinite end waiting patiently to embrace us.

I cannot say that even my medical career has ever made me comfortable or accustomed to the cessation of life. My very being rebels against it. Though a gentleman may hope to meet death with fortitude and honor, what are these to the limp form that lies behind to mock the courage and dignity of the one who is gone? Many are the terrors that beset us, even at home in the comfort of a dressing gown and with a glass of port wine ready at hand and with a coal fire leaping in the grate. I think often of that old hymn recalled from my youth asking for divine aid "for those in peril on the sea." But mariners at least know that death stalks them daily in the form of wind and wave, of rock and reef. What prayer is there for the man of comfort, the man of confidence, or the man who feels immortal and arrogant in his youth, not dreaming that behind him a fearful form may follow carrying his shroud? It is the daily peril of the ordinary that can swallow us. Was it any wonder then that Sherlock Holmes sought not merely enlightenment in his wanderings, but adventure as well, and had for his companion, not the ever compliant and well-meaning Doctor Watson, but that man of the jungle and the hunt, that man for whom civilization is folly, Colonel Sebastian Moran?

This definitive step that I am about to take forces me to ask myself whether I believe all the doctrines that the Roman Catholic Church asks that I believe in order to be a Catholic. The dogmas and doctrines are so definitive and backed up by all of the mighty theological apparatus and ritual of the faith of near two millennia of practice and conquest. Was it enlightenment when Christianity left the middle-east and penetrated to the dark forests of the German and Frankish lands? Did this great faith merely fill an ideological vacuum? The message of the cross and the man who hung upon it managed to push aside the dark Pagan deities of Europe and advance into Scandinavia and beyond across the steppes of Russia.

Do I believe then only because this great force overwhelms me so that I dare not imagine any belief system that can compete with it? Does Christianity invite me or compel me to believe? Is it the rewards of heaven that I seek rather than the bliss of thoughtless oblivion that will make no further demands upon me, not even the duty to rejoice? Or is it only the fear of hell, the existence of which is only testified to by a religion that I do not dare reject for fear that it is right and that it is not enough for the human race to suffer from all the deprivations of our earthly life, but in addition that an unnamed multitude must suffer even greater pains after death so as to vindicate the honor of God and to make some fruitless recompense to God as Father for allowing His Son to be crucified for our sins? Was it a mere paternal indulgence all along for the Father to go along with His Son's folly in loving the human race rather than exclusively a tiny subset of those who might be found pleasing because they belong to a chosen people, however that chosen people might be defined?

The texts of scripture allow both an expansive and a narrow reading in this regard. Many Christians prefer to tighten the latent strictures as much as possible so as to exclude as many people as possible from heaven and to doom as many as possible to hell. Our English so-called Glorious Revolution under Oliver Cromwell was succeeded by the debauchery of the Restoration period under King Charles II. In the oscillation between these two regimes we observe two sides of the Christian equation represented here by a vicious Puritan and a self-indulgent voluptuary, both of them Christian: one Protestant and one nominally Catholic. Perhaps both of them are sharing a common fate of perdition at last.

Where shall I place myself in relation to my own country's history? I dare not stand aside from this turmoil because each side demands that I become one of their mutually exclusive company or to suffer the consequences of abstention from making a choice and affirmation. Shall I seek the path of least resistance or is my final testimony of belief so filled with lacunae as to be meaningless? Can I hope to solve the theological conundrums that millennia have not put to rest so that one must even make a choice regarding whom to believe? Even to resolve these matters of belief is not depository or sufficient for salvation because the question of whether one has lived a sufficiently virtuous life to merit heaven rears its head in opposition and pushes any confidence in the atonement of the blood of Christ aside as inadequate, not perhaps in itself, but certainly in one's experience of the ongoing folly of humankind, since so many people evidently leave this life without the requisite repentance.

I hesitate to reach the comfortable position that satisfies so many Christians that great majority of the human race, no matter what missionary efforts have been made, will be damned, if not by one sin then by its opposite. The rich will be condemned when prudence and thrift yields to greed and the poor will be damned when deprivation yields to envy and resentment. Thus does the world turn about on the axis of human mistrust and the generations pile on top of the previous generations with little moral progress made despite the claims of religion to advance the civilization of the human race; all leading inevitably to the installation of the Kingdom of God at some indefinite future date when in one great judgment all will be assembled to hear the sentences read. It is this model of a supreme judicial forum that for me is the least appealing aspect of the faith that I hope soon to profess, one that is motivated less because I believe than because I fear not to believe.

From the Journal of Sherlock Holmes

April 10, 1892
Egypt

We have left behind the lands of jungle and of desert and are again in a land that has been changed substantially by the occupation of man. Indeed, in Luxor, the Valley of the Kings, even stone has been impressed by mathematical ideals in the shape of the pyramids. These great monuments are symbols of man's desire to transcend death by his own efforts. How contrary is this to Christian belief! To the Christian the acceptance of death is the final act of humility. To accept death and know that one's elements will disperse is to accept the fact that our bodies were always derivative and merely lent to us. We are not finally substance, but only form, only a design or pattern. We are like a standing wave in the rapids of a river; the pattern remains although the waters are always changing. What does it matter then if we are dispersed finally at death into those elemental substances that were gathered over the years into our bodies through the consumption of food and drink?

As we age we find that we become at last strangers to ourselves. The mask of our visage finally bears little resemblance to that of the freshness of our youth, which once formed our eternal image of ourselves. Death enters us slowly as we age before we die so that when the inevitable parting comes at last, it may be the easier for we are already not what we were. If on the other hand we die in our youth it is only so that we may reach maturity sooner in the fairer land of heaven. We leave to God the memory of what we were and it is God alone who may call us forth again in due season. It is said that ghosts exist and that those who have died by violent means may try and go back to the things and places that they knew only to find that they have no home there. The world rushes on and the memory of even the powerful is no more. To see the pyramids is to witness the erosion of the years and what was meant to be eternal is only a ruin beset by the sands. The earth knows best how to deal with the dead and those who are not buried outright and taken from our view are soon effaced by time itself.

Yet for all of these reflections we have come to Cairo, that busiest of cities. I reported at once to the British Embassy so that I might inform Mycroft that I have arrived safe and alive. My full account of my mission must wait until the day of my return to England, but by a pre-arranged code I gave him to understand that my mission had not been successful and that the Sudan would resist any alliance with England. I knew what this would mean. It would mean war, but when I could not say.

The declaration of wars is the final act of human futility. War is the failure of law and the end of any hope of reconciling diverse interests. It enthrones the defeat and death as a god and surrounds it with the panoply of glory. Each succeeding army through the years knows this to be the grossest of lies. The young are used to gratify the vanity of age. I have always believed that if wars were to be fought by old men they would not last long. The very comedy of those limping coughing scarecrows going at each other would show the stupidity of it all. No, we use our young to fight our wars so that their wasted lives may further embitter us against the enemy. We use what is most precious to make the other side seem inhuman while we forget that their young are dying also.

I cannot wait to get to France. I have been too long away from the comforts of European civilization. I need to feel about me the song, the poetry, and even the foods that I have known for much of my life. My time in Asia and in Africa has only confirmed me in the belief that no one person can be the universal man. We may escape prejudice but we cannot escape the bias of locality and custom. To throw the net of our aspirations too wide is to emerge with nothing in the end. Even Shakespeare, that most universal of authors, still shows the bias of an Elizabethan mind. We can but articulate what we have assembled through the course of our lives and in a tongue that is the product of the lives that have gone before us. There is no way to unify all of mankind in all the miniscule aspects of life and to attempt to do so will only cheapen the variety of cultures, melding them into a prosaic commercial trickle and not a river of progress.

I can see now the value of distance. Men are brought into conflict by too much intercourse. It is better that some lands should remain distant and unknown. This will seem contrary to the command of Christ to spread the faith to every region of the world and to the ends of earth, but it must be remembered that the ends of the earth seemed smaller then and might be presumed to reach only to Rome which heard of Christ before the death of the last apostle. The original commission of Christ was then in a sense completed within a generation.

Jesus once told St. Peter not to make too close an inquiry about the fate of St. John. Peter had his mission and what was it to that mission if St. John were to remain until the end of the world. Since St. John wrote these words, perhaps he believed that he would indeed witness the return of Christ. Similarly, it is not the business of the Church to fear for the salvation of those who died then and still die today without an explicit proclamation of faith. The condemnation in the gospels refers to those who have affirmatively rejected Christ when His message should have been met with welcome. It does not refer to those of other faiths who have heard the word of God from within their own belief systems.

If this is a daring pronouncement I must still make it or subject God's will to save mankind to the accidents of life and the dullness and resistance of the human intellect. I believe that the Grace of God is the universal solvent and that how it finds its place within the soul is within the providence of God and not the dispensations of Christian missionary zeal. If Jesus is indeed the alpha and the omega, the beginning and the end, and the living Word of God, then he dwells already within all men and women. He is in advance of those who would announce his name to the gentile and to the heathen alike. It is rather for us as Christians to honor the presence of Christ within the alien when we encounter him and by doing so awaken what lies within him as seed. To call any man or woman a sinner is an act of presumption and only the saints may do so, but only when referring to themselves.

April 16, 1892
Last Days in Cairo

When I made my report to the British garrison at Cairo I laid some emphasis upon the fact that I had been treated most civilly by the Kalifa and that he had even taken the trouble to provide an escort to assist our passage down the Nile to Egypt, lest we be molested by roving bands of robbers. Our goods had been welcomed by local merchants along the river and we had been well paid, so well in fact that Colonel Moran and I need not look for financial assistance from London in the year that lies before us in France and in Monte Carlo.

I am sad to say that my report did nothing to sway British prejudice against the Kalifa as I might judge by the expression of the Major who received my report. He clearly felt that I was a naïve tourist and that behind the actions of the Kalifa there lay a subtle contempt for the British if not a calculated insult. The Kalifa may well have desired to play the role of the bounteous host to show the extent of his power, but that power was quite real. The British would meet stiff resistance if they chose to invade the Sudan and I told the Major so. The devotion of the desert tribes to the Kalifa was no less than to his predecessor, the so-called Mahdi. I fear that we can imagine only with difficulty the sense of insult that those who follow Islam feel in the face of the triumph and progress of the Christian nations. Many no doubt feel that their hour has arrived and that the time for jihad is at hand. It seemed to me the part of wisdom to refrain from igniting that powder keg through any aggressive action.

I was of course thanked for my report, but I felt that my own observations were perceived by the authorities as irrelevant. The army would do what armies have always done. They would seek out war and would find a pretext for invasion. I saw that I could do no more here. I looked over at Colonel Moran and noticed that he wore as usual an aspect of benign pity for my heroic delusions and a sardonic satisfaction that I was witnessing firsthand the short-sightedness of the military mind, which when matched with the pompous desire to exercise power in the civilian government of nations, foments all wars.

We returned to our hotel and orders were given to pay those who had served us well on our journey from Abyssinia to Egypt. Our journey on to Alexandria will not be trying. From that lovely city we will take a ship for Marseilles. I shall be glad to leave Cairo with its stuffy colonial teas. We had been hosted by several of the local wives of the officer corps. They looked properly horrified as Colonel Moran described our journey for them from Tibet to Egypt. He did not dwell on those aspects of the long odyssey that appears in my spiritual journal, but rather upon our hardships and occasional brushes with danger. I am afraid that he even embellished them simply to witness the wide eyes of our hostess and her friends. He added a most colorful account of a visit to a harem that never occurred and I must say that he skirted the borders of delicacy by doing so. I am afraid that his account drew heavily from his reading in "The Arabian Nights" and even from the salacious tales of "The Decameron." It was not that he shared any overt revelations but even his silences and averted eyes seemed to suggest matters that had the ladies' fans waving swiftly to hide their blushes and I noticed how intense the interest of his audience was and how reluctantly they bid us ado, when we desired at my instigation to return to our hotel before midnight. The Colonel chuckled in the carriage that conveyed us from the suburban villas back to the center of Cairo.

"The trick of all narrators, Mr. Holmes, is to give the audience what it expects, to reveal what they already know, but then to take them just that little bit further still. If we told those women the truth we should have sorely disappointed them. I gave them back the world of Islam and of China that would meet their expectations because it was my desire to be believed. It is no easy matter to speak the truth, the whole truth, and nothing but the truth. For this reason all legal proceedings are exercises in the formalism of perjury, for what witness ever tells the complete truth. To know the complete truth is not within human capacity, and if we did know it I doubt that we could face our own complicity in the evils that we claim to abhor. You no doubt find me to be a skeptic and a cynic, whereas I view myself as one of the few realists and you, Mr. Sherlock Holmes, as being almost as romantic as the ladies we entertained this evening over a proper tea. You would no doubt have bored them with revelations of your spiritual struggle. I could not endure the prospect of watching them feign interest. I knew that their dreams tonight would be the richer for my inventions. I wonder which of us, for this evening at least, was the more charitable."

After a significant pause he continued, "I will go further still in elaborating my position. Think of all the books that have ever been written. Many are more excellent than those that are purchased with avidity at the booksellers, yet they have been suffered to decline into obscurity. On the other hand many books that are flying off of the booksellers' shelves will in twenty years be thought of no more. Immortality is not to be purchased, even in print, but is subject to the whims of fate. There are of course so-called classics, but might not a time arrive when public taste is so degraded that few will take the trouble to even read them? We do not for the most part read for the truth, Mr. Holmes, but to be amused and to fill an idle hour. Perhaps a time will come when the printed word will be as ephemeral as the notices upon billboards. A sort of word-inflation might then exist just as there are currency inflations and watered stock. Each man or woman will then assemble a set of favorite authors to support his or her particular bias. The very concept of general truths will then be passé."

"Men like yourself who strive valiantly for truth will be seen to be the fools that they are. Do not think that your efforts will be rewarded with everlasting fame! The records of your cases will be seen as quaint problems that arose during the dusty reign of our midget queen and you yourself with your strange habits will be perceived as a mere case-study in eccentricity. You are I know disappointed that your mission to the Kalifa has failed. I on the other hand knew that it could never succeed. The British position on the Sudan is to use the issue of the slave trade to justify an intervention; yet if that same government was asked why it does not object to the outrages of that monarch across the English Channel, the infamous King Leopold of Belgium, whose policies in the Congo have already cost the lives of millions of black natives, in what is deemed to be his personal domain, it would be answered that no sovereign may interfere in the actions of another sovereign. It is the mutual respect granted among iniquitous sovereigns!"

"I on the other hand hope that a day may come when all nations will acknowledge the rights of man, not that I expect them to sacrifice their own interests to vindicate them, but it would be a source of comfort to know that iniquity and exploitation might at last have a clearly delineated face so that when one nation appropriates another's dignity and enslaves its citizens to serve the economy of imperial power, it may not speak of its benevolent intentions when the results of its dominion only destroy the rights of men rather than spreading the supposed benefits of civilization."

"You, no doubt believe, that you have left the jungle behind and have now returned to civilization do you not, Mr. Holmes? Hah, I thought so. I tell you this, that civilization is itself a jungle and the beasts that prey there are the great statesmen and businessmen of our age. Democracy is a façade used to keep the masses in check lest they realize how little control they have over their lives. There is no greater obstacle to the righteous revolution than to get the people to realize that it is they who have chosen their masters or in the case of a monarchy to speak of the beloved virtues of king or queen."

"Only rapacity finally rules, Mr. Holmes. You have said that I am a hunter and so I am. I have learned how to fell a beast that is greater than I am with a single shot and why, because I know that if I do not stop its charge at once that it will destroy me. There will be no second chance. I look my opponent full in the face and I squeeze the shot off slowly; I watch it fall. I use its very fury against it, for by charging me it has abandoned its cover and given me the advantage. Similarly, the task of all social reform is to unmask social evil and to makes its agents charge. Once the evil is out of cover it can be destroyed. This is the only power that the poor possess: to make their misery visible even as your Christian Jesus showed His wounds to identify himself to his followers after he was said to have risen from the dead. Well, we are all dead right now because European civilization itself is dead. The great houses of Europe are the charnel houses of old ideas. The day of mere brute force is coming; oh yes it is! The European empires will soon assault each other, perhaps any day now, in a general European war and what will be left is a world of smoke and ashes."

He fell into silence then, which was just as well, for we had forced our way through the teaming traffic of this city that is alive with commerce even at night and arrived at last at our hotel. We were no longer beset with the street vendors. I saw their hopeful faces falling away behind our carriage once they knew they would not make a sale. All day the streets of Cairo are thronged with trade, yet few there are who can purchase a meaningful selection from the sheer variety of goods that are offered for sale. What system is it that makes a world of goods go seeking for the dollars, pounds, franks, and marks that lie in the great vaults of Europe and of America? Perhaps, the Colonel was right in this at least, that a time may come when the world will find a new axis and not swing about the western nations that have so long dominated world trade. Will Christianity survive the fall of the western economic world? This is the great question that among so many others I will take with me to France.

April 19, 1892
Alexandria

We have arrived at our fourth sea. I smell again that odor of life and of death that every seaside town carries. There is always abundance and superfluity in the sea, and a continuous motion, not of waves and winds only, but of trade and commerce. I shall always think of Alexandria as a white city containing too much light, as though it bore within itself the source of its own illumination. To see it at any season would be astonishing, but to be in Alexandria in spring is to taste heaven. I have not felt this quickening in some time, this sense again that life holds great possibilities. Perhaps it is simply being within a city that was once among the intellectual beacons of the human race.

Perhaps it is simply seeing the sailing craft of every shape and variety bearing the treasures of many places. In any case I feel that time is drawing me on once again and that my road leads somewhere that there is a purpose for my life.

It is a false humility that despairs of dreams. Disillusion and despair are not the same as detachment and resignation. The first are the fruits of the spirit of discouragement, while the latter are a conscious decision to pursue the greater ends of God while sacrificing the goods of this earth. I sometimes think that God has showered us with gifts so as to invite us to look beyond them to their source. God may at times be too indulgent, for many are lost in this world, which being all too lovely seems to be an end in itself.

Yet the beauty of the earth must never be denied, even while acknowledging disease, suffering, and old age. Life is forever arising again out of the humus of the past and hope springs with it. Already I can feel the green fields of Provence beckoning to me. The gentle language of the troubadours will soothe the quiet afternoons and I will wander the village roads and see the sheep grazing in the meadows. It will be grand simply to sleep again in a feather bed and not to waken at dawn to the sound of the camels in camp and to face the long and weary desert roads again.

How much I have asked of myself in this last year. What was a strain to that old campaigner, Colonel Moran, was agony to me. My tall and slim body was ill-adapted to the rigors of travel by camel caravan. I seem still to feel the swaying of the great beasts below me. My very insides have been bruised and battered. How I long to sit still. I plan to spend a great deal of time in the laboratory. All chemists know that there are mysteries within creation that only respond to close inspection. Chemistry seeks the vocabulary of creation. There are substances and compounds that may either enrich life or destroy it. Even poisons have their use in small quantities though and for select applications. I have long believed that the organic molecules have infinite uses and coal-tar in particular fascinates me. I hope that I may discover something of utility to mankind. I feel a desire to make some sort of concrete contribution to accompany my metaphysical speculations in my journal in my daring pursuit of God. Only then will my strange odyssey be completed.

Besides, I am not yet ready to return to England and to encounter Professor Moriarty. I must have time to go over my journal and to see if its many facets form a whole. I have not feared to be contradictory, for only by risking contradiction may we be sure to have missed nothing. To be comprehensive and conclusive is to risk premature consistency and error. I must have my conclusions well in hand if I am to convince such a strict a judge as Professor Moriarty will be upon my return.

April 21, 1892
Alexandria

I visited several Coptic Churches today. The role of Alexandria in the early struggles of Christianity is not to be diminished. During the first centuries of Roman persecution it was the East and Africa that defined the nature of Orthodox belief, for it was here that the battleground of ideas existed. The Gospels failed to resolve all questions regarding the nature of Jesus as the Christ and the relations to His Father. Almost all views were adhered to in good faith by various factions. It took the contributions of two Doctors of the Church, both Patriarchs of Alexandria, to define and defend the orthodox position.

These men, St. Athanasius and St. Cyril, defended the idea that God is One yet possesses three underlying persons. In addition, Christ's nature was held to partake of two realities: a human nature and a divine nature, but these natures were not two and separate, but instead were so united that Jesus was not two people but one person with two natures miraculously joined into a single unity, the hypostatic-union. The significance of these distinctions is critical because if God was not crucified for our sins, then the suffering of Christ as a merely human tragedy could not suffice as a general atonement for all mankind. Only by totally infusing the Godhead into the human could an eternal redemption be realized.

Similarly, from earliest times Mary was referred to as the Mother of God, the Theotokos. She was not merely the mother of the human nature of Jesus but of the one Jesus who was both man and God. Christianity is astonishing precisely because of this blending of incompatible concepts, the breaking down of contradictories in order to reunify them. This is the scandal of faith in its purest form: it cannot be understood; it can only be affirmed.

Yet these distinctions were recognized as critical by the early Church because the entire mission and substance of Christ to both belief and to mobilize activity requires it. The entire Sacramental order rests upon the Divinity of Christ, who shares his divinity with us *in personem* by becoming in flesh and blood of the Most Holy Sacrament of the Altar and forgives our sins in Confession because He takes them as God upon Himself. If the two natures are not one in Christ, then a fatal dualism enters into the life of the Savior and His teachings lack unity depending to which nature they are attributed.

It was a wonder for me to be present at Alexandria during these days since the city provides a perfect coda and conclusion to my eastern journey of faith. There is a clarity here that is absent in the industry-ridden capitals of Europe. I am tempted to remain in one of the lovely monasteries here, but I have my own tasks before me and already Colonel Moran is again chaffing at the bit to get on to Monte Carlo. I can but yield with as good a grace as possible. The heat of the day makes me somewhat lethargic and I have developed a persistent cough in recent days that I do not like.

Extract from Dr. Watson's Notebook

The following is an extract from notes that I kept regarding the case in hand in Rome in the year 1898.

I have heard from Holmes. His message was short and to the point but vastly encouraging. The price of the shares in the Greater Dutch Canal Company has begun to climb. Moreover the purchases were made not in England but on the exchange operating in Amsterdam. In addition to this news Holmes' agents report that Charles Augustus Milverton has been seen recently, after an absence of some weeks, at his home in Mayfair. There is every reason then to assume that the exchange of papers has occurred and that Baron Maupertuis has succeeded to the Murillo Papers. He has not yet made them public, but Holmes expects rumors of the publication to occur at any time.

Regarding the state of his health and recuperation, I was relieved to learn that Holmes has for once been complying with the orders of his physician and that he has put on some weight. The news from Devonshire is also excellent. Holmes has received word from Professor Moriarty that the horse, Silver Star, has been found in the south of France. It was run in a breeder's cup race in Biarritz and won. The Professor knew that in order to collect stud-fees that the Baron would need to again establish Silver Star's reputation on the continent, but under a different name. The Professor has therefore been following the sporting news from many countries to find a horse that matches Silver Star's description. The Professor made a trip to Biarritz and was able to trace the horse to a local stable. The French claim to have purchased the horse in all honesty, but an investigation is being made. In any case, the Professor was delighted to have recovered the fine animal, which will shortly be transported back to England. The Professor has hopes that it may run in next year's Wessex Cup.

As for Sir Henry and Lady Beryl Baskerville, there have been no further attempts upon Lady Beryl, but Wiggins continues to be on guard there and will, no doubt, remain so for some time to come. He is no doubt enjoying the life of a country gentleman by proxy and will return to London fat and happy after enjoying the excellent cuisine and the Devonshire Crème desserts served regularly at Baskerville Hall.

I am no thinner myself since I have been enjoying the wonderful Italian fare here since my arrival. I have been helping Inspector Hopkins with the journal left behind by Cardinal Tosca and we are making progress although there is nothing decisive as yet. The means and manner whereby Cardinal Tosca first met with agents of Baron Maupertuis and later invested Vatican funds has not yet come to light. It is possible that the Cardinal used some inner code, one comprehensible only to himself, to leave a record, or it is possible that the money involved was kept out of the usual account books altogether. An audit is being performed and we have hopes that it may reveal something.

Dr. Watson's Narrative Continues

It was customary for me to keep notes to help me to reconstruct the case later in writing up the popular accounts of my friend, Sherlock Holmes. My skills as a chronicler had improved over time. In my early years though I would often need to date cases by memory and this resulted in sometimes assigning certain cases to years in which they did not occur. After publication these errors were sometimes pointed out to me by Holmes with some amusement on his part.

"Really, Doctor," he would say, "I trust that your records of the medications that you have prescribed are in better order or else you may have prescribed laudanum for pneumonia instead of toothache."

I would reply with some asperity that my medical practice was quite orderly and that Holmes must remember that I was only an amateur author.

"Ah well," he would say, "The dates are unimportant since it is the fact patterns alone that matter to future historians of crime detection. I trust that your accounts will be read someday only for technical reasons, long after their romantic appeal has faded."

I took umbrage at this, pointing out that romance is eternal in the human breast and that in any case I trusted that I had not neglected essential details.

"No indeed Doctor," he would answer. "Your accounts have been quite adequate I assure you. I have on one or two occasions attempted to write up my own cases and I perceive that the task is not an easy one. Need I add that your accounts are quite flattering to me? I do wish though that you might have kept certain details private. What must your readers think of a man who is as slovenly as you portray me and who lounges about Baker Street in his dressing gown lamenting that the days of the great criminals are past, for all the world like an opera diva recalling her better days? You seem to suggest that I would have long ago profited by the attentions of an alienist or a follower of that fellow Mesmer for my mental disturbances."

I answered that I meant no harm but that he must admit that his habits were singular and somewhat irregular.

"As are those of most people," he replied on one occasion. "We are all a bit mad you know. Indeed it is our signature habits and eccentricities that distinguish us from one another. Show me a man or woman who is normal in all respects and I will show you a very dull individual. I will go so far as to say that the most difficult crimes to solve are those committed by bland and boring people. They leave behind no imprint of individuality, no singular clue. Their motives are only the most prosaic and mundane. It is for this reason that I have always preferred the unusual crimes for it is in them alone that human nature reveals some new facet to the criminal investigator. Where would we be if there were only pick-pockets and forgers abroad in the fog–lit streets of London by night? I assure you that I would long since have ceased to be a consulting detective if that was the case. I am a connoisseur of the unusual. I crave the most outré of human experiences. Though I do not share his vices, I am in sympathy with that chap Oscar Wilde and with the author Huysmans who wrote the books 'Down There' and 'Against the Grain,' in my hunger for strange sensations. Life must constantly renew itself, my dear fellow, and it does so by change. Change is the child of discontent. For that reason it is to the restless and the unhappy men that we owe what progress mankind has made over the centuries. The well-adjusted individual is fat and contented with the circumstances of his life. Such people may chuckle warmly at a jest, but they contribute little to the advancement of wit. No, give me a man like Kierkegaard or Schopenhauer; it is they, the discontented ones, who are forced to seek solutions to the problems of human life."

I answered that there would be fewer problems if philosophers were not so adamant in discovering them.

"Ah well, your point is well taken. Where should we be if all men were questioners? We must as a society have at least some measure of resignation and content or else there would be a state of permanent revolution among us. Life requires its Clydesdales to pull its heavy loads as well as a few nervous thoroughbreds such as I am to provide amusement upon a weekend afternoon at the track. It is proper that life should attain a collective harmony. To disillusion all men and even to demand a perfect articulation of the principles upon which their lives are based would never be possible nor would it even be advantageous. I will even go so far as to say that there is a function in evil itself, for could we ever know virtue if there was no vice with which to compare it. We live in a world of opposition. We only perceive distinctions by the rule of contrast. I have often told you that you possess the genius of stimulating my own abilities as a detective by your persistent and apparent inability to solve the problems that are presented to us. This is a case in point. I assure you that I doubt that there would even be a Sherlock Holmes if there had not been at my side a Doctor Watson. You feed my abilities, such as they are, and I shall always be grateful for your inestimable services in that regard."

As so often before, I had to be contented with this oblique and ambiguous sort of compliment that often seemed more of an insult than a commendation for my long years of devoted service at his side. Yet, I was happy to serve him still and to make allowances for a temperament usually associated with artists for that is what he was after all. In spite of his repeated assertions that detection was a science, it has always been my opinion that it is more of an art. To deduce from generalities is often to be in error. Sherlock Holmes' genius was in recognizing the exceptional when it presented itself to him. It was the official police, in fact, who practiced the science of deduction alone and as a result their conclusions were frequently wrong.

Imagination was the key to Holmes' success. His ability to adapt and to change allowed him to enter into the very substance of a crime and to inhabit the mind of the malefactor. He had through the years attempted to convey that ability to me, but art is finally a matter of insight and spontaneous inspiration in the artist. It may not be too much to say that art simply happens and as such its prior existence within the artist's mind will be forever unattainable. In this sense true art is seen in always going beyond its own foundations. Something emerges that is even greater than authorial intent can supply. The evolution of new forms of expression is the history of art.

So it was I who was the scientist, not Holmes; he was the fabulist. My habits as a doctor precluded the ability to break the rules, which for Holmes was his métier. It was this fact rather than any inherently deficient degree of intellect that often made me blind to a solution when all was clarity to Sherlock Holmes. It was no affectation that I was often mystified by his methods until they were explained to me, for his methods were always tailored to the unique circumstances presented by each case so that no real generalization of his techniques was ever possible. Beyond a few aphorisms such as, "It is a classical mistake to theorize without data," his instruction was pointless beyond preparing me to be an adequate narrator of his adventures in my publications after the solution was revealed to me.

The same could not be said of Inspector Stanley Hopkins. He had indeed learned much from Holmes through the years, but it has always been my opinion that the truth was that each man shared the same innate prior ability as an artist of crime, although Hopkins in a lesser degree of course than Holmes. It was those matured abilities that the Inspector brought to bear on the problem at hand in Rome. So successful was he in fact that within a week of our prior conversation he was able to report that he believed that he had found the key. The audit had been performed and it clearly showed a pattern of dispersals to a fund for relief in the Low Countries. The money had been forwarded to the poor coal-mining region of the Boranage in Belgium but certain letters from the local Bishop indicated that some of the money could not be traced. It was Inspector Hopkins's opinion that certain amounts had been siphoned off as it were for investment in the Baron's unnamed scheme.

Whether the Cardinal knew the details of the plot to bring disease to England we shall never know for sure, but he was at least negligent in asking for details beyond the promise of a high-yield on the money entrusted to the scheme. Whoever killed the Cardinal no doubt was looking for the pass-book; for every account, even one toward such a nefarious end, must still leave some sort of paper-trail, the dominant law of the science of accounting. It is a sad comment that the Cardinal may have paid with his life rather than surrender the pass-book and other papers that would provide a trail of evidence. We knew of this because since his death there had been several subtle intrusions into the quarters formerly occupied by the Cardinal. Though some destruction had occurred there was no evidence that the papers had been found.

For the rest, we would not have been successful in our mission but for a piece of extraordinary good luck. We were surprised one day at breakfast by a missive conveyed by hand to us from the manager of the hotel saying that a Franciscan Friar of the Capuchin Order had stopped by on the previous afternoon and desired to speak with the two Englishmen. He would not explain his business to the manager, but he had carried with him a box. He had promised to return the following morning. He might appear on the hour, so the Inspector and I went upstairs to our room for our morning ablutions and were gratified when we had scarcely concluded them when our phone rang to announce that our visitor had arrived.

A short time later there came a knock on our door. We opened it and greeted the friar who proved to be short man of Austrian extraction wearing the distinctive cowled robe of his order. We bade him to take a seat and though he refused an offer of anisette accepted some tea and biscuits. He had brought with him the box that he had carried with him on the previous day. We were of course curious as to the contents, but allowed the diminutive friar to tell his story in his own way, a technique that was habitual to Sherlock Holmes and that was in turn practiced by those educated, as we both had been, in his methods.

"I do not know if what I bring you today will help, my dear English friends, but I have with me something that was entrusted to my care by the late Cardinal Tosca; may his illustrious soul find rest. Another of my order was his confessor, but I was his friend. We studied together in our youth at the Gregorian Institute in Rome. He of course went on to achieve the honors of the Church and is called venerable, while I have been only a humble instructor in a gymnasium in Napoli. Upon my retirement from that position I was given charge of a small parish here in Rome. You can imagine my surprise when my housekeeper announced one morning that the great Cardinal Tosca was below in the courtyard and had asked to see me. I was flattered of course, since it had been some years since we had met or corresponded, and I was surprised to find that he even knew of my presence in Rome."

"He was shown in by my housekeeper with many courtesies and I rose to greet him and to kiss his ring. He waved aside all formalities and asked that I resume my chair while he in turn sat on my small sofa near the window. I was able to observe him clearly in the light and I could see that he had received something of a shock recently for his eyes would ever and again go to the window as though he expected to see someone outside. I could not explain his nervousness for our parish although poor is not given to crime and in any case even criminals in Italy are not as impious as to rob or to assault a Cardinal, a Prince of the Church."

"Yet his manner attempted to hide his trepidation. He expressed his sorrow that so many years had passed without any communication between us, but his duties had been many and had left him little time to pursue old friendships. Now a time had come when such deficiencies must be remedied for he was getting no younger and the thoughts of the Four Last Things must finally come to preoccupy all men. I recall that I asked at this point if he was ill. He said that he was not, but the hand that he raised to emphasize the point trembled as with an ague. He saw at once that I noticed this and placed his hand down upon the very box that now stands before you and that he entrusted to me on that day. He explained that it contained a pilgrim statue and that it was his desire that it remain in our Church for one year for the edification of our parishioners and that it would bring a special blessing to them."

"It was a humble statue of no great artistic merit, but our faith teaches us not to judge by appearances. He assured me that its presence in our church would not only benefit us but that we would be doing him a great service as well by displaying it since he desired that during that year we would all pray for him. I could not refuse such an entreaty from an old friend, so I immediately accepted."

"The statue was of St. Jude, the patron of what are called lost causes. I had it placed in a small niche in the back of the church. There is has remained until this last week. We keep our Church always open, for there are no great treasures to steal and during the time that the statue has remained with us there have been only the local women and workers present who come to early mass. The statue became a favorite with many of them and I may truly say that it has brought to many people the blessings that had been promised. Sincere prayer is always heard by Saint Jude, who was of the same family as Jesus, and he may intercede in all matters with Our Dear Lord."

"It was truly a tragedy then for us when we heard of the death of Cardinal Tosca and knew that we could not return the statue to our benefactor on the feast day of Saint Jude as had been arranged. It appeared that the statue must cease its pilgrimage then and remain with us. We did however continue to pray for the repose of the soul of Cardinal Tosca and that he would, if it should be the will of God, convey to us in some manner what further disposal we should make of the statue when its time in our custody should draw to a close."

"Only this week we received an answer to that prayer, but not one that we had anticipated. An elderly sacristan in attempting to dust the statue lost his grip upon it. It fell from its niche and shattered. Within it we found some papers and what is evidently a claim on certain funds in Holland. Here, do you see?"

He opened the box and laid its contents before the Inspector and myself. Inspector Hopkins caught them up with a barely suppressed cry of triumph for they indeed proved to be the link we had hoped to find to the Baron. The sum of the account was an astonishing figure. The account had been opened in the central bank of the Vatican and the funds and securities deposited there might be withdrawn by any designated representative of the Papacy. No doubt these papers and the pass-book was what the servants of Baron Maupertuis had sought since the death of the Cardinal and his refusal to surrender them may have resulted in his death, thus sealing his lips forever.

"I have come to you, Gentlemen, because the Cardinal's

former confessor informed me that you are investigating the death of my friend, Cardinal Tosca. You will know then how best to use these papers. It has been my effort to return them since their discovery in due season to the officials of the Vatican bank but in a manner that will not compromise the memory of my friend. It is my hope that I have done the right thing in coming to see you today." We assured him that he had done quite right and that his contribution to our investigation might prove decisive in resolving any lingering doubts as to who might be responsible for the Cardinal's death. He accepted our reassurances with a humble nod of his head. Shortly after this he withdrew and we heard his shuffling steps receding down the corridor.

The Inspector clapped me on the back exclaiming, "We have got it Doctor!"

We spent the remainder of the afternoon going over the papers with the aid of our translator. They clearly indicated that vast sums had been deposited with Baron Maupertuis who might act with full agency powers to invest them as he saw fit. The Baron in turn pledged the return of the funds upon demand with the proviso that a reasonable period of three months would be allotted in order to liquidate shares in securities and to process the proceeds through normal accounting procedures. The proceeds could be picked up in person or be directed to a destination of the principal's choice, acting as trustee. Several separate letters further explained that Cardinal Tosca could communicate with the Baron through an agent in Rome who would identify himself and bring proof that he did indeed represent the Baron; but that person was not named, nor could we locate anyone who had witnessed the meetings that had occurred between this agent and Cardinal Tosca. In any case, the papers were quite adequate to state a claim on the funds.

An audit would show where the funds had been invested. Since the deposit was made in the name of the bank as agent and not Cardinal Tosca in his own person, his death was irrelevant and the deposit with the Baron was unaffected by the Cardinal's death. The Baron might have hoped that as the months passed and no claim was made that the intermediary institutions would assume that the funds had been embezzled or simply disappeared, and the Baron may have hoped that no claim upon the proceeds would ever be made. The temptation to use those funds then to supplement his own might have made the Baron treat those entrusted funds as his own and to invest them in the Greater Dutch Canal Company. If he had done so, he would be guilty of a severe breach of fiduciary trust and one that would allow for his prosecution under Dutch law for fraud and conversion.

Soon after this, Inspector Hopkins and I wired Holmes in London with the results of our investigation and that to the possibility of bankruptcy by our scheme a new nemesis now stood poised over against Baron Maupertuis, that he might be prosecuted for withholding funds due to the trustee of the bank acting as agent for the Roman Catholic Church and sent to prison.

We received an immediate answer from Holmes with his urgent congratulations to us and his assurance that Mycroft would be informed so that a deeper investigation of the Baron's financial practices might be instigated in Holland through the intercession of the British government and with the aid of Scotland Yard. The worm had turned and the cards were now being dealt to us to be played as we decided to play them. There only remained for us then the task of informing His Holiness of the progress that we had made. We therefore sought an appointment for a private audience with the Pope and it was soon granted. The night before the audience with His Holiness I thought of the strange way that Cardinal Tosca had spoken to us from beyond the grave. I cannot say whether accident or the intercession of St. Jude was operative, but it was in a contemplative frame of mind that I returned to Holmes' Journal.

From the Journal of Sherlock Holmes

April 25, 1892
On the Mediterranean en route for Marseilles

I am again at sea and feel again that peculiar sense of infinite possibility that the sea always conveys to me. The great oceans of the world unite all lands and from the deck of a vessel there is always the illusion that the continents are but a step away from each other for in voyaging the waters seem not to partake of the realm of space but only of time. Each day one wakes to the same circumference of sky and water. There are no distinguishing marks of mountain or of valley. The whispering foam of the ship's wake seems to be like a streaming and joyful pennant held in the wind. The sense of progress seems to be an illusion. The ship appears to stand still and the waves breaking upon the bow seem to be the agent of the progress of the sea and not of the ship. It is as though the world is unfolding before one like a succession of images. The days grow longer until each finally becomes indistinguishable from the others. The shipboard routine, particularly for the idle passenger, makes time seem to stand still. Ah, were that only possible!

How often I have wished to step off of the earth for a time, to find a place where I might look back upon my life and see it as God must see it, from the perspective of infinite distance where it might assume some cohesive form rather than resembling a series of accidental encounters. We are too close to our own lives to evaluate them. The issues of each day so oppress and preoccupy us that we cannot imagine what it would be like to change, not merely at the branches but at the trunk. Religion speaks often of conversion or repentance with both conveying some manner of radical reorientation for one's life. The original Jewish idea of a covenantal relationship between God and His people was always brought face to face with periods of exile due to sin. Christianity, based as it is on one's fate in an after-life, has supplanted exile with damnation. The Jewish idea was that God's own faithfulness would never cast anyone away forever because the fate of the people and of the individual was one and the same. To be outside of the community was already to perish in the desert.

Early Christianity took the imagery of exile or alienation and applied it radically to the individual. The sin of Adam and Eve was seen as entailing such a radical break with God that only Baptism followed by a life of heroic virtue could prevent the final sentence of death from being read out on the Day of Judgment. The latter history of Christianity can be read as one long commentary on the strictness of that sentence. Martin Luther assumed that faith alone would be adequate for salvation, while John Calvin went beyond even early Catholicism in its presumption that the majority of the human race had little hope for salvation. The early monasteries were filled by those who held this life in scorn and as a result had placed all their hopes on the conviction that this earthly life is only a sorry prelude to an even worse fate.

Messages of hope have always seemed risky when dealing with an omnipotent being that could crush us at will. Human concepts of fairness or equity simply had no standing in the courts of the celestial legions occupied in the constant praise of God. Christianity might be considered to be a victim of its own texts. The graphic visions called forth by the concrete thinking peculiar to Hebraic thought and expression made God a terrible reality, one that was active in all causal relationships. Morality was more than merely a drama of ethical choice; it encompassed every aspect of life and was more than a distant and speculative metaphysics such as that of Descartes or before him of Plato and of Parmenides, each of them seeking the nature of that which unites all things. To the Hebrews the physical and the spiritual were so infused by God as to be inseparable. The question arises then whether the God of scripture is God as He actually is or whether the God of scripture is God as intuited through the lens of Hebraic cognitive and cultural presuppositions. Shall God be defined according to our own categories of thought? But on the other hand if human conceptions have no ability to approach if not to penetrate to the core of God's essence, then God becomes a stranger to us and from estrangement an even greater fear and mistrust of God would arise.

In any case Christian history gradually made way for critical inquiry that finally resulted in what is today called the secular world. Religion in consequence lost its claim for absolute allegiance and the other disciplines emerging out of the cloudy confines of philosophy left theology behind, a province of the middle ages with only a tenuous grasp on the way that the post-renaissance world is practically run. Repentance became identified with what one does in preparation for death. Even repentance is more an act of surrender than it is an act of affirmation. We wander in circles like the early Israelites in Sinai. Each year we say that we will break forth, that our shackles will fall away and it will be possible to stand tall and strong before God and say, "There, do you see, I am what you meant me to be, I have arrived at the full stature of man!" Instead, each year finds us making a beetle's progress across a barren plain.

I raise my eyes to see the shimmering snows upon the distant mountain ranges and I think, "It is too late! Already the sun is in its late declension. I will be caught by night still crawling forward and what will then be my fate? Worse still! Am I even going forward at all? Is not my life more like that of the mindless progress of the carpenter ant who bustles about seeking every nook and cranny only to move on? What means this mountain of books that I have accumulated at Baker Street yet had so little time to peruse?" Am I like Don Quixote, am I living a quest very like his own?

The one advantage of youth is that it contains within itself the treasure of all the years that lie ahead. As one grows older that treasure is gradually spent until a day comes when one's former balance appears to have been overdrawn. To sit amidst the rubble of the years and to be unable to recall even one complete day is horrifying for it seems to imply that life never happened at all. For this reason men raise monuments and fill their days with achievements as a testament to the eternal. What military general does not wear upon his very person the insignia of his rank, his postings, and his medals of valor? Our fear is not that posterity will forget us, it is the fear that we have already forgotten ourselves, that our lives are as strange and inconsequential to us as they are to the rest of human-kind. It is bad enough to have suffered in this life, but to know that our endurance has not even been noticed and will soon be forgotten; that is too much to bear! If there is no God to preserve our days and even our sins in His memory, then we are like those mindless dandelion seeds that float about in every wind. The slightest breath changes our direction and even if we should find rest, a breeze may come and we will be torn forth again and sent aloft.

For these reasons, to seek the definitive and to find it by my own efforts; that has been my life's quest. Truly the heretic Pelagius, who put such trust in our own unaided cognitive and spiritual resources, has at least one disciple in this age and he has been Sherlock Holmes! I wonder if I shall ever comprehend that first principle of our faith, that redemption is not something that we do for ourselves. We appear before God naked and trembling, not in fear, for we trust in His mercy, but in the awareness that even cooperation with grace leaves the honor to God and not to ourselves, that our merit is always secondary and derivative. I will go so far as to say that even sin serves the function of proving to us again and again our stature before God and the vanity of any ambition to be like Him, except as he makes us so by Divine grace.

Yet to persist too far in this vein would be to accept predestination of result, viz. that Divine grace determines the will and to accept the Calvinist view that virtue is impossible and that the effect of Divine grace is such that all human actions that would be meritorious are such by God's action alone and not due also to human cooperation with the dictates of that grace. That position of course is heresy because such a doctrine denies human free-will. The true teaching is that of the Communion of Saints within the corporate body of the Church, which is animated by the Holy Spirit. The Holy Spirit so infuses the Church that it is the very life blood of the Church and even its soul! The same God so dwells within us that our very debts are an occasion of joy in heaven, for from the fullness of God all is made whole and complete. There is no lasting debit on the balance sheet of heaven; the sacrifice of Christ has paid all in full. It might be said that hell is for those who prefer to keep a separate book of accounts and that the eternity of hell is spent summing up again and again one's individual merits and trying to add them up to a total that would be equal to God and by doing so to make His love superfluous.

April 28, 1892
En Route to Marseilles

The problem of reconciling God's supreme power and goodness with the world that we experience has troubled all philosophers and theologians. The problem lies in our use of words to assign attributes to God. To say for instance that God is omnipotent exceeds the particular history of God's choice of the means to exercise that power. The history of salvation in fact shows the continual frustration of God's intentions by the actions of men and women, both individually and collectively. The history of salvation is nothing if not a succession of "second chances." In fact, if God were to be defined at all by any word within the compass of the human mind it would be a word that shows that very character of thwarted love. God appears to be defined by His Faithfulness just as mankind is defined by its unfaithfulness. Love appears to constantly expand its compass and to be always in advance of man's rejection of that love. This is why the very concept of Divine rejection at the last judgment in such words as, "Depart from me you evil-doers to the place prepared for the devil and his angels ," seems to contradict all of God's prior dealings with humanity.

One possibility of course is that the passage in question had a didactic purpose, to stimulate charity and that excessive language was used in order to motivate compliance by the disciples. Another possibility though is that the passage in question shows something essential in the very metaphysic of God. That essential quality of God is that He cannot divorce himself from human misery wherever it is to be found. To associate with God then, let alone to share the Divine life of the Trinity in heaven, demands that we share that characteristic to some degree and that sharing is made manifest by simple, concrete acts of charity. For that same reason, every failure to be aware of the suffering of others is directly contrary to God and places us along the path that leads to ultimate selfishness and the imprisonment within our own nature, our own vanity and self-sufficiency. This is the broad path that leads to destruction, and it appears to be a natural one, for which one of us does not think first of his own good before considering that of others? It is the function of Divine grace to separate men and women from the fear that makes us so considerate of our own comfort and pleasures that we have neither the time nor the resources to alleviate the needs of those who surround us.

Those needs are often pressing and direct. Every human contact is an opportunity to make inquiry into the state of our neighbor, not out of an intrusive desire to shame our neighbor, but rather out of our own inner need to participate in the largess of God. This is why it is that luxury ultimately robs us of our freedom. To the degree that we increase the cost of our own maintenance through excessive desires, we cheapen our ability to be of use to others because our residual resources that may be shared will be so much the less. This means in effect that the richest man is the one who requires little to sustain himself and whose desires approach as far as possible the desire of the God who uses all of His power so as to be deprived of that power, who uses his dignity so as to lay it aside and to assume human nature, and who uses eternity so as to encase it not only within time but in every marginal action of goodwill.

This strange definition of God explains why God's rule does not encompass the confines of hell, for God may not enter into a realm the very definition of which is the lack of charity. Hell and those who choose it is a narrow chasm wherein each person's good would be an affront to the all-encompassing greed of his neighbor. In hell, each desires to be everything, so that no cooperation is ever possible to attain community. There is no alleviation from a pain that is so self-induced. I will go so far as to say that hell is not a place but rather something contained in the great emptiness of a soul that has been emptied of the God who alone can fill it with Himself and in doing so to unite each soul to the company of all other souls so that the good of one becomes the good of all and that each one exists only to share any good as soon as it is received. Everything circulates then like the blood does within the body.

In contrast to this is the centralization of power and wealth. Such a concentration causes the flow of grace to cease and the body to die. It is the very characteristic of a dead body that the blood pools in the extremities and that gravity defeats the action of the heart. When the heart fails within us, the heart of charity, then it is that the soul dies. It is then not death that is to be feared but only the fear that makes of death an absolute. This is why the martyrs such as St. Lawrence could mock death, for they saw clearly that death has only the thickness of a coating of mercury upon a mirror. Whoever looks into a mirror seems to be looking into infinity and to imagine that through the face of the mirror there is infinite depth. He would long to enter into the beckoning but shallow world that stands before him and see himself reflected in all his glory, but alas he looks into a flat surface and the real world is always behind him! Real depth is to be found not in the thin veneer of death the only function of which is to deceive us and to awaken our fears. Depth is to be found only by living within the eternity of the present and to know that the thin membrane of death is penetrated in an instant and that after that we will endure as we have always endured with our preferences intact, if we wish it so.

But what shall we be in that moment, one branching out into eternity? Will we be found with charity within us or will we rather find ourselves seeking still that flat surface whose narrow confines seemed to contain all that was or could ever be? If that should be the case, we will go about looking frantically for a world that never was because it was our illusion, an illusion in which it was we who were always God, for the sin of man and of woman in Eden was not in seeking to be like God, but to wish God to be as we imagined Him to be: one who could be controlled by our perceptions and placated by our actions, or even simply ignored because we were sufficient to ourselves.

Even now we burden God with our conceptions and the

limitations we have placed upon His mercy. It is possible that naked again, as were Adam and Eve in the garden, and seeing our nakedness clearly, we will finally accept the clothing that Divine grace offers to our infirmity and in doing so we will find that we are after all in heaven. The Manichean dualism that has been so long resident in Christian thinking and that gives so much attention to evil merely gratifies the vanity of the Devil and the minions who with him form a sort of heavy sludge in the cosmos. It is characteristic of evil that it is frozen and immobile, rooted in a great negation of all that is. Evil reverses the order of goodness whose character is dynamic and productive of new life and of variety. Nature manifests this in the remarkable variety of plant and animal species. Life grasps at every nook and cranny for a place to take root, whereas death lays barren great swaths of fertile and elaborated structures of community. Evil destroys relationships of cooperation and of mutual dependence. In nature even death provides the soil for new life to spring up so that what is an individual evil becomes for the plurality of beings a source of nutriment.

The sacrament of the Holy Eucharist and the death of Christ on the Cross are a mirror image of this life proceeding out of death. God Himself, through the Second Person of the Divine Trinity, who is the principle and agency of all of creation, takes upon Himself death, willingly so as to serve the needs of all men and women and to purge from within them the last remnants of death. A fire is lit within the vessel so that each soul flows with a common flame, not of its own making, but derivative from God. That fire is a cleansing force that purges the old so that from its ashes a new birth may quicken.

By exalting the sons of men, all lesser creation receives its vindication also. The death that was so necessary to life will, for so the Holy Scriptures state, be supplanted by a new order of creation in which death and all of the powers of darkness will fall away like the sheath that protects the flower until it may burst forth again in all of its glory. Creation will blossom, but not to know only the glory of days, but to move constantly to new states of renewal, to penetrate ever deeper into the mystery of God.

Evil shall be left without its function of servitude and by becoming absolute in itself, even death will change. What was formerly the final refusing remnant of the divine command to the angels of service to creation, that command will be transformed so that the evil ones might serve the will of God still, by an inverse means of threatening that which is good; it will now pass and evil will be allowed to be the pure principle that it always aspired to be. Non-being will be enthroned in its own inertia and to no end. It will shrink into itself until in mere frustration it will concoct all of those punishments that God forbears to administer to them, for the punishment of hell is simply the achievement of evil's own ends, which are by definition self-defeating. Hell is simply getting what evil wants and for the human soul it would be getting whatever it wants if what it wants is not God.

This formulation of eternal life or death is the same as that of St. Augustine when he said to God, "You have made us for yourself and our hearts are restless until they rest in thee." The natural capacity of all created beings is defined by God prior to creation. This is the true meaning of predestination properly understood. That we do not create our own natures, nor do we have the capacity to define what is good and evil for ourselves; rather, we find an order in things not of our making and are subservient to that order. Our freedom is then perfective of our natures when it cooperates with that order that reveals the will of God for us and it is frustrated in its own goodness when it resists that order, which if merely imposed by God arbitrarily would make of the universe only a vast and intricate machine.

God allows evil to exist so that love may be possible, so that beings who might choose otherwise would willingly love God, for love may be invited but never commanded. The commands of God are then not the orders of a tyrant, but a guide to the avoidance of evil. This is what Jesus meant when he said that we should, "Take my yoke upon you, for my yoke is easy and my burden light and you will find rest for your souls." Evil is then strenuousness to no purpose, whereas goodness, when it is freely embraced, creates that fittingness, that appropriateness, that harmony, that shows that it alone is natural and within a greater order known only to God in all its fullness.

All of the above thoughts are a rehearsal for the confrontation with Professor Moriarty that is no longer a distant prospect, but must soon occur. The Professor will no doubt point to the features of his desolate asteroids to show that in his view the universe consists only of colliding bodies of mindless matter. The study of truth then for him is the mere mapping out of various trajectories and the measurement of forces. He will say that all judgments are void and that good and evil are metaphysical concepts that are the illusions of the human mind, that if we could only see ourselves clearly we would note that we as the knower are irrelevant to the cosmos as that which is known.

Professor Moriarty would say that all knowledge is only a mechanical translation of what lies without us into the form of neural-bonds within the brain and the vanity of the coded-references of languages and of mathematics. He would entertain the possibility of epistemology, but would deny the relevance of all metaphysics. He would say that the only function of man is to know, but that even that knowledge is finally purposeless for there is no final end to anything but only a purposeless elaboration of forms. If I asked him then why he makes the effort to know anything at all, he would state that there is no reason beyond at best a desire to escape ennui while waiting for death. If I should tell him that such a motive seems to be present in the minority of men and women and if I should point out to him that drunkenness and vice seem to satisfy many, he would no doubt say bitterly that his own cranial capacity has been his undoing and that he is condemned to wish to know. If this should be true, then I share his curse. The desire for knowledge has also been my own fate. Yet we have come to such different conclusions! Which of us shall then prevail? Is the Professor capable of changing his own axioms at this late date? Shall I abandon the treasury of European philosophy or the religion that has nurtured and made possible most of what we call Western Civilization?

Ah well, the event must await my return. Until then I shall spend my time in France to complete at least some work that may justify my life and contribute something to the good of men and women by examining the chemistry of the coal-tar derivatives. Perhaps, I may glimpse within the strange intricacy of the organic molecules some equivalent to Moriarty's order of astral motion. It will give us at the very least some common-ground as scientists where we may meet upon my return. Perhaps with a common bond in nature with its regularities we may find as well a synthesis as regards human nature and destiny. Philosophy leads one to the door of religion but we must open it ourselves.

Dr. Watson's Narrative Continues

I interrupted my reading of Holmes' journal for the day had come at last for our audience with the Pope. I hardly knew how to prepare for such a meeting and was grateful to have at my side Inspector Stanley Hopkins who was so consumed with the results of our investigation and the desire to communicate it to the Pope that he was not as anxious or concerned as I was who had a more personal communication to make to the Holy Father. We had our usual excellent breakfast, no longer the prosaic eggs, bacon, and kippers of England, but enjoyed instead the bounty of the cooking of Italy. I had gained some pounds since my arrival and I therefore suggested that we walk to the Vatican rather than taking the coach provided to us for our use since our arrival by the British Embassy.

It was a lovely morning in spring and all of Rome seemed washed in the pale sunlight that brought out every facet in the marble facades that are seen everywhere in Rome. Simply to feel the air of Italy is a gift for one such as I who have spent so much of my life in the dank and foggy airs of London with the stale miasma of the Thames River and the press of humanity all about me. The center of the British Empire is perhaps the first of what will become more common in great cities in the centuries to come. It is characterized by the unnatural growth and agglomeration of people until all ties of community are broken. Hampstead Heath is all that remains of the commons that used to be attached to every village in England. It was on the commons that the urban and the rural met. The food supply was never distant for such communities. Compared to that way of life modern London is like a great fungus that draws not only upon the English countryside for sustenance but upon the entire world for resources to feed its voracious appetite. Through the years I had grown to loathe the dark confines of the commercial heart of empire. I was only too happy to sell my Kensington practice and to seek respite on that "Riviera of England," the coast of Cornwall.

To be in Italy was an opportunity for me to realize fully why the great English poets sought out the Italian climate. How I wished that I could prevail upon Holmes to live out his retirement years here, but for Holmes there would always be the need to be close to England and to the scene of his many cases or so I believed at the time. Even the unsavory districts of the East End of London were for him the place from which to view humanity in all of its diversity and depravity. The squalor and ignorance bred in the very heart of commerce was to him a symbol of the age in which we lived and he would never rest until he might ameliorate in some way these plagues upon human life. Unfortunately he had now put his own life at risk through his many labors. The consumption that wracked his very bones lay like a shadow over the life of the great detective. How glad I was to be able to help him by undertaking some of the tasks of the investigation and I could only pray that he was resting well in Baker Street so that this most recent flare-up of his malady might pass.

We arrived at Saint Peter's Square with its great arms and columns that invite the faithful of the world to the greatest Cathedral in Christendom. We were met at the very door by the Pope's own secretary, a Cardinal of noble birth and a distant descendant as he informed us of the great St. Charles Borromeo of Milan. He led us through an obscure private passage into a small garden built against the hillside. Our audience with the Pope was to be private in nature and to be held in these very informal surroundings. Our revelations were of a most intimate nature and perhaps this fact accounted for this break in the normal protocol of audiences with the Sovereign Pontiff. But I could not help but feel that this unique event was also a distant tribute to Holmes himself and a sign of the personal esteem in which he was held by the currently reigning Pontiff, Pope Leo XIII.

We were shown to two brocaded chairs that seemed misplaced in the natural setting of the garden. It was there that we were joined after no great interval by His Holiness. He accepted our homage briefly as ceremony demanded but with a businesslike air bid us to resume our seats while he took a seat also just opposite to us. He was a tiny shrunken man but I could feel the great intellect and vitality within him that belied his years. During his Pontificate the Church had progressed into the modern age. The long reign of his predecessor had been a prolonged and tragic battle to sustain the prerogatives of the medieval Church. Though the present Pope still considered himself to be a prisoner of the Vatican like his predecessor, Pope Pius IX, there was no further appeal for military aid from France or Austria to regain the Papal States as there had been under the former Papacy. No Christian blood would be shed for an earthly claim. This may be taken as a sign that the Popes of the future will feel with a greater intensity the need to minister to the entire Roman Catholic Church and that the dominant role of the Italian clergy to the Universal See of St. Peter will be broken. If that should be the case, then history may record that Pope Leo XIII was the first modern Pope. How strange that as the Papacy has lost its earthly ability to resist aggression by the new nation-state system of world government it may have returned to the authority given it by Jesus and not by the Emperor Constantine.

The gift of Jesus to the first of the Popes was to Saint Peter and it was simple in nature and recorded near the end of the Gospel of Saint John. Jesus asked Peter, "Do you love me more than these others do?" When Peter said to Jesus that He must know that Peter loved him, Jesus admonished Peter to feed His sheep and to confirm his brothers in the faith. The primacy of Peter then is one of mission and less of power, a mission to confirm the entire Body of Christ in what has been taught always and everywhere by the collective Bishops of the Church under the guidance of the Holy Spirit. The Pope is then not a legislator or even an executive in his functions, but is rather the Universal Pastor of Souls. What he has received is what he sustains and protects. His function is one of confirmation and not origination. He creates nothing new, nor is his function one of prophecy, but is rather to adapt by speaking again in the time of his Pontificate those great truths that are the substance of revelation and to shepherd faithfully the flock of Christ.

It is not inconceivable that the Pope might even leave Rome one day, for where Peter's chair rests there rests the Church. The one who governs in Peter's place is part of the organic structure of the Mystical Body of Christ. The entire Church gathers about him as once the little children were bid to come to the feet of Jesus so that he might embrace them in all of their unassuming needs and trust. Every Christian is admonished that unless we become like little children we shall not enter the Kingdom of Heaven. This is only another way of saying that our acceptance of heaven must rest upon conditions set by God and not upon our own machinations. The Kingdom of heaven is a gift and who is better at accepting gifts then little children whose immaturity and limitations preclude obtaining them through their own efforts. I could see in the manner of the present Holy Father that he himself was uncomfortable with the panoply and encrustations of Papal grandeur, which is only relevant at all if it is seen as an effort to picture the majesty of God so that even His servants may manifest His glory. Beyond that ceremonies become encumbrances to the soul and an insult to the humility of Jesus Christ.

This much I retained from my Protestant upbringing. But I

found that morning that I was no longer bitter towards the Roman Church. I could see how a possible reconciliation of all branches of Christianity might actually be possible and why the Popes and the entire Catholic Church prays unceasingly, as did Jesus at the Last Supper, that all may be one. This unity is essential because the Bride of Christ, which is the Church of God, is one. There is no harem in the Kingdom of Heaven but only the one Eternal Wedding Feast when Jesus will present the Church as one collective whole to the Father. It is within the Church that each individual on earth finds his or her home. This is what is meant by the old Latin phrase that outside the Church there is no salvation. It is simply a reflection that the Grace of God determines the borders of the Church and that within those borders salvation is assured. Only one who willingly excludes himself from Divine grace is eternally lost. The mercy of God is ever open to appeal. The gate is narrow not to exclude then but to tell us that we enter that gate naked of all baggage and that we must rid ourselves of every encumbrance that might bar our entry. The world for each of us is passing away.

As a physician I have always thought it strange to speak of one who is dying as though that were not true of all of us every day of our lives. We are passing closer to Eternity with each second; the final gate becomes closer. The result is that a life which is so often spent in the acts of accumulation is in direct opposition to what should be our life course, which is to rid ourselves of everything but God. It is often said that the vice of age is miserliness. As death approaches, the organism clings with greater vigor to all that it was. The semblance of youth is created by clothing the wizened bones in fine garments. The eye that has known desire still hungers for the pleasures of the flesh. Above all else, one is jealous that one's name shall not be forgotten. This explains the ardor for tombs, inscriptions, and epitaphs. How swiftly are these memorials effaced by the waves of time! I think often of that marvelous verse by the American poet Henry Wadsworth Longfellow in this regard: "Morning returns and the steeds in their stalls stamp and neigh as the hostler calls. The day returns but nevermore returns the traveler to the shore and the tide rises the tide falls."

The Pope opened our discussion that day by expressing his concern and assuring us that he would offer his Mass that day for the recovery of health of his friend, Mr. Sherlock Holmes. He then went on to inquire about the results of our investigation. We explained that the late Cardinal Tosca had invested funds in Holland from the Vatican Bank and that we believed that they might even now be recovered for the Church. His Holiness thanked us and asked that we would share the details with his secretary who would see that the proper Vatican officials were informed. He then went on to express a grave concern: "My dear Sons," said he, "There is a deeper matter. We need to know how these funds were used. Did they have anything to do with Cardinal Tosca's death?"

Inspector Hopkins attempted to put the matter with some delicacy, but the Pontiff waved aside these amenities. "You must understand that our faith does not shield us from an awareness of the evils that are present in the world. Nor are we surprised when evil finds its way even within the ministers of the Holy Catholic Church. As men we ministers of the gospel share all of the follies of the rest of mankind; it is only our office that deserves respect, not because of our actions, but because Our Lord has promised not to leave us orphans and that He would be with us through his Holy Spirit even unto the consummation of the world. You may then feel free to share with me all that you have discovered of this affair holding nothing back."

We then proceeded to share with him all of the details of the plot of Baron Maupertuis and how we had been fortunate enough to abort those plans. We stressed that we could not ascertain just how many of the details were known by Cardinal Tosca and that his murder, for such we felt it had been, might have been simply to prevent the need to return the Vatican funds as well as to insure the no word of the plot would ever reach European officials from the mouth of the Cardinal. To these revelations, the Pope listened with great solemnity. He was silent for a time, perhaps in prayer.

He then remarked, "In the effort to do good, we often work great evil. The ways of power, even of spiritual power, are always dangerous. We are drawn always back to the humility of Christ who promised that the poor we would have always with us. No earthly scheme for general reform will bring heaven down to earth. Our Lord's kingdom is for the little ones who understand him in their hearts. I am afraid that our brother, Cardinal Tosca, may have forgotten this. I wish for you to know that he was a man of great zeal, perhaps too much zeal. We have known him since seminary days. Even then he had the highest of aspirations to create justice, often to the neglect of prayer. He was of the opinion that since God knows all of our ways that prayer was superfluous, that our petitions were vain, and that God's will would be achieved even without our daily cooperation. I fear that Cardinal Tosca harbored a latent streak of Jansenism. It is not humility to deny free-will but an insult to the creator. Our dignity and freedom are not impaired by Divine grace but perfected by it. God does not despise us nor does He treat us as automata to be pushed about by his providence. Rather he does as Scripture says, he stands at the door and knocks, and it is we who must open the door, which we do by simple acts of prayer and the exercise of daily charity. This was evidently not enough for our brother, Cardinal Tosca."

He turned aside for a time before continuing, "I blame myself. Had he been posted to some obscure diocese he might have better discerned the true nature of the Kingdom of God among the peasant women and the working men. It was his desire instead to deal with the powerful of this world and to set up an order of economic collaboration that would bring glory to the Church and create justice and equity on an earth that will never know these things completely. The comfort of the Church is of another order entirely. That comfort is to bring peace to troubled souls; not the least numbers of such souls are to be found among those persons who are wealthy powerful. The way of the cross cannot be avoided and to seek to do so is to court disaster. Our Lord assured us that no servant is greater than his master. I fear that Cardinal Tosca desired in a sense to succeed where Christ failed and to eliminate all earthly suffering. This shall never be the lot of mankind. The state of the world in the last days will be if anything worse than they are now. We still live within the time of the green wood and have yet to see what will happen when the wood is dry. It is our constant care to avoid the illusions of progress and to recall that the Prince of Darkness has been allowed this time to try our souls so that our virtues shall be perfected and so that our defects may be brought humbly before God for His forgiveness. This is the mission of the Church and the call of our ministry as the heir of the teaching office of St. Peter. As you see, gentlemen, the strain has shrunken our poor body. We are very weary. Please pray for me."

Soon after that he rose to depart but before he did so I requested his blessing which he readily bestowed upon us both. As Pope Leo XIII was about to bid us goodbye, suddenly I was certain of the course that I wished my future life to follow; the past months had wrought an immense change in my previous religious opinions with the result that I spoke up in that silent and peaceful hour and told the Pope how much it had meant to me to meet him and that I chose that moment to request from the Holy Father that I might be admitted into the Roman Catholic Church.

"My dear man you are most welcome. May I ask if you have been baptized in the name of the Father, the Son, and the Holy

Spirit and by water? Good, very good. Your return to Holy Mother Church is then a matter of receiving instruction in the faith and in your willing profession of faith to all that the Church has passed on from the Holy Apostles."

I asked if that might be done soon and in Rome. "Yes of course my dear Son. I shall give you an introduction to a most excellent priest of your own country who is teaching at the Gregorian Institute here in Rome. He is a member of the order of the Jesuits, a most learned man. Come to me in a month, will you do so? I shall then receive your profession of faith personally in thanksgiving for your efforts in resolving this matter of Cardinal Tosca."

The Inspector and I bowed to the Pontiff and awaited his retirement to his private chambers before taking our own departure. We walked back from St. Peter's to our hotel in silence. I could hardly refuse such a gracious offer as that which he had been made to me, but I knew that it would delay my return to London. Still, I knew that Holmes was receiving excellent medical care from Dr. Moore Agar and that my presence in London was not strictly necessary. Inspector Hopkins explained after we returned to our rooms that he could use the extended time to complete his own investigations. He had not given up the possibility that he might trace the assassins of Cardinal Tosca and his superiors at Scotland Yard had suggested that he might use his time in Italy to study a criminal secret society whose reach extended even as far as England itself.

Thus it was that we each settled into a regular routine in the days that followed. I made daily trips to the magnificent Gregorian Institute while the Inspector went about his own affairs with the assiduity of a bloodhound on the trail. I found that my instruction from the good Padre was not as demanding as I had feared. Indeed, he was startled at some of the matters that I discussed with him that were derived from my reading of Holmes' journal. Our discussions as a result had an intricacy and a breadth beyond that of the usual catechumenal instruction. The study of one's faith is in any case a lifelong process; a faith that is not challenged from time to time must be of a most mechanical and mundane nature. Faith is not so much blind as it is an attitude of trust and of patience. Not all can be revealed in an instant. Even the apostles were told that they had much yet to learn but that they could not bear it at the time. Even as late as the event of the Last Supper the followers of Our Lord expected a glorious victory and not the bitter death of Jesus on the Cross. Even now there are Christians who forget that we are yet upon the road and would wish to begin to celebrate victory in a premature manner. There will always be the empty silence of Holy Saturday between the Crucifixion and the Resurrection to eternal life.

The month of my instruction in the Roman Catholic Faith passed swiftly. I continued to hear from Holmes from time to time regarding the progress of the Greater Dutch Canal Company. The price of the shares had increased dramatically since they had first been offered to the public before I left England. There could be little doubt that the Baron was bent on gradually acquiring a controlling interest in the company as Holmes had foreseen. I was surprised though that the Baron had yet to make the Murillo Papers public, but then he was no doubt waiting until he had acquired as many shares as possible in the company. It was then, with no surprise that I read one day in the foreign edition of "The London Times" that the papers of ex-president Don Juan Murillo of Costa Rica had been discovered and the contents would soon be published in book form.

The copy of the text of the article is before me now as I write. Its text reads as follows:

"It has just been revealed by a scholar at Leyden University that he has come into the possession, through the gift

of an unnamed patron of the university's history department, of a most valuable find that may have the most dramatic effects upon certain events of the present day. Though these papers have yet to be examined in detail their import is to show that during his detestable reign over the small nation of Costa Rica the dictator Don Juan Murillo was favored by contributions from well connected business interests and military aid from the United States of America so that he might remain in power to advance the interests of various large American companies. The railroad that was constructed at that time, one that linked the two major ports in Costa Rica was apparently built and owned by an American consortium, which had the sole interest in not only the railroad itself but was given permission by President Murillo to run the two ports in question as virtual extra-territorial possessions of the United States of America. In addition, President Murillo was bribed to reduce the normal tariffs assessed on the produce of certain American companies with stock in the said railroad while retaining those tariffs for European goods.

While these offenses are in a certain sense the product of actions taken in the past, their effects continue at the present time. The trade advantage to American production remains and several treaties may have been violated. A wave of outrage is likely to ensue in many quarters and many on the continent have already called for an immediate investigation into other past American practices of sharp-dealing. Your correspondent has not been able as yet to procure an interview with the American ambassador who has been deluged with cables from outraged investors of European firms. Many lawsuits are in the air. The issues posed though are unlikely to be settled by private litigation since government policy at the highest levels during the administrations of several Presidents is also indicated. It is too early to tell what effect this may have upon the confidence of the electorate in America, but there can be no doubt that each political party there will blame the other for the corruptions of yesterday.

The full tale that emerges is an ugly one. The railroad in Costa Rica was built with Italian labor that was little short of slavery and even British subjects from Manchester and Leeds were among those who met their deaths from yellow fever in the swamps and low mountains of Costa Rica in order to build the railroad that is now used less for mining transport and more to service fruit exportation to world markets. The recent American ambitions to build a canal in Central America will of course make the current railroad of less strategic importance, but since its operation has already brought in vast profits to its owners, some of those profits will undoubtedly be invested in any projected American canal project. Whether it will rely similarly for its building upon brutal labor conditions is a question that many people are asking? Suddenly all eyes are upon American policy at this juncture. Will the nation that fought to free its Negro slaves now impose slavery and even death upon workers drawn from Europe in order to build a canal that will allow America to dominate trade with Japan and China? The answer from Europe thus far has been a resounding no!

The best current competitor to America since the failure of the French concern of some years ago is a Dutch bid to build the canal. Shares in that company are now being bought with zeal by many Europeans in order to show America that Europe is not to be treated as a decaying continent to be left behind by American industry. The price of the shares has gone up since these revelations, boosted by patriotic zeal and each independent European nation now stands with little Holland to challenge the American behemoth. The major stockholder in the Dutch company that was recently formed is Baron Maupertuis of Amsterdam, the well known banker and trader with the Dutch

East Indies. Your correspondent believes that this gentleman summed up the situation best.

When he was interviewed yesterday Baron Maupertuis stated, "Europe will not be thrust aside through Yankee arrogance. It is time that the so-called Monroe Doctrine was challenged. Europe demands trade with the East. We shall obtain it. If the first of the world's great modern democracies is in fact a domain of plutocrats, then we in Europe will lay bare its national hypocrisy. We shall build the canal. We shall open it to all nations. We shall not allow America to have a key to the portals of world-trade. We shall not allow the taskmaster to impose a new slavery upon our workers, nor shall we submit the sovereignty of our ancient kingdoms to that upstart hegemon, America. We shall see which nation will build the Canal!"

This was the article that I read that day in Rome. I could see at once that the world was radically changing. The competition between the nations of the world for influence and supremacy in trade and power was growing. The insatiable desires of the supposedly Christian nations had set each at odds with each. Only a balance of mistrust remained to unite Christendom. I could see why the Islamic lands felt it their sacred duty to spread the faith of Mohammed that would transcend all national borders and unite all believers in one vast community of the Ummah the service of all believers in Allah.

How strange it was that the spirit of the Crusades had made the peoples in Europe who had embraced Christianity forget that Jesus had told them that he who takes the up the sword will surely perish by the sword. It was the sword and not the cross that had became the emblem of Christianity in the modern age as Christians prepared to slaughter Christians in a great war that would finally settle all differences. Since the 16th century there had been no unity among Christian peoples. Even those countries that still remained Catholic had attempted at times to dictate to the

Church. France and Spanish Austria had long been engaged in a war of desire to represent their own national versions of the faith as normative and binding for all members of the universal Church. Even Lutheran Germany had become a shattered people divided along the lines of the faith of the Princes of its often warring principalities.

Meanwhile Russia, Greece, and the Balkans were severed from the body of the rest of Christianity in their claim of Orthodoxy that had torn down the supremacy of the Papacy and the Universal See of St, Peter that alone can unite the One Church of Jesus Christ. The article that I had read seemed to foretell that America would soon be isolated with its all-embracing ambition to control its hemisphere. The Latin nations would someday unite to oppose the northern aggression. Had not the vast octopus of American enterprise already terminated the land rights of its native inhabitants? Would it stop then after having reached the Pacific Ocean? What could contain America, the nation that above all others desired to be universal in the sweep of its power? The universal aspiration to power of the American demos might finally make it aspire to a *Pax Americana,* the first universal world empire since the fall of Rome. As such it will someday come into conflict with the Catholic Church, which recognizes the rights of all people to a form of government including self-determination in the secular realm.

Of course the universal claims of the Catholic Church are not to rule over God's earth, but to be the spotless Bride of Christ and to follow Our Lord in the path towards salvation. How different is America, that land that would build paradise upon the earth in the famous pursuit of happiness through material means. This is the fundamental error of American thought: that it believes that happiness is an adequate pursuit that may be obtained by material struggle. It is a nation born in the Pelagian mindset for happiness is a gift and not a possession. It may not be sought through effort, but only received as a gift through conversion and prayer. Happiness is always in front of us. It is never a permanent possession for even the greatest happiness must end with our deaths. Our task then is not to strive directly for happiness, but rather to open a space within us so that God may fill it with the only gift that will never be taken away, the gift of God Himself who alone is our final happiness. I could see that even the ambitions of the evil Baron Maupertuis had succeeded in awakening the slumbering European nations to the threat posed by America, the greatest secular power the world has ever known as it is soon likely to become.

America will never be a truly Christian nation. Rather, it will undermine Christianity by proposing an anti-gospel of power, arms, and violent conquest. The borders of America have always been defined by what the Americans could take from others, first the Indians, then from England, and finally from the Mexicans. It is a nation conceived in war. Its national anthem is about triumph in war. Americans will never accept the defeat and humility that is entailed in embracing the Cross. They will instead attempt to exceed grace by placing others upon the cross instead of in imitation of Jesus Christ who accepted its humiliation willingly.

America is if anything a nation founded on the principles of Deism and Freemasonry as may be seen by the number of its Presidents who were Freemasons. America believes that it is the *Mysterium Tremendum* spoken of in those arcane gatherings. It makes idols of its Founding Fathers and its Constitution has replaced the gospels with the rule of man rather than the rule of God. America is the final product of the thoughts of the Deists and the French Philosophes such as Diderot that resulted finally in its mythology of Manifest Destiny. America imagines that it is the new chosen nation of God with the mission to subdue the world even as the Jews conquered ancient Canaan by driving out the Hittites and the Amorites. America is an idol unto itself and will do anything to avoid confronting its own nakedness and emptiness. No man or any collection of men may be as God. I will go so far as to say that Americanism is the last and the greatest of the heresies. America is the great beast; the Babylon of old has been restored!

Wherever American business interests lie, there the people need to tremble, for their lands and produce will be extracted to feed the greedy maw of the American gullet. I have watched as the last of the native tribes of America have been brought to heal on reservations and read in the year of 1890 of that final disgraceful slaughter at Wounded Knee that must forever cause a blush of shame to any American who learns of it. How was it possible that men like Crook, Sherman, and Sheridan were given the power to decimate whole peoples and to displace them if it was not innate in the American character to endorse their course of brutality and theft towards the Indians? America is only the latest example of the danger of initially promising ideas. What mankind conceives out of its own being is usually evil. Only when we listen to the natural law and to the Church are we safe from error. However, even the Church itself has known periods when it sought its own power and glory apart from Christ. It is that scandal that has led to the fragmentation of Christianity.

To be a convert as I was soon to be, I wished at last to confront the sins of the Church's members and of its leaders while retaining and professing faith in the Church as conceived by God. Conversion of heart is not merely an individual phenomenon but one in which the Church itself must always be engaged. The Church grows by the infusion of its new members who enter with an excitement and passion that has sometimes been lost by older Catholics. The vision must be always new and a general repentance offers a brighter tomorrow for those who will reach deep into the coffers that hide the true treasures of the Church. Its majestic teachings and its perennial hope for the salvation of all men and women must be constantly rediscovered. It was my privilege to be in Rome in the spring and to find my life anew. This may account for these far-reaching observations. I am astonished at my temerity of judgment, but in actual fact I was merely taking the next step in a lifetime of groping since the great disillusionment of my days in Afghanistan that brought a wound that has both physically and spiritually troubled me ever since. I do not know if Sherlock Holmes intended any such end as my full profession of faith in the Catholic Church when he sent me to Rome, but providence undoubtedly used this occasion to crystallize my intentions into one great act that resolved the aspirations of many years.

The days passed swiftly as I neared the day that I would be received into the Catholic Church. I knew that what I had undertaken was only a beginning of course, but I longed to see that it was accomplished and to return soon to England and to my friend Sherlock Holmes. I worried still about his health. His few terse telegrams and letters assured me that all was going well, but I would not rest easy until I could see again his lean and commanding form filled with the energies of old. Until that time of reunion I sought the comfort of his presence by continuing to read the words of his journal that was about to record his time spent in France. I had long been a victim of his often malodorous chemical experiments in our rooms at Baker Street. It would be rewarding to know that those sacrifices of my personal comfort had not been in vain if they had led him to stumble upon some discovery that might aid mankind is some fashion and perhaps ensure his own survival from the ravages of that ancient scourge of tuberculosis into the bargain. What lives might be saved, what genius might be preserved, and how much sorrow and loss might be prevented by just such a discovery!

From the Journal of Sherlock Holmes

May 1, 1892
Arrival at Marseilles

It is the first of May, a day to commemorate the Blessed Virgin Mary who is honored by the Church as the Mother of God, the Theotokos. It is the belief of the Church now solemnly defined that Mary was conceived without the burden of Original Sin. This gift of divine favor is such that Mary alone, although fully human, is not born with that inclination to evil known by all other men and women as the result of the sin of our first parents. Mary is thus in a unique position in the order of creation. Her cooperation with Divine grace though free is not burdened by that inherited openness to the suggestions of the Devil that are shared by all other men and women; in this sense she is a new creation, a second chance for all of humankind. She is not strictly speaking of the spiritual lineage of Adam and Eve. She exists on an entirely unique level.

This gives the Blessed Virgin Mary a quality that the Catholic Church does not worship but rather venerates and appropriately so for her unique and substantial nature is to be the bearer of Divine grace for and to the Church and through it to all of humanity. She is its model and example. She is already what the Catholic Church as a whole aspires to be: holy, perfect, and unblemished in the eyes of God. Since the Blessed Virgin Mary offers no obstacle to the action of grace and is in complete accord with the will of God, He has chosen to bestow all graces through her. She is in a sense the window through which God sees the world. Her Divine Son, also born without original sin, unites all things in Himself, for final presentation to the Father, but those actions are bestowed through his Blessed Mother. She is the Holy Gate to the city of the Celestial Jerusalem. She is known as the Mother of Mercy for she opposes no soul but welcomes all who come to her so that they may lay aside the burden of their sins.

These images are more than mere metaphors. They answer a deeply felt need within all men and women to be loved and to be gathered up as a mother gathers her children to bring them home, to nurture and protect them from harm. The Blessed Virgin Mary has no part in the Evil One. Though he once even tempted Christ to that very lack of trust in God's bounty that led our first parents into sin, there is no record that the devil ever tempted the Blessed Virgin Mary. Her fullness of grace is such that she is preserved inviolate. Before her the powers of hell bow in terror and submission and her eventual triumph on the last day is secure.

It will be asked why if the Devil did not tempt the Blessed Virgin Mary, how would he dare to tempt Jesus Christ, who after all is God. This raises a subtle point in theology but I believe that I have an answer. The entire point of the Incarnation was for God to assume the burdens posed by evil, not the least of which is temptation to cooperate with evil. It was essential then for Christ's human nature to be tempted just as it was essential for Jesus to assume the penalty of sin although he himself was guiltless. Only in this way can God do for us what we may not do for ourselves.

These events are not merely historical or symbolic; they have an efficacy that only actuality may claim. For God to enter into time is to penetrate a foreign realm with Divine Presence. It is as though God entered into a dark cave and turned it into the very sun. Light drives out all darkness, which then falls backwards. I will go so far as to say that God has left the devil with no remaining ground upon which to lay an exclusive claim or from which to take a stand. God has staked a definitive claim upon the souls of men and women and upon the universe as such. If I may take a legal metaphor as an example, prior to Jesus Christ the devil had a perfected tenancy upon the earth surrendered to him by God to do his worst and to see if his version of reality might gain the willing submission of men and women. The devil was allowed this God-like rule so that Evil might be allowed its fullest range of expression and activity. Though this is all a mystery of course it does make sense. It is like a fire that may be extinguished by allowing it to burn up the sources of its combustion. In like manner Evil was allowed free reign upon the earth so as to exhaust any potential claim upon creation.

If it is true that Evil sprang forth out of creation without prior cause, then Evil is the invention of creation and not of God. Evil is what happens when contingent being assumes the prerogatives that belong to Absolute Being alone. To close off that process prematurely is to allow it to slumber like ashes and embers only to arise again. No, in order to defeat Evil it must be allowed to do its worst, to flame up and then in the very moment of its triumph to reduce it to nothing, to show Evil's absurdity and vanity by making that vanity manifest. This was the purpose that was attained by the Incarnation and by the Death of Jesus Christ on the cross. It is not that God cannot simply forgive us without atonement, but to do so without bearing the cost would be to make of reality a mere shadow-play. For God to simply write-out a writ of forgiveness would be to reduce our own suffering under the assaults of Evil to nothing. It would be unworthy of God to stand blithely aside from His creation. If that were so then the devil might as it were claim that if given a free chance he might still have achieved his ends.

Instead God does what at first must appear absurd; He

takes the burden of Evil upon Himself! Heaven itself is shaken and the harmony and ease of the Blessed Trinity is altered to embrace what is foreign to itself. God so penetrates creation with love that Evil must fall back to the drear edges where Being and even beings cease, there to retire into a frozen immobility of ultimate defeat on its own terms. It is as though God allowed Evil to dictate every term of a contract and then signed it in God's own blood and when the devil looked at the contract he found that every term brought about God's victory and the devil's defeat.

Christianity is more than mere mythology, a mere way of looking at things; it is an actuality. Christianity in other words does justice to the world that we encounter, a world of the irremediable actuality of things. The brutality of cause and effect is such that when life flees it does not return. The reason that Michelangelo's Pieta is so poignant is because of the finality of the crucifixion; because it manifests so truly and exactly our own experience of life, that what is lost is not made whole again. If the suffering and death of Jesus has mere sign value, then the Incarnation is a shadow-play. The suffering and the death of Jesus was real and it was complete. Jesus does not simply bounce back into life as though death was a trampoline. By embracing even death and death as a sinner, Jesus submitted to the possibility of final extinction and banishment from God. Only by seeing the death of Jesus as an act of complete trust in God can we assume that same posture when we ourselves come to die. Death for us then is just what it appears to be, final and irremediable, and after all appropriate to a contingent being. We can trust to something more because Jesus trusted in something more. Death as we know it is what it means to have been excluded from the Tree of Life in the Garden of Eden. We may know good and evil but we cannot of ourselves be our own point of origin. Our life must and always will be derivative and it will be lived hereafter in God or not at all. In other words God is our life, we have no other, and to pretend that we do is of the very nature of the pretence that is Evil. Evil then is an absurd pretention that might thrive for a time in a space and time surrendered to its control, but that must vanish finally when set against the backdrop of eternity.

The gift of God in Christ though is far more than an unmasking of Evil's pretences; it is an action that appropriates from Evil even the shred of dignity that it might still claim, a hopeless quest to elude omnipotence. God, in making himself subject to sin, transforms Evil from within its very self. Evil is turned inside-out and the Devil is left with only the great hollowness within which it may claim to still exist. This makes of our time on earth in these latter days, knowing that our salvation has been accomplished, none other than a period of quarantine until we shall be ready for entry into heaven. May that time be short! This is the final prayer of the Church in the Bible for at the end of the book of "The Apocalypse of St. John," also called "The Book of Revelation" the Church prays, "Come quickly Lord Jesus."

May 7, 1892
At Anchor in the Harbor of Marseilles

Our ship is at anchor in the harbor of Marseilles and we are in quarantine here. It is a mere precaution in our case since we have no plague cases aboard. We must remain here for a week and I shall spend the time profitably in reviewing my own manuscript. I am afraid that it is rather formless, but then it does not follow a preordained plan. If I had known what my thoughts would be and was merely laying out a preconceived theology I need never have left the comforts of Europe behind me to seek the adventurous quest of my Asian journey. Even now I wonder if that odyssey was worth the infinite effort involved. I realize that it is only by the providence of God that Colonel Moran and I were able to travel in such dangerous regions and still remain unmolested by bandits and brigands. The comforting rule of Anglo-Saxon law did not follow us and even the might of the British Empire was as smoke drifting over the land. I have been among cultures now far older than our own. How they must look down upon us and our modern ideas! The juggernaut of British trade as enforced by its navy is impressive and the British Soldier has even penetrated into the Punjab and the mountainous regions beyond. Still our colonial rule is only a violent fever that the peoples of those lands pray will soon pass and perhaps it shall.

We British imagine that the entire earth like us hungers for what lies upon distant shores. We cart everything about like a coster-monger. We have not learned to make-do with what lies at our doorstep and to live within the means that locality dictates. From this restlessness comes greed and untrammeled desire and from these in turn comes war. We must someday develop a blessed sense of limits. I wonder if it might be possible to reward efforts that diminish the outer impact of all that we do and to reward minimalism instead.

What if health for instance should be defined not by a fleshy body and a ruddy countenance, but by a body whose resources were adequate to its tasks with less superfluous flesh? Such an athletic economy of means would not be forever in advance of itself and the danger of overproduction would end. There would be no need to fear those ghastly economic cycles that create so much suffering among the working masses. I am certainly no economist, but I do believe that I have found the root-cause of such cycles. What are they but analogous to a receding tide that leaves the clams and starfish gasping for the water that carries their oxygen to them? That phenomenon is peculiar to shallow beaches and does not occur when the depth of water is greater and the beach drops off swiftly. It is then the lack of sufficient depth that is the problem with our economic structures. The maintenance of a servile working-class and the pressures of competition keep wages artificially low. The workers have no cushion to aid them to survive in times of receding economic tides. The formula is a simple one viz. the pain of an economic contraction is proportionate to the degree of inequality in a society. If the economic strata are leveled, no sector of the populace must bear disproportionate pain.

The other cause of economic panics, as they are called, is over-production compared to the ability of consumers to absorb the goods by purchasing them. Excess production over consumption causes prices to fall and inventory to back-up. Once again, the payment of adequate wages would ensure that human needs and wants would assume a constant and predictable level and production schedules could be adjusted accordingly. The working classes would be able to enjoy periods of blessed leisure and to live a life that is truly human. The last and final slavery of deficient wages would end. The squalor and depravity that feed on poverty would cease. The need of nations to subjugate other nations in order to obtain trade advantages would be lessened if not eliminated. It seems obvious to me that scarcity is less a matter of the natural order than it is a human creation. The land itself dictates the number of persons that it can comfortably support. Should we not listen then to the land and disperse the human race to under-populated regions and to the ends of the earth? But having done so to stop and cultivate what lies near at hand.

It should not be necessary to be the universal man. Surely even faith in God may show diversity proportionate to God's complexity. I believe Christianity to be the truth, but to violently impose that truth upon foreign peoples seems to me to doubt that God's sacraments are only the witnesses of grace. If grace does not exceed the sacramental sign and overflow it then the abundance of God is constrained by formal structures and priests become magisters and not ministers. The words and forms of sacraments are for us and not for God; the vehicle of communication is not the source of the communication. If God does not exceed His law and is not greater than the temples that purport to house His Divinity, can He be God at all?

How we do brutalize each other in God's name! Can that be the will of God? Surely not! We are jealous of our own dignity and not of God's sovereignty when we oppress others with our faith rather than simply to announce it and to allow the attractiveness of God to do as he said and to draw all men to Himself by His Cross in a manner that we may never understand. Divine grace must by its very nature exceed the sacramental order. If we are busy about our own souls then that grace will be quite enough for us.

Proceeding from these theological conclusions I am content to leave Colonel Sebastian Moran to his own counsel now that we have arrived safely in France. I shall go inland to Montpellier and the ancient university there while he plans to go on to Monte Carlo to the great casino there and to return to the baccarat tables that have so often been his undoing. I in turn plan to engage in the quiet of daily walks in the countryside and to pursue my long dreamed of chemical research into the coal-tar derivatives. We shall see what bounties there may be in that grim but complex sludge of old plant-matter deposited in the earth.

I find a certain charm to exist in the test tube. Nature speaks to us in the still small voice of science and it is only by slow degrees that we come to see the intricacy of the plans of God. Chemistry is as it were the coded language of God. If inorganic chemistry may be considered as God's rough-sketches in the art of creation, then organic chemistry represents the full-flower of God's creativity. All of life stems from the intricacy of the bonding formations of the carbon atom. The vast chain of being rests upon the pedestal of this humble atom as does the energy of the earth. Life is not an addition to the universe but a natural product of the potency that lies within matter itself. But who instilled that potency? Shall we ever imagine such variety as mere accident and not as a product of some infused design? God creates by instilling the potential of action and then allowing that potential to become manifest. All of creation may be considered to be a single great unfolding event. Creation is a kaleidoscope in which the patterns that we see are infinite while the actual constituent elements and their relations are finite and discoverable.

We should not be scandalized at the exchange and transformation of matter and of energy and the transient nature of the individual. If individuals were to persist in any form, then all change would cease and life would cease with it. The life processes are one of maturation followed by decay. We are cyclic creatures with a beginning and an end. The horror of death is not that we surrender our last elements to the universe from which we have drawn them, but that the dynamic that has infused matter for a time appears to cease with its final form which is frozen into immobility and decay. But were we ever really the bone and sinew and gristle of the body? If that were so then we are only the product of chickens and turnips. Nonsense! We are that transforming power that reduces to a persistent but altering form all that we have ever consumed. Even our memory is not finally the sum of us, for the faculty of memory may fail.

What are we then? We are, I believe, two things: first we are that principle that activates matter as a flame does a candle, change the candle yet the flame remains the same, for it is an active principle and not a passive substance. Second, we are a being in relation to God who contains us within His own memory. Our being exists in God who not only encloses us but interpenetrates us so that God's life is within us through the Holy Spirit. For this reason we persist, for what exists in God may not vanish, for God will not permit it to vanish. That death which seems so definitive is really a step of the flame of our life from one candle to another. Only if the flame is extinguished by being deprived of the life of God that is oxygen to the soul is the flame extinguished and what that darkness is we cannot say.

Perhaps a soul without God is analogous to the slow fires of decay in a compost heap that feeds upon its own substance. Perhaps Evil finally acts as a process that consumes but creates nothing but formless energy and the sheer sludge of matter without soul. It is a festering without fertilization. Nothing new ever arises from Evil but only the destruction of what is. Evil is the low, rumbling groundswell from which virtue breaks forth as the budding seedling arises from the soil. Perhaps in its own way it serves the function of definition for would we recognize the good without its opposite?

At precisely those times when we would wish to get beyond good and evil altogether we are forced to realize that we are subject to a world of opposition; that only the mind of God is absolute. We cannot stretch beyond our reach. Though we are now like God in knowing good and evil, we do not know these things in the manner of God himself who alone exists beyond all that is created. God precedes good and evil. If there had been no creation at all there would be no predicate of good or evil for there would only be God alone and to God no assignment of qualities may be made by a contingent creature. God's nature is such that God in Himself is neither good not evil for such terms cannot be attached to what precedes all definitions. Good and evil are terms of the relationship between creation and its God. The center-point has no direction. Rather, all creation is defined as good or evil by its distance and direction in relation to God.

The inner relations of the Holy Trinity exceed our grasp, so when we speak of them as good it is only by analogy. The Holy Trinity that is God is of such harmony and unity that God is spoken of as one. Yet that One is engaged in no great solipsism, but is so engaged as to be Love itself and to create what is good in relationship to itself. All language breaks down of course when dealing with God. The Christian religion is finally a matter of promise and covenant and not of knowledge.

In legal language heaven is spoken of as an inheritance and the fruit of a compact between God and man as restored to his former status by the death of Christ on the cross. This is why the Gnostics were always on the wrong track, for Christianity is not a matter of prior knowledge followed by action; it is instead action followed by knowledge. Jesus said that if we act out of love then the Father and the Son will come and dwell within us. Our task then is to make a temple for God out of our daily actions undertaken in the Holy Spirit of God, the source of all life.

We are forever in a period of advent in this life. All of our acts are a mere preparation while God does the rest. In the last analysis our knowledge is confined to the elements below us, what is above us can be felt but never contained within the grasp of our clear vision. We can at best intuit truths that lie beyond us. For this reason we are assigned a task in life and that is enough for us. We do well if we fill that tiny niche of relations that surrounds us in a way that embraces justice and love. This action in faith is the only antidote to despair, for if adequate knowledge were demanded of us, who might rest secure? Our short days allow us only a sample of life's great potential and even a man such as William Shakespeare must finally hang his head and mourn for his unwritten plays.

If our lives are ever to be sufficient for us we must relinquish finally our unfinished lives. It is a bitter task. In that final hour we will imagine all of the opportunities wasted and even our greatest achievements will appear as straw. All that is required of us though is that the flame, though guttering, should not be extinguished by despair. What is purgatory but the great onrush of the oxygen of God to feed the tiny flame of residual grace within us and to burn away forever all that stands between us and God! For who would dare approach God in the rags and tatters of His life?

If God clothes not the soul, it is naked indeed. The nature

of Purgatory is truly conceived when the Father welcomes back the prodigal son and bids his servants to clothe him and to bring a ring for his finger and sandals for his feet for he is alive after all. The great prayer of the Church is for all souls, so that they may come to that blessed event, to be eventually clothed by God in splendor. This sense of theological optimism is our best assurance that we are not mere playthings of chance in a mindless universe, a universe that is unaware and uncaring for our existence or our preservation.

May 9, 1892
We Finally Disembark at Marseilles

Our period of quarantine is over and our ship has been cleared. In an hour we shall disembark. I shall soon bid adieux for a time to Colonel Moran, but we have agreed to meet again when my time in Montpellier is over. He will of course inform the Professor that we are again upon the Continent. I trust that my dallying in France may not cause the Professor to assume that I fear to face him at last. I must however complete my own mission in its due season and part of that mission is to make some contribution to chemistry. May my researches prosper since I long to see England again after a final return visit to Rome. Only then will I be prepared to confront Moriarty in his lair in Devonshire. I have not rehearsed my arguments for I believe that I will know in that hour what I must say to my formidable foe. For that reason, I intend to enjoy my days in France and to relish this late spring in the life of an aging consulting detective. I am not immune to that feeling of spring that fills the sweet airs of Province. Here the sun and the sea nurture the finest vintages. May I follow the example of the poet John Keats who thirsted for a beaker warm with the wine of the Deep South to restore his own ailing health after he contracted consumption!

This journey has been trying to my own constitution. I have always feared consumption. Even as a lad in Yorkshire I can recall how broad a swath that grim reaper cut through the long winter days and nights. Many of my classmates perished young. I myself have shown occasional symptoms of late. I have suffered from fevers at night and a general sense of malaise. At first I thought that I might have acquired some tropical malady, but both the Colonel and I have been well-dosed with quinine so as to avoid the dreaded malaria.

I have said nothing yet to Colonel Moran of this for fear that he would use it as an excuse to prematurely end our journey, but now that our journey has reached a proper terminus I may shift my attention for a time to my own health. I shall remain in the salubrious climate of southern France until my symptoms abate and devote my time to chemical research which may advance the prospects of a cure of that dread malady tuberculosis, which took the life of my dear mother in her youth. I seldom speak of her even to Watson but she is always close to my heart. Her loss was the great trial of my youth and the great severing event that in many ways took my father from me as well, for he blamed her death upon an unstable religious temperament. It was then that he became the rationalist that he later became. He looked only to the material order to answer all questions. He locked his own heart up and placed it in the grave with her whom he had loved. His sons were left to their own devices and each of us has pursued his own unique way of life. Is it too much to say that each of us has a wound of which we do not speak? Shall we ever heal that wound until we gather again as brothers and speak of what is past? I shall never surrender that hope.

But, the porter is here now to receive our luggage; I must close. I trust that my journal with its many abstruse musings may be of some use to me so that I may recall at the appropriate time my thoughts and theories about Good and Evil. I do not claim to have resolved all of my doubts but rather to have at least formulated my faith such as it is. I leave the rest to the design and mercy of God. I hope that I may soon be restored to health so that I may return to England and to the great task of confronting Professor Moriarty and perhaps convincing him that an abiding presence surrounds and sustains us and promises that our intuition of a transcendent meaning in human life has some ground after all that may compel belief.

Dr. Watson's Narrative Continues

I had reached this point in my reading of Holmes' journal as I recall just before the day of my acceptance into the Catholic Church and I recall that I chose to stop there for a time. I had probed in the company of Holmes as deeply into the mysteries of life as my poor physician's mind might do. Though my knowledge of theology and philosophy did not approach that of Holmes, I still felt adequate to profess the faith in all honesty and to receive the sacraments then open to me as a member of the Roman Catholic Church. As a doctor I found it comforting that the sacraments are medicine to the soul. I felt happy that I might not need to reach the rarified distinctions drawn by Holmes in order to be a good Catholic, but still I found it comforting that his great mind had wrestled with questions that I might never think to ask, yet I might still know that these questions had found an answer of sorts at his hands. It did not add to my faith then to read Holmes' writings, but it allowed me to release some of the doubts that perplex and trouble many minds that suffer from the itching of the intellect to know all things.

The 19th century has been one in which rationalism has appeared to surrender its supremacy to the doubting mind. The result has been that religion that in the past had claimed to explain and to answer our ultimate questions has become primarily a matter of pure emotionalism as seen in the American revivalist movements. Many charlatans of religion first create an atmosphere of religious terror by describing hell in the most visceral manner; they then proceed to offer a specious solution in one great moment of conversion and definitive redemption. The entire process is often the fruit of three days of emotional excess directed towards bestowing some meaning into the dull lives of the rural masses. As a finale to the days of preaching, there follows a period of hysterical manifestations of supposed gifts and healings and then the entire spiritual circus moves on to another district. Although it is possible that some order of grace may possibly work through such phenomena, the results are a scandal to those who do not share this unique and fevered sort of religious experience. Certainly the traditional churches have always looked askance at these elaborate occasions displaying behavior that often approaches hysteria and madness.

There can be no substitution for me for the sound doctrines of Catholicism and the clarity of established ritual. Whoever has heard the majesty of Gregorian chant or listened to the polyphonic harmonies of the great composer, Palestrina, must wonder at this new group of religious sects that were then springing up like New Orleans jazz music across the American landscape. America is the land of syncretism followed by new inventions in all fields. Americans seem never to be satisfied unless they have recreated something in their own image. No wonder that Henry James left that land of railroads and commerce to find some remnant of dignity in England. Holmes has often said that I am the very embodiment of the stolid British character and perhaps I am exemplifying those very traits by these pronouncements, but there it is. I will not dwell in this narrative upon my private emotions that day in Rome. Let me say only that I felt the dignity of being accepted into the Church by the Pope himself and to participate in a Mass said for my intentions and that of Holmes by the Holy Father on that day.

This final action of my conversion completed my mission in

Rome and I felt free to return then to Holmes in London. I took a walk about Rome after mass on that that special and never to be forgotten day and after thanking Pope Leo XIII who again surprised me by requesting my prayers. I do not think anyone can imagine the burden sustained by any Pope in order to shepherd the Universal Church of Christ in this vale of tears. I went that day to the Trevi fountain as well and saw the young people throwing into it their coins and hoping to find love. I found myself speculating regarding what their expectations from life were, standing as they did not merely by the fabled fountain but at the gates of life with everything before them. Catholics are advised to keep the prospect of the four last things always near to consciousness so as to avoid sin. They are death, judgment, heaven, and hell. This grim reminder is really no more than a logical product of what the church views as the transient character of all of human existence. Every day is to enter the lists in spiritual battle against a massive assault by the distractions of the world and the wiles of the Evil One and His minions. To the young these matters appear to exist so far in the future that they have little relevance, but in fact they are woven through the fabric of every hour of our existence. They form our character, alter our relationships, and even determine the destiny of nations.

To advise the young on these matters of course is to seek to traverse an insurmountable gap. The blood of life is still hot within them and experience has yet to temper the scope of their dreams. Everything seems possible when little has yet been attempted and they have yet to encounter the resistance that time and circumstance will place in their path to oppose their undaunted will. The aged suffer from a different malady regarding time. Nothing seems to be as urgent when the time to enjoy the fruits of one's endeavors grows shorter. That which in youth had loomed up as only an improbable disaster becomes a yearly expectation that one may soon join those who are falling all about one into the realm of the shades. Our grip upon all the familiar objects and places that once enabled our lives and tantalized our hopes can slip away in an instant with the result that they seem to become cloudy and insubstantial, too frail to support the demands that we make of them. As a result any admonition to meditate on the Four Last Things becomes superfluous to one who thinks of little else.

I mention these things so that my readers can appreciate how welcome it was to me to be summoned forth from my domicile in Cornwall so as to engage once again in that endless succession of cases that seemed always to find their way for solution to my friend Sherlock Holmes. How strange it is to see the entire process of life from the perspective of age. The human condition never changes and each generation makes the same errors and finds in its own way a path forward. I still feel in many ways like a young man, yet in recent years I have noticed a difference. At a certain age there comes a desire to sum up one's life and to sort out clearly what is important and to set aside one's past failures and to find some sort of peace with what one has made of one's life. This is often not a pleasant process. If nothing else one realizes suddenly that the infinite horizon that once stretched before the startled gaze of youth has diminished unawares. Instead of infinity and the slow procession of the hours the years rush by with ever greater speed as they become fewer and more precious. Suddenly the lazy river of time becomes a torrent and the last decades of life become a rush towards the cataract of our extinction. At the same time one's body and face grow strange. Whose face matches the unaccustomed visage staring back at one from the mirror? All of the pains of life seem to be etched upon the countenance with each line traceable to a year spent in the pursuit of vanity. This time of life was described so well in the phrase of Shakespeare as that of "Bare ruined choirs where erst the sweet birds sang." That age is upon me now.

At first there is an impulse felt within to thrash about like a fish in a net. Surely one might make one great effort and suddenly time will return what it has stolen away! But no, such efforts are in vain. One's life is only that. The years of infinite choices have been traded for the irrevocable etchings in the metallic tablet that we each carry forward into death. Worse, that tablet may have little written upon it but only a dull succession of days spent to no real account. Again the words of Shakespeare are apt here. "Life is a tale told by an idiot full of sound and fury signifying nothing." Such is the state of the man who sees his life only in all its tawdry triviality without the mercy of God who alone might in some fashion make of this life of straw and dross a garment worthy of eternity.

I believe that Purgatory is simply the state of seeing one's life just as it was without illusions and seeing how far it is from what it might have been. It is then that God comes to our aid so that we are able to see in the virtues of others the merits that may remedy our deficiencies. Those who suffered in silent rooms with cancers and the crippled and the wounded who accepted their sufferings with grace and dignity are those who will save the active and the powerful. When the secrets of all hearts are revealed how different will we assess the order of merit in others for we will see them then from the perspective of God. How sorely will we be tried at that moment! Will we accept mercy in that dread hour of the great test or will we gather about us the pathetic rags of our self-regard and persist in being our own god unto ourselves? We pray in the Lord's Prayer to be spared that test, when our self-regard must be subordinated to the order of God where the last shall be first and the first shall be last.

I spent a final week in Rome before departing going to Mass daily in the small Church where the statue of St. Teresa in Ecstasy resides. This phantasia attempts to portray spiritual ecstasy through a figure that might have been painted later in the style of Dante Gabriel Rossetti. The impish cherub who pierces St. Teresa's soul with an arrow is far removed from that unseen God who was her only true passion. Still the figures in the sculpture are arresting. Perhaps only the transports of carnal love may explain to our animal natures the suspension of all of the faculties when met by God. In any case this statue was to be my last memory of Rome. Inspector Hopkins and I took an evening train for Switzerland. Summer was almost upon us and I desired to return to Holmes and to persuade him to leave stifling London and return with me to the fresh airs of Devon and Cornwall. I had heard little from Sherlock Holmes in weeks. I could only assume that all was well. This illusion was promptly shattered though.

As we disembarked from the train in Zurich I thought to purchase a copy of the Times of London. I opened it in the cab on our way to our hotel and the headlines leaped up in what appeared to be scarlet print before me.

It read: "MURDEROUS ATTACK UPON SHERLOCK HOLMES." I turned at once to Inspector Hopkins who sat beside me in the cab.

"There has been an attack upon Holmes!" I cried. He was as dismayed as I was by the dreadful news. He immediately asked me to read further. The article went on as follows:

"In Baker Street last night there occurred a most regrettable incident. Mr. Sherlock Holmes, the famous consulting detective, was wounded by the bullet of an assassin. Reports are coming in hourly from Whitehall where Mr. Holmes is being treated by Her Majesty's own physicians. Mr. Holmes was taken there rather than to either Charing Cross Hospital or the hospital at the University of London so that he might be kept under armed guard during what all of London hopes will be his quick convalescence. Hourly reports are coming in as to his condition. Reports thus far state that the bullet has been removed, but Mr. Holmes has yet to regain consciousness and his recovery if he

lives is likely to be a protracted one. Scotland Yard has traced the bullet to the empty dwelling across the street from Mr. Holmes' own rooms in Baker Street. The weapon was German in origin and it is thought that the attempt may reflect the tensions that exist between the German Empire and the government of these islands. That Sherlock Holmes should be the chosen victim may give some indication of the international renown that has come to him in recent years and the fear that his talents might be used to thwart Germany in its international designs. The German ambassador has been contacted by the Home Secretary demanding full cooperation in the coming investigation. The diplomatic situation is quite tense and may remain so for some time and may further strain relations between the two countries of Germany and England; these are, as our readers must know, times of great international mistrust. It is only necessary to recall the current tension between the Dutch and the Americans over the prospect of building a canal in Central America to bridge the oceans in order to see that international mistrust and competition are in the air. We can only hope that Mr. Holmes recovers soon and that this incident will not bring further conflict in Africa and throughout the world by the contending world powers."

I put down the paper. I reproached myself bitterly. How could I have left Holmes alone at this critical time and in his weakened condition? I could only despair at his prospects of recovery. A gunshot to even a healthy man leaves infinite prospects of infection. Could Holmes hope to throw off the many microbes attacking his body when wounded? I only hoped that I might get to London while he still lived. I was about to hammer on the side of the carriage to instruct the driver to return us at once to the station when Inspector Hopkins reached out his strong arm to restrain me.

"Wait, Dr. Watson! We are almost to the hotel and we may send a wire from there in order to ascertain how Holmes progresses. You have received a deep and lamentable shock and need time to recover yourself. Please do as I say." I sat back in the carriage weakly. I was indeed in no condition to proceed.

We arrived at our hotel a short time later and we both rushed in and quickly located the desk of the concierge. I immediately demanded a telegraph form and quickly dispatched a message to Mycroft Holmes in London to forward to us complete and immediate news of Holmes' condition to our hotel. Inspector Hopkins advised that we adjourn to the dining room bar for a brandy while we waited for a reply. The bar was sparsely occupied. Besides ourselves there was only an elderly Swiss burgher smoking a long-stemmed pipe and engaged in conversation with the man attending the bar. He was evidently sharing some witticism since both the bartender and he broke out in occasional laughter. The old gentleman turned briefly as we entered before dismissing our presence petulantly as an unfortunate interruption and returning to his story.

Inspector Hopkins and I took a table at the opposite end of the room for I was in no mood to hear laughter at such a time. A waiter came to our table and we both ordered a double brandy. We sat then in silence over our drinks. Inspector Hopkins had the good sense to be silent. A thousand thoughts ran through my mind. Had Holmes been a victim to Baron Maupertuis at last? Was it possible that that blackguard who was once called Stapleton had tracked him down in London to seek revenge? It even crossed my mind that Professor Moriarty might be responsible in some way. Perhaps his reformation had not been as sincere as Holmes had believed it was.

I was turning these matters over in my mind and about to call the waiter to order another brandy when I noticed that Inspector Hopkins was concentrating on the elderly raconteur across the room who we had noticed upon entering. No doubt Inspector Hopkins was following the tale being told in a loud voice by the wheezy old gentleman across the room from where we sat. The gentleman in question had continued subliminally to irritate me during my cogitations because he had only increased the volume of his narrative since we had entered as though intending to include our unwilling selves as members of his appreciative audience. I found the entire matter an example of the ill-breeding of continentals. It was just then that the old Swiss gentleman concluded his story. This prevented me from protesting to our waiter about his conduct. The erstwhile raconteur then paid his bill and rose to leave. At last I could return to my thoughts uninterrupted.

But this was not to be the case. The man in question walked brazenly towards us as though about to enlist us in conversation. I knew only too well what a burden such a boor might be. We should never be rid of him! I therefore rose immediately to ask the *maître d'hôtel* to intervene and I had reached down to look for my hat and walking stick when I was addressed by the old Swiss gentleman in a familiar voice.

"Leaving so soon Watson? Surely you can spare a few moments to hear of my journey here and how matters are progressing in London."

I gasped and fell back in my chair. The room seemed to sway before me for there shaking the hand of Inspector Hopkins and gazing down at me with humor mixed with concern was none other than Sherlock Holmes! The voice was unmistakable. It was indeed Sherlock Holmes.

"My dear fellow, do not take on so. It is indeed I. Dear me, I can never resist these little impromptu dramas. Please accept my most heartfelt apology. Buck up now. Here, *garçon* three cognacs! Ah, Inspector Hopkins, how well you look. You must help me with our friend Watson. There now his color is returning. Watson, old fellow you look splendid, I see that the Italian air agrees with you."

At last I gasped out, "Holmes! You are alive."

"Yes, alive and better still quite well my dear friend. Let me assure you that Dr. Moore Agar is quite pleased with my progress. He feels that I have mended as well as I might in the non-salubrious airs of London and that a trip to Switzerland was advisable to enable me to continue my recovery. I was able to manage a month in Davos and it has worked wonders."

"But Holmes, what about the attack made upon you in Baker Street?" I demanded

"It was a ruse my dear fellow, a pure fabrication, but I assure you a most necessary one. Ah here are our drinks. A toast my dear friends, to our reunion, may we be strengthened in our quest, for there are still dangers ahead for us all."

We each raised a glass. My first shock had passed away and a great joy filled my heart for it was the Sherlock Holmes of old who stood before me. He was thin and pale but I could see indeed that he was on the mend. He had again that avid look of the wily sight-hound seeking its prey. Simply to have him with me again was to feel that anything was possible; the mystery of life was made lighter because he was in the world. His great mind was always in advance of my own speculations and I had grown to accept this and to forgive any temporary jolts to my equanimity. His sense of the dramatic was often ill-timed, but I knew that in some strange manner I had come over the years to enjoy being startled by his surprises. What is the magician without his illusions after all?

"Now, my dear Watson, if you have quite recovered yourself I think that I can explain matters to your complete satisfaction. Let me begin by telling you how much joy the news of your reception into the Catholic Church has brought to me. As you well know my own religious quest was not an easy one. I began as the foremost of skeptics as you will recall from the days when Winwood Reade was my inspiration. I found his bleak assessment of life comforting, for by making stolid endurance of our utter aloneness in the universe the final test of honesty and virtue, I once hoped to be reconciled to my own chronic unhappiness. If there is nothing to hope for in life, then misery becomes the norm and one need not feel that one is missing anything. Such a grim belief also relieves one of a sense of responsibility for events and of the need to make an effort to improve the world by our actions. In addition there is certain pride at being able to accept this great vacuum with a stiff upper lip."

"I think my first insight contrary to my former disposition came when I realized that if there was no God then who was there to witness the heroism of my stoicism except only my fellow mortals who were swimming about in the same soup of the human condition. It was little comfort that my ashes would be revered by people who were all quite busy about preserving the ashes of their own reputations. For a time I considered the charms of the sensual life as providing at least a partial recompense for present ills, but I could see even at a distance that the sheer complexities of the avid search for pleasure can be so exhausting as to make the quest futile in producing any true or lasting happiness. You will recall that I turned then to cocaine to directly manipulate the brain so as to achieve a sense of purpose and victory without any true goal or purpose. The result was similar to a dog chasing its tail. I finally gave up that quest through sheer exhaustion and also because I grew tired of witnessing your sour look of disapproval of my indulgence in dissipation for which I can never thank you enough, my dear fellow."

"After your arrival as my companion in Baker Street I began gradually to find in the little problems that came our way a sense again of value in my life. I could see that the application of my unique skills might bring some respite to the sufferings of my fellow mortals. The path to recovery after that was comparatively easy, for once having accepted that life might have an actual purpose, to awaken our compassion for others, I began to wonder if my own dogged atheism was not more of a pose than a conviction. Why not at least imagine that just as there is conservation of energy in the universe then why not assume that there is a similar conservation of moral force as well, so that no good deed ever ceases but is preserved within the mind of God? I admit that it was only a beginning to the development of a religious consciousness, but it was a sensible one. My task then was to find a religious tradition that seemed to offer the best version of what such a God might be like."

"I began with the assumption that the God I sought would be bored by receiving a simple servile obedience; I also abjured a God who would revel in His own glory. I desired a God who was as moral as He bids us to be, a God of infinite compassion and tenderness for erring men and women. I am happy to say that such a God exists and is represented by the humble figure of Jesus Christ who came not be served but to serve. Once having glimpsed such a God, no other contenders even came close to winning my allegiance. After that it was a simple matter to locate the Church that had been constantly announcing the advent of Christ for almost two thousand years and whose succession and uniformity of teaching reaches back to the first apostles."

"I arrived at this conclusion gradually though. I proceeded to follow an historical time-line backwards into history. I became first a High-Church Anglican as I had been taught in my youth to be while living at home in Yorkshire. You may recall something of this early conversion process although I kept my comings and goings secret from you at the time. I then heard something of the Oxford Movement and of Cardinal Newman and I read his *Apologia Pro Vita Sua*. I found his arguments to be persuasive and his own transference of loyalty back to Rome seemed to me historically sound and liturgically inviting. At last I too returned to the One Holy Catholic and Apostolic Church, which has its origin in Jesus Christ and its continuity in The Holy Spirit. Jesus Christ sustains His Church in every age; it is a Church of sinners seeking their God despite its opulence and antiquity. And now you are also one of its members, dear friend!"

I was very pleased by his words and by this succinct account of his own conversion process. It still seemed miraculous though that he had so suddenly and unaccountably appeared in Zurich when I thought he was dead. I told him so at the conclusion of his narrative. He waved my wonder aside before continuing.

"There is nothing miraculous about it. I wanted you to have time to enjoy your Italian holiday and to complete your process of reception into the Church. My first intention was to join you in Rome, but there were matters of great importance to finish in London and I was delayed in my planned departure for Switzerland. I did however wire Inspector Hopkins that I hoped to join you both soon and he has at my request kept it from you so that you might be surprised by my arrival there. It is no small part my lingering vanity that I still delight in the ability to catch you unawares. Imagine my surprise when I had news of your planned departure for England earlier than I had expected and when I had planned a stay of some months in Switzerland. I had to rush things. It was then that I thought up my little scheme to elude pursuit and came away without fear of danger from certain quarters. I had sufficient time for a partial convalescence, but it is now necessary that we proceed at once from Zurich. There are serious days ahead for us all. "

"Baron Maupertuis is now the controlling force in the Greater Dutch Canal Company. He has been buying up shares slowly in order to keep the stock price from rising precipitately. The shares owned by Sir Henry and by our little cabal were sold only last week at a substantial profit. With our own influence now at an end the Baron will control the board of directors and he will no doubt desire to begin negotiations at once with the governments of Columbia for the Panama isthmus route or with

Costa Rica. Our engineers have already plotted several possible routes for the canal. All is in readiness for surveys to begin. It is now that we must spring the trap on the Baron. We must show that the papers published by Baron Maupertuis are forgeries. To do this we must leave for America. No, not a word, Watson! I assure you that I am quite up to the trip. Our ship leaves Plymouth within two weeks. We shall return to England and you shall have time to visit your lodgings to see that all is in order in Cornwall before we leave. I shall meanwhile make a brief side-trip to Baskerville Hall to check on Sir Henry. I will then join you in Plymouth and we shall be off."

Holmes turned then to Inspector Stanley Hopkins. "It is my hope that you will be able to accompany us to America as the official representative of Scotland Yard. We may have some difficulty explaining our knowledge of these matters to the Americans and it will be of great assistance to have you with us to back up our own accounts. I am also in possession of several depositions signed by officials of state thanks to the aid of my brother Mycroft." Inspector Hopkins readily assented to this when he heard that Holmes had already been in communication with his superiors and that all permissions had been obtained in advance for him to accompany us to America.

That was the substance of our talk that day. We spent the remainder of the afternoon walking about the city and soon retired, keeping early hours for sleep, since our train was scheduled to leave at dawn. We enjoyed the amenities of our excellent lodgings with a meal of sauerbraten and roast pheasant with potatoes. Holmes ate heartily. I could see that he was indeed a healthier man than the one that I had left four months ago in London. He slept well and without that dreadful cough that had at first so alarmed me. I read for a bit that night and then I also drifted off to sleep with thoughts of the adventures which lay ahead for us all. Would the Americans react as Holmes had planned with a renewed call to patriotism and demand that the canal should be built by American interests? Or would Baron Maupertuis manage to out-compete the Americans and build the canal himself. If so, he would undoubtedly use human beings like cattle to accomplish his goal. I could only imagine the many men who would die from yellow fever and dysentery under his command of the project. The prospect lay ahead then for a titanic struggle to breach the continent of the Americas with the fate of world trade in the balance. Even should the Americans succeed over the Dutch, would it be a benefit to mankind to open up the Far-East? Surely, China and Japan had done well enough before the advent of Western intervention in their affairs. I also thought of Central America. Did those native peoples benefit when their tribal cultures were opened to the West. The Monroe Doctrine thus far had proved to be a license for a version of American colonialism. I often thought that a wholesome diversity among peoples should be respected but alas even the Catholic Church has been at times an aid to colonial rule. Nations must learn to leave providence to God. Surely the tide of grace is not confined by the gifts of the sacraments. If Baptism is a sign for the human reality of incorporation into the Church, God still lives in some manner in the hearts of all men and women of good will. I believed that God would find a way to save all men and women in due season despite their circumstances. God is not limited by the extent of our reach, nor is He constrained by historical accident. Even St Augustine, that often bitter Church Father, has seemed at times to have built a wall about God in his desire to maintain God's honor and to vindicate the supremacy of the city of God, but since that city is finally built by God alone in the hearts of men and women, God alone may set the outer boundaries of His Kingdom. The church has perhaps taken too much upon itself by the phrase: *"extra Ecclesiam Nulla Salus."*

he next morning we caught the early train for Strasbourg, France. How strange it was after all of these years to be again with Sherlock Holmes in Switzerland. It was only a short distance to Meiringen and the Reichenbach Falls, but that site was no longer for me a sacred shrine to mark the final burying place of my friend. Instead, he sat beside me alive and well talking with animation with Inspector Hopkins who was giving him all of the details of our investigation of the death of Cardinal Tosca. Nor was Professor Moriarty lying dead beneath that fearful cataract. He was also alive and living in Devonshire. Life had spared these two great antagonists and they had made common cause to defeat a man who embodied the very roots of unprincipled evil, Baron Maupertuis. Such evil does not see itself against any background of good and evil; instead, men such as the Baron make their own ends that to which all other men must bend.

Wherefrom comes that all abiding will? To make of one's own desires an absolute while knowing that one is only one more poor creature upon the earth; surely such monomania is a sort of madness. Where are the doubts that beset most men? Where is that sense of desperation that most of us feel when we realize that however great our efforts the results will wither as our energies are dispersed to the winds and our bodies must dissolve finally into its constituent compounds after death? Surely, Ecclesiastes is correct and all is vanity. Such men though know nothing of this. They are like a blind force of nature, a whirlwind or an earthquake, and for that very reason they must be opposed by all rational men.

Soon we had left the highest peaks behind us. We came to Basle and then to Freiburg in Swabia. Soon we had left the German lands behind as well and arrived in Strasbourg where we halted. Our connecting train was to leave in a two hours. That gave us time to wander through the ancient streets of the city and to get thick sandwiches and refreshments to fortify us for our continued journey. Our next train was an express that would take us through

Lyon to the channel while by-passing Paris. We were racing for the channel ports for we had much still to accomplish before our boat was to sail for America.

How I longed to see my little cottage again! What a strange year I had spent and how different it all had been from what I had anticipated. What was to have been a short visit to Holmes in Devonshire had grown instead into what would be our longest adventure together. I wondered at the time if I would ever be able to tell the world about its strange links and twists. If so I would use the occasion to explain the true heart of my great friend and explain that the deepest struggles of his life had involved the exorcism of his own doubts and fears about human existence? Perhaps, I thought then, it would eventually be published many years after the present storm of events had passed when it could do no harm for I had come to know the strange fact that entire nations must often be kept in ignorance of how close they have come to mutual destruction. There are illusions that must be held by all nations simultaneously if life is to go on; otherwise the hearts of all men would freeze in terror, because civilization, which seems so secure is really only a thin and swaying footbridge held up by the most delicate of cables swaying over an abyss.

What force will finally tame the savage passions of men? If the social contract that binds each nation is not extended to all nations, then we shall certainly someday die from simply our fear of each other. Security and peace are the prerequisites for all progress and we have possessed it throughout most of this century. The war between the American states has shown the entire world the vast carnage of passions unleashed in the name of ideas and to preserve a way of life. I have often thought that America betrayed its own principles when the right of people to associate as states was denied for surely that was what was ultimately at stake in the recent American civil war. The states of America are after all not mere territory. They are people in association with loyalty to the sovereign states that collectively created the union. To assume that such a compact was thereafter irrevocable would be to assume that the people can be deprived of freedom, for what is freedom if it is not ongoing in time?

The Union victory was an act of imposition and not of willing adherence and it will leave scars on America that I fear will never heal. Instead the Union victory only succeeded in creating a new nation based upon force. As the center grows in power individual freedoms will diminish until they will become a mere formalism. The people of America will speak of freedom, but their lives will be subordinate to the new economy of the great corporations and trusts: the rail-roads, the oil trusts, and the banks. How strange that what began as a democracy will instead become in time merely another empire! Will the people find a way to return to themselves the powers that they have surrendered to these abstractions? Or will they finally wake to realize that each man has become only a cog in the great machine of commerce? Will the states then unite in order to restore freedom and force the great behemoth to its knees? Maybe the people will call for a new *Magna Carta* to restore the rights that have been stolen insensibly away from the citizens until a mere shell is increasingly all that remains.

"What are you brooding about Watson?" Holmes broke in upon my thoughts. "It can only be about our journey to America. Let me assure you once again that I am quite able to make the trip and in any case you will be at my side to foresee and prevent any excesses or is it perhaps that you are still nursing your ancient grievances towards that republic? How well I recall your conflict of mind at the time of America's civil war. On the one hand you abhorred slavery and kept a picture of Henry Ward Beecher upon our walls at Baker Street yet you abhorred the necessity of a war that severed the nation and resulted in so many deaths of brave young men."

"It was because I thought then that the slaves might have been freed by other means while still retaining the freedom of the states to self-determination and economic security," I answered him sorrowfully.

"So you said at the time. But I fear that slavery, a moral atrocity, was the very basis of the southern economy at the time and history responds to present ills and not too distant visions of regional equity," Holmes remarked.

"A form of slavery still persists though in the northern industrial cities of America. Are the laborers in the great factories there not slaves?" I asked with indignation.

"Good old Watson, you are ever the staunch laborite! But you must learn to moderate your speech or you will develop a reputation as one of those bomb-tossing anarchists? I fear that freedom will always exist within a social context and it will always be raw power that dictates the freedoms allowed to the individual. We are going to a new land, a land defined first and foremost by the dollar and by the laws that support American prosperity. America is of all lands a nation based upon the laws and the laws unfortunately are the creation of the propertied class. I have always thought it too bad that America does not possess a single constitutional monarch rather than an elected head-of-state. The virtue of a monarchy is that the sovereign is not an abstraction, but a designated human being with the right to rule over the people of the nation. The King or Queen must recall that he or she exists to follow the natural order and to live up to what is asked of a monarch, the service of God and of his people."

"America in contrast speaks with awe that it is the people that institutes governments among men and not God who generously provides that sovereigns in monarchical governments should exist. When the people are spoken of in this way *en masse* they are reduced to a mere abstraction. If any smaller group of 'the people' demand redress of wrongs it is then a simple matter to call them rebels against the established order and in the name of 'the people' to subdue those who demand actual freedoms as opposed to an exalted but vapid and empty abstraction. Alas, I fear that Rousseau was the progenitor of every tyranny that the world will ever know in the future because it was he who spoke of a 'general will' that can never be directly ascertained, even in a democracy. It will now only require that the proper formula should be produced, that of speaking patriotically 'in the name of the people' in order to justify any tyranny and to silence or curtail opposition and dissent. But who are 'the people' if they are not actual living individuals acting in concert to achieve a given end?"

Inspector Hopkins laughed at our discussion. "Gentlemen, gentlemen how ardent are your passions and how spirited your discourse. Is this an example of the lively nature of debate that persisted through the years within those hallowed walls at Baker Street? If so, then the public has missed in your brief narratives half of what has occurred there."

I was about to point out the difficulty of writing a sustained narrative and of keeping the point of the problem presented by the investigation foremost in my readers' minds when Holmes explained the situation better that I could have done.

"You have placed your finger upon a most central point, my dear Inspector Hopkins. Watson and I have often disputed regarding how our adventures should be written down and displayed before the public. I took the initial position that the art of detection is a science and should be explained with all of the dryness of a mathematical proposition of Euclid. Watson on the other hand maintained that the virtue of the story of detection lies in precisely that sense of the unknown that awakens awe and wonder as did Aristotle in his Poetics. For this reason he chose to dwell upon the minutiae of character in his writings and was never happier as an author than when emotions of a most extravagant nature were being exposed. There is also something innately chivalrous in the good doctor's nature. His men and women, particularly if romance or vengeance is in any way involved, are creatures of another age when the rules of chivalry and courtly love were the order of the day. I fear that many of his readers have been women and that one of the reasons that Watson has portrayed me as a dry-as-dust confirmed old bachelor was to prevent any actual coterie of admirers from dogging my every step and sending me scented handkerchiefs in the mail. I am afraid that I should long since have needed to give up my practice as a consulting detective if Watson had not insisted that my heart belonged to but a single woman as a candidate for my affections, a lady who had departed for the antipodes yet haunted his readers' minds with an abiding sense of romantic possibility. This discouraged any attentions that might have come my way from Victorian mothers seeking a suitable match for their daughters. Few mothers would care to act as do those matrons portrayed so well in the excellent novels of Jane Austin if they thought that they were arranging a match with a confirmed cocaine addict who lounged around his rooms all day in a dressing gown smoking obnoxious tobacco and conducting malodorous chemical experiments."

"But Holmes," protested Inspector Hopkins, "I have been to your rooms and the good doctor has not deceived the public, for your habits are indeed quite unique."

"Ah, but it is a matter of the degree of emphasis is it not, Inspector? Because I have my own habits need they be made manifest upon every occasion? No! It was done to spare me unwanted romances and to create about me a certain forbidding and mysterious aura to attract readers but simultaneously to repel coquetry. I hope that in some future narrative Doctor Watson will take the risk of simply telling the truth about me by appealing to that special reader who will take the time to know me as I truly am, not as seen through the distorting lens of superfluous romance. I in turn am willing to moderate my own demand that detection should be viewed as only a science, for clearly that is also untrue. In fact I will go so far as to say that the most singular gift that I possess is that of insight into human motives. If I was as inhuman as Watson has often portrayed me to be then I would never have been able to solve most of the problems presented to me. Detection requires the knowledge above all of human nature. The truest detective is above all else a psychologist and a student of the soul. The remainder merely requires consistency in reasoning from cause to effect. I would also recommend for aspiring sleuths that they acquire a deep knowledge of the crimes of the past. It is truly said that there is nothing new under the sun and the same rule applies to human aberrations. I have always maintained that the real reason that Jack the Ripper was never apprehended was that he was so dull and degraded in mind. Surely wanton brutality is the most mundane of motives. It creates nothing. There is no nurturing of individuality or of invention there, but rather a reduction of each victim to a mere mass of flesh randomly chosen. Evil of that caliber betrays such a manifest absence of what defines the human that the criminal is finally only engaged in an act of the self-portraiture of an empty vessel. The crime scenes become a mere way to shock and to dismay those who first come upon it. The crimes of Jack the Ripper and of his kind are not even crimes stemming from the humanity and passions of the criminal. They are not exercises and demonstrations of boredom and of that great inner emptiness, which is the final character of all evil. Evil is an abyss and none but God may ever hope to fill it or to transform it. When evil comes to desire that its own emptiness should itself be God... well, that is when evil shows itself and its nature most clearly. The devil desires not merely our service you see but finally our love although he cannot love us in return."

"Why then, Mr. Holmes, did you never solve the case of Jack the Ripper yourself?" asked the Inspector. I had also wondered at this for no crimes had ever more perplexed the

British public at the time of their occurrence than those horrible assaults upon the street women of Whitechapel.

"There is a very good reason why I did not do so, Inspector. The reason that I did not solve the crimes is that Jack the Ripper was not an individual but instead the representative of a type of man that will always exist among us. To apprehend him and to dramatize his individuality would have been to create a throng of imitators. You will note that his crimes finally ceased of their own accord. Why, you may ask? Because the attention afforded to him was the purpose of his initial design. It was never the crimes themselves. They were purposeless, mere symbols, canvas on which to paint. It is the very nature of all purely destructive forces that they finally exhaust themselves for their aims are sterile. Only the forces of generation and growth are self-sustaining. No doubt the person who was Jack the Ripper finally collapsed inwards at last just as a fire does when it has exhausted its supply of fuel. The truth is that crime, insofar as it approaches what is termed "mindless criminality," finally becomes pointless. Its rewards are at best derivative. It is hard for a person, such as I have made myself through long study, to solve crimes of that merely brutal nature, for they are by definition less than human in their conception and execution."

"Why for instance was my nemesis instead a man like Professor Moriarty and not a brute like Jack the Ripper? The answer is really quite simple. Professor Moriarty was an example of principled evil and as such his motives and reasons could be comprehended and a solution could be reached and his crimes solved. His great intellect was why I knew that he could be reached by reason at last. The intellect despises boredom and craves purpose. I made it my task to supply that purpose for him."

"By the way Watson, how are you coming in your reading of my journal narrative? Not finished yet? Dear me I should have thought...but then again it cannot be easy to traverse the thoughts of my entire life in a series of short and interrupted sittings and I have kept you rather busy of late. I wrote my journal so that I could record the inner struggles of my entire life. Surely, if such an account is worth reading at all, then it is only right that it should demand some close attention by the reader. Besides, it is after all not for common consumption. Indeed I doubted if any eyes but my own would ever peruse it and perhaps no others ever shall after you, my dear fellow, finish with it. When you have finished it you will have the conscience of your friend Sherlock Holmes finally laid out before you. I believe that you will enjoy my account of my final struggle with Professor Moriarty, one that occurred not on the brink of the Falls of Reichenbach, but over a far greater abyss, that of hell itself.”

Such was the nature of our conversation as our train sped across the lovely French countryside. How strange it seemed to speak of crimes and of darkness when traversing that lovely land. Holmes subsided into silence and I was happy to see him fall asleep. It was important that he save his strength for what lay before us in America. The Inspector also nodded off at last and I decided to return to Holmes' journal and to his account of the year that he spent in the city of Montpellier that was then many miles south of the train on which we were speeding towards the English Channel and home.

Book Eight

Montpellier France
The Coal-tar Research

From the Journal of Sherlock Holmes

May 10, 1892
A Parting of the Ways

Our goods and mementos made it through customs in France without issue and Colonel Moran and I sent our luggage on to our hotel. We will spend a final day in each other's company before parting. We found an excellent waterfront restaurant that faced the busy harbor. Through its windows we could observe the activity of the boats and ships and small vessel traffic upon the clear blue waters of the bay. Our meal was an excellent one, a crab and oyster quiche, a *specialite de maison*. The Colonel was in high spirits now that we have returned to what he would call civilization. Upon my remarking that it was I who was the novice at desert living while he had known these privations for years and should therefore be more accustomed to them; he smiled and answered.

"But you forget Mr. Holmes that this journey was not my choice but yours. The game that you have pursued was entirely of the mind. Now that our ideological safari is over I can ask you whether you might not have done better to discuss these abstractions with the Dean of some cathedral in Bath or Canterbury rather than dragging us both across Asia and Africa in your search for enlightenment."

"I went to see the people. Faith does not exist in a vacuum, but is embodied in the human heart," I replied.

Colonel Moran snorted at this and said, "Were there no hearts in England that you could consult? For myself, I have long since made my peace with the human condition and have no expectations for futurity. There is no reward in discomfort for its own sake in my philosophy. There is something though that I have wanted to ask you for some time and I will ask it now. I believe that it is Christian doctrine that the sacrifice of Christ upon the cross works the full satisfaction due to sin. That is so? Ah, excellent! Then pray tell me why it is that Christians go out of their way to seek out desert places and undertake various obnoxious penances rather than simply enjoying their lives as best they may. Surely such actions are superfluous in the face of the work of God, which has already accomplished everything for sinful man."

The question was an excellent one and one that has misled many Christians of the past in the form of the Quietist Movement of Spain in the 16th century and even in the central doctrine of Lutheranism, salvation by faith alone.

I therefore answered him as follows. "You forget Colonel Moran that the doctrine of grace demands that grace must be in some manner efficacious. The signs of grace are a changed manner of life so that we may more resemble Jesus Christ in all our actions. God does not drag a supine humanity into heaven in their present state. Heaven would seem an unnatural condition to the soul of one that was still attached to evil passions and pursuits and in full cooperation with his lower nature. It is of the essence of freedom that it should be exercised in some fashion. The choice or submission to the penances and observances recommended by the Catholic Church adds nothing to the essential glory of God. They are of infinite benefit to us though for they remind us of the true nature of things and of our subordinate status before God. By ridding ourselves of undue attachments we also open space as it were so that God may fill it. This was explained most gently by

Jesus to his friend Martha when Jesus said, 'Ah Martha, Martha, you are busy about many things. Your sister, Mary, has chosen the better part and it will not be taken from her.' Mary understood you see that our first function as Christians is contemplation of God through observing Jesus, whose life and teachings will not only show us our tasks, but aid us to accomplish them in due season."

He sighed comically. "It all sounds rather strenuous to me. Of what use is suffering voluntarily imposed? I should have thought that the world already had sufficient opportunities for suffering without our election and exaltation of it. And while you are waiting on God what about the many manifest evils in the world that must be met on their own terms? As I see it your problem with the Professor is that he and I have gone about making it a better world by eliminating certain evil men and women. I ask you once again to observe that petty crime was never our object, but rather to impose a private tax upon oppression. If that policy was evil because it also gave us a good living and therefore was self-serving, what of your Christian desire for salvation and those who cater to it, is that not the greatest selfishness of all? Even to imagine that God exists and to simultaneously maintain that he cares for some poor ape-creature on an obscure planet, hah, is that not the greatest of blasphemies towards any God worth worshiping? Is not true humility admitting the inconsequential importance of our lives?"

I pointed out that to use our physical size and power as a measure of our celestial worth was hardly an appropriate scale with which to measure God or to estimate what God valued, but he gave little weight to my objection.

He continued, "The mercy of Allah is one thing, but to assume that God would become one of us? Surely that is too much. I on the other hand am content to realize that man is a beast that preys upon its own kind. We are nasty animals, Mr. Sherlock Holmes, whatever you may care to believe. I at least and the

Professor as well prefer to climb the food-chain by preying upon the strong and not upon the weak. I would never say these things to some simple working woman in Soho who needs the comfort of her chapel and the illusions of her faith to sustain her. I do say it though to you for you hold yourself out as a vigorous Christian apologist who can tolerate the strain of my objections. I take all of human history as my witness that I am correct. The primary function of religion as it has always appeared in history, with the possible exception of Buddhism, for which I have some respect, is to give power to a set of religious functionaries who then lord it over the mere believer. Kung fu Tsu, called Confucius in the west, was at least honest about this. His entire system is one of emulation of the noble few coupled with a chain of command that unites society. There is no nonsense about individualism and rewards and punishments in eternity."

"Confucius tells us how we must live now if a society is to prosper. His message is to remind us of the power we possess to create from within the gamut of our own resources a proper dignity and for the most noble of us to sacrifice so that the masses will have something to emulate. The result of this process of active and disinterested virtue is that society improves. The sage lifts the masses by seeking a reward that is confined to the mere knowledge that he is acting virtuously. Things in the state of nature advance to the degree that mankind advances. We claw our way out of the swamp and mire of savagery over the course of centuries and not within the period of a single human life."

"Look at this bay beyond our window. The tide is out and the tiny clams pursue their tasks but have no consciousness of themselves as individuals, nor do we for we eat them. They are part of a larger scene for us, part of the activity of the bay-front as a whole system of biological interactions. Now look at the ships and the sailors and stevedores, the huge cranes unloading produce. What do you see? More clams but at a higher level of evolution and with a greater range of purpose. If we could but realize that we are part of the great tidal movements of history that are as careless and indifferent to our individual fates as are the tidal flows that sweep over this seashore, we would at last have comprehended our relative place in the universe."

"We are not simply, to use of a phrase of yours "contingent" vis-a-vis God, we are contingent even to one another. Each of us imagines that he is in some way the center of the universe. What is God but a projection of our illusion of importance and centrality? We worship God because we dare not worship ourselves because we know that we will die, that in an instant, yes an instant Mr. Holmes, that great bubbling brain of yours will, through oxygen starvation, be reduced to the equivalent of any piece of meat on a butcher's block. One instant you will be speaking with the eloquence of St. Thomas Aquinas and explaining a syllogism; and the next instant you will be to an outer observer reduced first to an irreparable silence and in a few days to so much stinking offal to be swiftly rushed below ground lest it be an offence to the nose. That is reality, Sherlock Holmes! So now you will understand why I do not value your Christian pretences and why I at least abhor the desert places where you hoped to find God. I prefer a well-lit bordello and the short but delightful company of female flesh after an evening of good food and drink at the Grand Casino at Monte Carlo."

I will not say that I was not shocked by his vehemence. Knowing him as I then did I was not scandalized by his reduction of human motives to the most banal. I will even say that I admired the courage that he showed in at least enunciating a belief in the sole efficacy of this world's comforts for I knew that many think as he does in their heart of hearts, but out of a hypocritical delicacy they forbear to say so.

"Your position is admirably stated, my dear Colonel," I answered. "You are even to be congratulated at the equanimity that allows you to maintain it. If you are indeed complacent in contemplating with fortitude your own extinction and the loss of those pleasures that are so dear to you, which must come at last, very well, but you do not I believe have any children, nor do I. May I ask if you would with such blasé composure consign a child of yours to the ground, never again to see its bright countenance looking in innocent wonder up at you and at this glorious world? If you are as you say a true Epicurean you must finally join Lucretius in his despair. Read his book, 'On the nature of things!' The man who is truly aware must have compassion for others even if he has little or none for himself. You may accept death readily, but would you ever presume to do so for another whom you held dear?"

I allowed time for him to consider that question before continuing, "If it is true that you and the Professor believed in truth that your crimes were justified when you committed them, that may excuse you from moral culpability, at least as applied to your own culpability before God; however they manifest, do they not, a desire for a better world that can only be achieved by ridding the world of its malefactors. Yet you must know that after killing many people who are stained with blood and oppression you must finally confront your own bloody hands. What will you do then but need to kill yourselves as well for he who takes up the sword must in turn perish by it. The wars of history, however they might be justified, only lead on to other wars. Only peace begets itself with more peace. Such is the woe and futility of the man or woman who will beat evil on its own ground and by evil means, so that he must become at last what he hates in others."

"In contrast Christian acceptance of a death by martyrdom is not resignation, but instead an act of hope and of love. We embrace the death that claimed our Savior as an end that is appropriate to the human condition as we have received it, as one that is tainted by sin. Our belief in the sinless Christ is our hope that our own sins may find dissolution in the Blood of that unique

Sacrifice. The very inappropriateness of God dying for men is our assurance of its truth. No more daring doctrine has ever been stated in the history of human grappling towards truth. Its very disproportion is the greatest argument that it is true! That the infinite could care for the finite, this great suspension of the prerogatives of God, is that not the most startling thing ever thought or expressed by the mind of man? Yet, we maintain it by faith."

"The Christian is not spared the agony of death and its great degradation, but we are made able to bear it for if death is a scandal to our conception of our own dignity and our marvelous capacities for science and art, what is that degradation to the assumption of human nature by God Himself in the personhood of Jesus Christ and then to actually know death, for it is an article of faith that Christ died. The mystery of Holy Saturday when Christ lay in the tomb is that for one day in the year the tabernacle in all the churches of Christendom are empty. For one day we have the universe just as you would have us believe it always is, one that is empty of a caring God and one where God at least to us is dead!"

"But on the very next day of Easter Sunday the churches throughout the world rejoice and proclaim the living God of the Resurrection. The entire Church of God renews itself in the hope that just as flowers grow again from the soil with every spring just so shall we in turn and in God's own time find ourselves again! Even our very bones and sinews will be knit together so that our individuality now cured of all ills and limitations will exist once more and be recognizable as uniquely us."

"You forget in your exposition, my dear Colonel, that you are not a clam but a man. Very well, be a man then and recognize your own dignity as such. The very individuality that allows you to even take the position that God, at least as Christianity presents him to you, does not exist is the best proof that God does in fact exist! Your own being, in all of your complex human nature, is the best argument that God exists! God tolerates such unbelief as a sacred right of all men and women. The God that we propose to faith stands at the door and knocks; he does not arrive with the great panoply of grandeur. God's grandeur is reserved for creation. When He appears as Himself, He appears as a servant. Jesus referred to himself as 'the Son of Man' so as to show His complete identification with the human race in all of its frailty and folly and even in its sin for which he alone paid the price of death."

"The nature of God is determined by His actions is that not so? Apparently God is humble in his magnificence so can we be less? If it is degrading for man to die it is because we feel within ourselves the desire to persist and to grow always in the knowledge of God. It is characteristic of man and woman that we are never finally satisfied. Only God may suffice for us. The measure of our hunger is the measure of our certainty. We believe because without belief we cease to be human. The penances that are undertaken by us add nothing to God but are of great value to us because we are reminded by them not to be easily satisfied even by the riches of this marvelous earth with its many blessings."

"I sometimes think that only the Christian knows the true value of the pleasures of the earth, which are only sinful because they enslave us and manifest a lack of due charity and proportion. It must be recalled that the first commandment is the one most often broken by man. God asks simply that we recall that He is God and there is no other. To contemplate God is to see all things in their proper relations. To see God is to recover our sanity as a species! The problem of evil is that evil is so absurdly pointless. The devil hates nothing more than to be laughed at. After all, what does it cost us, who are doomed in any case to die, to accept death as the price of our own limitations and to entrust our futurity to God?" St. John said, 'Beloved, we are God's children now; what we shall be has not yet been revealed.'"

"Even if that promise has been most imperfectly lived by

the Catholic Church itself in the person of the Pope and his Bishops, to whom the Church of God has been entrusted, it is of little concern to us for the life of the Church is the Holy Spirit. To blaspheme against the Holy Spirit is to doubt the supreme efficacy of that Holy Spirit to complete the task of mankind's redemption until Christ returns despite our negligence and imperfections. Only final despair can blind us forever to the light of God because all else will finally be made whole! For this reason heaven rejoices more in the conversion of the greatest sinners, for those who seemed most lost demonstrate most clearly the power of God, so that in the end all will be restored and we shall join the Holy Trinity in the love that is our very nature and element. This is the view of life that the Catholic Church proposes for our belief. I think it is more attractive, my dear Colonel Moran, than all your casinos, brothels, and your clam-strewn beach. Forgive me if I prefer to cast my lot with the poor woman in her humble chapel in Soho who needs her consolations for I need them too."

The restaurant had gone strangely quiet as we two battled over our quiche and Pinot Noir. I dare say that not every diner in the place cared to explore their futurity with such vehemence, but this entry in my journal shows that just such debates that are often put off to the hours of our final decline may occur to some persons in the full vigor of their maturity when there is time to manifest the results of faith in their daily actions and not in words alone. But I trust that even in one's final hours that a reassessment of the values that have governed their lives is possible and that no one is to be despaired of when God may yet encounter them, perhaps even within death itself, for what do we finally know of death and what that final and brief separation from the body may entail? It seems the better part of prudence to trust in the mercy of God rather than to ourselves to decide upon the ultimate fate of any soul...

Colonel Moran did not reply to my final discourse and since

our place in the restaurant was needed and the plates heaped up about us testified to our satisfied appetites, we left off our discussion at least knowing that we had been honest with each other. I must say that I bear a certain degree of affection for Colonel Sebastian Moran after our long journey. I do not believe that he is far from faith. He has the gift of demanding much from life. Such men must finally wonder if all that they have known is adequate. Faith springs from dissatisfaction with the dull order of events. This is why we go to desert places to find God at last, just as I have done in the course of my Asian journey. It is not that God is not to be found in all places, but that sometimes it is imperative to seek God where one would least expect to find Him if we are truly to find Him at all.

May 11, 1892
Marseilles

This morning the Colonel and I had a champagne breakfast at our hotel. Unlike our discussion of the previous day we kept to neutral topics and I can say that I even enjoyed the Colonel's company. He is a man of great charm and occasional saturnine humor. He has an extraordinary quality of observation and attention to detail and it is undoubtedly those qualities that have made it possible for him to survive in his many military campaigns and when he is stalking wild game. He favored me at the end of our meal with an observation that may prove helpful to me in the future.

"It is imperative when hunting tigers that the shikari understand clearly and bear it always in mind that the tiger he is hunting is simultaneously hunting him. There is a corollary to this, the tiger will always appear where one least expects to find him. I was surprised to discover that this observation derived from my days spent in hunting big game has been echoed in the realm of metaphysics that is so dear to you by that most excellent philosopher Friedrich Nietzsche. The quotation from him is I believe that if you look too deeply into the abyss, the abyss will look into you."

"And what meaning do you assign to that rather intriguing phrase?" I inquired.

"That there are matters that are best left alone," he answered. "It has always been my desire to be a happy animal. The tiger for instance is like a kitten when its needs are met. It is never happier than when it is resting after a kill. During my days as a hunter I learned to respect my quarry enough not to disturb a tiger at rest. There is no sport in mere slaughter. I prefer the hungry foe, when it is nervous and suspicious. A beast like that will attack when menaced or even slightly threatened. It is less cunning and more impetuous and likely to blunder. The key is to retain the initiative by applying unrelenting pressure on him. It is then that the beast will turn. I always prefer a shot right into the beast's chest, never the head. The bullet travels deep and the great heart is often pierced. The whole point of honor in hunting is to give the tiger a chance to escape if it wishes. I don't kill anything that isn't looking at me when I fire. I want it to know why it must die and who is pulling the trigger."

He sat back then in his chair while smoking a cigar. "But I am curious. What meaning do you assign to that phrase of Nietzsche, Mr. Holmes?"

"The word abyss is I believe of the greatest significance," I answered calmly. "You will note that it is personified and therefore presumed to have the ability to take deliberate action. It is therefore a conscious agent. I suggest that even if Nietzsche did not believe in God that he was at least well acquainted with the devil. The abyss you see is not mere vacuous space; it is the great emptiness and aloneness of human life in the face of existence. If there is no God, then everything is alien to us."

"Unless one is a happy beast," interrupted the Colonel smiling.

"But is that ever really possible?" I inquired. "Even you, my dear Colonel Moran, have a code of ethics that even governs your behavior to the tiger. You are human despite your insistence that you are a beast. Do you believe that the tiger is similarly motivated to ever give you a fighting chance?"

He thought for a time before replying, "Perhaps not, but I am not responsible for the tiger only for myself. I choose the aesthetic if you will of an honest kill. Perhaps it is because there is a beauty and symmetry in nature that I respect. You find nature to be cruel while I see only the balance that is attained by its every action. When I come to die I hope that I will be eaten by a tiger. It would be some comfort to me to know that I am part of one of those great beasts and not a perfumed corpse reposing in a walnut coffin in Westminster. I don't want to be pampered by a nursemaid when I am old and fed gruel while I cough and whimper like a child. When I am old I shall enter the jungle and make of the tiger my final friend. I hope that I may meet him with the same fortitude and pride as that of his many brothers that adorn my homes in the islands of the Dutch Indies or the Malay Archipelago. I prefer to choose my own fate and to carve life up into a pattern of my choosing. I have always been impatient with metaphysics but I do understand beauty."

"Beauty is always individual and unique. May Plato be damned with his eternal forms! I care nothing for his insipid forms and ideas. They are mere busy-work for scholars. If Plato stood at my side with a gun contemplating "tiger-ness" and not the individual beast rushing upon him then he would know that ideas are not real, there are only singularities. For that same reason I care nothing for 'the good of mankind' and all other abstractions. Every act of kindness or malice stands on its own and is irremediably itself. This is why your concept of atonement for sin is nonsense. Sins are never forgiven. They enter the vast compost-heap of history and finally they are so overlaid with new events so that even the worst wars and atrocities become irrelevant and forgotten with time. You would make God out to be some great bookkeeper of the cosmos. I could never admire such a God. I prefer one who has the good taste to be indifferent to our individual fate."

"I know that when I face my tiger that I am alone. Do you think that the beauty of the scene by a river is spoiled for me because one less wildebeest is drinking there? Do you think then any God that exists beyond those bags of frozen gases and exploding suns cares for you? How many old maids fear that God is peeping out from behind his curtain to see if they are taking a pinch of snuff or a thimbleful of brandy! I should think that if there is a God that he would be beyond such trivial occupations."

"We owe the conception of a personal God to the Jews. My quarrel with the Jews is their extraordinary self-delusion. Why should God speak from Sinai when he might just as well have thundered from the Himalayas to the Tibetans? The Jews are the acme of small-mindedness in their pretense to be a chosen people. While they were sacrificing sheep and goats and washing their arms to the elbows Rome was busy conquering the world. Do you think that even Pilate killed Christ because he was angry with him? Christ was killed because he was spoiling Pilate's morning with some boring Jewish matter that he as governor could not even understand. Pontius Pilate was a typical bureaucrat. You can find his like in any county postal inspector. Am I to believe that the universal destiny of mankind depends upon what happened that morning because of a minor riot in an obscure province of a dead empire? We would all do well to forget history and perhaps philosophy as well because until we do mankind will forever be subject to what is finally merely literature."

I ignored the blasphemy for I could see how, when seen

from outside, one might take the view of Colonel Moran. Religion can never be judged objectively because it demands a commitment that must precede understanding.

I replied, "You deny then that there is a perennial human nature and that revelation is accepted not as a history of a tangential event but because that event finds its echo from within our very being. Your jaundiced view pre-determines the judgment that you have reached. You seem determined to rebel against the universe as a sort of modern-day Lord Byron. I on the other hand suggest that God's inversion of our expectations is the precise reason for belief as I stated yesterday. Christianity and its success is a most unnatural phenomenon. It tries our patience and frustrates our desire for closure. It is open-ended even with the strictures of its dogmas for it exists in the waiting for an event that we cannot determine. Christianity is a subject whose predicate is indefinitely delayed."

"The question is when will Jesus Christ return? We are bid only to keep our lamps filled with oil and thereafter to be kept burning. The Church settled down in its first centuries and exchanged eager expectation for the regular pulse of the liturgical year. The Church is satisfied to possess the Holy Spirit now. It has not forgotten Christ of course, but is sufficiently busy with acts of charity and the sanctification of sinners to keep its attention fixed upon its mission. The rest it leaves to the Father. The Church desires nothing more than the imitation of Christ who entered the abyss in complete acceptance like a lamb led to the slaughter. You say that you wish, my dear Colonel, to be reincarnated in the muscles and sinews of a tiger after your demise. Well, St. Paul bids us to so put on Christ so that we may share his fate both in death and in life. I submit that the possibility of incorporation into a risen Christ who is God is superior to being nutriment for the very beast that has snuffed out your life. It is you who are the romantic idealist, Colonel Sebastian Moran, and I, Sherlock Holmes, who am the realist. Perhaps you have more in common with Plato than you suspect."

The Colonel was silent for a time and then burst out laughing. "By Jove Holmes you are everything that the Professor always claimed that you were. I just think that I have you by the whiskers and you come back at me roaring. Perhaps I have found my ultimate tiger after all. Allow me to drink your very good health for we cannot tarry here longer or I will miss my train and disappoint the young ladies of Monte Carlo and the eager hands of the rich men at the gaming tables. Let us part then if not as friends at least as former comrades-in-arms who care to question the ways of fate. A toast then, to your very good health, Mr. Sherlock Holmes, I hope that you may meet success in your researches at the university!"

I accepted his toast and wished him well in return. My toast was a simple one. *"Bon chance!"*

Within the hour I had bid his train farewell at the station in Marseilles as it sped eastward along the *Cote d' Azur* I caught my own train shortly afterwards which took me the 168 kilometers from Marseilles to Montpellier.

May 12, 1892
Montpellier

I have arrived at last at the place that I shall call home for the indefinite future. I have installed myself in the *Hotel d' Midi* near the *Place de la Comedie* in the center of the city. I have not chosen this place by chance. Montpellier is the site of one of the oldest universities in all of Europe. It has a most excellent medical faculty and the climate is conducive to my recovery. In addition, the university is as renowned for its school of theology (the great St. Anthony of Padua once taught here), which has certainly become lately my avocation if not my regular profession.

I have no professional credentials in this latter discipline of theology, but I hope to audit a few classes in systematic theology in order to correct any misapprehensions that may still linger in my own thoughts about God and the Christian religion.

The quest for religious certainty would seem to belie the necessity of faith. In this sense all theology might be deemed to be a vain pursuit, particularly for the Catholic layman whose role in the light of the authoritative Magisterium of the Pope and Bishops would seem to lie in mere acceptance; but one must always articulate one's belief if only to oneself. If one has no language of the soul, then one's faith becomes not a matter of passion and conviction but rather a pale surrender to a series of phrases that finally become meaningless. It is beneath the dignity of man to assume such a posture before God. God must be in some manner known if only in His attributes before He may be loved. In addition God must be loved before He can be served for service without love brings no merit. Still we must always rely upon God's Divine grace to mediate our inevitable shortcomings.

If religion is a mere formalism, it is doomed to be inauthentic and hypocritical. But if religion is a mere matter of individual feelings, then there is no communal structure in the Church. But if there is only Church and structure, then there is no use for the private prayer and acts of charity that are the sign of God's actual union with the soul. The growth of the spirit takes place within the parameters of the Church, but it is still an individual experience.

To know the parameters of faith is the *raison d'être* for theology. Christian Theology already implies belief and Baptism. One must be already within the Church in order to comprehend her. The mere recitation of doctrine without love is to merely set forth a series of formulae that may fail to convince because there is no answering voice from within the soul based upon its own experience. For this reason men like August Compte, who was born in this very city, aspired to what he calls in his writings, "positivism," a sort of secular religion The problem of course with a strict empiricism is that without categories of experience the mind is unable to proceed. A stream of unrelated data would be a mere chaos of the senses. Apprehension requires that the mind pay attention and how may it do so if it is not already discriminating and sorting the impressions that flood in upon it.

All perception is therefore a process of selection and of neglect. If all impressions have equal weight then we would perceive the world as a vast monolith or as a single massive wave. The whole would always eclipse the parts; everything would be one massive and indescribably uniform white-light with no rainbow that would allow for separation and discrimination. The mind is the crystal whose facets break up the light of knowledge into the rainbow of perception. The trained mind is the one with the most facets that may be break down into mere particles the flood of the possible into actuality realized in time. In this sense knowledge is a matter of good taste, of assigning the proper value to all things. Only when everything is broken up and distinguished may it be reassembled within the mind of the philosopher. It is then that the synthetic function comes into play and new relationships are formed. Finally the mind reaches beyond itself into categories that may be termed transcendent. These are the categories that Plato termed ideas because they are names, not for things, but for abstract relationships.

To return then to theology: theology cannot claim to know God in Himself for such knowledge would require an intuitive apparatus that is beyond the mind of man in his present state. We can at best know the relationships of God as seen through the prism of creation and to respect God's Will to be manifest in dogma when religious language assumes the imperative mode. God will never command what is evil or impossible. Thus, the purpose of theology is to tell us not what God is, nor is its function to prove God's existence; rather, the purpose of theology is to tell us how to perfect human nature that when combined with God's mercy will save our souls and bestow upon us a state capable of direct apprehension of God in the Beatific Vision of heaven.

I take comfort here in knowing that the coat-of-arms of the city of Montpellier celebrates the Blessed Virgin holding the Infant Jesus and sitting on a throne. It would appear that the Virgin Mary has been placed over the rules of trade as expressed by the money-changers of the temple. In the gospels we seldom see the anger of Our Lord, but His wrath is visited upon the money-changers, perhaps because they play so central a role in human life. He who controls money may control what money can buy. The money-changers of the temple even controlled access to God. Some have gone so far as to say that the modern priesthood has gone beyond being servants drawn from within the community of the Church and that priests have set themselves up as the new money-changers in the temple of the Catholic Church. It must be admitted that this observation has been true at various times in Church history, but at the same time there have always been faithful pastors of souls whose devotion to their flock has been exemplary and devoted, even at the cost of their very lives. There is in the last analysis then no caste system in the Church but only a diversity of functions.

The same is true in the larger community caught up as it is in the commercial relations of life. If commerce may be blessed by God in the form of free and honest trade, then even commerce may wear the guise of charity and serve the pursuit of Christian virtue in daily life. Since most men and women must live engaged in the daily occupations of living and of raising children, it may comfort them to know that they may serve God by carrying out these mundane affairs with proper devotion and subordination to the mandates of God's laws. The impulses of the heart often lie within the ambit of charity, a charity belonging most properly to the cohesive structure and acts of the Catholic Church collectively and as a whole, but also present in the secular pursuits where charity assumes the individual form of personal acts of love performed out of love of God and neighbor. Thus religion and government can reinforce each other to create a peaceful and prosperous social order in which the individual is not overwhelmed or rendered as a mere insensate cell in a larger body.

May 15, 1892
I Walk About the City

It is a lovely spring day. I awoke with that marvelous sense of purpose that for me is happiness. Yet I feel no pressure. I know that my strength will be sufficient for the day and that knowledge is adequate for me to feel contented. I have not yet presented myself at the Medical Faculty. Mycroft will be forwarding my credentials from England within the week. I have been in touch with him by telegram and letter. He was not pleased with the results obtained in the Sudan, but he was kind enough to let me know that he realized that I had done my best and at great personal risk. He did not comment upon my marginal and supererogatory observations that I believed that we must deal with men like the Kalifa with respect and that we must attempt to enter into their view of matters. I am afraid that Mycroft is wedded to the idea of efficacious force in all matters concerning the empire. It will do no good to ask him to take a wider view. It is a peculiarity of power that it narrows the imagination. Having a ready force at one's disposal seems always the shorter way to deal with conflict, although it seldom is. To see humanity and dignity in the enemy and not to characterize him according to one's own preconceptions is not easy. Above all it is essential to avoid contempt and underestimation of the willingness of the enemy to continue to fight. So much I have learned from Sun Tsu, the great Chinese theorist of the laws of war. I doubt if many modern statesmen ever read it. Ah well, perhaps I may do more when I return to England, but for now matters are settled. My short career as a diplomat is over.

Mycroft reports that Watson's wife is ill. He still maintains our old rooms as a sort of shrine at Mycroft's request. I have requested that Mycroft transfer some funds to help Watson in his present needs. The funds come from the sale of some property in Yorkshire that Mycroft and I share. They are the proceeds from a sale of property that came to us through a contingent remainder on properties adjacent to the family's main estate at Sigerside. I directed Mycroft to sell this property to meet my needs on the journey before leaving England. I requested that my share of that estate should be given to Watson in case of my premature death. I am sad that I cannot be by his side now, but there are still reasons of personal safety for me to remain away. Mycroft and Scotland Yard have done all that they can to keep an eye on the Professor's movements without arousing suspicion. He appears to have become a stolid country gentleman. He has become so by purchasing the racehorse stables at King's Pyland, a grimly humorous move on his part. He has chosen the site of what was once the scene of a victorious case of mine in the matter of Silver Blaze from whence to plan his great conspiracy against the British Empire.

No one can say as yet what that crime will be. Apparently he did take one trip to Amsterdam but the reason for that trip may have been only of a business nature. The Professor does have many investments abroad it appears and I might add that he is busy seeing to the management of the plantation in the region of the Dutch East Indies for Colonel Moran in his absence. Beyond this nothing has been discovered. At least there is no sign that Professor Moriarty is engaged in any crime that will actually occur prior to my return. The Professor evidently trusts me to contact him immediately upon my return and I believe that I can now assert that the Professor will keep his part of our wager. If he has delayed this long to accomplish his ends, I may rest assured that he will continue to restrain the execution of his grand design until my return to England. I must say that I always assumed that he had exaggerated, that his claim that he could destroy the British Empire with a single crime was all bluster; yet I am uneasy at times for the precise character of the Professor does not lend itself often to such specious claims. But I must not allow these dismal thoughts to oppress me. A time of freedom lies ahead for me and I must use it to some account.

My plan is to attempt various syntheses of the various compounds derived from coal-tar. So complex are these molecules that they have any number of useful properties from dyes to drugs. They are a great unopened book of nature's possibilities and perhaps I shall append a useful chapter. It is ironic that I should be dealing with coal-tar since a significant part of the wealth of the Holmes' estate is derived from the family holdings of coal mines in Northumberland. These mines are now owned by my brother Sherringford who inherited them through the descent provisions of primogeniture. Mycroft and I receive remittances from time to time from the Holmes' tenant-farms in Yorkshire that collectively make up the estate of Sigerside and from a small family shipping company operating out of the Port of Whitby. We do not play an active role in the management of these hereditary properties having left these choices of management to Sherringford. He is a man who delights in management and rejoices in figures and books of account. I doubt if either Mycroft or I could do as well to manage our own affairs as does Sherringford who makes up in assiduity what he lacks in imagination and human warmth. He is a stout Tory and a great opponent of the Chartist movement and of Irish Home Rule. He uses his position in the house of Lord's to maintain and spread his views and to preserve his properties with minimal taxation.

I recall asking him once why property plays so great a role in his life. He answered, "Because, my dear Sherlock, property is all that there is. The individual passes but property remains."

I fear that my eldest brother's religion is the laws of England. He does keep a Bible and occupies the family pew on a Sunday, but his copy of Blackstone's Commentaries on the law is more thumbed than the family Bible. The Bible's binding is stiff with lack of use as I noted many years ago in one of my brief visits to the family estate. But these are not thoughts for a lovely morning in spring when all of the beauty of nature is both priceless and free. I shall stop writing now and descend to my breakfast of croissants and fresh fruits and then be off and walk about this most interesting metropolis.

Evening—

I have had a most glorious day. I could not have found a better place for the tasks that lie before me. Perhaps only one who has spent most of his life in England can imagine how clarifying it is to the mind to exist in a land of sun and balmy breezes. Montpellier lies upon the plains of Languedoc along the River Lez. It is a city of waters bathed in the sea air. The sea is a mere six miles away and its influence can be felt even though it can only be glimpsed from the higher vantage points of the region. The river on the other hand is a constant presence as it purls through the town. The abiding impression that I have had on my first day is of light and clarity. This is a land of fertility and joy. All things amenable to reason seem possible here.

One should never underestimate the role of climate and geography upon the character of a people. Here I would say the city has a climate where reason and optimism must prevail. It is fertile yet not given to excess. The quest to find a balance between appetite and reason seems to me to be the goal of life. It may account for what Watson has attempted to portray of my cat-like abstemiousness. I am innately suspicious of the passions and of what may be termed "enthusiasm." I prefer an edge to my pleasures and a clear boundary to my desires. Perhaps this is because I fear that there is something in man that will spread in all directions if not confined in some way. Yet such is the paradox of my nature that I chaff at confinement. I am forever fighting the inherent lethargy of my own nature which at times overcomes me. I am easily discouraged by the prospect of time. I fear nothing more than to be made immobile, yet I desire at times to bury myself among my books and papers at Baker Street and to allow the somnolent roar of London to carry me off into the obscure regions of thought and speculation.

I have known of the despair of the gin-soaked denizens of East London. How often have I seen the painted faces of the women in the gas-lit streets and wondered how they might appear in the clear light of the south. Certainly fog and darkness add charm to many doyens who have known better days. Passions thrive on the artificial beauty of the east-end music halls and the assumed cheerfulness there that hides the pain of the lot of the working poor. I do not condemn them because their pleasures are few and their days short. It is only in a land such as this in the south of France though that one may grasp the true measure and stature of man and woman. In such a place I long to break out of those limits that serve to encase both body and mind simply in order to be equal to the majesty of the landscape before me. Yet even here in this lovely land violence has known its time and left its traces.

It was here that the great scandal of the Albigensian Crusade against the Cathars took place. Even now there still rages in the theological faculty the ancient battle between Jesuits and Dominicans, both orders quite orthodox yet different in spirit. The

Dominicans have what might be termed a rage for reason, while the Jesuits are at heart romantics and mystics. The Jesuit doctrine of Probableism makes some allowance for our imperfect moral knowledge and the need for practical action in an imperfect world. That doctrine allows one to choose without the luxury of moral certitude the best of several alternate courses. A Jesuit confessor attempts to inspire the penitent with a higher vision and through gradations to approach sanctity. The Dominicans on the other hand pounce upon error to root it out and lose sight of the groping soul in their desire for an imposed clarity that may exceed the soul's present powers to attain or to actuate.

The Jesuits will never forget that St. Ignatius of Loyola was hauled before the Inquisition to answer for the suspected heresy of Quietism in his book, "The Spiritual Exercises." The Jesuits have always aroused ire in many quarters for it is the desire of the order's members to penetrate the world with grace and to labor always for the greater glory of God. The Jesuits are often found close to the men and women of wealth and power, because the Jesuits know that to change the world one must re-direct the forces that determine that world. Jesuits are practical strategists and do not feel that they are abandoning God when they seek the betterment of man. The Dominicans on the other hand were cognitively closed-in upon their own stringent nature in dealing with the people that they sought to convert through their preaching with little regard for the private and individual character of each soul.

The fate of the Cathars is a case in point. The Cathars were of the same mindset as all dualists such as the early Gnostics and the Manicheans of the third and fourth centuries. Dualist thought attempts to isolate evil and in doing so to exalt it as a separate force and to purge God of any complicity in physical evil by positing two separate principles as being at war as though they were equal. Orthodox Catholicism on the other hand accepts the insolubility of the problem of evil, which is answered not by defeating evil but by using it through the mystery of the Crucifixion of Christ to attain the redemptive will of God. This is not to say that God wills evil directly, but rather that God comprehends evil in way that evil may never comprehend goodness. Darkness is the absence of light and may only exist when light is blocked in some way from the universal illumination.

There is a misapprehension that the vast distances that surround the constellations are void of light. This is not so. Rather, it is only in the blackness of space where we can apprehend the emptiness where light travels but is not reflected back from any object. Light must in some way interact with what is not itself a source of light by means of reflection if it is to be seen. Where this interaction does not take place, we see only darkness. In a similar manner the soul remains in darkness unless acted upon by grace. The Cathars believed in the need for certain perfect ones to act as a source of light for the others who were relegated to a class saved by a mere fiat of God rather than because of their own perfections. The version of dualism practiced by the Cathars in other words detracted from the dignity of human nature shared by all men and women, which posits the possibility of active salvation for each man and woman without exception. Calvinism is at heart similar to Catharism because it also posits an elect made perfect by grace and another group that is irretrievably damned. These doctrines make a mockery of the mercy of God and attempt to pre-determine a soul's state in eternity.

The Jesuits on the contrary assert that moral improvement is always possible for every soul, leaving the rest to the mercy of God. They are not Pelagian, because the Jesuits put great emphasis upon God as the active agent of salvation, but they yet retain the vision of heroic action by the soul in response to the love of God if properly exercised by the imagination. This strict orthodoxy has made the Jesuits immune from the usual charges of heresy. Indeed if there is a Jesuit heresy at all it would be that they love the world too much and in their desire to find God everywhere some have approached a religion of pantheism and animism. This very trait though made the Jesuits great missionaries in India, China, and Japan. The universal Godliness in all things could be made conformable to the Hindu mindset with its many Gods that penetrate every aspect of life. The Chinese likewise found in the admirable clarity and balance of Jesuit thought conformity to the teachings of Kung fu Tsu and Lao Tsu. Finally the Japanese with their elaborate sense of the virtues contained in the minute ceremonies of Shinto that reflect the greater world-order in miniature valued the Jesuit mantra of finding God in all things.

The great temptation of reason is always that reason presumes too much. Even when applied to human conduct it is finally inadequate, but when applied to God it exceeds its own powers. For this reason, religion must always finally be a matter of the heart, a heart guided by reason but not encompassed by it. I will go so far as to say that God has left the universe unfinished and open to new possibilities. The best answer to all determinisms is to realize that they rest upon the positing of a closed universe in which all forces may be numbered and assigned a direction and strength by an omniscient being; but, if God has allowed an opening to exist, even if it is only a hairsbreadth wide, for chance and for chaos to reign, then there is room for the indeterminate and for freedom. Perhaps God prefers a slight asymmetry to exist in his creation and if God prefers it so then who are we to impose upon the creator our demand that He should always act in a predictable fashion? If that demand is to be allowed, then it would be we who are dictating the nature of God rather than God who is seeking to elevate man, which is certainly a blasphemous reversal in metaphysics.

What was Peter's temptation to Jesus but simply to suggest that the cross was unworthy of him? It was the same temptation as that of the devil who bid Jesus to accept victory in this world by feeding mankind with bread so that no further effort would be required in dealing with a contingent world where crops sometimes fail to grow and sharing is required. This was the temptation for Jesus as God to simply mandate sanctity by implanting an irresistible grace in the souls of men and women and by that means to ensure their salvation. There is no human freedom in such a plan. Jesus said in reply to the devil that God's word is adequate to exact a free and willing compliance from men and women for true human dignity demands that this freedom must exist.

Jesus was next tempted to avoid the very character of the Incarnation by retaining the prerogatives of divinity by casting himself down from the height of the temple only to be rescued by angels. Jesus refused this temptation by asserting that trust in God requires that no test by man should be put to God, but rather that God should have our absolute trust. It is for this reason that orthodox doctrine bids us to hope for a salvation that may never be certain on this earth because it is hope in God and not certainly in ourselves that must sustain us. We must leave ourselves open in complete trust to the mercy of the God who loves us.

Finally, the devil urged Jesus to rely upon that mercy alone without undergoing His earthly ministry and sacrificial death and to enjoy the magnificence of this world without restraint by serving the devil in preference to God. Again Jesus said no to this temptation by saying that it is God alone who must be served and as the Son of Man by virtue of the Incarnation Jesus was no exception to this general rule. This world can never demand our strict and absolute allegiance; we must use it with care and restraint. True Christianity always denies to itself the temptation of the easy solution. This is not merely a rule of practice but of belief as well. The Nicean Creed is not so much an assertion of perfect clarity in belief as it is a refusal to adopt the positions of the various heresies that would impose a specious clarity where there can only be mystery. Men have sinned most when they have assumed a degree of theological clarity to exist that is denied them by God. Reason as often as the passions betrays man to sin. At least the passions leave man face to face with the humiliation of his own brutish excesses. We are more likely to be saved in the end by humor and its rebuke directed at our follies than by our supposed comprehension of God.

It is said that the devil cannot bear to be made ridiculous and for this reason he is often depicted with horns and a tail. It must be remembered though that the devil is a fallen angel, one with a darkened intellect because he has turned away from God, yet his status and faculties are unimpaired except through his own wickedness and the desire to revel in his suffering. The devil scorns the passions of men and delights in reducing us to mere brutes, to bury our hopes in ashes. What is death itself if not the final degradation of mankind's pretentions? God alone sets at naught all of this by sharing our condition and by redeeming it from within humanity and not from any mere outside fiat. If the Incarnation had never occurred, then the dualists might be correct. A perfect God would then need to mechanically redeem imperfect man. But man is created, as is the universe, in an indeterminate fashion so that spontaneous actions are possible. What appears at first to be a flaw in creation is actually what makes it fascinating and capable of exciting wonder in us; for if God were a mere standing-wave that we might describe and define, then God would not be God.

God's nature is expressed in the phrase, "I am that I am" which is not, as it first appears to be, circular in nature. It is instead the fact that God wills what he wills and is pure spontaneity and freedom and abundance. God alone requires no cause to set Him in motion but is instead activity posited upon no higher power. The great metaphysical question of why is there something rather than nothing may be resolved by simply focusing upon the word "why." The question assumes a position that is denied to man, to question the wisdom of what is. This question is denied to reason for it transcends reason. The being who asks the question already must exist and cannot posit a non-being that is now forever denied to it by God. The more proper form of the basic metaphysical question then would be to ask: why would a Perfect Being create contingent beings that are by definition imperfect because they are God. Of course a contingent being may be less than perfect but still conformable to its nature and unmarred by sin. Whatever evil may be then it is more than simply being metaphysically dependent upon God for its existence. Evil always implies the rejection of a gift, a state of being less than what God created it to be, because God always creates in love and for love. God does not demand our degradation. He does not create us to be ground into the dust. Even death is seen as an enemy and not part of the essential nature of human existence. We are born for immortality and only evil can make us prefer our own extinction or to visit upon ourselves. This is what is meant by the phrase that the wages of sin is death. We need only look about us to realize that this is so.

God creates because he prefers to do so. In the face of this reality all questioning of metaphysical alternatives must cease. We have the world that we perceive all around us and the laws that we are daily discovering through science and that must be enough for us to accept the conditions posed by our own contingent nature. Beyond this it is a capital mistake to seek to go, to extrapolate beyond analogy in our contemplation of eternity. This insight was said best by Saint John when he spoke in admonition to his flock. "Beloved, we are God's children now; what we will be has not yet been revealed."

May 20, 1892
First days in Montpellier

It is one of those warm Mediterranean days with the air absolutely brilliant that draws artists to the south of France. The fields are rich with the shoots of early grain. The heavens seem to invite the mind of man to transcend its usual dull preoccupations and the heart awakens to many possibilities. I shall keep my tour of the *Musee Fabre* for one of those days of summer clouds and heat-lightening when the moisture of the sea comes inland with the rains to wash the dusty streets and to leave them steaming in the returning sun. I went to early mass at the 14th century Cathedral of St. Pierre. The great church was filled with the usual pious women and old men who are always the backbone of the Church. I went up to the altar after Mass and lit a candle before *Notre Dame* for the intention that my stay here in this lovely city may serve some good end and that I may discover something useful in my research.

The desire to create and to discover is no small part of human happiness. No one wishes to pass through life as a great vacuum that absorbs experience and leaves nothing behind. The quest for some earthly legacy seems to me more than mere vanity. It is the godlike in our nature. We desire to share and to distribute being and to rejoice in the sheer abundance of life. It is true that science seems to be an impersonal study, but there would be no science if we did not first observe, then question, and finally use the infinity of our imagination to propose explanations. The experiment however always contains within itself the germ of its own result. Even when the expectations of the scientist are thwarted, that disappointment only draws the imagination to go back and to seek a new hypothesis leading to a solution.

It is not a bad thing to entertain this desire for knowledge; without it man would be only a dull parasite adapting mindlessly to its host environment. Even the lowly sponge is active, filtering the waters for tiny organisms to sustain it. Nothing in life is ever static, yet we have within us a desire for rest and for complete knowledge. If we should have the misfortune to ever attain it though, if our road of seeking should ever end, if all might be summed up in some final formula written down once and for all, then life as we know it would cease. For this reason, I will go so far as to say that restlessness and dissatisfaction should be welcomed in our lives. On such days we rise early, the earth beckons to us, and everything seems possible. It is the very spirit of youth that thrills within us then and it must be preserved at all costs as we age. Woe to the man or woman who finds that all needs have been met, who finds a home so suitable that the urge to move ceases. The often preferred question uttered by a child to its parents each morning is, "What shall we do today?" Their young eyes are filled with the delight of expectation.

Often I have seen in the eyes of the denizens of London the dull pain of knowing precisely what each day will bring. Even pleasure cloys the palate if it becomes the norm and not the reward at the end of effort. We are born to a life of seeking and it is best that it should be so. Time ceases to be noticed and valued when it is infinite. Nothing destroys the sense of progress like knowing that there will be no end. If mortal life would never cease, then one might always put off living and repenting in an infinite regress of promises to amend. There is no sadder word than tomorrow. Let life begin for us today! To grasp each day like a terrier shaking a rat, to toss it in the air before worrying it yet again, to draw out of it each breath and fragment so that each day is filled with the wine of creation, to live like that would be to be truly alive.

Nothing that God could ever do to man would be crueler than to have granted us a premature eternity. We could never bear it. Only God is forever new and exciting and until we are ready to perceive God as He is by transcending our greed, our fears, and our vanity we would be unable to perceive that wondrousness. To see God without the practical faculties created and honed over a life-time would be impossible. God's simplicity would appear to us to be trivial for God does not consist of compounds but is only and always God. He alone is the great singularity.

At the same time, the perfections of God would so insult our own vanity that we would have been forced to flee from His Face without the moral probation granted to us by our earthly existence, as scripture attests when it says that no man can bear the sight of God and live. All such language is metaphoric of course, but it may explain why we are asked even by a God of love to endure the human condition for it is that very condition that tutors us in the language of love that is the sole *lingua franca* of heaven.

Later—

After several days spent enjoying the delights of the city such as the exquisite Arch of the *Porte de Peyrou*, I got down to business today. I visited the University's School of Medicine and met with the director, a great jovial Frenchman named Dr. Pierre Cardet. He read my records and letters of recommendation after adjusting a pince-nez to his aquiline nose. It created a somewhat comical effect and I was put to a great effort to repress my laughter. I had the misfortune to have him glance up at the height of my amusement and his pince-nez fell to the floor. He immediately divined the source of my amusement and to my immense relief he laughed.

"You are amused Monsieur? I do not look like the director of a great medical faculty? I look more like a member of the bourgeoisie is that not so? My father was a mechanic and I alone of my family have joined the ranks of the professional class. Social distinctions are not so great here in the south of France as they are in Paris or in London. We have a tradition of heterodoxy here. Even our medical school embraces what is progressive and new. We embraced early the water-born theory of cholera transmission while most medical schools still spoke of the dangers inherent in breathing bad air, of miasma. I see here in your records that you are a chemist and not a physician. You will not be held in less esteem for that fact here. I am happy to be able to accept you and to grant you laboratory access during your time here in Montpellier."

He read further in my application materials. "Hmm, I see that you wish to do research in the derivatives of the coal-tars. Very interesting! I shall follow your progress closely since I also am fascinated by the possibilities inherent in just such compounds. I also see that you have published a most interesting study upon atavism and have even done work in philology by deciphering medieval palimpsests. I should not be surprised by the variety of your interests for you are also the famous detective are you not? Ah excellent, you may then be added to the list of many great men who have done work here in the university. Are you aware that the great author Francois Rabelais studied here as well as Nostradamus and that the zoologist Pierre-Joseph Amoreux and the chemist Antoine Jerome Ballard lived here. We value a diversity of gifts for we feel that the university must be open to change. We have not allowed the venerable history of the university to make us stodgy and backward looking. We have here a minimum of requirements, preferring that new knowledge should always be encouraged, without setting up the often arbitrary borders of academic discipline and undue respect for seniority. We believe in turning loose the inquiring spirit of youth, knowing that time corrects all things. I shall give instructions then that you are to receive all the aids that we may supply to your research. You may attend lectures if you choose without charge during the period of your fellowship and there will be no fees for your laboratory expenses. You will retain all rights and patents to any discoveries that you make. We ask only that we be allowed to publish the results in our journal. Is this agreeable to you? Excellent! Then allow me to show you our facilities and to introduce you to your colleagues."

I was taken around the university grounds and met everywhere with the same courtesy. The laboratory is an excellent one and will answer all of my requirements. Tomorrow I shall begin. I will first attempt a fractional distillation of the major compounds. After that I intend to begin synthesizing as many new derivatives as possible. Then each must be tested with various reagents. I am afraid that many months of effort lie ahead for me. I shall not burden this journal though with my results but will record them in a separate series of notebooks. I will record here only my thoughts and spiritual progress as I have done throughout my travels. May success crown all my efforts!

June 1, 1892
The Jardin des Plants de Montpellier and *La Serre Amazonienne*

Today I took a brief holiday from my research to visit the oldest botanical garden in France founded in 1593. I could not have chosen a better day for my excursion. The sky is clear again and warm and all of nature seems filled with life. One may learn much of the nature of God through the study of plants. They turn always to the sun as does the holy soul when it turns towards God for aid. It has always seemed folly to me to assume that plants are unconscious and take no joy in life. Who has witnessed the expanding glory of the rose and not thought that in some manner unknown to us it is thanking God for the gift of being a rose. Who may look at the simple daisy in the field and not see in its simplicity a metaphor for virginity or seen a reflection in the charms of a courtesan in the lush beauty of an orchid? It has always seemed to me that God acts as a gardener towards all of created things and I take it to be more than a mere accident in the gospel that the women who first came upon the tomb of Jesus and found it empty presumed that the risen Jesus was a gardener.

Christianity includes the dogma of the Resurrection of the Body as one of its primary articles of faith. What must a risen body be like? Surely it must be like a newly flowering plant still wet with the morning dew, its petals still fragile and tentative as they blossom forth into a hitherto unknown eternity, its leaves still tentative and uncertain seeking the sun. I like to think that the words of the gospel, "*Noli me tangere,*" spoken to Mary Magdalene after the Resurrection of Jesus, were not meant as a rebuff to the ardent Mary by asking her not to hold him, but were rather the spontaneous utterance of the human-nature of Jesus still present and active even after the Resurrection. It was more than Mary holding Jesus bound to the familiar embrace of earth; a great separation was taking place already and a similar transition will take place within us as we enter eternity leaving our former relations and limitations behind us. This new condition is incommunicable to us in our present state. All of our experience is bound to the life that we knew and to the people whom we loved. If we do not relinquish the hold that these things still maintain over us we become like those lost ones that we call hungry ghosts that haunt the places to which they are still bound and to which they cannot bid a final farewell. The human nature of Jesus was only then adapting to the strange new air of an eternal life, still shaking itself out in the sun, still burdened by the remnant of its mortal chrysalis and only about to spread its untrammeled wings.

If even the words of mortal literature are such that the reader must contribute something to complete the author's intentions, then should not the word of God stimulate our imaginations as well as our minds? Perhaps more people would hunger for heaven if it its image had not been degraded over time by the wheezy organs, the dull sermons, and the stale proprieties of a benighted clergy too accustomed to their religion to appreciate how strange its claims must seem to the uninitiated. To become too familiar with religion is often to create it in our own image with all of our own dull complacencies. To break religion free from its prison and to make the Holy Scriptures speak anew it is necessary that we feel within ourselves the passion of a Mary Magdalene whose first reaction to the Risen Lord is to catch hold of Him in an embrace of passion for He had returned not only as the Jesus she had known, but as the Eternal Lord of Heaven and Earth.

I spent hours today gazing at the sheer variety of blossoms and thought of all nature's excesses. Surely if all is accidental and flowers exist merely to attract the pollinating bees with no reference to human beings at all, then why include the sheer wonder and variety of the minute and detailed designs in each species of flower? Pure functionality would, or so it seems to me, fall into the same dreary sameness as so many of the creations of man. I have often wandered just as I did today in the dank garden of the slums of London. I have seen how the buildings in Whitechapel have decayed into a bleak sameness. Even the faces that surrounded me there and the eyes that met mine only to glance away again showed me the bleak unity of human despair. I have doubted at times that any sin, no matter how grievous in that Garden of Eden so long ago, could ever account for the fallen stature of men and women when they are said to be made in the image and likeness of God. To locate the time of our highest stature in the distant past shortly after an individual creation is less persuasive than that we are still in process of formation as human beings either though evolution or through cultural progress.

It would be easier for me to believe that we were ugly monkey-like creatures and had long betrayed our lowly origins in our subsequent history and that instances of human goodness are the great exception; that it is only now that we are just approaching the light of day and the realization of our full humanity and of our potential nature. Perhaps all of human history has been a matter of tunneling through mud and the great religious teachers of all lands are those who have intuited, since they could not know, that a world of light might once have existed and that the true flowers of our existence might spring forth again, maybe not today, not even soon, but at some distant era to be presided over by a generation far removed from our present time of troubles.

If that was true, then there would be no need to account for sin. Sin would be the norm for men and women in our present state of degradation, the temporary environment of our souls at this incomplete state of our evolution. Brutality and callousness would simply be what one might expect of most people and virtue would be the great anomaly. But who can believe this? If this was so babies would emerge from the womb with claws and fangs and not be the tiny weak beings that they are, oriented towards and rightfully expecting nurture, kindness, and the presence of a stable social-order to receive them and to guard them through their long period of maturation. Some sort of civilization must have always been present in human history.

When I first wrote my paper on atavism, the regression of mankind over time, I dared to explore the possibility that sin has so encased our nature that we are not evolving in the only dimension that really matters, in the moral direction, in our degree of innate kindness and compassion. If our great factories, our mines, and our steel mills are indeed the great wonders of the age and our signal accomplishments as a culture, then a great night of the spirit is descending upon us all and we will only use our technical progress to wage more efficient wars until we finally cease to exist upon this planet. If that should be so then the garden of this earth that is still touched and resonant with beauty and the plentitude that descends directly from the hand of God will have been destroyed by the very beings who might have abided with reverence and with wonder in peace over the face of the earth.

I have heard that the American Indians are one of the few races of mankind who have learned to live at peace with the earth, taking from it no more than what is allowed to be necessary for their sustenance and survival. I think it is the best interpretation of the words of God to Adam and Eve that they might eat freely from all of the trees in the garden except the one that would bring death to them, because it exceeded their mortal capacity to absorb its supposed nutrients. Perhaps that sense of our innate limitation was the reason that God held something in reserve. The primal weakness of man and of woman is that we crave excess. We abhor limits, even when those limits are set by God and for our own good. Our fatal curiosity is even now our undoing. We will not accept a good as a gift if we can snatch it up and by doing so claim that it was really ours all along so that we need not refer all things back to their cause and give thanks to God.

After the act resulting in Original Sin Holy Scripture says that we were thereafter barred from the Tree of Eternal Life by an angel with a flaming sword lest we eat of it and live forever. God in His mercy gave us the inevitability of death, the one limit that no man or woman may transgress. This paradoxical gift was our last chance to be so humbled that we might once again know our place as created beings so that we might like the flowers turn toward the sun that alone gives us life. We are not our own source of illumination; not even the universe as a whole can be our source of illumination, even if we possessed perfect knowledge of all of its motions and perturbations and could control them. Perfect power and predictability are the source of all idolatry, the vaunted ability that we hoped for so as to be equal to God. All sin is part of the great refusal to give thanks for what does not depend upon us.

If we return to the creation narratives in Genesis we are

faced with a fundamental potency in all things to become what their natures dictate. Sin begins when that fundamental order is violated by being taken from the overall context of harmony that unites all creation. Even darkness might be seen as a great waiting, a setting forth of the stage for the play to begin. Darkness it is said brooded on the face of the deep until God said, "Let there be light." Similarly if we did not exist latently in the mind of God we would not have been endowed with that Godlike character of thinking. With God to conceive anything at all is to do the thing because nothing stemming from God can be evil. God does not debate alternatives. If God by definition can only will the good, then His will is determined forever by itself. In its first incipiency it has already weighed all consequences and assumed the burden of the choice before the choice is even made. Only by such paradoxical language can we realize that God foresaw our redemption before we ever sinned. The Cross of Calvary hovered over innocent Eden.

I will even go so far as to say that the Tree of Life was always the Cross of Christ. How else are we to explain that men have been trying to crucify themselves and each other ever since our origin in Eden, for surely our genius has always been to devise and to induce new methods of suffering upon each other and in consequence to enhance our guilt before God? In this lovely world one would think that we would have simply blundered our way into happiness by now; instead history is one long nightmare of power, greed, and pillage. And when we are not tortured by others we torture ourselves with fears, regrets, and recriminations. So at the end of the 19th century, we oare not evolving as nature has done; we are instead a festering agent or a plague to the earth. Our cities are great boils erupting across the clear skin of this living world. So intensely do I feel this that I have vowed to spend my last years as a beekeeper so that I might in some way foster and help to fertilize the living plants.

Nature speaks to us in the bees. I have often noted that the hive is a great harmony presided over by the females. In nature the females raise the young and preserve the species and they often have much to do simply to prevent the males from eating their own young. Maleness deprived of devotion and fatherhood is dullness and savagery. The bees know this. The male principle in bees is reduced to its lowest common denominator of the mere passage of the genetic legacy followed by the death of the drones.

Yet in the Judeo-Christian perspective we speak of God as a Father. Why did Jesus so characterize Yahweh? A proper religious conception of fatherhood must by its very nature include as its primal characteristic the act of protection and the nurturance of life. For this reason I hold that to engage in warfare is to be most unmanly, because war is oriented toward destruction rather than toward creation and nurturance. True manhood is known by its wisdom and benevolence, by the time and effort that it takes to foster life and to show reverence for all things.

I have always thought that the command, once placed in the mouth of God, that man should subdue the earth must be one of those later cultural accretions that have blurred the image of God and obscured its true wishes for mankind. Any cultivator knows that when we subdue nature we only kill it. Nature may be aided, even guided in fertility and growth, just as the gardener may put up a trellis for the vine to embrace. No good gardener tramples upon the flowers to subdue them. Even fields of wheat are gently combed by the thresher to remove the grain, as a lovely woman combs her hair so that it may shine forth in splendor. Men subdue the earth at their peril. Rather, it is the earth that shall someday subdue us until at last we lie beneath it to await the summoning voice of God on the last day.

June 10, 1892
My Laboratory

During this last week I have spent countless hours synthesizing the fractional coal-tars. Each must be tested for its own unusual properties and then broken down into its constituent elements. I have often thought it strange that the properties of a compound exceed the character and energy potential of the elements of which it is composed. Think only of the difference between water with a chemical formula of two parts hydrogen to one part of oxygen and then compare it to hydrogen peroxide where the elemental proportions are equal in composition. How different the chemical properties are! Often the properties are enhanced; for instance the methyl form of mercury is more deadly than its elemental form in it pure state. Combine inert nitrogen with the carbon atom that is the very source of life and with hydrogen the simplest element and one produces cyanide. Elements are often gases yet the compound is often a liquid. The non-intuitiveness of science explains why even today so much eludes human knowledge. To judge by appearances has misled many. Only slow testing and synthesis of observation may produce reliable results. Nature is teased out of its secrets.

My ultimate hope is to find an agent that will cure consumption. Truly I would know that I have benefited mankind if I might solve the dilemma posed by tuberculosis. It is truly a vicious illness. The body's own defensive response kills itself by sheer exhaustion as it attempts to contain and to wall-off the invading bacillus. In attempting to limit the evil of the disease, the body becomes an evil to itself. At last a wall of spongiform tissue is created with great vascular crevasses supplied with blood. Coughing causes these tissues to break away in yellow bits of tissue called rales. In the final stages of the disease a blood vessel may burst and the tubercular patient then drowns in his or her own blood. Few germs toy with their victims in this way but rather kill swiftly and hence mercifully, but this lethargic and patient bacillus kills by degrees. It may take years to kill the patient and not the days or even hours as in the case of cholera. For this reason, victims of tuberculosis have a special name. They are referred to as consumptives just as victims of leprosy are called lepers.

The life of a consumptive is one of abiding fevers and progressive weakness. The fire of life becomes at last a flickering flame similar to a dying candle. It often takes the young in the very glory of their early maturity. For years I have wanted to address this disease that took my poor mother in her thirties. I shall labor for a year if I can manage to remain so long away from England. Even my entries in this journal may have to take second place for a time so that I may devote all of my waking hours to the notations of my work. Only then may I face Professor Moriarty at last and dare him to do his worst. I can only hope that he will continue to honor his word in the meantime and refrain from executing the scheme that he has no doubt devised until I have returned to England for our final duel of wits. I am glad that Colonel Moran has left me to pursue his pleasures since I do not need his taunting words about me now. I need all of my resources to address the tasks that lie ahead. May God direct my hands and mind so that I may find a cure at last for this dread disease or at least some advancement to rid mankind forever from one its most lethal foes.

Dr. Watson's Narrative Continues

Our train had arrived at last at Dieppe on the French coast. On the following day we were to take a coach to Calais and cross over to England by way of Dover. We left Dieppe and settled in for the night at a lovely inn on the Channel. After a dinner of oysters and a very fine flounder in cream sauce topped with almonds Holmes motioned to me and we took a walk outside together leaving Inspector Hopkins to an after-dinner drink of Benedictine before the Hotel fire. A thick sea-fog was blowing in off of the channel but it was a warm night. The sun had just set over the sea. We walked for some minutes in silence before Holmes spoke to me.

"You have not asked for details regarding the supposed attack upon me in Baker Street, but I think that you should know that we are both in danger. It is one of the reasons why we are leaving for America. Never since the year of 1891 have I been in such jeopardy."

"Surely the Baron is not as great a danger as was Professor Moriarty in 1891," I suggested hopefully.

"On the contrary, he is a far more dangerous man. It was never Moriarty who I feared you see; it was the men who worked under him. I knew that Professor Moriarty did not desire my death. Why else would he have come for that interview in my rooms before we left for Switzerland and how are we to explain his patience at our confrontation at the Reichenbach Falls? His threat, that if I succeeded in bringing destruction upon him, that he would do the same for me, was a mere gesture because he could not be sure how far I would go at the time. He could not have thought me so stupid that I regarded him as a mere thug. The whole conversation between us was a bout of verbal jousting to test each other's knowledge of the real character of the man who stood before him. Each of us had come to realize that we were in our own way *sui generis*. Each of us had despaired of ever finding another opponent worthy of our steel, yet even after years of move and countermove each of us doubted that the other was really of the same intellectual caliber. I am happy to say that we each passed the test and emerged from that meeting in Baker Street with the knowledge that we could depend upon each other not to go to extremes. Otherwise I would have taken my stand in England where I had Scotland Yard and Mycroft at my side. The whole purpose of our flight to the continent on that occasion was to give Moriarty an excuse to pursue me so that he might escape from the authorities who might otherwise have felt duty-bound to arrest him along with his gang."

"I have always wondered about that matter," I remarked. "How is it that after his return to Devonshire that he was not prosecuted?"

"The reason is simple, my dear fellow. It was because I obtained for him a royal pardon conditioned upon his remaining crime-free during the time of my absence in Asia. It was my correlative contribution to the wager between us. Just as Colonel Moran kept me under guard during my journey, so I had the threat of revocation of his pardon over Professor Moriarty should he break out into active criminal conduct before my return from my travels. I knew that he would probably not refrain from planning his great scheme to destroy the British Empire during my absence, but I knew that he would at least refrain from its execution and from lesser crimes. It was essential to our contract that each of us surrender something of the total freedom we might otherwise have enjoyed."

"But you say that you did not fear Professor Moriarty, why was that may I ask?"

"I had begun to realize that most of the crimes of Professor Moriarty hinged upon one common factor. I had observed as much over time. His victims were always men and women of wealth and power and each crime had within it an obscure ethical core. The Professor was, if I may describe him as such, a mobile version of the French Directorate under the French Revolution. His function was to kill, blackmail, or steal from the patrician class. In his own mind he was engaged in performing a service to humanity by destroying those whom the law could not reach. Many a respectable villain met his end through the machinations of the Professor. My early metaphor comparing him to Napoleon was not the best one I might have chosen. He was more like *La Guillotine*. The entire essence of his organization was to employ common thieves and cutthroats to achieve the ends thought up by the Professor and executed under the leadership of Colonel Moran, a man who shared his radical ethical views. You must remember Watson that the Professor originally came from humble roots. He never forgot his resentment of the class structure of England that might have condemned him to a life of penury and servitude if it was not for his genius. As it was he obtained a first rate education because he had a sponsor who recognized the talents of his stable boy and paid for his instruction and schooling."

"Who was that patron? Did he ever tell you?" I inquired with casual interest.

Holmes turned to face me before answering. "It was my father," he said quietly.

"It was your father?" I exclaimed in astonishment.

"Yes Watson, Professor Moriarty's father was the head horse trainer at our stables in Yorkshire. He was an itinerant

Irishman and he knew horses better than any man alive, or so my father claimed. His son, James Moriarty, was a quiet and sullen youth. A birth injury had left him slightly stooped and with a decided physical weakness and he was I am sad to say a figure of fun to the village youth. This drove him inward upon himself. His mother had been a former governess however and she had schooled him at home. He was from the beginning a quick learner. My father once noticed him reading in a corner of the stable-yard where he worked with his father as a groom. Rather than resenting the boy's idleness, my father found the sight amusing. He inquired what the boy was reading and upon discovering that it was Euclid he broke out in a hearty laugh as I was later told. My father was a stern man but not a prejudiced one. He was not as stuffy as my brother Sherringford who inherited my father's title, but not his disposition. My father was a nobleman of the old cast, a man of the land, deeply attached to his yeomen farmers, his horses, and his hounds."

"My father set him a problem on the spot. 'My boy,' said he, speaking to the young Moriarty, 'I will set you a little test. I shall have a horse run about the track and I shall ask you to calculate his speed without a watch. Can you do it? If you can, I shall see that you get an education for your body that will sustain you over the hurdles of life.'"

"Well Watson, need I tell you that Moriarty passed that test. The fence posts of the track were at uniform intervals. It was for the lad a minor calculation after measuring the number of feet between the posts and noting their total number to calculate the speed over the complete course run by the animal. My father kept his word. He would often thereafter glance at the academic marks achieved by young James and not content at ending his course of learning with the rudiments, he sent him on to public school and eventually to university."

"Then why did Professor Moriarty resent the upper classes

so? At least one member of that class seems to have treated him quite nobly indeed."

"Well Watson, my father's democratic spirit was not a universal one. The young Moriarty was treated like a dog in the public school where he was sent, his bold and sensitive spirit was mocked by students and tutors alike, and his stature and physique made him unable to defend himself against the kicks and blows that were motivated by their jealousy of his many achievements for he often took firsts in every subject offered. His knowledge of mathematics was so advanced that at last even the head-master of the school took him in hand to promote his interests. From that hour all abuse stopped, but it had already worked its mischief and left the young man with an inner canker of resentment and hatred of the class that had so oppressed him in the persons of the young noblemen who were his fellow students."

While I was still absorbing this startling revelation Holmes went on to give me details from the life of our other chief opponent from the days in Baker Street.

"Let me now turn to Colonel Sebastian Moran. He was raised in the provinces of India and not at home in England. The education of Colonel Moran from the beginning was to be a soldier on the frontiers of empire. His father was a diplomat in Persia. The Colonel excelled at horsemanship and languages, but otherwise cared little for books. He was though in his way as much of a rebel as was the Professor. He had developed great affection for the peoples that were governed by the English and never looked down upon them as mere wogs and coolies. He spoke familiarly with them and knew that the people of Asia have cultures that are far older than our own. This intimate knowledge and familiarity made his later tasks as a soldier difficult to execute. He found that he was killing men who were far nobler than the barracks-room brawlers whom he often commanded. At last he caught one of his sergeants beating an elderly Indian to get him to betray one of his countrymen. The Colonel grabbed the stick away from the fellow and proceeded to beat him in turn to within an inch of his life before he was pulled away by two young captains. There was a great fuss made of the incident of course and for a while it looked as though the Colonel would be court-marshaled and broken in rank, but because of his status as the son of an illustrious father he was allowed to quietly resign and still retain the rank of Colonel. He had after all suffered wounds in Her Majesty's service, so he was pensioned off. He therefore found himself as a comparatively young man at liberty and with an assured income."

"Soon after this he left India for the continent and it was there that he met Professor Moriarty in the Casino at Monte Carlo. The Professor it seems had devised a system of gambling by simply watching the play. He needed a brash young fellow though to execute his plan and he explained it to the Colonel who thereafter became his partner. Needless to say that they both left Monte Carlo richer than before and had in the interim cemented a fast friendship, perhaps the only close relationship that either of them had ever known. They found that they were both of a common mind in believing that the ills of this world cannot be righted by persuasion but only by the use of force and by the cunning use of power. The money that they had earned gambling became the basis for a criminal enterprise unlike any that the world had ever known. Its reach was international and its effectiveness was such that within three years it had eliminated some of the worst scoundrels and dictators of Europe. Several anarchist organizations were suspected of course in the slayings, but it was Moriarty and Moran all the time. The rest of the story you know."

I was astonished to hear the details of the strange web of relationships that had obtained between Holmes and men whom I had always believed were his greatest foes. This new insight explained at last why Holmes had been so confident in his wager with Moriarty, a matter that had puzzled me in my reading of

Holmes' journal.

"But Holmes, you say that we are in greater danger now than ever before, even when dealing with Professor Moriarty. I can see now why you had just cause to rely upon him and why it was that you were willing to run the risk of that fateful meeting at the Falls of Reichenbach, but what is it that you fear now when your plans are falling into place just as you outlined them to Sir Henry and to me?"

"My dear fellow, I trust that you know that I never exaggerate in such matters. I have only truly feared a few men in my life and those without exception have had ample reasons to work towards my destruction. There were lesser men among them of course. There was that sullen chap, Jonas Oldacre for instance, but I believe he is still serving his sentence in Reading Prison. The ones that I have most feared are Baron Maupertuis and that dreadful fiend Roger Baskerville alias Stapleton. Both of these men are still alive. I have therefore arranged this ruse of a murderous attack made upon me to buy us time in order to escape to America. Each of my enemies will conclude that another has done their work for them and that I am in a hospital at death's door. I have arranged that a great fuss is to be made about the attack upon me in the press and my supposed critical condition. Prayers are being offered for my recovery in many quarters and Her Majesty has been quoted as having expressed the gravest concern for my welfare in this extremity. It has all been quite dramatic and I almost wish that I could stay and observe the daily drama of my vacillations in recovery. The whole thing has all of the features of an Italian Opera, but it has been all been no mere joke I assure you. The story has been designed to buy us precious time to depart for America without interference and while there to complete our plans."

"And what about after that," I asked in concern. "Will we ever be really free of them while they live?"

Holmes turned to face me. "There is always a price old friend for attempting to face down evil. We can only hope that we will not have to pay the complete price with undue heroism. The desire to find a place of safety, some quiet refuge from terror and discontent, is as old as mankind and perhaps even we may be graced with a safe harbor at last. We put to sea in a storm last year and survived. We can but face this new storm bow-on and hope to come through at last. Come along Watson; let us go inside now and to our beds. Inspector Hopkins will be wondering what has become of us."

The next day we crossed the English Channel to Dover. Its white cliffs and ancient castle stood out brightly in the sun and I smelled again that glorious and familiar smell of England that always greets the wanderer home from the sea. We did not tarry long in Dover though but caught a train at once for Southampton. We had a private compartment reserved and we refrained from trips to the dining car until we had caught a local train out of Southampton for Exeter. Holmes had provided each of us with some small elements of disguise to prevent any possibility of recognition for all of England was alive with newspaper accounts of the supposed attack made upon him. We were to arrive at Exeter after dark. There we would separate. I would proceed to Cornwall and Holmes would proceed to Grimpen-on-the-Moors. He had arranged for a private carriage to pick him up there and he and Inspector Hopkins would then proceed to Holmes' own cottage to procure the necessary items for our trip and to see that all was well at home. He would then proceed to Baskerville Hall to acquaint Sir Henry with our discoveries and our plans. Holmes had of course written of his plans to Sir Henry to prevent any surprise when the news of the attack might filter out even to the remote provinces.

After all these matters had been accomplished Holmes and

I were to ultimately meet in Plymouth prior to the sailing of our vessel for America. We would be traveling under assumed names aboard ship and Mycroft had managed to procure passports for us so that we might arrive in New York under those same assumed names. The reputation of Sherlock Holmes was well-known even in America. We would of course have the means to prove our real identity should it be necessary and we had the papers that would allow us to do so, including a personal introduction from the Lord High Chancellor and one from the Prime Minister and also from the Home Secretary.

So it was that I bade farewell to Holmes and to Inspector Hopkins in the compartment as our train pulled into Exeter. We left the train separately as a further precaution. A fog had rolled in with one of those brief summer rainstorms that are so common in Devonshire. The air was fresh and moist and I found my own way to the platform where another train was to leave for Cornwall and within the half-hour I had caught the milk-train for Plymouth. My last sight was of Holmes and the Inspector sitting on a bench awaiting the slow and ancient train that serviced North Devon. Holmes' hat sat low upon his brow and his chin was muffled by his great-coat. The Inspector sat smoking his pipe and all about them flowed the silent eddies of the farmers and cottagers leaving Exeter for their homes out upon the moors. I thought then of my own cottage, now so long vacant, and wondered how I should find matters there upon my return. The swaying of the train after I boarded was like already being at sea and I soon drifted off to sleep.

The train arrived in the tiny Cornish station of Treddannick Wollas before proceeding on to Truro. A local coachman was dozing in his rig before the station. I roused him and soon we were trotting down the lanes of the village. The fog had passed with the night and the heat of the day was melting the last mists that hovered over the bay. It was only a short distance to my cottage that lies in its own private park. We turned in at the drive that makes a small semi-circle before the house. I paid the driver who had unloaded my luggage as I gazed at the well-remembered door. It was inset into the frame of the solid Country Tudor-style structure and was framed with ivy that climbed the stone walls. The driver soon left me and I was alone. The somnolent sound of bees came to me and I heard again the distant lapping of the sea on the sand-beach at the rear of the house. Turning the key in the lock I entered and placed my hat and walking stick on the entrance table. I walked on slowly through the hall to my sitting-room. There were my familiar books, neatly dusted by my charwoman and still in precisely the same place and attitude where I had left them almost a year ago. I recalled that I had been quite deep into Murgatroyd's, "Diseases of the Tropics," a book that I had been reading when I had received Holmes' urgent summons and there was my advance copy of the strange romance that had been published by a former client of Holmes named Bram Stoker. It was entitled, "Dracula." I would certainly have taken it along with me, but I had expected my visit to Holmes to be one of only short duration. Events had sped us along ever since and here we were well into the year of 1898.

I sat down wearily in my favorite armchair, turned on my reading lamp, and lit my pipe. I had wired my charwoman from Dover and expected her momentarily. She would build up the fire for the room had a decided chill and needed airing. I had already decided to spend the day by the bay in my small garden. It has marvelous and with an open view of Truro Bay. One could see the small tidal estuary to the left and to the right one could see the opening to the greater sea beyond. On a stormy day I would watch the waves breaking on the cliffs that guarded the entrance to the bay. There was a small channel in the center and a fleet of dory fishermen plied the local waters. Fresh fish were in consequence always available in the village and the local inn served the best fish-and-chips in Cornwall and the salmon in dill sauce at the local hostelry was a wonder.

It was all coming back to me now, my quiet and happy life. I had long ago adjusted to the rhythms of the place and the great world of events had seemed to be far away. I did not think then of what was happening on the margins of the great English Empire or what play from America was crowding the West-End theaters in London. I did not care if there was a revolution going on somewhere in South America or whether a mutiny might threaten among the troops guarding the Punjab. For me there was only the bright summer sun and the opening lilies and morning glories, the geraniums lining the walk to my door, and perhaps a visit from the local apothecary and a game of whist with neighbors after dinner. How had I given up all of these things to face again the always strenuous adventures by the side of Sherlock Holmes? Even he had spoken of retiring soon after the dawn of the new century; in spite of his protestations though I wondered if he would ever take up the beekeeping that he had once said he contemplated. But then at the dawn of life we dream of entering the vast swarm of events and of making a difference in the course that the world will take. We imagine our last years in the colorful garb of completion and of satisfaction and with no regrets.

There I was, at the time when the illusion of bending the world to one's own will should have been long past and Holmes and I planned to enter world affairs to a degree presented by no other case in which we had ever been involved. Even the matter of the Bruce-Partington Plans seemed to be only a small matter compared to our projected trip to America with the Murillo Papers. How far off seemed those days when Sherlock Holmes would expend all of his efforts to solve some trifling matter such as that presented by what I called, "The Adventure of the Copper Beeches." Now, I reflected, our clients were the august figures of the Prime Minister and the Pope!

But who may turn aside with a clear conscience, I asked myself then, when history summons? We tend to forget that even great statesmen have private lives. I could forgive much in them now for I see clearly that even men who have sought power and influence must have had times when they would rather have withdrawn into obscurity, as I had once done so as to live in a tiny cottage by the sea. How blessed to have no interruptions and to greet the dawning of each day with the innocence of a child for whom the day's adventures seem to partake of an eternity. How long are the hours of our youth! Even a day then seems to last forever. No wonder that death seems to children to be a mere abstraction. Life seems unending in our youth, even as in spring the first leaves seem to be invincible. Who can imagine in that pale dawn of the year that they will someday wither in a matter of weeks and thereafter will be blowing in the winds and fall to lie irrevocably in the earth?

My own autumn as I write these words is upon me now. I no longer read with patience Goethe's paean to the indulgent passions of youth, "The Sorrows of Young Werther." Even the poet Percy Shelley with his sighs and high-flown redemptive aspirations for mankind have paled upon me with the years. There are times now when I can only grasp the works of Rabelais or Fielding or seek in the genial humor of Stern's, "Tristram Shandy," for some wider view of life, but alas my time of Ecclesiastes is upon me and will not relinquish me to entertain fonder notions of life and death.

I read Gerard Manley Hopkins and Francis Thompson now containing poetry with lines such as these: "Margaret, are you grieving. Over Goldengrove unleaving?" and I feel that old ache of autumn and the deep poignancy of all life: that each of us was once a child but will never be again. Were the tyrants of the world once only sullen infants who might have been changed if they had been met with love or were they even then plucking wings from butterflies? Was the later voluptuary early out chasing the neighbor girls with unsought kisses? Was the future saint lingering over her nightly prayers and weeping because of the cruel slights of nature? Life is such a mystery to us that even faith can never explain it fully. We see indeed in a glass darkly and must wait for all to be made clear to us as I trust that someday it will.

There was a sound of a key in the lock and a great rattling at my back-door which always sticks. My charwoman had arrived at last and I rose to greet her. She was a fine hearty Cornishwoman named Clara.

"Good heavens Doctor Watson," said she. "As I live and breathe sir it's that good to see you as I can never say. I told my husband, 'See here,' says I, 'You won't believe it but the good doctor as I works for is coming home; that he is,' and here ye be. Well, I hope that you will find all well here. I did as you wished and tried to keep it as it was before you left. My, but it's coming on a year now since you left, ain't it? Well I can't say as you have missed much here for nothing has changed of consequence, although we are all a year older and that's the truth on it sir. But look at you, Doctor, with your fine tan. You've never looked healthier if I do say so myself. I always say that I would love to see Italy before I die, all those statues and things, but my mister, he don't like foreigners and all their strange way of talk and such."

I have given a brief example of her style of speech that was relaxing to listen to in its way. It was like a rushing stream going over boulders, following its own course. It was not essential to pay attention to details in her speech, but only to follow the general drift and to put in a comment now and again to re-direct the discussion back to the matter at hand. I was grateful that day however that she did not ask me for details of my absence which might send her off again as she tended to embroider whatever statements I might care to make on any topic. She could not read, so I hoped that she would know nothing of the supposed attack made upon Sherlock Holmes. Our provincial newspaper seldom follows events in the larger world beyond the county, so I trusted that even gossip would fail to carry the news to her and that I would be spared the burden of long explanations.

Once she had assured herself that I was satisfied with her upkeep of the cottage, she busied herself preparing a fine breakfast for me of eggs and kippers. She had also brought along some Cornish Pasties for my dinner. She asked me though how long I planned to stay and I was forced to tell her that I was soon to be off again within the week for America. She shook her head in a comical fashion and went on about "that Greek fellow what could not stop voyaging once he started."

She left me alone at last and I was able to review the papers from my solicitor who had been handling my bills and business affairs in my absence. I was relieved to see that all was well. The sale of my medical practice had left me well endowed with the funds to live comfortably and I was able at last to delegate the more onerous tasks of daily life to hired professionals. I had no idea how long I would be absent in America, so I took the time to pack all that I might require for an extended trip.

Holmes had given me only a few days to complete my tasks before I was to leave for Plymouth where we would meet our vessel for the crossing to America. I had the whole summer's day before me though, so I went out to the lawn in the rear of my cottage that runs to a steep incline that descends down to the bay. A fresh breeze had sprung up I recall and the trees that were swaying over my head created patterns of sun and shade on the greensward. I sat down in my comfortable garden chair and took in the shimmering waters of the bay before me. Its shoreline was an intricate one with many coves, each with its own sandy beach. A great rock stood in the middle and the breakers that entered the bay would froth about it, waving its kelp like the tresses of a mermaid. The waters took on a most delightful color of opalescent green as the clouds passed.

I know that I will never grow tired of the tidal music of the sea. Each season of the day brought change, and yet the rhythms were predictable, the result being a vast symphony of light and sound. How welcome it all was. I closed my eyes and was soon asleep. I felt as though suspended upon the summer air. How far away seemed any speculations of ill intent and evil seemed but a brief illusion in a momentarily troubled sleep and perhaps that is true. I often thank heaven for the brief hours of respite that sleep provides for us. They are not the least part of the joy of living. To hover on the brink of consciousness without that settled purpose that demands that we arise and meet the duties of the day; surely that is to know the purity of happiness for one who has led a busy life with many responsibilities.

I awoke to find that the noon-hour had already passed. The gentle morning breeze had fallen away and it was quite warm. I had fortunately moved my chair into the shade of the great elm tree in my garden before falling asleep, but now the sun shown full upon my head. The sun had crossed its zenith. The waters were now a rich blue color and the bay quite calm; all of nature was at peace.

I arose and went inside and poured myself a stone mug full of milk and sampled the blueberry pie that Clara had brought along with the savory pasty that would be my dinner later. I thought of sauntering into the village, but I preferred not to risk the danger of inquiries. This visit to my home must be as though I was a ghost come back to haunt the place it had once known. The search for a home can take the better part of one's life. I had lived most of my life in London, but it was never really a home to me. My people were from Scotland, yet that was not home either, tainted as it was by the painful memories of my youth. Few places on earth are not marred finally by conflict and if that conflict touches one deeply, then the blood of one's kinfolk will cry from the soil that has received it. For this reason I had come to believe that a home is a creation and not a legacy. A home is a place that one discovers and creates. It is better to leave the past behind with all of its bitterness and the accumulated hatreds of the people and the many injustices that we all suffer.

God may forgive sins, but the earth still bears the marks of our collective memory. When I was in Afghanistan I could see its immense and bleak beauty when I first arrived, but soon it was tainted for me by the blood of my mates, the young lads who died for England. As I was young myself then, I did not understand why English lads must die so far from home. Finally I came to understand that it was not for England that they had died, but for the men who equated the extent of British power with the land itself. The only justified war I now believe is one to repel an immediate invader. To fight for the supremacy of British trade so that British products may be purchased and raw materials obtained on the cheap is not a war for one's native land but for a system of trade and an unequal one at that.

Perhaps I cling so to the margins of the sea because the great oceans know no sovereign. Britain's claim to rule the waves is mere vain hubris. It seems to me that governments of all sorts are absurd abstractions meant to hide the intentions of those who rule. True freedom then, it seems to me, exists in the absence of bonds, in reducing the formal relations that seek to command our loyalty, until there is space at last for individual freedom. To the man who seeks freedom, misanthropy and solitude become the goal at last for all of human relations tend to involve one and to draw one into citizenship or membership in some tribe or other. Every loyalty enhances the possibilities of conflict. Even love within marriage can be an invitation to friction as the emotional nerves are there most exposed and begin to rub against those of one's mate. At some time I believe that we need to shift our loyalties away from men and women and to seek God alone. Even those we have loved must be seen only in the penumbra of that all embracing love of God.

It is well that we die to the world in old age by losing our friends and family members before it dies to us. Otherwise we would be forced to watch in horror as each succeeding loyalty is changed with time. Even our close friends may become strangers to us as they alter with the years and old loves may turn to the ashes of resentment or indifference. To escape this fate we move about restlessly during our lives, always seeking a home, but never finding one for long. Blessed are those with short memories then for they will be least likely to regret the inevitable dislocations of life. They will not hunger for a past that is already lost to them.

Ritual and tradition may make a place tolerable for a time. By enacting rituals we embed ourselves in non-provable certainties. A community is created by its shared beliefs and by placing the blame for its sins and poor judgments on aliens, those who are not accepted by the community. Men seem always to require an enemy in order to define a friend. Perhaps the only way to love all of mankind is to never see any of its concrete examples. The hermits went to the desert for a reason. It is easy to believe in the stature of man as a creature of God when we are alone. Then only our own sins are before us and we may seek the immediate healing of God for them. To forgive others though, oh what a task that is! To invoke the love of God towards an enemy is surely the greatest task for a Christian. It seems to demand of man more than he may perform and for this very reason I believe that here and here alone is the primary truth of the Christian message. Absent forgiveness in even the most extreme of cases and the willingness to die at the hands of whoever wishes finally to take our lives, we may not yet join the God who forgives all things. To be a Christian and to escape martyrdom must therefore be   the exception.

To hunger for a universal justice upon the earth is to be

drawn again and again into conflict. Soon one becomes what one abhors, a murderer if only in our hearts. A man is lucky beyond measure if he may live three-score years and ten and know that his survival has cost no other man's life. So often each of us exists upon a pile of corpses. Even the consumption of goods is to participate in the labor and weariness of the man or woman who produced them. I refuse to wear cotton because I know that it is often the fruit of the labors of a slave in America or in India. To finally take a principled stand on any real issue is to be sucked into the maelstrom though. At any time there is a war going on somewhere, a war raging to redress past grievances. How sad it is that what is most noble within us condemns us to disregard the pain of our enemies.

I think that the reason that Jesus advised us in the gospels that the Christian must be a stranger even to his own family was this simple recognition that we must forgive those who kill us and even call our enemy our brother; but it asks too much of us to watch as our wives and children are killed in front of us. The death of a kinsman bears for us a greater bitterness than our own death for we must continue to live and to remember. The cycles of violence upon the earth may someday require generations of celibates to break the chain, or alternatively the assassins must become so cloyed with gore that they cease to slaughter out of sheer exhaustion. This is why Jesus said so clearly that His kingdom was not of this world and demanded that no sword should be raised to defend Him at Gethsemane when he was arrested.

It is said that we are baptized into the death of Christ and so we are. The Christian in this most bloody world must wake each day to know that it may be his last. For this reason, it is no small matter to practice universal charity and to live as Jesus did without a roof over one's head, but that may be asked of us at any time. I will go so far as to say that Christianity is nothing more than the application of a rigorous logic to human events. If one must choose to be either Cain or Abel, if there is no other choice, which will we choose?

It must always be remembered though that God put a mark upon Cain to protect him and not to condemn him. God had already forgiven him. We must imagine that Cain would have rather, if he repented at all, have drawn the wrath of the world down upon him if only to have assuaged his own guilt; but this was denied to him by God. The fate of Cain is that he was condemned to live and to wander upon the face of the earth. All people shunned him, and rightly so, for we fear the beast in our own hearts. The murderers among us remind us of the savagery that lurks within our own breasts. Christ then did not need to die then to appease the wrath of God, but instead to satisfy the wrath of men towards its other!

God asks always that we forgive each other. God takes the place of Cain in the person of Christ. The posture of the Christian is always then that of the bereft figure of the Blessed Virgin Mary in the *Pieta* of Mary holding the dead body of her Divine Son and doing nothing in revenge and seeking no recompense for the wrong done to her. This is the image which accuses the world in its very silence because it calls to our attention that our sins should never have come to this point: that this innocent death was made necessary to redeem us. To that image there is no answer but to finally throw down our arms and drop to our knees and weep collectively for God's forgiveness. Christ's death is God's final word to man and woman. He can speak no other word and still be God.

How hell must have groaned in knowing its defeat then, for the Evil One was a murderer as it is said from the beginning until now, even that evil was encompassed by God who accepted its fruit and allowed it to destroy what was and will always be most precious to God and to us as well, the Beloved Son of God. In that act Personified Evil lost all of its grandeur and pretense. It could no longer claim itself as a victim of God's omnipotence. Even the self-inflicted suffering of hell then became pointless, for it was now self-administered to no end of victory. The truth is that Evil is finally left with nothing and it is that nothing that it then embraces for all eternity.

I see now as I recall these thoughts that unbeknownst to myself I had become a metaphysician as well as a physician during those years of our strange adventures together. To think about the truth must be something that can be communicated to others as Holmes' Journal had communicated itself to me. Otherwise we would not be able to recognize truth when we are presented with it. I had not merely read the journal during that past year; I had allowed it to penetrate into my own doubts, hopes, and speculations. It remains with me still for I had changed. I had finally entered into that realm where our deepest thoughts and fears reside. Perhaps it is the mere habit of living and being forced to accept the contradictions of life that makes most men finally yield to life's limitations. There is a quiet resolution to accept things as they are and to use pleasure and forgetfulness to numb the silent ache of existence. There are men though who live in a constant inner monologue that demands that some answer must be given to the great inscrutability of our being. Sherlock Holmes was one of these.

I have watched men die. One minute they are before one and the world of light is cascading down about them and the future although uncertain reaches to the horizon from their youth to old age and suddenly there is a gunshot and they are gone, gone utterly. Later as a physician I witnessed the same sudden eruption of death and knew then that I could not restore what only an instant ago was intact, solid, vital, and exploding with perceptions and plans and then suddenly it became nothing...

To truly realize the horror of death is to catch one's breath in each moment of existence. I hesitate to write this sentence. Will

I survive until its completion? Will some sudden rupture occur, some untoward clot of blood, some skipped beating of the heart that will not resume, afflict me before I reach the end of this sentence? Blessed is the man who can ignore his own mortality. Some might say that to think too deeply on this is an exercise in morbidity but to never think of these things is barely to be human.

The short days before we left for America stand out for me now as most precious ones. Each dear object seemed to glow with an inner light. To look upon my sitting-room was like looking into one of those fabulous eggs made by Faberge for the Czar of Russia at Easter-time. Each object seemed to be placed with a purpose, although they were only placed where they were by the habits of long usage and conformably to my custom and convenience. A man leaves, even in disorder his signature upon a room in which he lives with each object lying where it was last of use to him. Many of the grand essays of Michel de Montaigne take note of the silent process of daily perception. Sherlock Holmes always used to call my attention to the particulars in any crime scene. A story can be read in the objects left behind and there is no human drama but leaves its traces. We are that with which we surround ourselves. I knew that the reunion with my home was to be a short one and that danger might await us soon. I told myself then that even if I might never see my home again, I might at least remember that last peaceful evening by my own fire.

From the Journal of Sherlock Holmes

June 28, 1892
My Research Continues

My days have now assumed a pleasant routine. Each day begins with a walk by the Aqueduct of Saint Clement along the river. Afterwards I sit in a café and eat a baguette and have some of the strong coffee of the region. I then go back to the university and spend the hours when the sun is warmest bent over my test tubes and retorts. I leave at four and take an early dinner and then spend the evening on my balcony with a book overlooking the street scene below with all of its drama and romance. I am reading a marvelous history of the region and a rather lurid novel by Emile Zola as well as *Les Miserables* by Victor Hugo, which I am sorry to say I have only now found time to read after getting the requisite dispensation because lamentably both books are by authors who are listed on the *Index Librorum Prohibitorum.*

It us an odd fact that western religion thrived best in those eras where the majority of the population was illiterate; this observation is not to imply that the nominal Christians of those times never heard the testimony of Holy Scripture read and explained to them, but the attraction and catechesis provided by artistic means in stained-glass, sculpture, and music as well as in architecture may have done more to support church membership and to win converts than an independent reading of the word of God. Vernacular translations and the printing press changed all of that. The greatest threat to Christianity came when the faith of the people was less culturally induced and was more of an individual choice. It was only recently for instance that critical methods were applied to the source materials of Christianity and it became possible to separate science from theology. The source of sovereignty was relocated from divine appointment and began to rest with the people in their own perceived interest by forming democratic movements and governments.

I am haunted by the thought of the many classical works that I have promised myself to read one day. I know their rough outlines of course, but I have yet to complete many of them. My old lodging in Baker Street is littered with half-read books I am sorry to say, but then no one can hope to read all of the books that one wishes to read in one short span of life. I fear that a comprehensive view of the human condition is impossible to attain and that at best I can only follow as I so often do in a case a series of indications towards a probable solution of the human dilemma.

It is much like my research in the laboratory. Each step suggests another, but the final end is not in view. I may only advance the study of coal-tars but a short distance and leave to another the final breakthrough if one is even possible. I labor more out of hope than conviction, but such are all human endeavors. Everything we do in science is but an essay, a partial revelation, a vision half unveiled. The struggle to create and to discover flows from a spring within us and sometimes that that flow ceases and who may ever know if it will ever come again. One day the writer puts his pen down and does not take it up again, the painter leaves a sketch unfinished and his pallet dries, the final experiment is tried by the scientist and found to be inconclusive. The torch passes then to another. How many lives are ever really completed to our satisfaction? Some lives are barely begun before death claims them and for the rest all remains a prelude, an overture, a preparation for life. If each effort that we make is tentative and its finale incomplete, what if we are tempted to make no effort at all?

The daily round of life for the great majority of mankind is a struggle for survival. There is little time for higher culture or for indulgence, let alone for fashionable indulgence or even for improving literature so as to raise the general level of our awareness. War, disease, and famine still claim countless lives. Even the religions of the world that serve to make misery bearable are predicated not on escaping suffering but on giving it meaning. The great question of humanity addressed to God is encapsulated in the single word, "WHY?" To this question the silent heavens seem to provide no answer. Christianity alone worships a deity that shares the human condition, not to alter it, but to enter into it and by doing so to transform our lives.

The promises of heaven have been trivialized through the years by making them a reward for good conduct. God does not act towards us as though we were canines being taught to fetch. The full importance of human actions and the full stature of humanity in the eyes of God are proclaimed by the fact of the Incarnation of Jesus. This was why the great Arian heresy was such a threat to the early church, because if Jesus possessed only a human nature and not a divine nature as well, then the crucifixion and the resurrection would lose its general application to every living soul. Jesus would have simply been a very good man and God would still remain outside of the human condition rather than within it.

Suffering from the Christian point of view is still to be opposed rather than meekly accepted as the price of living or as a supposed punishment for a sin committed by our ancestors. The story in Genesis is not a tit for tat story of retribution as it is so often understood even by Christians. The real message to be learned from Eden is that men and women elected to be like God by experiencing good and evil, we entered into complicity with the agony of God at the recalcitrance of creation and into the paradox that what was created to be good manifests evil as well. Genesis does not answer that question rather it poses it to us so that humanity can provide an answer.

We do not look to religion as a mere instruction manual; it is deeper than that. Religion is about human nature reflecting upon our collective experience and realizing our own inadequacy to provide a definitive answer to the problem of evil. We look finally to God when we despair of ourselves and God in return comes down to earth as a savior to show us how to be truly human in the figure of Jesus Christ. In spite of His miracles Jesus did not change the world. Pontius Pilate remained in office and the Roman Empire crushed Israel and dispersed the Jewish nation like seeds in the wind until the final days. Jesus left us only with the Church that is made up of ourselves and with His sacramental presence in Holy Communion. As the true Son of Man Jesus proclaimed his identification with humanity in an intimacy that no mere covenant, however faithful it might be, could ever provide.

For all of these reasons Christianity is a scandal and will always remain a scandal that puzzles the mind even as it challenges the will. It poses an ethical standard that is so exalted as to be virtually unattainable yet it simultaneously provides a solution and a remedy for human failure and sin in the forgiveness of God and the atonement of His Son. Precisely how these opposing factors will be judged by God in the final instance at our death will always exceed our competence to define and demarcate, although we never stop intemperately trying to do so. We are told to enter heaven by using the analogy of the narrow gate to Jerusalem, but we still prefer the wide gate that promises an easy entry with all of our baggage intact; just how precisely narrow that gate may be is up to God to determine, not to us.

Instead Christianity, in the admonitions of Jesus, refuses to bargain with us so that we might guarantee at least a back row ticket in the theater of eternity. Our lives are eventually stripped as bare as December's trees by time and circumstance and we are left at last with only our bare and skeletal boughs to present to God for all of our supposed certainties and virtues. There will never be a science of salvation. We are not left with certainty but only with hope. The great task of our lives is to resist despair when we witness the failure of human history to amend itself, even with the assistance of Divine grace. The good are too few and the evil are too many so that when the entire human race is added up the final equations found to be wanting and only God can supply the difference in the equation.

Then there is the whole question of endings. Who may say that anything is ever over? There are always the fragments left unformulated in any idea. Here in Languedoc there was a sudden resurgence of Gnosticism among the Cathars long after the Manicheans were history. Every idea recurs because it is still rooted in the human mind as a possibility. That is why there can never be a final triumph in human affairs and utopia never arrives. We build only to destroy and what is destroyed is again rebuilt. The old lament the passing of the old ways that have become familiar to them, and the young push aside the collective wisdom only to learn again what has always been known at one time or another, but since forgotten. Dares one laugh at this spectacle when we are all players in the same great human saga?

The history of Christianity has been one long speculation about the hour and the day of the return of Jesus to claim His Kingdom. At the end our memory becomes a prison for us. How great becomes the burden of all that we have ever known and loved! We carry about with us all of our prior-selves, each one waiting its hour to awaken again and to claim the whole of our remaining life in order to pursue whatever unfulfilled goals and visions he or she once possessed. To die with that cacophony of claims still echoing in one's ears with each one begging for just one more day in order to find itself again is a tragedy. But it is surely a greater tragedy to make an untimely end of our lives too soon and to be ready to die before our final hour has arrived at last. So we ask ourselves which life is most successful and complete. Perhaps it is the one that consents to the limits already imposed by providence and by time? To labor always, yet to expect no harvest in return, seems to me to be the best guarantee of our perseverance in virtue and in hope. I leave the ultimate result to God and to the hour of my homeward journey...

Dr. Watson's Narrative Continues

It was strange but the journal kept by my friend seemed to answer a question for me just as I was ready to pose it. I had been lamenting that I needed to leave home and to resume our struggle posed by the case at hand and Holmes seemed to suggest in his journal that to be finally satisfied with anything is premature. Perhaps it was a blessing after all that I had been dragged back into active life once again. I awoke on that morning when I was due to leave for Plymouth with a renewed sense of purpose. The train was wheezing at the station when I arrived and I was no sooner aboard than it began to move. It seemed to take infinite effort and to protest all the way, but soon we were flying through the green fields of Cornwall. The trip was a short one and I saw Holmes through the window of my carriage before the train came to a stop at the Plymouth station. His face was muffled and his collar was up, but I could see the piercing eyes and the stern nose of my companion as well as the commanding form that he always managed to project. I could feel the air of suppressed excitement and energy within him and my own melancholy faded with the rising mists that had veiled the summer day.

We soon hailed a carriage that took us to the pier. Our boat lay at rest in Plymouth harbor. It was a substantial steam-boat of some two hundred feet named the Waterloo. Holmes had booked us each a comfortable stateroom with an adjoining drawing-room. His own luggage was spare as always. He often chided me at my desire to bring along some of the comforts of my abode and far more books than I could ever hope to read on the journey no matter how protracted it might be. We took our final steps on English soil and were soon aboard. Our purser explained the workings of the ship and at last we were left alone to unpack and to adapt to our new surroundings. I was no stranger to the sea and the routine was a familiar one, but each voyage has about it its own special nature and no two ships are ever the same.

I have never lost that sense of admiration for the sheer design of ships. A well-constructed ship must resist forces that impinge upon it from all directions. It must yield to those forces but still triumph over them. It must be light enough to float, but strong enough to resist the impact of tons of water. It must steer a course through wind and wave and still secure what comfort it may for its passengers. The grace of its design is a thing of beauty. Nothing is wasted aboard. There is an economy of space and all items must become one with the ship as a whole or be jostled about. A ship is for me a model of the economy that must prevail in the well-ordered life that must resist all gales and currents in order to chart a straight course to its goal. No small part of my favorite reading has been chosen from Clark Russell and Joseph Conrad and I have even read that odd American, Herman Melville, and that new chap Jack London. These men know what life is for they have crossed the great waters. A true man of the sea may never be provincial for he has seen the varieties of men and cultures firsthand. He knows the great unity that is the human soul and can see past the accidents of place and manners and pierce to the essential core.

The result of my continuing fascination with ships was that I needed to be up and about the ship at once. Holmes smiled and yielded to my importunity and we were soon out on deck to see the ship cast loose its bonds to the land. Our pilot-boat saw us safely out of the harbor. Small-craft yielded before us and a few resentful scows that chugged along-side of us after yielding steerage way to the sound of our great steam-horn that echoed back from the surrounding hills of the harbor. We soon cleared the breakwater that was left in our wake. For a time the town of Plymouth was visible on our starboard-beam. The wind freshened on our faces and I smelled again that lovely smell of the open sea. Holmes and I sought shelter behind a bulkhead that broke the full force of the wind for I was in danger of losing my hat. We each took a deckchair so that we might see Lands End before England vanished from our sight. Meanwhile, Inspector Hopkins was engaged in an inspection of the ship to see that all was well and I noticed that Holmes kept alert throughout our conversation for any sign that we had been recognized or followed aboard.

At last he said, "I believe that we have made our escape handily, my dear fellow. I am happy to report that I was able to visit my own domicile safely. We ended up disembarking at a station before our usual stop and were met there by Sir Henry's coach and taken directly to Baskerville Hall. The servants had been instructed to maintain strict secrecy regarding my visit. I was able to slip away on the following night to visit my own abode and to obtain the articles that I will need for this trip. I then returned to Baskerville Hall for the next two days. I trust that you enjoyed your own visit home?"

I told him how much it had meant to me to see my home again at last.

"Yes, your journey has been a protracted one and I ask that you accept my apologies. I must say that I did not expect matters to require such an extended presence on your part, but I could not imagine leaving you out of such a vital case, the summit if I may say so of our career together. Your presence has been as invaluable as ever to me and so it will prove in what lies before us in America. I have heard marvelous tales of the beauty of the west, but I am afraid that the buzzing of the great commercial hives holds little interest for me. The dull pragmatism of the American character seems to me to have been adequately covered by De Tocqueville and I have little interest in witnessing it firsthand. But we have little choice. The matter before us requires some delicacy and I could not entrust it to any other hand than my own. But we will come to all of that in the days ahead."

He continued, "No doubt you are curious regarding the welfare of Sir Henry and Lady Beryl. I am happy to say that Lady Beryl has quite recovered from her ordeal and is engaged as before in her charitable works in the community. Constable Wiggins still resides with them and was able to report that there have been no untoward incidents to date."

"Where then do you believe Roger Baskerville is?" I inquired.

Holmes shook his head. "I can make no assertion whatever in that direction. If I have any maxim at all to apply to his behavior, it is this: that he will always do the unexpected. That is the reason for Wiggins' protracted stay. The man may strike at any time or he may long since have absconded to parts unknown. In any case we must exercise all caution for we may very well encounter him again."

He was silent for a time before continuing. "Did I mention that Professor Moriarty was there to greet me? No? Well he was. I spent some time with him alone and I was able to bring him up to date on developments and to receive his counsel on some important points. He has kept the return of Silver Star quiet and the utmost security is maintained now about the stables. At my urging he has agreed not to run Silver Star in the Wessex Cup this year until we have settled matters with the Baron. I wish the Baron to be able to believe that he can rely on Professor Moriarty's silence in the belief that the horse is still absent and in custody."

"But the Baron promptly sold it to a breeder after its abduction," I objected.

Holmes smiled. "That is a fact that he presumes the Professor does not know, thus the presumed continued efficacy of the inducement so that the Professor will remain silent. If the Baron should discover that the Professor has regained his horse, then the Baron might take some other action against him. It is my hope that Baron Maupertuis has put aside any concern that the Professor might cooperate with the authorities in an investigation of their former criminal partnership, because mind is now on other matters In any case, I have had Inspector Wiggins extend his protective services to include the region of the Kings Pyland stables and he has noticed nothing amiss to date. No, I think we may rest easy on that score and we may leave England knowing that our clients and friends are safe. It is now we who must take the offensive. The tide has turned in our favor and the next sally shall be ours to make."

"You found everything safe at your home also?" I inquired.

"Yes, there have been no break-ins. I arranged for its occupancy in my absence by one of Sir Henry's servants. He has kept up the garden and given the place an air of habitation. There is little there in any case to steal since all of my records are retained in London. I would not like anyone to take my old books and pipes though, and there are a few articles of furniture that I would not care to lose. I also possess a few manuscripts and charters on loan from a private collection for which I am responsible. I am afraid that my researches in that area will have to be deferred. I had hoped to collaborate with Dr. Mortimer during my convalescence of last year and we were close to some remarkable revelations. By the way, I saw Dr. Mortimer during my short visit. I am afraid that he haunts the Baskerville Estate like a resident ghost and I felt obliged to make my presence known to him. He was delighted of course and proceeded to demand that I abandon any nonsense (as he termed it) in which I was engaged and that I join him at once in his excavations. He wished me to come down to his villa and to see some items and artifacts that he has found. I had a great deal of trouble putting him off, since I was afraid that even the appearance of acquiescence would involve me in a web of obligations from which I could never hope to extricate myself in time for our hurried departure. I therefore allowed him to summarize his findings thus far and listened to his tentative conclusions."

I expressed some interest so Holmes continued. "It appears that he has found the site of an old Druid grove or meeting place. This alone would be of interest, but the most intriguing element is that his excavations there have also allowed him to retrieve some artifacts of tin that show a decidedly Chaldean influence. He has yet to submit his finds to any experts in the field, preferring first to obtain my own opinion, and to author a joint paper with me. He fears that we will have to share our find if it should become widely known and that then the effect of our own publication would be diluted by the secondary opinions of experts in the field. It is even possible that they might airily dismiss our discovery altogether since it flies in the face of established opinion. Dr. Mortimer is I think quite right, that we should bide our time until we have fully elaborated our thesis. I was happy of course that some proof has at last been found to support my own speculations. I assured the good doctor that I look forward to our collaboration upon my return. This mollified him to some extent. I complimented him upon his efforts thus far and insisted that his name appear first on any subsequent publication. He agreed to continue with his diggings and to catalogue each item as it is found for my review upon my return. It will make the entire matter easier. My own contribution will be to look at the evidence presented and to attempt a synthesis of the whole into a connected narrative of events. How was it that the Chaldeans found their way to the South-West of England? Did they bring with them any of their own religious beliefs and did it in any way influence those of the Druid people or the Picts that they found inhabiting these shores?"

He went on to describe his method for a general anthropology of religion.

"It is of capital importance to the study of the religious mentality to trace how any religion becomes eventually rooted in the folk-experience of the people. You will recall Watson that upon my return from my travels in 1894, when we met again at last after so many years, that I then appeared in the guise of an old book-seller and that I had in my possession a volume entitled, 'The Origin of Tree Worship.'"

I recalled the incident well. It was incorporated into my account of our reunion related in my account entitled, "The Adventure of the Empty House," in which I announced to the world the fact of Holmes return after his long absence. Holmes' revelations had recently shown me that this account had been inaccurate in many respects, but I could not have known that at the time. I could not have known for instance that the episode with the air-gun and Colonel Sebastian Moran had been a ruse devised by Holmes to account for his long absence. The supposed murderous attempt on the life of Sherlock Holmes by Colonel Sebastian Moran that was included there was merely to add a credible codicil to Holmes' delicate handling of the Ronald Adair Case for that young man's family. It served an additional purpose though, which was to explain Holmes' absence to the world in a coherent way by providing a plausible excuse for his lengthy sabbatical from his work as a detective. Many important cases had failed to be solved in the interim because Sherlock Holmes was not there to give his aid. There would surely have been a public outcry if it was thought that England's greatest detective and public asset had been engaged upon a matter of a private series of adventures and of chemical research however productive those might have been and no matter what personal significance they might have had on Holmes' own life. We often forget that great men and women have the same private needs as the rest of us.

Sherlock Holmes had become over the years both a national treasure and even a national monument and I fear to say that many people had forgotten what I knew so well, that Sherlock Holmes maintained, often with difficulty and risk, a very precarious mental and physical balance throughout his life. His physical constitution was menaced by the consumption acquired in his youth in Yorkshire and his mental and spiritual struggles, although unknown to the public, were equally severe and at times threatening to his survival and tranquility. These special conditions required the constant presence of an understanding friend and physician in attendance and I had been only too happy to play that role through the many years of our acquaintance and collaboration. Part of this role was to hold back from the ever-curious public certain data that might compromise other people during their lives or betray information that might affect international relations or prevent Holmes from carrying out certain delicate assignments.

During my musings Holmes continued his discourse about the omni-presence in culture after culture of the phenomenon of tree worship. He seemed happy and to have warmed to a subject that although obscure and fanciful to my way of thinking, clearly meant something to Holmes and played a part in his own philosophy of religion. I suggested that we discuss the matter more at length over lunch and a bottle of claret since I did not wish Holmes to take a chill by remaining on deck. He agreed at once but before we went into the dining-room he pointed in the distance. Over the waters I could see the low-lying finger of Lands End. It was sinking into an early fogbank that rolled along the coast. The sun shown upon the blue Atlantic ahead of us and I could only hope that its golden sheen was a portent that as we pursued our westward way we would meet with success on our American expedition.

Our lunch together proved to be a memorable one. Holmes was in the best of spirits. The dining-room of the vessel was decorated with all the splendor and luxury of the age in which it was constructed. It was substantial in size and its wainscoting was of the finest walnut. Holmes had chosen a vessel of medium size that was adequate to meet the waves with comfort but not so large as to resemble a veritable cross-section of society floating about upon the ocean. I am afraid that the elegance of our vessel's appointments was also reflected in its price, but Holmes waived aside any hesitation that I might have had on that score.

"Our journey, my dear fellow, has been subsidized by Sir Henry in return for, as he worded it, a partial payment of his debt of gratitude for our efforts in restoring his wife to him safe and sound. He would hear of no lesser means to be employed in order to reach our destination. I trust that your fillet of sole almandine is up to the mark? Excellent! Pray allow me to refill your glass. This is a very satisfactory Riesling. The Germans excel in their white wines even over those of the French. One must take these little enjoyments that life affords to us when they are present and give thanks, for misfortunes are certain to return in due course. I have always tried to balance my Rabelais with a goodly helping of Schopenhauer. But let us continue our discussion of tree-worship and in that connection of Dr. Mortimer. The man is quite beside himself with joy at his recent archeological find. His talk is all about pottery-shards and tin-engravings."

Holmes turned to Inspector Hopkins who had joined us for lunch. "Dr. Mortimer, my dear Inspector, has been since medical school obsessed with some theories of his own about Devonshire and indeed about humanity as a whole. He is one who believes in a golden age from whence our species has been in a process of decline ever since. One need only think of the genius of the Greek and Roman writers to find support for his views in various tales about Atlantis. What literature is more to be admired than the works of Aeschylus and of Sophocles in their grasp of the human condition? Who today is more eloquent than Seneca or Cicero? Truly we live now in an age when only the poets retain the glory of the English language! Where now can we find the eloquence of Donne or of Milton? What further degradation of language may yet lie before us when all discourse might become only the bland assertion of a few facts of science? Only mathematics, the chosen domain of Professor Moriarty, may then be adequate to describe the new world of time and space and few will find it an adequate language for our more spiritual thoughts."

Warming to his subject Holmes continued, "For myself, I prefer the glories of our English tongue even to the French. It is fertilized and fallow with the influx of England's many invaders and the lure of commerce. Our words contain roots from Latin, Greek, Saxon, and Nordic sources and if my own pet theory is correct, then the Cornish language possesses elements of the Chaldean in its roots. It is for this reason that Dr. Mortimer assumed that I would gladly drop everything to proceed with him to his diggings in the ancient barrow that he has discovered. He was quite right in his knowledge of my interest in linguistic roots. If I had not greater matters in view right now, it would indeed arouse my most intense interest. Let me assure both of you that I had quite resigned myself to a settled existence upon the moors. This case though has been smoldering for years and I could not say when the moment of spontaneous combustion would occur. I knew that it was too early for me to retire, but on the other hand I could not hope to continue at the pace I had so long maintained. So here we are and we must make the best of it. If all goes well we may all return soon to more congenial pursuits. Besides, a forced visit to America is not entirely amiss. I should hate to leave this life without some visit to what is termed 'the New World.' We must attempt to fathom the peculiar greed and simultaneous innocence of the American character and see whether the many immigrants who flock there, only to meet exploitation by American industry, had not better have struggled on in the Old World that at least has the virtue of having abandoned its historical illusions."

"The European nations live now in a permanent state of readiness for siege. All is a balance of suspicion and the pursuit of relative power through the possession of colonies. The royal houses are each precariously balanced over an abyss and what unfortunate event might start the landslide that could engulf their royal houses and their subjects alike in ruin is anybody's guess. We rejoice in the wonders of the age. Electricity is everywhere and all seems bathed in illumination by it except the darkness in that lies in the hearts of men. You see I agree with Dr. Mortimer that we may be going backwards, not in our technical achievements, but in our knowledge of ourselves. We are confusing ourselves with our engineered products. How long, I wonder, can it be before we become mere appendages to our industrial constructions and become victims of the golem that we ourselves have created? Mary Shelley's great work, 'Frankenstein,' may be prophetic, but whereas her creature was a parable of man's protest against a personal God who seems to have abandoned him, our creations are embodiments of our fears and hopes and our godlike aspirations. Not least of these is our insane love of weaponry. The use of our implements of war must be constrained within the bounds of a sensible diplomacy or they shall become monsters indeed!"

I was accustomed to Holmes' far-ranging discourses that often united the most disparate topics into one sustained vision. It was a habit of mind that was in no small part responsible for his success as a detective that he could unite into one image or construct facts and observations drawn from a multiplicity of disciplines. Had his views been less comprehensive and been confined to mere chains of linear deductions many a crime would have remained unsolved. I had learned from experience that the best course was to allow his mind the freedom to roam at will and to follow his diffuse observations as best I could. In time the picture would become clear and what had first appeared to be mere blots of color and obscure shapes would, through the skillful use of his mental brush strokes, at last reveal a complete landscape of thought and I would then be able to see the balance and proportion of the whole.

Holmes sipped from his wineglass and proceeded further with his discourse. "It is perhaps natural for historians to divide historical periods into segments, but we must remember that there are indefinite transition periods. Seldom does a new age dawn swiftly. There are of course those dramatic single episodes and events such as the signing of the *Magna Carta* that seem to denote instantaneous change, but the ground had long been tilled and seeded for *Magna Carta* by prior events. After one of these earth-shaking moments it may take years for its final results to become manifest. The Thirty Years War waged between Catholic and Protestant kingdoms did not after all break out the day after Luther nailed his theses to the cathedral door a century earlier. The defeat of the Manicheans did not end religious dualism as we may observe by the rise of Catharism in the South of France in the twelfth century. Christianity did not end the practice of Judaism, which went on to entrench the Torah in the elaborations of the Babylonian Talmud and the extensive network of Yeshiva Schools that teach its doctrines. Similarly, it has always been my belief that the Egyptian religion interpenetrated the entire eastern Mediterranean and that the Phoenicians with their extensive trading fleet might have carried such beliefs even to the shores of Cornwall that was at the end of the known world of that time."

"We assume that the Druids were only a native growth, forgetting that the Celts were a migratory people and were to be found throughout England, Ireland, and even in the Brittany region of France. The history of religion is a matter of the interpenetration of doctrinal elements and the mutual influence of other faiths. Is it a mere accident that the Moslems speak of the Jinn and that Jews and Christians refer to the angels and even to a supposed race of giants in the Bible? These giants, strange hybrid-beings, the children if so they may be called of the unnatural intercourse of the sons of heaven and the daughters of earth, are they mere phantoms of the mind of man or did they ever really exist? We have yet to discover the roots of our own variety of hominid. Who may say that the Neanderthals were blood-thirsty cave dwellers rather than peaceful wanderers in search of food? Is it not far more likely that they were gatherers and eaters of roots and berries who were clubbed to death by our own more advanced Cro-Magnon forebears?"

"Men like Doctor Mortimer attempt to answer these questions by seeking in the earth for clues, but most bones are now only dust and who can really deduce much from a few old pots and pans? If Baker Street was to fall into ruin and centuries hence some avid bone-hunter was to excavate 221B Baker Street he might conclude that all Londoners engaged in chemical experiments, smoked clay pipes, and kept tobacco in Persian slippers. No, gentlemen, I fear that we must resign ourselves to living on the farther shores of history. The past before the last five millennia is lost to us. Our origins have forever vanished and remain for us only as preserved in myths. We must turn to Gilgamesh and to the story of Eden to ask from whence we came."

"`We shall perhaps never comprehend the pre-existent plan of God for human beings, nor shall we know the influence of other cultures upon the genesis of Genesis. We will never understand those cultures that revered serpents for their wisdom nor will we be able to trace the reasons for the choice of the sacred author to choose that particular beast to represent Satan. There are anomalies that point to authorial choice of material and fictional composition and synthesis rather than history being in play in composing this account of the origin of evil among humankind. If the serpent was only made to crawl on the ground after the first sin in paradise, then by what means of locomotion did it first approach innocent Eve? Religious belief that must rest upon textual support alone must still ask questions implicating form and genre in order to decide how the text as a whole is to be properly understood. Selected Biblical quotations removed from their total context of meaning are bound to be misleading and to provide an insecure base for embracing faith and for filling in the gaps in our understanding. The act of belief must rather be so rooted in our own contemporary conditions and the difficulties of life that it is a natural outgrowth of our daily struggle to form out of our life experiences some sort of integral construct to guide our lives. The moral instinct in man is primal. We would suffer from guilt even had we been given no divine mandates to violate. We make laws to validate our own need for order in our lives."

"This raises the question of whether human societies might have deduced the Ten Commandments without divine intervention on Sinai. If there was no word for adultery prior to its prohibition, then how could the textual command have been understood? Did God concern Himself directly with the minute strictures of Leviticus and Deuteronomy? These appear to contain so much that is extraneous to our contemporary moral convictions that their only functions appear to be to differentiate the Jews as the chosen people from the rival tribes of Canaan. Is it not far more likely that the content of these books was the result of the long elaboration of Priestly practices that were created over time to formalize the fundamental need to relate in a concrete fashion to an unseen God? Surely those elaborate modes of worship were not the demands of a vain and insecure celestial monarch who demanded worship. They are instead more likely to be the efforts of men to reach out towards a God whose nature is such that we can approach Him only through mystery and in the darkness of faith.

If I may say so, the true sense of the goodness and mercy of God is shown by His good humor in enduring our worship. The wonder is that He ever turns aside from the celestial choirs to listen to the cacophony of our inadequate songs of praise."

"It is a sad feature of human arrogance that we insist on burdening God with our own obsessions and that we are willing to kill each other to vindicate our own tentative approximations of the nature of God and of the features of the world to come. This is not to say that all religions are equal in their respective insights, still less is it to deny the unique character of the revelations contained in the Bible. Rather, it is to fully appreciate that the definitive revelation of God to man is contained neither in the Judaic laws nor in Levite rituals but only in the very flesh and blood of God becoming one with us and the indwelling of God's Holy Spirit that is to remain with us until Jesus returns to the extended body that is the Church. To imagine Christianity as a mere textual creation of words and assertions is to miss the entire point of the Incarnation of Jesus with its concrete restoration of the fullness of the stature of man. Human beings now live within the final age, the one preceding the final revelation of man in glory with God and incorporated within the very life of the Trinity. Compared to this august vision, any trivial reward called heaven is the equivalent of offering a treacle treat to a child as a reward for its good behavior. Surely redemption is more than this. The Church is more than mere fellowship coupled with sanctimonious practices. The Living Church is God living among us."

"That the historical Church demonstrates still the universality and the reality of sin should never blind its members to the exalted calling that their faith imposes upon them individually and collectively. The Church is always more than itself. It is the life of God within the Church that gives the Church its sacred character and is the source of its power and significance for mankind as a whole. That is why the life of the Church is always grace as is also the life of each individual man and woman. It is this grace that calls forth belief from within us; it is not imposed from outside of us. It springs up from within us. It is as natural as anything else that we observe in human nature because it rests upon the promises of God to us. The desire to worship is so universal that man tends to honor whatever appears to be a source of life and of majesty confusing it sometimes with the gentle splendor of God."

The inspector interrupted Holmes at this point with a question. "I have attempted to follow your line of discourse, Mr. Holmes, but if faith is as natural to mankind as you assert, how can we be sure that God is not merely a projection of our own desires?"

Holmes smiled. "Your question assumes that to desire something is always a matter of wishful thinking, but think for a moment Inspector, we desire food yet it really exists, we desire beauty and we find it all around us. It is no indictment of a thing's existence that we desire it. But most of our desires for the essentials of life are met with partial fulfillment. If we feel the desire to worship and to reverence God from deep within ourselves, then there must be an object worthy of such an attitude."

"Such as a tree?" asked the Inspector smiled archly. "I believe that your research has explored, as you mentioned earlier, the subject of tree worship."

"It is true that I have studied the subject and it is a fascinating topic to which I will return in a moment but first let me handle your implied objection first. You are saying, are you not, that though we must worship something, that something does not need to be a conscious spiritual entity such as God? Faith in the specific vision of the deity represented by Christianity would then appear using your implied way of thinking to require more than a mere natural resolution of the problem of positing a creator or showing reverence for trees. You will recall that the Deists for instance believed in a supreme being as a source for creation but stopped short of giving that being any specific attributes, let alone a personal nature and a concern for men and women. Similarly, to worship a tree as a source of fertility and power need not imply a belief that the tree cares for man or has a plan for human destiny. My argument then for the Christian God becomes an extension of my original assertion that worship is natural to human beings. The next question becomes then, what sort of object is worthy of such total esteem and obeisance? Surely, the object of worship should be the highest conception that we may attain. It must possess every excellence of truth and beauty. The attributes of God then should be a summation of all good qualities and those qualities should be present in the highest degree for to worship anything less would leave open the possibility that a more excellent being might take the place of our first object of worship thus making that supreme reverence that we had exhibited for the former object premature. It is natural then for us not only to worship but to worship only that being who manifests every quality of excellence in its most superlative form."

Inspector Hopkins frowned with concentration. "I follow you thus far, but I still insist that our mere desire for that last in a line of better objects of worship does not guarantee that our desire will ever be satisfied by arriving at an absolute perfection."

"But bear with me yet a bit for my thesis is only partially before you. To continue then with my demonstration: we have established that the final object of our worship must possess to the highest degree every excellence that we can imagine. A corollary of this is that to find a defect in our object must of necessity disqualify it from worship or at least to defer it while we wait for a more appropriate object of worship. We may still reverence it for whatever partial good it may possess and manifest, but we must withhold worship in deference to that final object, which by definition will display no defects. Of course this assumes for a moment that we even have the ability to discern such excellence since we ourselves are flawed, but let us take it as an axiom essential to our discourse upon this topic that man may judge relative excellence when he finds it, that all of our judgments cannot be awry though we may mistake any particular instance. We must believe in our ability to distinguish goodness and evil or all moral and theological discourse comes to an end. Philosophy has certain terminal positions which if adopted cause thought to grind to a halt. Adamant skepticism, the doubt that we may know anything with certainty, is just such a philosophical dead end. It requires its own act of faith, viz. that the mind of man is inadequate to its tasks. I prefer to keep the discourse of ideas flowing so I posit that we may indeed know certain matters with certainty or at least with a high probability. Let us continue. If we may be certain that excellence exists in any quality, then we may go further and imagine a locus of all those qualities and in the highest degree in a single Being, that Being then becomes our *a priori* definition of God. What then must be our next step?"

"I have no idea," admitted Inspector Hopkins.

"Well it is obvious is it not? We must allow for the candidates for our choice to pass before us as we seek to discover if any one candidate may embody, as far as His reputation and admitted character admits, of those qualities that we have assigned *a priori* to our conception of God. Please note that we will never know God's every excellence until He is seen face to face and even then only insofar as He gives us the ability to progress in that comprehension. Our perception of God shall always be confined by our capacities and those capacities must grow or be extended to encompass their object. Since the excellence of God is by definition limitless, then our capacity to appreciate and to worship must be confined to our furthest capacity at any given moment. This implies that heaven must encompass a sort of infinite progression as we find an increasing aptitude arising within us to appreciate

God or if time itself shall cease in the realm of eternity, then we must simply await the advent within ourselves of those capacities that God will bestow upon us after death, capacities that now exceed our imagination."

"This is why it is said that 'Eye has not seen, nor has ear heard, nor has it entered into the heart of man what God has prepared for those who love him.' That phrase is profoundly and essentially Christian. Christianity makes no attempt to delineate the character of paradise even by metaphor. That fact is no small measure of its unique credibility. As we march before us the various religious systems of belief, I think that we may quickly eliminate those candidates that embody a God who is *prima facia* an inadequate object of worship as judged by our innate moral sense of good and evil, a legacy from our choice in Eden. This must lead us quickly through all systems of animism and magic because in these systems it is man who manipulates God in order to achieve a given end set by an act of the human will. The practice of Christianity on the other hand adapts our conceptions and desires to God and not those of God to us. The final purpose of all prayer is to reconcile us to the will of God. Even our petitions must always have as a final codicil the same petition that Jesus made in the Garden of Gethsemane before His death when he said to His Father, 'Not my will but Thine be done.' Christianity follows this attitude of Jesus Christ in humble submission. To allow God to decide for us what is appropriate and to entrust even our lives into His hands. In other words, we do not put God to the test. Rather, having eliminated for ourselves all claims to worship of any candidate for 'God' whose character is such that He could not possibly be God, we are left with only one candidate finally standing and to that candidate we lay down what remains of our pendent judgments as to His nature as being already inadequate to comprehend Him. At that point man leaves knowledge behind and enters upon the path of faith that may in all justice demand from us anything that we possess."

The Inspector shook his head. "Well if that isn't a mouthful Mr. Holmes! As the years have passed I just begin to think that I have arrived, that I have your compass, and then you are off again and I realize that I am still the same young Scotland Yard bloke who first studied under your tutelage. It is hard enough to follow your lead in your criminal practice, but now here you are in advanced metaphysics. Well, as I say, you do beat me, indeed you do."

Holmes smiled. "You underrate yourself, my dear fellow. I assure you that you are adequate to the demands of my argument. Let me continue for a bit. All men and women have it within their capacity to submit to something greater than themselves. It is merely a matter of doing so. I assure you that during my time in France I learned more from the men and women gathered for Mass each morning, in their prayerful attitude for we seldom spoke, than from many a learned text. I asked myself what it was about them that spoke to me when I saw them in earnest but humble contemplation after Mass. Was it not that they were simply present? These people simply made an appearance so as to worship God. They had made found in the humility and the humanity of Christ an answering something within their own nature. They brought to the altar whatever was in their lives, their tiny concerns, or their abiding hunger for God. All alike were laid before God in prayer. They realized that they would never understand all things, but in this life understanding is not a prerequisite for admission to heaven (we Catholics are not Gnostics after all). Their devotion was a matter of reversing the sin of Eden by waiting for God to reveal everything in His own time and season. The essential Christian attitude is that God may be trusted. This is the essence of a covenant as opposed to a contract; it is simply to trust God unconditionally. Without trust no true covenant can ever be made."

"Yes, Mr. Holmes, but every contract has a damages clause, if I recall correctly. What then, pardon my temerity, if God should prove unfaithful and our trust in Him proves to have been misplaced after all?"

"But we need only return to our *a priori* definition, do we not, in order to answer your question? A God who would break His word must be a most imperfect god and thus not God at all," answered Holmes. "But in any case just as one must believe in something to worship, so do we have a desire for trust. What baby does not justly assume that it shall find the breast that answers to its hunger? Trust is essential to the very structure of human life."

"And we are often disappointed," muttered the Inspector sadly.

"So we are, but not by God, but only by imperfect men and women," said Holmes quietly.

"But see here, Mr. Holmes, if God is omnipotent, why then does he not simply stop all the suffering, right now and at once by whisking it away by divine fiat?"

"Well, if He did so then we would both be out of business; is that not so Inspector?" Holmes laughed. Then he was serious once more. "You have placed your finger upon the crux of the problem of evil or rather upon the crux of my argument. We arrive at the unique Christian doctrine of God as the suffering servant as the most adequate candidate in our celestial review. Christianity does not escape the problem of suffering, but instead elevates it by taking it into the realm of heaven itself by bringing God down to earth in the person of the Son of the Father. God does not witness the plight of mankind from a distance, nor does He trivialize suffering by simply whisking it away and changing our natures in the process. Might we in turn not disappear in the course of that very 'whisking away' since many evils seem integral within ourselves? Instead God suffers with us and carries the wounds of the Cross of Christ, even within His resurrected body. The mystery of Christ is precisely that He does not end suffering, but embraces our condition and takes upon Himself our every pain even to the point of accepting death on a cross."

"Even our sins are embraced although they are not His. The entire concept of a savior is one of absolute acceptance of the real us while repudiating all in us that would separate us from Him. By this means we are cleansed and forgiven. What the Church speaks of as the temporal punishment due to sin is merely what it takes for us to realize and to accept, perhaps only within and after our death in the state of being called Purgatory, what has been done for us and to begin to contemplate the excellence of what grace has accomplished in our fellow human beings as well. I think of Purgatory as like a great art gallery presided over by God who acts as its curator. Purgatory as an essential article of faith of the Church is simply the realization within us, as we observe the majesty of God reflected in the sufferings and triumphs of trust in often the simplest of souls, of how God has always dealt with men and women by allowing them to confront evil and only by doing so to fully realize the good."

"The parallel doctrine of the Communion of Saints implies that the excellence of each of us plays a part in the redemption of the whole. St. Paul speaks of making up in his own body for what is lacking in the sufferings of Christ. What is this then but an admission that even the smallest of our limitations may in some way, through our own willing submission to grace, enhance the salvation of the world. Perhaps even the seemingly mindless suffering of the innocent and of animals is somehow caught up in this great primal mystery. Perhaps the consent of the innocent and even of the unborn, with a capacity not theirs at the time of their suffering, to the limitations imposed by circumstance and their acceptance in faith of their unlived lives covers a life of daily renunciations that they were never allowed to make through the long and tedious course of a human life."

"Much remains a mystery that will somehow later be revealed, but for now is this not the most worthy and appropriate vision of how God works that we may possibly entertain? A God who will embrace even what is least Godlike within us to accommodate our need, surely that is the most likely candidate for our proposed worship. I will go so far as to say that if even a possibility that such a grand conception might be true exists, then it should be grasped with all of our strength rather than to accept a facile atheism that leaves the problem of human suffering, particularly that of the innocent, unresolved and hanging as it were like a loose end to all of our instincts for final order and justice in the universe."

Both the Inspector and I were quiet after this. I because I had accepted that same Catholic faith within the last month and the Inspector because he was still searching and might have found the answer as well that night, an answer that might allow him to follow the path of his cousin, Gerard Manley Hopkins, and to embrace the Catholic faith. We pushed back our chairs then, knowing that we might have just heard what Sherlock Holmes had finally assembled as the preliminary summation of his religious views upon his return from his great journey of discovery.

There were of course great adventures ahead recounted in the journal before I could read the detailed account of his final intellectual dual with Professor Moriarty that was to be the fulfillment and summit of their momentous wager. I determined to await these revelations until I reached that point in Holmes' journal dealing with that final confrontation between those two great intellects. These adventures of the mind and of the heart still lay before me in my reading, while our present American mission also promised adventures ahead. I had previously resolved to encounter these important elements in the course of their formulation so as to attain the organic unity of his thought processes and the reasons for his conclusions, just as Sherlock

Holmes had laid it out in his journal and not to anticipate that resolution.

Together Sherlock Holmes and I walked out on deck where we stood for a time gazing out over the dark waters towards America and looking at the stars in their heaven. Somewhere in the darkness behind us lay Europe with all of its seething conflicts. I felt something of the hope that the very idea of America has tended to inspire in the universal hearts of men and women of all lands as our vessel pushed its bow wave ahead. Everything on that magical night seemed to be very good indeed. I felt reassured having Sherlock Holmes once again at my side and I experienced one of those surprising moments that often come surprising and unsought in our lives of complete peace and confidence in what lay ahead.

To Be Continued...

Note From the Author

As one who has always esteemed writers such as Graham Greene, Evelyn Waugh, and George Bernanos (each of whom was Catholic) it has been my hope that my own effort in The Confessions of Sherlock Holmes might be part of a venerable tradition. I would like to point out however that the position of a writer who incidentally is Catholic must be distinguished from that of a Catholic writer whose writings are meant precisely to reflect church teachings as such. There is a tension between these two positions that makes it difficult for a Catholic to be both true to his faith while remaining simultaneously true to the form and literary intent that must accompany any act of composition. It would be awkward and indeed impossible to write a cohesive narrative seeking to capture and comment upon human life and conflict if the writer had to simultaneously ensure that goodness and fidelity always emerged in clarity and triumph while its opposite was equally revealed in all of its inherent malice and folly. Fiction, even when dealing with theological reflection, as is the case with the present work, can never be a substitute for catechesis. The reader is therefore cautioned that in reading the present text no decisive conclusion be drawn that the positions of any of the characters reflect either the final views of the author or the official position of the Catholic Church. Literature embraces life according to its own limited perceptions as it is and even in its suggestions of a better world must always fall short, not only in displaying accurately whatever emerging forces may exist in human history, but in depicting all that has been revealed of a higher purpose and source to illumine us in our beleaguered world.

Thomas Mengert possesses a Masters Degree in English Literature with a special expertise in the complex works of the Irish author, James Joyce. His background in humanities and philosophy are combined in this probing novel. As a final Sherlockian synthesis, The Confessions of Sherlock Holmes is Mengert's attempt to understand the true depths of the best known detective in world literature, a hero to his many fans who find in his character and habits of mind an endless fascination.

www.ingramcontent.com/pod-product-compliance
Lightning Source LLC
Chambersburg PA
CBHW060225100726
47907CB00003B/513